ECHOES OF CONTROL

ISBN: 978-1-968727-01-7

To everyone who wished they had a hero, but had to save themselves instead.

A Note to Readers:
This novel is a romantic suspense intended for mature audiences (18+) and explores themes of survival, trauma, and healing. It contains explicit content and situations that some readers may find disturbing or triggering. Please proceed with caution.

- Depictions and recollections of past domestic abuse (psychological, emotional, physical, financial, and sexual coercion within a BDSM context)
- Ongoing stalking and psychological torment by an abuser
- Explicit sexual content and consensual BDSM power exchange dynamics (D/s) between the main characters as part of a healing journey
- Scenes of violence, including gun violence, injury, and murder
- Kidnapping and captivity
- Strong language
- Detailed exploration of PTSD, panic attacks, and trauma responses

A core part of the heroine's recovery and romantic relationship involves the consensual exploration of BDSM (Dominance/submission dynamics). These scenes are explicit and integral to her reclaiming her agency and sexuality, presented as a healing counterpoint to past coercive trauma.

Your mental health and well-being are important. Reader discretion is advised.

CHAPTER ONE

Sage

I frown as my headlights flicker, dimming for a moment before brightening again. That's odd.

The road is pitch-black except for the thin beam of my headlights cutting through the pouring rain, and the towering trees on either side create the illusion of being trapped in an endless tunnel.

The upbeat song playing on the radio is a stark contrast to the eerie drive. The volume drowns out the sound of the rain, and I feel less alone listening to the artists croon their songs to me. I pray that my phone doesn't lose signal — sometimes these back roads are dead zones. Luckily, there's only one road to follow toward town if the signal cuts out.

A few minutes later, the lights dim again. I mutter a curse under my breath as I switch off the radio and unplug my phone. It slips from my hand as I fumble with it. I catch it in time, dropping it onto the passenger seat, where I can still see the map from the corner of my eye. I just need to conserve some power.

Everything will be fine.

The town is twenty miles away, and I can only go in one direction. I can make it. I have to.

The sudden silence is heavy and oppressive despite the relentless drumming of the rain and the swish of the windshield wipers. I don't want to be alone with my thoughts.

My hands tighten on the steering wheel, my knuckles white. I'm one disaster away from a breakdown. I can feel it simmering below the surface. Car troubles, skeevy motels, and ever-present feeling of being watched — I have this growing need to scream into the night.

It seems like everything is going wrong. Sometimes I wonder if the universe is telling me I am making a mistake. A little insidious voice whispering, *see, this is wrong. You need to go home and beg for forgiveness.*

No, the universe or fate or that stupid voice can go fuck itself. Leaving is the best decision I've made in the last decade. Probably. Doesn't matter. If I return... I shiver. That's not worth thinking about. Besides, I've been zig-zagging across the country for months now. It's too late to go back.

Some days, I'm not sure why I'm still running. It's not like Jordan will find me here. He's all the way on the other side of the country, and even if he wants to track me down, how could he? I'm in an old beater that I paid cash for, using a burner phone with a prepaid plan so he can't call or track me the way he did with my old phone. Plus, I pay cash or use a prepaid credit card for everything else. I haven't even connected to my email or social media.

I'm safe.

But other days, when I can't shake the feeling of being watched, I worry that all my precautions are for naught. I know that he has powerful connections. From law enforcement to the mafia; people owe him favors, and I wouldn't put it past him to use those favors to hunt me down.

So, I run. But god, am I tired.

The check engine light flicks on and stays on. Fuck. Okay, that could mean anything. I once had a car in college that had a check engine light because of a glitch in the electrical system. Maybe this is the same as that? Alright, I just need to make it to the next place, get some rest, and it'll be fine.

I could take a few days, catch my breath, fix the car, and then decide where to go next.

Once I make it, that is. The brochure I pulled from a tourist display at the last motel portrays it as a lovely mountain town with lots of cute bed-and-breakfasts and small-town charm.

Though a bed-and-breakfast might cost too much, maybe I could find a cheap motel or a campground. There must be campsites out here. I'm not a fan of the wild, but my money will only stretch so far, and the odd day job won't cut it for long. Perhaps I can find an under-the-table job while I am here? Online want ads have been helpful so far. Or maybe it's time to consider getting a real job. Except jobs require ID. And Jordan has those scary connections.

I remember when his assistant disappeared, and he suspected her of stealing a flash drive containing company secrets. He was so angry that he found any reason he could take that out on me. And then, one day a week later, he was gleeful. He watched the news with a sick smile on his face as the image of his assistant flashed across the screen, the headline reading, *'Local woman found dead in her home after a break-in gone wrong.'*

I liked Alice. She was the one who encouraged me to plan my escape.

"Remember that, Sage," his voice cold, his eyes never leaving the TV, the maniacal smile twisting his handsome features, "I always win in the end." There was nothing that linked him to the crime, but even without his ominous words, I knew deep down it was him. He may not have done the act, but he knew people who had no problem taking a life.

It took me another year and a beating that almost left me dead to gather the courage to leave.

I need to give him time to move on. I will be free once he sets his eyes on someone new. I know that makes me a monster, wanting someone to replace me as his obsession, but I can't be his punching bag anymore. And it isn't like I can go to the cops. The same night he had the chief of police over for dinner, he dislocated my shoulder. They'd laughed as I screamed when he wrenched it back into place.

No, the only way I will be safe is if he is dead or he finds a new target. Until then, I need to become a ghost.

The battery warning light on the dashboard blinks to life. "Great," I mutter, my irritation mounting. *Ten more miles. I'm sure I can make it.* The phone on the passenger seat glows, but it is too far away to make out the map. I should have left it on the mount, but I must be almost there.

The lights on the dash are barely visible now, a faint glow as the electrical system continues to fail. Fuck, fuck, fuck. If it weren't raining and pitch-black, turning off the headlights to save power might be an option, but that's a stupid risk in this weather.

I keep driving, focusing on keeping my breathing under control. I grip the steering wheel with both hands, hoping to minimize the trembling of my hands. The minutes drag on forever. The endless trees and empty sameness make it feel like I am going nowhere. I can't tell if it's been a minute or ten. I dare not move my eyes from the road.

This feels like a never-ending nightmare. A continuation of the trouble from last night when a stranger pounded on the motel door and tried the doorknob multiple times. I sat petrified, willing the person to go away, praying they didn't pick the lock or try to break the door down. The shitty motel door didn't have a peephole, and I wasn't about to look out the window.

I don't believe in ghosts, but I swear my past is haunting me.

I didn't sleep much after that.

Now, my car is failing me in the middle of the woods. It's like a bad horror movie.

If I can make it to town, I can get some rest, find an auto parts store, and try to fix it. I've done it before with YouTube as my guide when I needed to replace the radiator.

Another warning light flickers. My eyes dart from the dark, rain-slick road to the dashboard, trying to catch the warning before it disappears. Oil? What the hell is going on with my car? I changed the oil a few weeks ago. It should be fine.

My headlights flash across a green sign proclaiming Deliverance is 5 miles away. I feel some of the panic leech out. 5 miles isn't far. I can make it. I can walk 5 miles if I have to.

As soon as that thought flicks through my head, the knocking starts.

My stomach sinks as the low, grinding noise grows louder, and I feel the rumble and jerk in the steering wheel. I don't know that sound, but it's not a sound a car should make.

I'm screwed. Why did I jinx myself? I don't want to walk 5 miles in the rain.

I pull off the road, wincing as the tires slide in the mud. The last thing I need is to be stuck in the mud, too. My heart races as I put the car in park and turn off the engine. Silence, save for the relentless pounding of rain on the metal roof. I close my eyes and take a few steady breaths.

There's nothing for it. I pull the lever to pop the hood and grab my phone. I turn on the flashlight app before stepping out into the storm. Thank god phones are pretty much waterproof these days. In seconds, the storm plasters my clothes to my body like a second skin, and I feel the biting cold down to my bones.

The light from the phone does very little to cut through the inky darkness, but as I peer under the open hood, nothing looks to be smoking or out of place. That's a good sign, right? Then again, aside from basic car maintenance and what I've learned from the internet, I'm not an expert.

I go to the car's passenger side and dig around for something to wipe the dipstick with. The napkins in the cup holder will disintegrate in this downpour, and I'm reluctant to dirty one of my shirts, but I don't have a lot of options. I reach under the seat and get lucky, pulling out an old T-shirt.

Back under the hood, I tuck the phone into my shirt collar for light, yank out the dipstick, and wipe it clean before plunging it back in. When I pull it out again, my stomach drops. No oil. Well, a tiny amount. I check again to be sure.

That's impossible. It was fine the last time I checked. Fuck. This is not good.

A car passes by, the first I've seen since getting off the interstate, its headlights illuminating the road before fading into the distance. I sigh and wipe my face with the back of my hand.

Five miles.

Maybe if the car cools down, it will start again, and the knocking will magically be gone. Like resetting a computer. I'm deluding myself, but I've got nothing else. I don't want to walk.

I slam the hood shut, not hopeful, but I'm too stubborn to give up without trying. Back in the driver's seat, I turn the key.

Click.

Nothing.

I try again. Another click. The engine doesn't even try to turn over. Fuck. I sit there, my breath starting to come out in heaving gasps as I stare in disbelief at the rain running down the windshield. Come on, Sage, deep breath. We can wait this out. I count slowly in my head, focusing on slowing my breathing.

Five minutes pass. Then ten. I try again. Nothing.

I pull the lever to open the hood again and step back out into the pouring rain. I stare down at the engine, wishing I knew exactly what I was supposed to be looking for. Why couldn't the problem be obvious? I glare at the dead car before pacing in front of it. I hear a second car drive by, but my mind is far too consumed with anger and helplessness to register it.

"Of all times to die on me, it has to be now? Right now?" I scream at my car. "What am I supposed to do? You expect me to walk? In this weather?" I let out a string of colorful curse words as I gesture to the rain, my phone still in hand, the flashlight on, so the weak beam flashes around. "Stupid fucking bucket of rust on wheels." I kick the tire, my voice shrill, on the edge of hysteria. "I take care of you! I get your oil changed! I don't abuse you, but—"

"Miss?" A deep voice calls out from behind me.

I freeze. Every muscle in my body locks up, and my already cold body feels like it has plunged into an icy pool. "Miss?" he calls again before tapping my shoulder. I can't help the shriek that spills from my mouth at the unexpected touch, and I spin around, my heart pounding, my hands instinctively rising in defense, causing my phone to slip. It hits the mud with a wet thwack, the light blinking out.

I take a step backward, my thighs hitting the car. Fuck. I have nowhere to go. The man standing before me is easily a foot taller than I am and outweighs me by at least a hundred pounds. Even in the poor light, I can make out his face—a shadowed, rugged attractiveness that makes my internal alarm bells scream danger.

Attractive men are not to be trusted.

"Whoa, whoa," he says, raising his hands in a placating gesture, treating me the way one might treat a frightened animal. "I didn't mean to scare you."

He steps forward, his hand outstretched, and my eyes dart for an exit. With the car at my back, I try to sidestep him, only for my foot to slip into the mud, sending me sprawling. His already imposing stature looms above me, heightening my fear, and I scramble backward in a pathetic crab walk, the mud squelching between my fingers.

So, this is how I die, the bitter thought breaking into the fear that clouds my mind, *on a dark stretch of road in the middle of nowhere.* Underneath the bitterness and panic is a kernel of anger, and I cling to it with all I have.

This asshole made me fall in the mud. What a jerk.

CHAPTER TWO

Reid

The windshield wipers beat a steady staccato as I drive down the winding road, matching the heavy tempo of the rock music playing. After a long flight, fighting through Seattle traffic, and a week guarding the rudest client to date, I'm eager to get home to my quiet house. But it's dark, and heavy rain forces me to keep my speed low. This stretch between Deliverance and the freeway is completely isolated. During the day and in the right conditions, it's a beautiful drive, but right now, I'm one wrong move from a potential car accident.

I should know; my buddy Maddox owns the only tow truck service and mechanic shop in the area, and the number of cars they've had to rescue and the handful of memorials on the side of the road is depressingly high. Locals are cautious, but tourists and teenagers, not so much.

A few miles outside Deliverance, my headlights illuminate an old car pulled off to the side, its hood up. I'm torn. If it weren't for the rain, I wouldn't hesitate to offer the person some help, but the week has been hell, and I'm tired. I could call Maddox and tell him to send out one of his boys. It's possible whoever is stranded already got a ride out of there, and the lure of my warm home is so tempting. But then I spot a bedraggled woman standing in front of it, seemingly having an animated phone conversation.

"Fuck," I mutter. Decision made, I pull over in front of her and get out, quickly getting drenched in the downpour. As I get closer, I realize she isn't on the phone at all. She's yelling at the car. Her soaked hair and clothes cling to her body, leaving little to the imagination. I force myself to look away from the delicious curve of her ass as she rants.

"Miss," I call, raising my voice to be heard over the rain. She doesn't respond, too caught up in her tirade. The colorful language she's using makes me grimace. If she were my sub, I'd have to punish that mouth. A spanking would do the trick, but alas, she isn't mine.

"Miss?" Her tirade cuts off, but she doesn't turn. Perhaps she is questioning whether she heard anything? The rain is rather loud.

I move closer and tap her shoulder. "Miss," I say again.

She spins around so fast that she nearly loses her balance, letting out a shriek of terror. She throws her hands up in a poorly executed karate stance; her wide eyes take me in. Panic flashes across her face as she looks me up and down and clocks my size.

Ouch. Despite my size I'm not accustomed to intimidating women.

"Whoa, whoa," I say, raising my hands in a placating gesture. "I didn't mean to scare you." But that does little to soothe her, and she steps back, causing her to slip in the mud. She shrieks again, losing her balance. I instinctively reach out to steady her, but she flails as my hands come near, so I quickly pull back. She lands in the mud with a heavy thwack. That doesn't halt her retreat as she scrambles backward.

Despite the awkwardness of her crab-walk retreat, it's not funny. I feel horrible about scaring her so much. I admit I am a large man, and we are on a dark, empty stretch of road surrounded by thick trees, but her reaction is out of proportion for being startled. I hold my hands up, palms facing her in surrender, and take a few steps back, trying to show her I'm not a threat.

"I didn't mean to scare you," I say, trying to project my voice over the downpour.

"What?" she replies, though I barely hear her over the rain. Her brows furrow in confusion, but that expression is far better than fear. Her eyes dart to the phone in the mud at my feet. I bend to grab it.

I take a cautious step forward, hands still up, the one with the phone holding it out as a peace offering. "I said, I'm sorry I scared you. I promise I'm not trying to hurt you. It looks like you could use some help."

She scrambles to her feet, eyeing me warily. "I don't need any help," she says, snatching her phone from my outstretched hands. She wipes the mud off it using the front of her shirt and presses a button to check that it still works before wrapping her arms around her rain-soaked body. The move appears to be in self-preservation rather than the need to keep warm.

Despite the rain and mud, her beauty is striking. Large eyes captivate me, but it is too dark to make out their color. My eyes drink in her features—the delicate arch of her eyebrows, her lush full lips—but the tension in her body reminds me she fears me.

"Do you know what's wrong?" I ask, turning my attention to the car before I make her more uncomfortable than she already is. Maybe if I focus on my reason for stopping rather than her, it'll reassure her I don't mean her any harm.

"I'll figure it out. I'm fine," she says, her expression mulish and her tone clearly signaling that I should leave.

I want to believe her, but her shivering form and defensive posture make that difficult. I'd feel guilty if I left and found out later that something bad had happened to her. "Can I take a look?"

"You a mechanic?" She asks, eyes narrowing.

"No, but I've—"

"Then no," she interrupts, her voice sharp. "Possessing a dick doesn't automatically grant car expertise, and my lack thereof doesn't mean I'm ignorant of vehicles."

I almost smile at her bravado. I can tell it's all bluster, though—like a wet kitten trying to appear fierce. She's trying to act tough, but I can see she's scared. That fear makes me want to protect her, even if it's just from the situation at hand.

"Do you?" I ask gently.

"Do I what?" she snaps, her hand coming up to move her wet hair behind her ear.

"Do you know what you're looking at?"

She shoots me a death glare, but her eyes dart to the side before she opens her mouth, clearly about to lie.

"I know enough."

"That may be, but I help at my buddy's shop when he gets busy. I know my way around a car. An extra pair of eyes can't hurt." I offer her a small, reassuring smile. Ma always told me to kill them with kindness.

She glares at me for a long moment before begrudgingly nodding. Progress. I turn and start walking back toward my truck, wincing at how uncomfortable my wet jeans are.

"Hey! I thought you said you were going to help!" she yells after me.

"Just grabbing a flashlight," I call over my shoulder; her little phone light won't be much help.

"How do I know you're not grabbing an ax?" she shoots back.

I pause. "What would I need an ax for?" I ask, then chuckle. "Oh right, if I wanted to hurt you, wouldn't I have already attacked you when your back was turned?" My sarcasm is punctuated with a raised brow, not that I was close enough for her to notice.

"Some crazy people like to watch the terror on their victims' faces," she says under her breath.

"What?" My brow furrows at such an odd comment.

"Nothing. You were getting a flashlight," she says, crossing her arms again.

I suppress another smile. She's prickly, and I like it. Usually, I prefer sweet and compliant. Bratty subs are not my thing, but something about her fiery attitude is endearing. I imagine there is a soft, sweet center beneath the prickly cactus exterior. One that a good Dom would need to work hard to unwrap, but the prize that lay underneath—I shake the thought from my head. This isn't the time. I need to get my head out of the gutter. She's already afraid of me. I don't need to give her an actual reason. She isn't a sub at the club. She's a woman stranded on the side of the road in need of help, not someone I should fantasize about.

I return with the flashlight, noting how tense she still is. She watches me closely, clearly ready to bolt at any moment.

"Goddamn, you could club a man to death with that thing," she mutters when she sees the size of the flashlight.

I snicker. "So, what do we have going on, Little Bunny?"

She doesn't disappoint as her expression darkens in anger. "Bunny?" she scoffs.

"You look ready to bolt," I say, still grinning. Good, anger is better than fear. I'd rather she found me annoying than threatening. "Reminds me of my niece's bunny. The thing is scared of its own shadow."

"I'm not scared of my own shadow," she snaps back, her posture straightening and her hands balling into fists before she looks off towards the trees, and her voice softens, "I just have a healthy dose of reality about what people are capable of."

Fuck, I hate that for her. My job sometimes involves dealing with the worst of society, and I know the kinds of monsters there are. "I'm sorry you've experienced that, Bunny," I say sincerely.

"Arrgh! That's not my name."

"You didn't give me one," I reply with a smirk.

"Just look at the damn car." She says, stomping her foot in the wet mud, causing it to lose any effect.

"Yes, ma'am," I say with a mock salute and a wink.

She growls under her breath, all traces of fear gone, which only makes me want to rile her up more. I'm not sure why, but her defiance amuses me. The more I smile, the more irritated she becomes.

That's it. Don't be afraid of me.

"Does it turn on?" I ask as I run the flashlight over the engine.

"Nope. Nothing."

"Dead battery?"

"Clearly, but I don't think a jump will fix it. It wasn't having problems before," she trails off, biting her lip.

"Before?" I prompt, looking up at her, but she ignores me, keeping her eyes fixed on a spot past me.

"There was an issue with the electrical, then the check engine light, and I hoped to make it to the next town, but then the oil light before it started making weird noises."

"Due for a change?"

"No!" she snaps. "I know how to take care of my car. It gets regular maintenance. I took care of the oil last month. This shouldn't be happening. The oil shouldn't be that low."

I frown as I move a few cables and hoses out of the way. "Hmm. Well, here's your problem," I say, shining the light to the side. "Your alternator belt has snapped."

She steps closer to see, pressing in next to me, forgetting her fear of me with the realization that her car troubles are far worse than a dead battery. "Shit," she mutters, staring down at the engine. Her prickly exterior drops for a moment, revealing someone far more vulnerable than she lets on.

"You'll need a tow," my voice soft and apologetic.

"Shit," she repeats, looking lost for a second before her defenses shoot back up, and she takes a large step away from me. I miss the press of her body immediately. "I'll call someone. Uh, thanks, I guess. You can, uh… I'll take it from here."

"I can call my buddy. He runs the only shop in town. He'll come get your car tomorrow, and I can give you a ride into town."

That was the wrong thing to say.

Her body tightens, and she takes another enormous step away from me, vehemently shaking her head. "Nope, I think not. I'm not going anywhere with you. I'll call an Uber. It'll be fine."

Something tells me she is lying about calling an Uber. "Okay then, order one and I'll wait with you until it gets here." I cross my arms and give her a challenging look.

"I…uh… its," I raise my brows in a silent dare. "I'll be fine here. You did your good deed, you can go now."

"You can't spend the night in your car."

"Wouldn't be the first time," she mumbles, not meeting my gaze.

I shake my head but don't argue. She's smart not to get into a car with a stranger. I can't fault her for that. I walk over to my truck, grab my phone, and use a T-shirt to dry my hands before dialing Maddox.

It rings a few times before going to voicemail. "Motherf—" I mutter, dialing again.

"What, asshole? This better be an emergency," Maddox growls when he finally answers.

"I've got a damsel in distress in need of a tow and a ride," I say.

"I am not a damsel!" she yells from behind me, startling me. I hadn't realized she'd followed me.

Maddox chuckles. "Sounds lovely. Just tell me where her car is. I'll get it in the morning. You give her a ride."

"Yeah, that won't work. She thinks I'm an ax murderer. Could your sister come out instead?" She scoffs, and I grin at the cute sound.

Maddox snickers. "Finally, someone not instantly charmed by the great Reid Mathews. She must have impecable taste."

"Just get Juniper here. We're about 10 minutes out from Deliverance on Pine Crest Road."

Maddox groans. "Fine. Let me text Juniper, and I'll let you know when we're on our way."

"Thanks, man. But heads up, I don't think she'll get in the car if you're in it."

Maddox is silent for a moment, picking up on the unspoken concern. "Fine, but you're driving me back. I'm not letting Juniper drive out alone in this weather."

"I don't need you dragging your friends out here." She grumbles when I hang up the phone.

"Tough, I'm not about to leave you stranded, Little Bunny."

She growls again, and I can't help the laugh that escapes, causing her to turn and stomp through the mud back to her car. The rain is lightening up, but it is nowhere near stopping. I follow behind her. "My car still runs," I call out. "I can turn the heat on while we wait for Juniper to get here."

"You go do that then," she calls over her shoulder, stopping at her car. She slams down the hood before pressing her hands on the top of it. I watch as her shoulders slump, and the pure exhaustion and defeat radiating from her posture worry me. But as if she pulls strength from some hidden reserve, she straightens up, turns around, and leans back against the car, her expression a mix of annoyance and hostility. All evidence of her moment of weakness is gone. I can't help but admire the strength.

"So what's your story?" I ask, joining her. I guess we'll just ignore the cold as fuck rain and lean here and wait.

"I don't have a story."

"Everyone has a story. But you don't have to tell me yours. I can tell you mine," I grin down at her. She can keep her secrets. For now. "By the way, I'm Reid." I don't bother putting my hand out to her. I've annoyed her too much to think she'll shake it.

I let the silence stretch on, hoping she'll feel the pressure to fill it. "Sage," she says after a long moment.

I nod in acknowledgment. "So let's see, I'm heading home after a job. I work for a security firm, mostly doing fieldwork. Short-term contracts guarding important people. Or those that think they are important." She snorts at that, and I suppress a grin. "The last guy—I can't tell you his name, but he was a real character. He has an obsession with those CB radios. You know the kind that truckers use. He says that the chatter on them nowadays is a bunch of trolls, but he has this schedule of a handful of truckers he is still in contact with." She says nothing, but the slight tilt of her head in my direction and the tiny smile tell me she is listening.

I fill the next 15 minutes with random stories about people I've met on different jobs. Safe things.

Her guard is still up when Maddox and Juniper get here, but the hostility is gone. The presence of Juniper must put her at ease because the prickliness she aimed at me is nowhere to be seen when she talks to Maddox, and she even smiles at Juniper.

It's a beautiful smile.

I let out a sigh when she leaves with Juniper. A ball of tension I hadn't realized was knotted in my stomach vanishes now that she is heading some place safer than the side of the road.

"Let's go," Maddox calls, already getting into my truck. "I'll look at her car when it gets to the shop tomorrow. You owe me for coming all the way out here in the rain."

I laugh. Maddox would have my back regardless of the weather. "I'll bring you pastries from Dezzie's shop." I offer as compensation.

"For the entire shop."

I roll my eyes at the request. "Done."

We spend the rest of the drive to town catching up, but underneath the conversation, my thoughts keep circling back to the condition of her car. Like she'd said, I did my good deed, yet something feels unfinished. I just can't put my finger on what.

CHAPTER THREE

Sage

I sigh, glancing at Juniper before looking out the window into the darkness. Juniper is a beautiful brunette with flawless olive skin, wearing a bright pink raincoat. Why am I not into women? Life would probably be easier. Maybe then I could have dated someone like Juniper, who seems genuinely kind.

She'd practically bounced out of the car to greet me with a hug despite the rain, and is now driving me into town, acting like we are already friends.

"You would have been safe with him, you know?" she says after a few minutes of awkward silence, broken only by the low music playing softly in the car's background. The rain drums relentlessly against the windows, creating a steady backdrop of noise.

I shift in my seat, acutely aware of my damp clothes and the thin towel on the seat, unsure how to respond. "Sorry for making you drive out to get me," I finally say. "I would've been fine on my own, but..." I trail off, unsure if I believe my own words. I probably would have slept in my car and woken up to a dead phone if I am being honest with myself.

Juniper makes a derisive sound, rolling her eyes. "Uh, yeah, right. Like Reid would've left you on your own in this kind of weather, let alone at night. He's got a savior complex. Same with Maddox, and half the men I know in this tiny town." She shakes her head, smiling ruefully. "But that's not what I meant. And don't worry about the drive. I don't mind, really. It's... you clearly don't trust men. Honestly, I don't blame you. But Reid's a good guy." She gives me a warm smile before returning her focus to the road.

I frown, staring out the rain-streaked window. I can see faint outlines of trees interspersed with the occasional house. The dense woods are further away now that we are on the edge of town. "Yeah, maybe," I mutter, not entirely convinced.

"It's smart to be cautious," Juniper adds, her voice softening as if she senses my wariness. "But if you ever need help, Reid, Maddox, and the rest of their friends are good guys. They'd look out for you, no questions asked."

In response, I offer a small, tight-lipped smile, appreciating the sentiment but still not ready to let my guard down. "Thanks," I say, my voice quiet. After another beat of silence, I clear my throat and change the subject. "Do you know of any motels in town? Preferably one that" I hesitate for a moment, knowing that she might ask questions, "won't make a big deal about ID or paying in cash?" I end with a grimace.

Juniper glances at me, curiosity flashing in her eyes. "You running from someone?"

"No, I uh... just uh," I stumble over the words, feeling bad about lying, no matter how many times I've tried to sell it. I clear my throat and try again. "No. I just like keeping a low profile," I say vaguely, hoping that will be enough. I'm not ready to spill my life story to a stranger, no matter how kind she appears.

Juniper presses her lips together but doesn't push further. "Yeah, I know a place. The Rosewood Inn. It's cute, and the owner's pretty chill. I'll give her a heads-up so cash won't be an issue."

"Thanks," I say, happy that Juniper isn't digging too deep. "That sounds perfect."

Juniper fills the silences with safe topics, and I find myself relaxing around a stranger for the first time in... I don't remember when. The road twists and turns, the houses getting closer together, interspersed with thick clusters of trees. I am almost sad when we reach the town limits because I know my time with Juniper is coming to an end. Despite the exhaustion starting to creep up on me, I feel lighter as I laugh along to a story she tells me about her brother Maddox, Reid, and a prank they played involving peanut butter.

When we finally reach the center of Deliverance, I'm fighting off a yawn. Still, the sight of the adorable town is enough to give me a slight energy boost. Tiny storefronts line the main street, their windows glowing warmly in the otherwise gloomy night with only a handful of people on the sidewalk. The few that are out are smart enough to have umbrellas with them. The buildings are old brick but well-kept, while string lights hang over the streets, twinkling like stars through the sheets of rain, giving the town a charming, almost storybook feel.

Juniper pulls out her phone at a stoplight and types a quick message before handing it to me. "Here, put your number in and send yourself a text so you'll have mine in case you need it. I'll send you the guys' numbers too, just in case. I promise I won't give them yours. I told Silvia you were coming, so you shouldn't have any problems."

I stare down at the phone screen before moving to the messaging app. I don't have my new number memorized and am not even sure I want to give it out. I turn the screen off and quietly place the phone in the cupholder of the center console. I already have the number of the shop Maddox runs, and once my car is fixed, I'm leaving.

I think.

I could have sworn there was a flash of disappointment on Juniper's face, but it's gone before I can examine it.

Juniper turns down a narrow side street and pulls up in front of a quaint little building with a bright Rosewood Inn sign swinging in the rain. The building is painted a pale lavender, with white trim and flower boxes under the windows, filled with dark purple blooms. Most of the cars in the lot are parked near the office, but a few are scattered towards the back.

"This is the place," Juniper says, putting the car in park. She glances over at me as I'm already gathering my things. "You sure you're okay? You don't have to tell me anything, but... you seem like you've got a lot on your plate."

I pause, my hand gripping the door handle. I consider brushing it off again, giving the same vague response, but something about Juniper's gentle tone makes me soften a bit. "Yeah," I say after a moment. "I've got a lot going on, but... thanks. For everything. I really appreciate it."

Juniper smiles, though there's a hint of sadness in her eyes. "Anytime. And hey, if you need anything, just ask for me. Everyone knows me. And I'm sure Reid already told you, but he works for a security company. If... if you are running from someone, they can help. I promise. They take on a lot of different cases, and sometimes," she takes a deep breath, "sometimes it's domestic violence or stalkers or whatever, and they can help people hide."

I nod, offering a small smile before opening the door. I want to believe her, but even if my problem could be solved by hiring a bodyguard, I don't exactly have the money for that. The rain hits me full force, and I quickly duck out, pulling my jacket tight around me and swinging the lone backpack I'd brought from my car over my shoulders. The cold air is a shock after the warmth of the car.

I jog to the office, the old-fashioned bell above the door jingling as I step inside. The front desk is unmanned, but the space is cozy—with worn wooden floors, floral wallpaper, and a few antique chairs tucked into the corners.

A young woman with dark brown hair in a high ponytail emerges from a back room, wiping her hands on a dish towel. "You must be the one Juniper texted about," she says with a kind smile. "Need a room?" I guess this is Silvia.

"Yes, please," I reply, trying to sound composed despite the exhaustion creeping in. "Cash okay?"

The woman nods. "How many nights?"

"Oh, uh, I don't know, actually. I... until my car is fixed, I guess."

She nods. "We'll start with one night and play it by ear, sound good?"

I smile back, my tension easing just a little. "Thank you."

She tells me the rate, and I almost question her about the cost. There is no way a room at a place like this could be so cheap. But I guess Juniper must have said something in her text.

Silvia hands me a key with a small wooden tag attached. "Room three. It's near mine in room one in case you need anything. Down that hallway there." She points to the hall behind her.

I take the key with a soft thanks and head down the hall. The hall is lined with the same floral wallpaper, a pale yellow with pale pink roses. There's something comforting about the quaint little place. It's far from a fancy resort I once stayed at with Jordan. That place was full of clean white lines with no personality, and instead of a key, it had a key card that I, or rather Jordan, would flash at the door. After all, there was no need for me to have my own key to the room. I shake off the memory and quickly insert the key into the lock. I'm safe here for the night.

Once inside, I lock the door behind me with a satisfying click, feeling the reassuring finality of the bolt sliding into place. I stand for a moment, back pressed against the door, my eyes scanning the dimly lit room. The air holds a faint scent of lavender, cedarwood, and a lemony cleaner—it's an unusual but pleasant mix.

The room is small but comfortable. A mix of the rustic charm of a bed-and-breakfast, yet the impersonal nature of a hotel room. A queen bed is tucked to one side, neatly made with soft cream bedding and a navy throw folded at the foot. Between it and the wall is a small, end table with a simple lamp casting a warm amber glow and a squat, bowl-shaped vase with cut flowers.

On the other side of the bed is a cozy-looking, faded blue armchair with a patterned throw pillow artfully arranged on the seat. Against the wall, under the single curtain, covered window, is a small writing desk and chair with assorted knickknacks tucked in one corner and a basket with stationery supplies in the other.

Opposite the bed is an antique-looking dresser with more cut flowers and knickknacks. The walls are painted a soft blue, and painted landscapes dot the walls.

The longer I stand at the door, the stronger the urge to check that the room is truly empty begins to grow. I rationally know that no one could have followed me here, and that he couldn't have entered in the short time between Juniper dropping me off; however, I won't be able to rest until I've checked everywhere. I move through the space in slow, deliberate steps, the carpet muffling my cautious footsteps.

I kneel, peering under the bed—just empty shadows staring back at me. The closet is next, its single door creaking slightly as I open it, revealing only a few wooden hangers swaying gently, undisturbed. A sigh of relief slips from my lips as I close it again. I check behind the chair and under the writing desk, despite the spaces being incapable of concealing someone. With each spot I check, tension ebbs, my mind quieting at the familiar ritual.

I step into the bathroom, where the bright fluorescent

light starkly contrasts the soft, warm glow of the main room. A small fan hums overhead. The faded blue shower curtain and lone forest painting provide the only pops of color in an otherwise stark white space. I give a rueful smile at the pristine white-tiled floor. At least I can see at a glance that this bathroom is clean. Despite the harsh brightness, I'm oddly grateful for the simplicity. I've stayed in some grungy motels, where it was hard to tell what lurked in the shadows. I check behind the shower curtain, then leave it open.

Just in case.

Returning to the main room, I exhale, a small sense of relief settles over me. I am alone.

I set my backpack down and dig out a dry pair of sweatpants and an oversized t-shirt. Both worn and threadbare but soft. Back in the bathroom, I turn the water on to the hottest setting before tossing my wet clothes in a pile on the floor. The small room fills with steam, and I climb into the shower, my cold skin prickling with pain at the shock of the hot water before the pain fades to a comforting warmth.

I stand under the water for a while, trying to wash away the past few hours. Reid's concerned face flashes through my mind, but I quickly push the thought aside. He's a stranger. No matter what Juniper said, it wasn't worth the risk. Better to keep my distance from men altogether. Besides, it's not like he's thinking about me now. He'd done his good deed. He's probably already forgotten me.

Stepping out of the shower, I wrap myself in a thick white towel, my muscles loose and relaxed from the warmth of the water.

I slip into my sweats and ready the room for the night. My bag is within arm's reach and shoes are lined up next to it in case I need to make a quick escape. The door is locked, the phone is close by, and I leave the bathroom light on, its glow spilling into the bedroom, casting enough light to prevent anyone from hiding in the shadows.

I collapse onto the bed. The thick blankets envelop me, warm and soft as I burrow beneath. I stare up at the ceiling, listening to the rain as it continues to pour outside, the occasional sound of a car driving by the only variation in the steady pattering of the storm. The cozy warmth of the room should lull me into relaxation, especially after an eventful evening, but my mind is still racing. I press my hands over my face, trying to calm myself, to push back the paranoia that lurks behind my thoughts. I am exhausted; everything feels heavy, but I am still too keyed up.

"I'm safe. No one from my old life can find me here. There's no trail." I whisper into the empty room.

Are you sure? The small voice that lingers in the back of my mind whispers. I force myself to take deep slow breaths, reminding myself I'm safe—for now.

Reaching for my phone, I stare at the blank screen. I haven't used it much for anything other than a map since I started running. No phone calls, no social media, and not a single text sent to anyone who might give me away. Every phone call and text I have received has been either for the previous owner or spam. And yet, despite every precaution I've taken, that dark sense of foreboding creeps, clawing its way up from my gut.

Shoving the phone aside, I let out a frustrated sigh, but it's no use. The anxiety grows, heavy and unshakable.

It wasn't just the car. A snapped alternator belt could easily be bad luck catching up with me, but the uneasy feeling lingers. Has he somehow found me? Did he mess with my car? There was that attempted break-in at the last place I stayed. The thought makes my stomach twist, and I get up and cross the room to recheck the lock on the door. My gaze drifts to the dresser; I could use that to block the door. I dismiss the thought as quickly as it appears. It looks far too heavy and old.

Okay, back to bed.

In the quiet that follows, I feel the weight of my choices—whether to run again or to stick around and try to build a new life. My instincts scream at me to leave, but I'm so tired of running. At least for tonight, I'll try to find a sliver of peace here in this tiny, rain-soaked town. After all, I'm stuck until my car is fixed, and that might take the last of my savings. I have a few more trinkets I can sell, but that's my emergency stash sewn into the lining of a few choice pieces of clothing. I'm not that desperate yet.

I focus on my breathing, counting down from 100.

But as my breathing begins to slow and I sink deeper into the bed's embrace, a sudden buzz shatters the quiet. My heart lurches as I reach for my phone, hands trembling as I unlock the screen and open the message from an unknown number.

Unknown Number: No need to worry, I'll take care of everything.

Googling the number doesn't give me any information. Something feels wrong. I hadn't given my number to Juniper, and this certainly wasn't Maddox or Reid. Maddox gave me his shop number; I didn't give him mine. Maybe they found my number in the car. But why such a cryptic message?

Me: Who is this?

There is no response.

A memory stirs in the back of my mind, one I'd long buried with others I'd rather forget. It sounded eerily like one of Jordan's phrases when someone came to him with a request. His way of subtly asserting control at the end of those meetings. I shake my head, banishing the thought. There's no way he has this number. It's a prepaid burner phone I'd picked up at a gas station, with no identifiable information about me tied to it.

No, it has to be a wrong number. A coincidence. Nothing more.

But why didn't they respond?

My thoughts spin until the early hours of the morning when I finally drift off to sleep.

CHAPTER FOUR

Reid

I push open the side door to Maddox's garage, the scent of oil and metal hitting me as I step inside. It's early morning, and Maddox is already elbow-deep under the hood of an old truck while one of his employees is taking a tire off a red minivan, filling the air with the whir of the impact wrench. The heavy metal door slams shut behind me, catching Maddox's attention. He steps away from the truck, wiping his hands on a grease-stained rag he pulls from his pocket as I approach.

"Hey, man," Maddox greets, "Didn't expect to see you this early. Did you bring the pastries?" He asks, despite the obvious white box in my hands.

I ignore his question and drop the box off at the breakroom, grabbing a Danish for myself and a turnover for Maddox.

I return as Maddox is drying his hands and pass him the treat.

"Thanks, man, but why are you here so early? I didn't expect you until 10 or 11."

I shrug, running a hand through my still-damp hair. "Wanted to talk to you about that woman's car—the one from last night. Sage."

Maddox raises an eyebrow. "The one Juniper had to go pick up 'cause she thought you were some kind of ax murderer? Yeah, I remember." He chuckles at me.

I give a small laugh. "Yeah, her." I cross my arms, my expression growing more serious. "Something was off with her car.

The alternator belt had snapped, but it didn't look like normal wear and tear to me. Looked like someone had cut most of it, leaving a bit to hold it together. Not frayed or old like it would be if it just wore down."

Maddox pauses, the turnover halfway to his mouth. "Cut? That's not something you see every day. You sure?" he motions for me to follow him to his office.

"That's why I'm here," I reply. The loud sounds of the garage dim as soon as the office door closes. I sink into the stiff black office chair that looks like it's seen better days, the yellow foam padding peaking out in places. Maddox takes a seat behind his desk. The piles of paperwork scattered around his desk flutter in his wake, and one precarious pile threatens to topple, but he reaches out to catch it. "I want you to look and see if I'm overthinking it. It just didn't feel right. The cut was too clean, and Sage mentioned the oil pressure and check engine light came on before the car died. That doesn't make sense if it was only the alternator belt."

Maddox's frown deepens, and he sets the turnover down, forgotten. He leans forward, placing his elbows on the only empty space in front of him, hands clasped together, his expression contemplative. "No, it doesn't. A snapped belt wouldn't trigger an oil warning unless something else was going on. Could be a coincidence, but I trust your gut. It's been right too many times to count."

"That's what I'm worried about. Honestly, I hope I'm wrong."

"I'll have to take a closer look. Anything else seem off?"

I pause, my gaze drifting toward the wall behind Maddox, glossing over the hodgepodge assortment of charts and posters he has tacked on the wall. "She was skittish. I get it—dark road, big guy like me showing up out of nowhere—but this felt like more than that. Like she was already running scared. Wouldn't let me help at first, kept insisting she could handle it on her own. She was tense the entire time."

Maddox grunts, his brow furrowed. "Juniper mentioned something about that. Said the woman asked for a place that would let her pay in cash. Didn't want to give out too many details about herself. Pretended to give Juniper her number."

"Yep, Juniper told me that too."

He quirks an eyebrow at that. "Pretty rare for someone to put that much effort into staying off the grid unless they are on the run."

Unease is growing in my gut. "If she's running from someone, and someone tampered with that belt, there could be more going on than we realize. I didn't have time to dig around last night, but something's telling me this wasn't just an unlucky break."

Maddox leans back in his chair, pulling out his phone and unlocking it. "I sent one of the guys to tow her car in already. When it gets here, I'll go over it myself. If someone messed with her vehicle, I'll find it."

I nod. "I don't want to jump to conclusions, but the whole thing feels off. Even with a dead car, she was reluctant for me to take a look, and when I offered to give her a ride into town, she looked at me like I was about to throw her in the trunk."

Maddox lets out a dark chuckle. "Can't blame her. The world's a messed-up place, you know that more than most, especially for a woman traveling alone."

"Yeah," I agree, my voice dropping. "I don't know what her story is, but it's pretty clear she's on edge. The thought of someone driving a sabotaged car infuriates me. If it was, she's not safe."

"I'll handle it and let you know." His focus drifts to the paperwork on his desk, done with the conversation.

I linger for a moment, my concern still nagging at me. "Think she'll even listen to us if we tell her something's wrong?"

Maddox shrugs. "Hard to say. She might brush us off. But if someone tampered with her car, we can't ignore it. Maybe report it to the sheriff or something. Even though she's skittish, she deserves to know. At least then, the ball's in her court."

I grunt in agreement. "Yeah. You're right. I'll swing by the Rosewood in a bit, see if she's willing to talk more about what is going on now that it is day time." Grateful Juniper, oh so kindly, filled me in on where she took Sage, her suspicions, and the dozen demands that I do something. My phone vibrates in my pocket, so I pull it out. Make that a baker's dozen amount of demands.

Maddox gives me a quizzical look. "Juniper." I answer, "Asking for an update. I'm going to let her know you are taking your time." His brows narrow as he takes in the impatience under my poor attempt at a joke.

"You seem rather invested. Anything you want to share with the class?" he teases.

I scowl at the implications. "Just… worried."

"Sure, that's all. See if you can get something out of her. If someone's after her, maybe Heartwood can help."

I give a noncommittal nod, my thoughts swirling in my head. Involving Heartwood Security is probably the smartest course of action. But if she didn't want my help with her car, why would she accept it for anything else?

"Relax, I'll look at her car and let you know." Maddox says, dismissing me.

I give a brief nod before standing and heading to the door. "Thanks, man. I appreciate it." I say over my shoulder.

Maddox waves me off.

The drive to Rosewood is quick despite the usual morning traffic of people heading to work and tourists taking in the sights. I contemplate how I am going to approach her. Her car is the reason for my visit, but showing up at the inn might seem stalkerish. I know my reasoning is flimsy at best. However, it was a wasted effort, as Sage had already left for the day.

Probably a good thing.

I run my fingers through my hair.

Without Sage's number, I'm left with the choice of searching the town for her like the stalker I am trying not to be, or heading to the office and waiting for Maddox to call with an update.

Not wanting to give her a reason to fear me, I head to work.

CHAPTER FIVE

Sage

I rub my gritty eyes before massaging my temples. Could this coffee line be any slower? My cold fingertips are soothing against my forehead, the pressure helping to fight off the growing headache. I shake my head as if I can shake off the terrible night's sleep, but it does nothing to improve the fuzziness in my head. I groan and stretch my arms over my head, my body protesting the movement. The bed may have been soft, but my body ached from the lack of sleep. If it wasn't for that cryptic text, I might not have lain awake for so long.

If I am honest with myself, I probably would have obsessed over the car trouble instead. I did that, too, but the added layer of the unknown text message made it a stressful night of worrying about the car and paranoia about who the message may have been from.

I wait behind a portly man, willing him to hurry so I can get some coffee to go.

Finally! I skip the mug, opt for a to-go cup, and step off to the side as soon as it is filled before I doctor it with creamer.

See, I don't hog the coffee bar, unlike some people.

I take a sip, and the nirvana I was hoping for leaves me disappointed. I hide my grimace from Silvia. It's not awful coffee. Just far weaker than my sleep-starved body is craving right now.

Silvia is bustling around the common area off the side of the lobby, refreshing the small breakfast bar and refilling the ceramic cups of the guests staying for a relaxed breakfast. When I checked in last night, the room had been closed off, but now the double doors are propped open. Other guests mill around, filling their plates or talking to their travel companions at the small, round tables spread out around the room. This room lacks the floral wallpaper of the entry and hallway, but the rose theme is still very apparent with the multitude of cut flowers in vases throughout the room.

I wonder when Siliva finds time to sleep. Manning the desk last night and stocking the breakfast buffet could only mean late nights and early mornings. Does she have other employees? So far, I see only her. She glances my way, but I turn my head before she can catch my eye. In my periphery, I can see her start to approach me.

Time to go.

Weak coffee in one hand and a chocolate muffin in the other, I walk to the exit, trying very hard not to look like I am running away from her. I stuff down the pang of regret. I don't need her asking questions I can't answer.

As I step outside, my skin pebbles in the cool air. After the warmth of the inn, it's like jumping into a cold pool on a hot day. The shock does more to clear my head than the coffee did. I take another sip. It may be weak, but I can't let it go to waste. Dark, twisted dreams tainted what little rest I managed to find.

I need caffeine. First stop, a coffee shop for a proper cup of coffee.

I'm sure I remember Juniper driving past one before dropping me off. I walk in the direction I think it is, alternating bites of the muffin and sips of the coffee.

Passing a trash can, I toss my trash and pull out my phone. A quick search tells me I am close. Just one more block.

The town has a cozy mom-and-pop vibe. Old brick two and three-story buildings, a handful painted in faded hues of blue, green, and yellow, line the street, their shop windows reflecting glimmers of sunlight and flashes of movement from within. Each storefront is unique—a florist with a small display of potted plants out front, their bright greens and pinks popping against the subdued colors of the buildings; a bookstore with its door propped open, letting in the crisp air, stacks of novels and paperbacks piled on a table by the entrance. Handwritten signs in the windows advertise everything from seasonal sales to town events, and the casual scrawl makes the whole place appear unhurried and personal. Despite the postcard-perfect scene in front of me, I find it hard to appreciate my surroundings. My thoughts are a jumble of half-baked plans and worries I just want to discard.

I take a deep breath and try to blow away the nagging worries and focus on the beauty and charm around me. Everything is lush and vibrant, with only a few puddles of water as the last remnants of the storm. I can hear birds chirping as they flit around in the sky and the chatter of other people walking down the sidewalk. The sky is a brilliant cerulean blue that you only see after a rainstorm.

This is an adorable town. I rub at the sudden ache in my chest. Longing.

The coffee shop is a two-story building with a faded red brick façade and dark blue-black accents, giving it a hipster vibe. A green and white striped awning provides the entrance protection from the elements. Through the large windows, I can see people on laptops at tables or settling into armchairs, talking in small groups. My gaze moves to the counter, where Juniper is waving enthusiastically, a warm smile lighting up her face. My cheeks flush as a few patrons turn to see who has captured Juniper's attention.

The jingle of a bell announces my entrance as I pull open the heavy door. Wonderful, if I didn't already have half the shop looking at me. My gaze passes over the people and focuses on the counter. The strong aroma of fresh coffee is the only thing keeping me from running back outside.

I suppose this is the downside of a small town—everyone knows everyone, and newcomers stand out. I am used to blending into the background, not standing out. But the scrutiny doesn't last long, and the hum of conversation resumes.

"Sage!" Juniper calls out with a welcoming grin as I reach the counter. She steps out from behind the counter, arms out for a quick hug. "Glad you made it in this morning." She says, as if we made plans to meet up or something. Her warmth seems genuine, and I manage an awkward hug in return before Juniper pulls back, chatting easily. "What'll it be today? We've got coffee, tea, smoothies, and the usual breakfast fare. You've got to try the muffins—they're fresh every morning from the bakery down the street. Best in the entire state, if you ask me."

"Uh, coffee. Caramel latte, I guess, extra espresso," I say, a bit off-balance from Juniper's energy.

"Coming right up!" Juniper says, heading back to the counter. She moves around the machines with an air of familiarity, chatting the entire time about nothing consequential.

I glance around, self-conscious, but the patrons seem busy with their own business. I approach the register and hand my cash to the young man working there, watching him ring up my order with a friendly nod. Just as he hands me the receipt, Juniper reappears, holding out the steaming cup.

"So, I noticed my phone didn't save your number," she says casually, giving me an easy out despite also calling me out. A blush warms my cheeks.

"Uh, yeah. I actually don't have my number memorized, and..." I trail off awkwardly. My eyes dart to the young man, who gives me a small smile before taking Juniper's place, making drinks while she holds me hostage at the register.

"No worries!" Juniper replies with a grin, her tone light. "Here, just give me your phone." Before I can think twice, I hand over my unlocked phone, watching as Juniper quickly enters her number and then calls her phone. She lets it ring once and hangs up, handing my phone back with a satisfied smile.

"I know last night wasn't the ideal way to meet someone, but you might be here a few days while your car gets fixed, and it'll be nice to know someone, right?" her expression earnest. Seems Juniper is a morning person, and my sleep-deprived brain struggles to keep up. "I work mornings here, but I'm free in the afternoons, and in the evenings, I'm at the bookshop over there." She waves behind her in a vague, that-away direction, that, if I hadn't already passed the bookshop, would have done little to tell me where it was. You're welcome to come hang out. I could introduce you to some of my friends or show you around a bit. They're nice, I promise. And I promise they won't ask questions."

"That sounds good, I guess," I reply hesitantly. "I need to check on my car, but, um, I'll text you?" I want to kick myself for posing it as a question.

Unfazed by my lack of enthusiasm, Juniper gives me a light squeeze on the arm before returning to work.

Once I leave the shop, I stand on the sidewalk for a moment, clutching my coffee, not entirely sure what just happened. I take a sip and sigh in relief. Thank god this place has good strong coffee.

I shake my head, a fleeting smile tugging at my lips as I pull out my phone and search the directions to the mechanic's shop. According to the map on my phone, it's a little way past Main Street but close enough to walk.

The morning sun casts a gentle glow over the street, warming the chilly air as I walk along the sidewalk. A light breeze carries the scent of damp earth and pine from the surrounding hills, mingling with the faint aroma of freshly baked bread wafting from the bakery up ahead and the delicious smell of the coffee shop behind me. I take my time, glancing into the windows of the shops I pass as I stroll down the street.

I hope Maddox has already towed my car and figured out what has gone wrong. At the very least, I need to talk to him about potential costs.

Papers taped to the windows of one shop catch my eye. Each one shows a picture of a different house with a list of amenities and costs. Must be a real estate office.

Maybe I should stick around for a bit. My eyes jump from listing to listing. Fixing the car might use up what's left of my money anyway, so perhaps I really should consider getting a temporary job.

Small groups linger outside the shops or walk down the street. There is no way everyone here lives in this town. This place seems to be very touristy, and Juniper has two jobs. I've waited tables before, and I know I can handle cleaning. As much as I hate relying on people, maybe Juniper could help me find something under the table. Thanks to her, I am already staying in the nicest place I've been to so far. The places willing to overlook ID tend to be in not-so-great areas. The Rosewood Inn is more of a bed-and-breakfast.

But troubling thoughts of my car still linger. The alternator belt snapping doesn't make any sense. I try to do as much of the car repair as possible to save money. When I had to replace the radiator, nothing looked worn. Wouldn't I have noticed that? Perhaps that was a mistake. A professional might have seen that it needed to be replaced.

I can hear the soft strains of music drifting from a cafe, the tables full of people, and a brunette waitress flitting between the tables. She looks like she could use an extra pair of hands.

Up ahead, I spot a large town square with a beautiful gazebo in the center. As I look closer, my eyes catch on a woman in a wedding dress, and I do a double-take, only to realize the bride is posing for wedding photos. The scene is sweetly surreal—lace and tulle drifting in the gentle breeze as the photographer clicks away, the town square a pretty backdrop. I slow my steps, taking in the peace, the way every part of the street is worn in and familiar, like a faded memory. There's a comfort to it, a sense that nothing has to change if it doesn't want to, that life here follows a rhythm all its own. This would be a lovely place to live.

My phone chimes. I snort a laugh when I see what Juniper put as her name in my contacts.

New Bestie: Maddox says your car just got to the shop and to give him an hour to do a full inspection.

Me: Thanks

New Bestie: Since you have time, you should check out the town.

Her next message is a location pin.

I bite my lip, considering my next move. This is the start of a connection, an invitation to be more than a casual acquaintance passing through. I should shut it down. Thank her for the update, get my car fixed, and go. But the longing for a home, a friend, to not be alone is strong. Maybe I can enjoy a temporary slice of calm before I have to move on.

Me: Where does this lead?

New Bestie: Go there and find out. I'll send another one soon =)

CHAPTER SIX

Reid

The vibration of my phone startles me. I look up from the spot on the wall where I'd spent who knows how many minutes staring at, lost in thought, and glance at the unfinished paperwork mocking me on my desk. Well, this has been a productive morning, I snark to myself.

I look down at the still-buzzing phone, surprised to see Maddox calling. With towing the car and doing a full inspection, I didn't expect to hear from him so soon. A sinking feeling settles in my gut as I slide my finger across the screen to answer. I hope Maddox is calling to tell me my suspicions are completely unfounded.

"Tell me you've got good news for me, man," I say, skipping the greeting.

"I wish I could, brother," Maddox replies, his tone dashing any lingering doubt about Sage being in danger. "It might be a good idea if you come here. Maybe bring Vaughn and Rhett."

"Fuck."

"Yeah, man, it's not good."

"Thanks for the call. We'll be there in thirty. If Sage shows up, stall her or something. I want Rhett to do a sweep of the car." I end the call and take a steadying breath before looking at the paperwork scattered across my desk. Normally, I'd welcome any excuse to put off the tedious task, but right now, I'd rather be drowning in paperwork than facing the reality that Sage might be in serious trouble. I'm not even sure she'd believe me.

I stand, leaving my papers untouched, and head downstairs to Vaughn's office. The office I share with the other field agents is sparse, with little in the way of personal touches. Just four communal metal desks grouped in the center of the room facing each other as if we were still elementary school boys, a couple of filing cabinets, and plain, functional chairs are all it contains. I rarely spend time here, preferring the field or working from home, and the space reflects that—impersonal, practical, and almost sterile. The rest of the building has an industrial feel, albeit a touch warmer than my office: exposed metal beams, concrete floors, and simple, utilitarian lighting.

Vaughn's office, however, is different and more welcoming. A few leather chairs are arranged in front of his desk for client meetings, and framed photos of his kids and some of his past clients line the walls, lending warmth to the space. I knock on the door frame before stepping inside and sinking into one of the leather chairs.

"Sure, come on in, Reid," Vaughn says dryly, glancing up from his computer. "It's not like I was in the middle of anything important."

Vaughn Heartwood is the second youngest of the five Heartwood brothers and co-owner of Heartwood Security. Most of his work involves either desk work or schmoozing clients to land large, long-term contracts. He is effectively the face of the company and the only one of the owners guaranteed to be in the office on any given day.

I rub the back of my neck. "Yeah, well, this isn't a social visit, unfortunately."

Vaughn looks at me again, his eyes narrowing as he clocks the tension in my posture. "What happened? Something go wrong on the job?"

"No, but I ran into some trouble on the way back." I quickly fill Vaughn in on the situation with Sage and the call I'd just received from Maddox.

"So, you want us to look into it and make sure she's okay? Maybe help if she's not?"

"Something like that."

Vaughn gives me an assessing look. "You like this woman?"

"She needs someone to look after her."

"And you want that someone to be you?"

"I never said that."

"If we determine she needs a guard, maybe I could assign Kane."

"You will not. She'd bolt."

Vaughn smirks, raising an eyebrow. "Not interested, huh? Sure."

"Fuck you, man. Let's go." Sometimes working for one of your best friends really sucks.

Vaughn chuckles, shaking his head as he stands. "Alright, I'll let Rhett know to meet us at Maddox's shop. Maybe have Blake begin an investigation of her and see what we are dealing with."

As Vaughn and I pull up to Maddox's shop, we can see Maddox in the open bay, leaning over the hood of Sage's car with a grim expression. Rhett and Blake arrive moments behind us. I nod to them and enter the garage, where Maddox turns as I approach.

Maddox nods at the men as they join him. "Alright," I say, crossing my arms as I brace myself. "What did you find?"

Maddox lets out a sigh, his eyes dark with concern. "You were right to be suspicious. I did a thorough inspection, and—it's definitely not wear and tear. The alternator belt didn't just snap on its own. It was cut—just enough so that it would hold up for a while before giving out."

I feel a surge of anger, but I force myself to stay calm. "You're sure?"

"One hundred percent," Maddox replies grimly. "And that's not all. I found a small puncture in the oil pan. Judging by the amount of oil left, I'd say it happened in the morning just before she started driving for the day. Whoever did this knew what they were doing. They wanted her car to get far enough before it broke down, leaving her stranded."

"Jesus," Vaughn mutters, running a hand over his face. "So someone sabotaged her, made sure she'd be out in the middle of nowhere."

"Maybe." I reply, "They probably didn't know exactly where she was going, but a woman stranded on the side of a highway isn't much better than the middle of nowhere."

"Think someone's been following her?" Rhett asks, eyeing the old car with a skeptical expression.

"She was jumpy as hell," I say. "Everything about her screamed she was running away from something, but if they were close by, wouldn't they have approached her before I got there?"

"Perhaps someone is tracking her phone and planned to ambush her in the middle of the night." Vaughn muses.

"It's possible," I say, "but she seemed smart enough to ditch her original phone, though I think she would have slept in her car had I not shown up."

"So, not smart enough to ditch the car," Blake muses.

My jaw clenches. "Not everyone has the money to just up and get a new car," I snap. Blake gives me a sideways look but doesn't apologize for the comment. He's good at his job, but he can be a bit of an asshole.

"Actually," Maddox interjects, "the car isn't registered to her. It's some woman named Mary Dawson. I found the paperwork in the glove compartment. Maybe she bought a cheap car but didn't finish the paperwork?"

"Maybe that's her real name?" Blake pulls out a notepad from his pocket and begins writing notes, walking around the car, already dropping into investigator mode.

Rhett steps forward, holding up a small RF detector. "I've brought this with me. I'll run a scan and see if we pick up any signals from a tracker. If there is one on her car, it'll show up."

I exhale, my fists clenched. "Good. I want every inch of that car swept. If there's even a hint of a signal, I want to know about it."

Maddox's phone chimes with a message. He pulls it out and scans the screen. "Juniper said Sage didn't know her own phone number when they exchanged info, so there's a good chance she doesn't have her original phone."

"Think we're getting a little ahead of ourselves?" Vaughn begins, "We can just ask when..." but Rhett interrupts him.

"Got it," Rhett says, reaching into the glove compartment and feeling around. A moment later, he pulls out a small black device, about the size of a flash drive. "Found it. This little tracker was stashed in the glove compartment."

My heart sinks as I look at the device. "Whoever she is running from doesn't plan on letting her go."

CHAPTER SEVEN

Sage

My phone chimes, and I smile a little, thinking Juniper has sent me another message. In the last hour or so, she'd already sent me half a dozen places to check out. It is effectively a virtual tour and perhaps a 'check out all the cool places, don't you want to stay?' though that could just be wishful thinking on my part.

I want to be upset at her pushiness, but it feels nice. Like, I actually have a friend.

I open the messaging app, wondering what is next on this little scavenger hunt she is sending me on. My smile falls. The message is from an unknown number. A different one from the one I blocked last night.

Unknown Number: "One of these days"

My heart stutters, each beat hammering with the implicit threat beneath those simple words. Memories I wish I could forget bubble to the surface. In each one, Jordan is leering over me, having just finished hurting me in some way. "One of these days I am going to tire of your fuck-ups." "One of these days I will not hold back." "One of these days I'll let some of my men have you."

My grip tightens on the phone. I force myself to breathe. Focus. Don't panic. It can't be him. He doesn't have my number. He doesn't know where I am. I have a new phone and a new number. This is just a random message meant for the number's previous owner. People get stray texts all the time, right? How many marketing texts have I received since I got this phone? There was even a phishing message earlier this week. Two cryptic messages from unknown numbers mean nothing.

Yeah, that's it. Just a mistake.

But the words don't quite soothe me; as sound as my logic is, it still feels hollow. I can't shake the sense that my past is closer than I want it to be.

I slip the phone back into my pocket, but my pulse continues to race, my body rigid with a familiar tension. I'm in a small town full of strangers, a place where no one knows me, but right now, it feels like a spotlight is illuminating me, broadcasting my location to the last person I want to find me.

No, no, no, I whisper to myself, trying to shake off the feeling. I'm safe here. No one knows where I am.

I realize I am standing still on a somewhat busy sidewalk. Keep walking. Everything is okay. Don't draw attention. Just breathe. Where is the next place Juniper wants me to check out? A little crepe shop.

I stop in front of a tiny shop. The front is not big enough for a table or chairs. Just a counter to take orders at opening to a kitchen in the back. But the large window allows passersby to watch the staff at work creating delicious-looking confections. A crowd is gathered at the window, waiting for their food to be ready.

I try to sink back into the game's allure, but the magic of this somewhat self-guided tour is gone. I type out a quick message to Juniper, letting her know I am going to check on my car and maybe I'll explore more later today.

I've regained my composure by the time I arrive at Maddox's auto shop. I cling to the idea that it is a coincidence. But a fresh wave of tension fills my body as I step into the garage and find a group of large men surrounding my car, talking in harsh, low tones. Aside from Maddox, none of them look like mechanics; their clothes fit more in an office than in a garage. Every muscle goes taut, and it takes everything in me to fight the instinct to turn around, bolt back to the inn, and lock myself away.

My gaze flickers between Maddox, Reid, and three strangers. One of them, a dark-haired man with tan skin, stands next to the open passenger door of my car, holding up a small black device. Is he going to put it in my car? The energy in the room is heavy; everyone is on edge. I feel the hair at the back of my neck stand on end.

Reid is the first to spot me, but wisely doesn't approach me. After last night, he clearly realizes I don't trust men. Or maybe he can see that I am about five seconds away from bolting. Perhaps I really am like a bunny.

"Sage," he says, giving me a nod in greeting. I can see that he's angry—the furrowed brow, the sharp slash of his mouth, and my instincts scream at me that I'm in danger. In fact, they all seem rather angry. Angry men, in my experience, are the worst kind of danger. I can't help the step backward.

I look at Maddox. He is supposed to be fixing my car, but the sheepish expression just adds to my tension.

I take a shuddering breath. "Everything okay?" I ask, bracing myself for the worst. Maybe my car isn't fixable, and I'd be stuck here. It may be a lovely town, but I want it to be my choice on whether I stay.

Maddox looks uncomfortable, shifting from one foot to the other. "No, things aren't exactly okay, Sage."

I narrow my eyes, glancing from my car to Reid and then to Maddox, who frowns deeply. "Did you find something unfixable on my car?"

Maddox hesitates, his eyes flicking to Reid before he answers. "It's more than that..." He struggles with his words, clearly out of his depth.

Before he can continue, a man with jet-black hair, an unreadable expression and a notepad in his hand with interrupts. "Maddox thinks someone cut your alternator belt and punctured your oil pan." After dropping that bomb, he goes back to scribbling down notes like he didn't just land a blow that leaves me reeling.

My eyes dart from Maddox to the black-haired man, then back to Reid, trying to understand what I'm hearing. Someone vandalized my car. Why? Who?

The reality of it is slowly sinking in, and with it, my carefully constructed shields start to crack. Or maybe it was already cracking? Last night, I turned my fear into anger and hostility, using it like armor to keep everyone at a distance, but now I can't summon anything to smother the fear.

It is different this morning. My emotions are pulled in too many directions. Juniper disarmed me with kindness, then there were those ominous text messages, and now I am in a room full of large men—all taller, all broader than me, and all watching me with expressions ranging from concern to suspicion. These men are even bigger than my ex, and that realization makes my skin crawl. My fingers tremble, and I clasp my hands together, willing myself to appear calm. I feel as fragile as glass.

I catch Reid watching me, his gaze narrowing as he takes in my defensive posture. My eyes flicker to the other men in the room. They're clearly picking up on my discomfort, too, and I hate it. I hate feeling exposed.

I take a fortifying breath and focus on exuding the persona of someone calm and collected. Shoulders back, arms open and by my sides instead of crossed, a mask of calm indifference on my face. If I need to, I can slip on what I call my arm candy persona. Polite smile, placid expression, gentle and demure body language. A role I played too many times to count for Jordan in public. But right now, I didn't need the simpering public persona; I needed the amour I'd don around him in private.

One stranger steps forward, extending a hand with a friendly smile. He has that classic all-American look—blond hair coifed just so, a charming, polished appearance, and a crisp black suit that is out of place in an autobody shop. In another life, I could imagine him among Jordan's golf buddies, the type who would wear chinos and button-downs and pretend not to notice bruises or ignore cruel words. His presence makes my skin tingle with an unease that runs bone-deep.

"I'm Vaughn," he says smoothly, his smile appearing warm and practiced.

I look from his outstretched hand to his face and can't help the involuntary step backward as if I expect him to lash out. I scowl, but I am not sure whether that is at him or my reaction to him. Perhaps both. *So much for calm and collected, Sage.* I move a little closer to Reid as though he'll protect me. Somehow, in my mind, I've already decided that he's the safest person in the room.

The devil you know, and all that.

Vaughn is not fazed by my reaction. He withdraws his hand and gives me a slight nod, his expression unchanged. He must be used to handling difficult people, I muse. That calm, unwavering charm only deepens my suspicion. I know this type too well; Jordan could keep a smile up as long as he needed to, fooling everyone around him.

I look back at the open bay doors. The exit is right there. I could leave if I need to. Maybe. I doubt they would chase me down if I run. And I want so desperately to get away from here.

CHAPTER EIGHT

Reid

I have to stifle the weird sense of triumph I feel over her reaction to Vaughn. She clearly doesn't like him, and the subtle move closer to me tells me that, on some level, she trusts me a little.

Vaughn has already stepped back, a quick glance enough to tell me he's handing off the point position to me.

"Vaughn's my boss," I say, nodding to him. "He owns Heartwood Security."

"Co-owns," he says with a wry smile. "My four brothers own the rest."

She raises an eyebrow, his attempt at small talk falling flat, her expression clearly reading, 'And what does that have to do with me?'

I almost smile, catching her subtle defiance. Her mask had slipped for a moment, revealing a flash of genuine fear when Vaughn approached her, but now she's putting that prickly shield back up. I prefer this defiant side. So many people resort to placating or fawning to keep themselves safe. But with me, she fights. She might be scared, but she's a fighter, and I respect that.

"Remember when I said I work for a security company?" Trying to redo the introductions and meeting her gaze head-on. "Vaughn's my boss, and these two idiots are my coworkers."

Blake ignores the comment, giving a slight nod of his head. In contrast, Rhett gives a mocking bow and tips an imaginary top hat, a grin on his face as he returns to fiddling with his device. Most likely, he was doing another scan to make sure there was only one tracker.

I'm glad Tessa insisted on sensitivity training for situations involving scared clients. Keep a respectable distance, de-escalate the situation, and use humor when appropriate to dispel tension. Blake never passed that class. Probably why he doesn't work directly with clients. Impressive investigator but shit with anything that requires tact.

Most of our jobs are routine security work or investigations, but there are enough cases involving people fleeing domestic violence or children in protective custody that we all—rather, most of us—know how to handle fragile situations. Those cases get to me the most—seeing the worst of humanity and knowing I can only stand guard, not dispense the justice these victims deserve. Yet here I am, inserting myself into a situation that feels all too familiar.

"Okay," Sage says. "Why are they here? What does any of this have to do with me?"

I can tell she isn't clueless, but her denial is evident on her face; she's grasping for a lifeline, a bit of normalcy.

"Like Blake said, Maddox found some really concerning things when he was looking over your car. Things done deliberately to put you in danger." I pause, choosing my words carefully. "So, he called me about his concerns."

"Why would he call you and not me?" she shoots back, her voice carrying a sharp edge as she plays up her annoyance.

I don't flinch. "One, he didn't have your number. And two, it was either call me and my guys or call the cops." I watch as the color drains from her face, further confirmation that she is running from someone, but I continue. "Sheriff Conner's a good guy, but I got the feeling you'd rather avoid creating a paper trail." She gives me a tiny nod, more of a jerk. "And since the cops have certain rules they need to follow before they can actually do anything... Maddox called us."

"And what can you do?" she asks with a bitter edge in her tone.

"Keep you safe."

She makes a derisive snort. "From what a broken down car? This doesn't mean anything. Maybe I drove over something and that caused all the damage."

"Sage," I say, keeping my voice patient. "This isn't normal wear and tear. You are clearly running from someone. And that someone probably tampered with your car."

She shakes her head, her face ashen, stepping back as though the very idea is too much to bear. "I... I can't. You don't understand. It could be someone else. Right? This means... this means... no one can keep me safe. How could it be him?" Her words trail off, her voice barely a whisper.

I want to step forward, to wrap her in my arms, and promise her everything will be okay, but I know that will only push her further away. Instead, I watch as she struggles to gather herself, and I'm proud when I see her straighten, drawing her defenses back around her like armor. "Are you... are you sure someone did something to my car? There's no way it could have just worn out? I've been driving a lot," she says, her voice strained. A last desperate attempt to hold on to her denial.

I nod. "I'm sure. But that's not all, baby." I feel a pang of regret as I let the term of endearment slip—a teasing Bunny was one thing, but baby has implications that I don't know if she's even open to—but she doesn't seem to react to it, perhaps too overwhelmed to notice. Her gaze meets mine, and I see something raw and unfiltered there—fear, resignation, a glimmer of defiance. And beneath it all, a flicker of trust.

I nod in Rhett's direction. "Rhett is one of our tech guys. I asked him to check for anything unusual. He has some tools that scan for different devices."

"Like a tracker?" She whispers, her voice high.

"Yeah, like a tracker," I nod softly.

"Did he... did he find one?" She asks, her eyes fixed on the small black device in Rhett's hand—the one he had pulled out of her car just before she showed up.

"He did." My face softens with apology.

Sage's shoulders slump, her hand gripping the strap of her backpack as her gaze drops to the ground. "Oh, fuck," she whispers, terror lacing her words. "I gotta go. He found me. He knows where I am. I can't... this isn't safe..." She looks at her car, her expression one of betrayal, and my heart clenches at the sight of tears in her eyes. They're filled with disillusionment and heartbreak.

I approach her slowly, my hands held up in a gesture of peace. "Hey, it's okay... I won't let anyone get to you. You're safe with me."

"You don't understand," she chokes out. "He'll make you disappear and then laugh about it. He's done it before. He isn't sane. He... he..." Her words dissolve into a shuddering sob, and before she can push me away, I wrap her in my arms, pulling her close and tucking her head under my chin. Her tears soak through my shirt, but I don't care. I rub soothing circles on her back, whispering soft promises that I will keep her safe.

"But... how?" she whispers, her voice broken. "No one can keep me safe from him. You don't understand."

"Bunny, my job is to keep people safe from those who want to hurt them," I murmur, and she lets herself lean into my warmth, her sobs subsiding slowly.

Before I am ready, she is already pushing against my chest, trying to create distance, and I reluctantly let her go. She takes a few steps back, wiping her face with her sleeves, trying to pull herself back together, to reclaim some semblance of control. I hate that she feels the need to hide behind walls. I want to be her safe place, the one person she doesn't have to hide from. When she looks up at me, though, there's a new wariness in her gaze, one that makes my chest tighten.

"Why?" she asks, suspicion clouding her face. "Why would you help me?"

She gestures back at her car, her eyes narrowing. "I obviously don't have the money to hire you guys." She looks up at me, her expression hardening. I can practically see her mind racing, making assumptions, bracing for the worst. "What do you want out of this?" her voice hard and demanding.

I'm offended by her question. The implication that I'd exploit her vulnerability is insulting. I bite back my frustration, reminding myself that she must have been around some of the worst people imaginable if she's gone to all this effort to disappear. It's only natural that she is wary, that she'd expect ulterior motives. I can put enough of the clues together to see that someone close has hurt her. Until she can trust me, she'll see threats in every act of kindness.

A not-so-subtle cough interrupts us, and I look up to find Vaughn standing nearby. Maddox, Blake, and Rhett have all drifted back a few paces, giving Sage and me a semblance of privacy. But Vaughn is still close, watching us with a knowing smirk, an unmistakable I knew you were into her glint in his eye.

This fucker. I've been friends with him too long not to see the gears turning in his head.

I scowl, annoyed but grateful for the distraction. Vaughn takes the cue and addresses Sage. "We have a special fund for domestic violence and child endangerment cases," he says. "We charge ridiculous fees to the clients who can afford it, and a percentage of that goes to help people who need it most."

Sage opens her mouth, a mixture of disbelief and confusion on her face. "But I don't need..."

"You do," I interject firmly, my gaze unwavering.

She looks away, her eyes distant. "Maybe it would be better if I left," she murmurs, the words almost inaudible, as if she were talking more to herself than to us. A flash of panic shoots through me as I see the walls she'd started to lower, rebuilding. "You found the tracker. Maybe... maybe that's enough. I could leave. Get far away from here."

"Your car's not in any condition to go anywhere right now," I say, my voice gentle but unyielding.

She hesitates, the gravity of the situation settling over her. I can see the internal struggle in her eyes. I am offering her safety. A chance to rest.

Uncertainty clouds her eyes again. "I... no, I couldn't ask that of you. Or of anyone, really." She glances down, and I can see her expressive face flicker through a range of emotions, her mind whirling with conflicting thoughts. Her resolve wavers, and she shakes her head, trying to regain focus. "No, I think it's best if I go. I can get far away from here and—"

"And spend the rest of your life running?" I challenge, my tone calm and steady.

She meets my gaze head-on. "That's better than waiting for him to just show up," she counters, her voice wavering but laced with a hard edge.

I take a step closer, my gaze intent. "Do you think I can't protect you?" my voice incredulous. A part of me regrets the flare of emotion. She doesn't know me. How could she think I could protect her? I'm just the asshole who refused to leave her stranded in the rain when she told me to go.

"It's not that," she murmurs, her eyes drifting to the side, avoiding my gaze.

"Then what is it?" I press gently.

She swallows, her voice a whisper. "I don't want anyone to get hurt because of me."

Vaughn, charming as ever, intervenes. "Look, Sage," he says, flashing a a cajoling smile that has her frowning in response. I have to hide the little kernel of glee at the fact that she doesn't like him very much. "Your car won't be ready for at least a few days, so you'll need a safe place to stay and a trained bodyguard. Heartwood Security can help with that."

She hesitates, glancing between me and Vaughn. "I... yeah, I suppose," she says, resignation creeping into her voice.

"Good, then it's decided," Vaughn says with a firm nod, as though he'd just closed a business deal. "I'm assigning Reid as your guard. Reid, bring her to the office after you're finished here so we can go over the details of her case." He glances over at Blake and Rhett. "Blake, Rhett? Let's go."

I can't decide if I should kick him or thank him for opting to head out with the guys.

CHAPTER NINE

Sage

An hour later, I step out of Reid's truck, my mind still reeling from everything that has happened. Last night, I'd refused to let him drive me into town, certain I'd never ride in his vehicle, and now here I am, not only sitting in his truck but letting him take me to an unknown location without protest. If I weren't still in a state of shock, I might be more concerned about willingly going to a place I don't recognize with a relative stranger. But that nagging doubt seems dulled, my mind too exhausted to put up a fight.

He parks in front of a large, old three-story brick building on the edge of downtown. The building has the same picturesque charm as the rest of the buildings in this part of town, but where other businesses have large windows displaying their goods, this building's tinted windows reflect the street. A small sign next to the door announces it as Heartwood Security. The building almost reminds me of an old warehouse, with an imposing atmosphere. Or maybe that impression has more to do with my current state of mind.

As we step inside, I'm struck by how the old exterior melds into the sleek, industrial vibe within. Exposed pipes line the ceiling, and bright overhead lights cast a crisp glow down onto the large reception desk that dominates the entry space.

Off to the side is a waiting area with two leather couches arranged around a low coffee table, which bears an obvious, fake plant in the middle and a small stack of outdated magazines, one of which I am almost certain has been out of print for years.

Behind the reception desk sits a beautiful woman with red hair pulled back in a sleek ponytail. She looks up and flashes Reid a bright, almost flirtatious smile as he holds the heavy door open for me.

"Hey, Reid," she greets him, her voice light and breathy, her tone instantly warm. "Vaughn said to go on back as soon as you got in with your... client." Her gaze flicks to me, lingering just a second before it returns to Reid, her smile unwavering. "Oh, and he said she needs to fill this out." She reaches for a clipboard with a neatly stacked pile of forms and hands it to Reid.

"Thanks, Lena," Reid replies. The smile he directs at her speaks of familiarity.

Something twists in my stomach, a sharp pang of something I haven't felt in years. Jealousy. I don't like the feeling; it's irrational and unwanted.

How can I be feeling this way? With Jordan, I'd learned to numb myself to these kinds of things. He'd had so many affairs that I'd stopped caring about them altogether. In fact, most days, I was relieved when he was distracted by one of his flings—it meant he might be too busy or too tired to 'deal' with me. I'd even hoped he'd eventually leave me for one of his girlfriends. But he hadn't.

And here I am, annoyed over the sweet smile from Lena and Reid's easy response. They work together, so of course they are friendly. Besides, I have no claim on him, and yet there's that possessive twinge.

I shake my head, trying to clear my mind of such nonsense. Thankfully, Reid doesn't seem to notice anything off about my reaction. Instead, he simply places a steady hand on my lower back, guiding me gently past the reception area, through a heavy door and down a hallway. His touch is firm and reassuring, and despite myself, I lean into it slightly, drawing some small comfort from his confidence. I love and hate how much I trust him already.

With Jordan there was always this lingering feeling that something was off, a sliver of danger that I had attributed to the excitement of a new relationship and subsequently dismissed. I trusted my head. He did and said all the right things, so I easily pushed aside any weird feelings of apprehension. With Reid, it is the opposite. I am so jaded from my experience with Jordan that I am looking for a reason to run, but my heart is telling me I am safe. I didn't trust my intuition before, and it got me into a heap of trouble. Maybe I should listen to it now?

I am pulled from my thoughts when Reid gives a quick knock before opening a door and gesturing for me to step inside. I hesitate, my eyes scanning the room as I enter.

Vaughn is sitting behind a desk, so this must be his office. It's the kind of space designed for clients, more for show than functionality. The wall behind him features a scenic landscape painting that attempts to create a calm atmosphere, and a low dark wood bookshelf, filled with books and binders, and a collection of knickknacks on top. The only window is actually behind me; rather, the wall behind me is entirely glass, facing not the outside but the hallway we just walked through. To the right of his desk, a large leather couch is against the wall with a small coffee table in front, and opposite, what looks like a bar. It makes me feel like I've stepped into an episode of 'Mad Men,' back to a time when men wore polished suits to work and shared a glass of Scotch. Vaughn's desk is polished to a shine and organized with small personal touches—a few knickknacks, a potted plant, and framed photos of a little blond, green-eyed girl who looks like a mini, cuter version of Vaughn. It makes the space feel a little less clinical, but the showroom vibes don't put me at ease.

I barely register sitting down in a leather armchair, my focus still on the details of the room, as if grounding myself in my surroundings could somehow make everything else feel less overwhelming.

Reid sits down beside me, passing me the clipboard with the forms Lena had given him and handing me a pen. "Just some standard information," he says gently, as if trying not to disturb the fragile calm I'm holding onto.

I take the pen, staring at the top sheet on the clipboard. My name. My address—or at least, where I'd been staying. I haven't written my personal information like this in so long. I hesitate, feeling exposed. This simple act will strip me of the layers of anonymity I'd worked so hard to build.

"Sage," Vaughn greets me with a nod, giving me that practiced, professional smile I don't like. I narrow my eyes at him, feeling anything but calm in the face of his carefully composed demeanor. The smile is fake. I don't know what he is hiding, but the fake smile sets me on edge. Not in the way that screams danger but in the way that says he has his own secrets.

This is a mistake.

"Look," I start, my voice sharp. "I was telling Reid that I don't think I need a guard. I'll be okay as long as I keep moving. You guys found the tracker, so if I just..."

"How long have you been running?" Vaughn interrupts, his tone gentle but firm.

I look away, my jaw tightening. "A few months." Over half a year.

"And how long do you think you can keep that up?" he asks. "How long can you afford to keep running?"

"I can find work when I need it," I snap. Not much longer. Even if I sell the last few pieces of jewelry I have tucked away, I will run out of money soon.

"Sometimes the cost is more than financial." Vaughn says softly, the showman smile gone and a more caring expression on his face. This feels more honest. "How long until all this running takes a toll on your health? What about your mind? How much of a toll has it taken already?"

"I don't know," I reluctantly mutter defensive, knowing that he is right. My mental health has already taken such a toll if the constant paranoia and nightmares are any clue. My gaze flicks between him and Reid. I feel cornered, and I don't like it one bit. "But I don't need a guard, just a place to hide." I insist, more fiercely this time, as if trying to convince myself as much as them. A small part of me can't help but like the idea of a guard. But that's not going to stop Jordan. I'd need a small army.

Reid exchanges a look with Vaughn, who simply nods, passing the reins to him. They did this at the garage too. Maybe they didn't realize I noticed, but I'm observant when I need to be.

Reid leans forward, rubbing his temples briefly before meeting my gaze. "Sage, someone tampered with your car." I can't help bristling as he lays out the last 24 hours piece by piece as if I wasn't there myself and fully aware of the current shitshow that is my life. "They cut your alternator belt and punctured your oil pan. Maddox thinks other things might have been done to your car. Maybe things in the past you had to fix?" He raises a brow, and I think back to all the little things that have gone wrong. Some of it was car-related that needed to be fixed, like the flat tire that curiously had nothing wrong with it other than being low on air, windshield wipers that had chunks missing from the blade insert, or the cracked radiator that when I really think about it was more of a puncture than a crack. Others are mundane, easily dismissed as carelessness or a random jerk. My favorite shirt vanishing, reappearing days later in the passenger seat, random items left on the car roof, or strange dust patterns on the windows. "Whoever did that wanted you stranded in the middle of nowhere, vulnerable and alone. They put a tracker in your car. They would have been the one to find you had I not stopped." He keeps his voice steady, but his eyes are intense as he studies me. I can't help feeling a little chastised. "You know who this is, Sage. You know what they're capable of. Otherwise, you wouldn't be running. We need to know what we are up against so we can help. I promise we can keep you safe."

My eyes dart to the floor, lips pressed into a thin line, arms crossed over the clipboard. I want to believe him. But I also don't want to see him hurt. Getting involved with me is dangerous. I need to dissuade him from the ridiculous notion that he can help.

I look back and meet his challenging look with a glare. I gather my anger and fear as if they are a weapon, using it to drive everyone away for their own good. "And what? I'm supposed to trust you?" The challenge is clear, my voice dripping with disdain.

CHAPTER TEN

Reid

A flicker of irritation sparks within me, but I force it down. This is fear talking, not judgment. Someone close to her betrayed her, causing her so much harm that she has learned to fear men. I don't need my years in security to tell me it was most likely a former partner. She doesn't know me, doesn't know that I'm different. And trust isn't something she can just hand over after a day of knowing me. It will take time, and I have to earn it, step by step, proving myself again and again.

"I know you don't know me," I say, softening my tone. "But I do this for a living, Sage. I protect people. We wouldn't have established a fund for cases like yours if we didn't care or know what we were doing. We have resources, a lawyer who can help with a restraining order," she lets out a derisive snort, a clear sign she doesn't think the law will be much help, but I continue. "We can help you hide, start a new life when it is safe." I let a hint of vulnerability slip into my voice. "Just... let me help you. Please." I have to choke out the next words, "It doesn't have to be me. Vaughn has other equally capable guards that work here."

Her expression is a mixture of wariness and curiosity. "But why? Why do you want to help me?"

I hesitate, then lean back, meeting her gaze with an honesty I hope will break through her walls. "Because I hate that I terrified the hell out of you last night. You were already scared, and I added to that, unknowingly or not." I say, my voice low. "You shouldn't have to fear anyone. I do this job because I want people to be safe. I am not naïve enough to think I can save the world, but I can't stand by when I know I can do something."

She gives a bitter laugh, her eyes flashing with a hard edge. "Newsflash—every man is dangerous until proven otherwise."

The weight of her words hit me harder than I expected. "I know. I'm painfully aware of how dangerous men can be. Hell, I wouldn't even have a job if there weren't horrible men in this world."

"I could go to a women's shelter. They would help me."

"You could," I concede, "but chances are if you go to any of the ones between here and Seattle, they will reach out to us for help." It's not a lie; what little I have pieced together has my internal alarm bells ringing, and shelters routinely reach out to us when they need additional manpower to keep someone safe.

Her gaze drops to the floor, her shoulders slumping as the bravado melts away. Her voice is barely a whisper when she finally speaks. "Fine. But I don't want to be a burden. I don't want charity."

A pang resonates in my chest, but I keep my face neutral. "You're not a burden, Sage. And this isn't charity. We can work something out that you'll feel comfortable with."

A faint blush dusts her cheeks, and I have to stifle a smile at the implication her mind must have picked up on. Not that I would abuse my position, of course.

"Lena's been complaining about needing help with filing," Vaughn chimes in smoothly, redirecting the conversation to safer waters.

"A job?" Her voice perks up, her eyes brightening. "Like a trade?" she asks, leveling a smile at Vaughn. I fight back the irrational jealousy her smile for Vaughn provokes in me. What happened to her not liking him? I know it's the idea of a job. It's agency in her current circumstance. But I want that smile directed at me.

Vaughn nods, taking back control of the conversation now that Sage seems more amenable to our help. "While you're here, we'll go over the specifics of your protection plan." He glances at me, then looks back at her. "Reid will be your primary guard. He's in charge of every aspect of your safety, and he'll be with you at all times until we're sure you're safe."

Her eyes widen, a spark of alarm crossing her face. "At all times?"

"Yes, all times. It's standard procedure in cases like this," I say, keeping my tone professional. "But we'll work out the details to ensure you're comfortable." I try to soften the blow with a hint of levity. "Think of me as your ever-present, highly trained shadow." I offer a reassuring smile, but she doesn't return it. Instead, she frowns down at her hands, her expression troubled.

"What if I need some time to myself?" she asks, her voice tight.

"That depends on what you mean by 'time to yourself.' If you're in your room or another location I have ensured is secure, that's fine. But a walk alone by the river or anywhere you're out of sight—that's not going to happen, at least not until we are certain you are safe." My voice leaves no room for argument.

"And it's just you?" she presses, looking up at me with a mixture of skepticism and frustration. Is she worried I can't handle it or about being alone with me? Probably both. "What about your normal job?"

"This is his job," Vaughn interjects. "He'll have some help from his team when it is needed, but he'll be your primary guard and the lead on your case."

She sits silently, absorbing our words, her fingers fidgeting with the clipboard in her lap. A mix of emotions playing across her face— reluctance, doubt, fear, and perhaps, a tiny spark of hope forming. It's frail, but it's a beginning.

She closes her eyes, her jaw working as she visibly wrestles with her options. Finally, she sighs, the fight draining out of her. "So... what now? Where do I go? I can't stay at the Rosewood Inn, I suppose." Her expression is anxious but resigned.

"No," Vaughn says, shaking his head. "We wouldn't be able to secure the inn properly. We'll need to get you set up somewhere safer, somewhere with more controlled access." He pauses, his gaze shifting between us as he considers the options. "You could stay with Reid at his house."

Her gaze snaps to me, a spark of anger in her tone. "Do you take all your jobs there?"

I stifle a smile at her feistiness. "No, usually we use a safe house. But the only ones we have available right now are pretty remote, and I don't think you need to vanish into the wilderness yet."

Her eyes widen, and I can see the protest forming on her lips, so I hold up a hand to stop her. "Just for a few days, Sage. Until we're sure, this guy isn't about to show up in town. All our homes already have extensive security systems in place. You could also stay in the safe room here. It isn't as comfortable, but it is secure. You still have choices."

CHAPTER ELEVEN

Sage

"Okay," I whisper. "But if I'm going to stay anywhere, I want some say in it. I don't... I don't want to feel trapped."

Vaughn nods, his expression respectful. "Of course. How about you look at one of the safe rooms and we'll discuss your options? Reid will make sure you have control over what you can, but, Sage, there will be times when you'll need to defer to his judgment." He leans forward, his tone softening. "This is your life, Sage. You should be able to live it without constantly looking over your shoulder. We're here to help you take back that control. But first, you need to let us protect you."

I nod slowly, taking in his words. "Can I see the room?"

Vaughn leads us down to the lower level and enters a code in a very heavy-looking metal door. It opens up into a nice enough room but what is effectively an impersonal studio apartment. "No windows," I murmur as I look around. At least there is a TV. I suppose.

"It's a panic room. We've installed something like this in several clients' homes. It has..."

"I don't like it," I say quickly, interrupting Vaughn before he can start his sales pitch. "I... uh... If you have a guest room, then I think I could stay with you." I direct my comment to Reid, trying to focus on not panicking. If I stay in that room, I know I will unravel.

We return to Vaughn's office in silence. I am getting close to my breaking point. Or maybe I passed that point a few hours ago and am drifting through this whole experience like a ghost.

"I know this is overwhelming." Reid begins, "But you don't have to go through it alone. That's why I'm here."

I meet his gaze and try to add some strength to my voice. I can fake this. "Alright. But you'd better not treat me like I'm made of glass."

My attempt at levity falls flat, but he gives me a warm smile anyway. "I wouldn't dream of it."

Vaughn's voice is soft as he addresses me again. "Alright, Sage?" This time, his smile doesn't feel like an attempt to calm me but rather a quiet assurance. I give a slight nod in response. "I need you to fill out as much as you can here," Vaughn continues, handing me the clipboard. "It's everything you can remember about the person we need to protect you from. It's okay if you don't know everything. Just fill out what you can. We'll have more questions after we review it, but I promise we won't overwhelm you."

The room falls away as I pick up the pen and write. At first, I balk at some of them—questions about past encounters, about specific incidents—but as I fill in each line, it becomes unexpectedly cathartic. I never told anyone what was happening.. Who would I have told? I had no one and nothing. The one friend I did have was already slipping away, wrapped up in her new partner, when I met Jordan. Maybe that's why he'd targeted me.

The murmurs of Reid and Vaughn discussing my protection plan fade into the background, my focus solely on the form in front of me. By the time I finish, the room has grown quiet. I look up, feeling strangely light.

Reid reaches over and brushes a tear away with his thumb. The touch feather light. I hadn't even realized when they'd started falling. It feels surreal.

"This is... um... everything," I say, returning the paperwork to Vaughn. My voice is thick, and I rub at my face, trying to erase the evidence of my vulnerability. I feel a wave of fatigue wash over me.

Reid, ever observant, stands and holds out his hand. "Let's get something to eat. We can go over the preliminary plan Vaughn and I discussed, and he'll review what you wrote to make any necessary changes."

My eyes dart to Vaughn and the paperwork. "You won't... share that with anyone, will you?" I ask in a small voice. A wave of shame hits me, and I want to wrestle the clipboard back before he can read it.

"I'll only share what's necessary with my team," Vaughn assures me. "You have nothing to be ashamed of, Sage. This isn't a reflection of you."

"It's just...," I trail off, swallowing hard, my voice still stuffy from tears I am trying to suppress. "I don't want you to judge me for it."

Reid's voice is soft but firm. "I don't judge you, Sage. Just the asshole who put that fear in your eyes."

I nod, murmuring, "Okay." I take Reid's outstretched hand, letting him pull me to my feet before pulling away and standing with my head high.

Reid gives me a nod of approval. "Good. We'll get through this, one step at a time."

"Remember, Sage," Vaughn adds, his tone calm and steady. "This isn't forever. Just long enough to make sure you're safe."

I give a faint nod, letting Reid guide me out of the office and past the reception desk.

As we step outside, I feel a wave of anxiety wash over me. I feel exposed. Is he already here? Watching me from the shadows. I stifle the urge to move closer to Reid. Any closer, and I'd be pressed to his side.

"Ready?" he asks.

I nod, forcing my expression into a calm mask that hides my fear. Internally, I am berating myself. I was fine this morning. Exploring the town with what I can only look back and see as reckless abandon. Now, I just want to hide and spend a few hours feeling sorry for myself.

We walk down the sunlit sidewalk to where his truck is. The day is deceptively bright, as if the world did not care about the darkness chasing me. Reid reaches for the passenger door of his car, opening it for me.

"You'll be safe with me," he promises, watching as I settle in before rounding the car and getting into the driver's seat.

"What did you have for breakfast?" Reid asks as he buckles his seatbelt, glancing over at me.

My eyes shift to the empty coffee cup I'd left in his cup holder before looking back at him, a little sheepish. "I had a muffin?" Reid raises his eyebrows, a playful glint in his eyes.

"Alright, Bunny," he says with a warm grin, "let's get some proper food in you. It won't fix everything, but some lunch from Tina's will help a little."

"Who's Tina?" I ask after a few minutes on the road.

"The nosiest aunt in the world," he replies with a laugh. "Makes a mean pecan pie, but still gives me hell for trampling her tulips when I was 5. Five bucks says she finds a way to mention it to you if she is there." I can't help the giggle that slips out in response. He flashes a triumphant smile my way before returning his focus to the road.

When we pull up to Tina's, I realize it's a tiny, bustling diner filled with locals. The place is loud, with the clatter of dishes and hum of conversations filling the air, but the energy is comforting. Reid waves at a few people, who nod or wave back, and I blush under the curious glances from the other patrons. But no one makes me feel unwelcome, which helps ease my nerves.

"Well, look who it is," a feminine voice says from my right. I turn to find an older woman, barely taller than myself, walking up to the hostess stand. "I had to field another call from your mother complaining that you haven't called her all week."

"Aww, Aunt Tina, you're not supposed to embarrass me," Reid says, a teasing note in his voice.

Tina huffs, crossing her arms. "If I want to embarrass you, I could tell her about the time you dug up all my tulips." He mouths, 'I told you so.' And I cover my mouth as a laugh slips out.

She gives me a warm smile as she shifts her attention to me. "Well, now, aren't you a beauty," she says with genuine affection. "Come on, love, let's get some food in you."

Without waiting for a response, Tina grabs a single plastic menu from the hostess stand and turns, clearly expecting me to follow. She weaves through the crowded diner until we reach a cozy booth in the back. From this spot, I can see all the entry points without having my back to the room, and an unexpected weight lifts from my shoulders.

I slide into the booth, but Reid doesn't go to the other side as I expected. "Scoot over, Bunny."

I frown. "I don't want my back to the door."

"That's fine. Neither do I. Scoot over." His tone is gentle but firm, and I shift down a bit with only a half-hearted sigh.

Tina places a laminated menu down in front of me but pointedly gives nothing to Reid. He leans over at my questioning look and whispers, "I pretty much have the menu memorized after working here when I was a teenager."

Tina snorts, "Worst employee ever." She shakes her head. "Terrible waiter. Unfortunately, I fired him before I realized he is a decent cook. You can thank his Ma for that when you meet her."

Reid continues to smother his laughter, and I don't have the heart to tell Tina we aren't exactly what she thinks we are. But the sense of family and warmth radiating from this place—Tina's teasing, the easy laughter—is foreign to me but nice. I smile, letting down my guard just a bit as Tina walks off after taking our drink orders.

As I glance over at Reid, still trying to look serious while holding back a laugh, a surprising feeling wells up in my chest. I am not sure what it is. It isn't sharp and biting like the jealousy that had flared up when I saw how familiar he was with Lena earlier, and it isn't quite annoyance at his teasing now.

It's something softer, something unfamiliar but not unwelcome. I push the thought aside, focusing instead on the noise and warmth of the diner around me.

Lunch leaves me feeling warm and sleepy. The burger was cooked to perfection, and now I'm ready for a nap. The plan he and Vaughn mapped out doesn't really require me to do anything. Just sort of hang out. I hate it.

The more Raid told me, Rhett looking into the tracker, doing a drive into Jordan's background, possibly sending out Blake to do some fieldwork, all of it just sounds so expensive, and I see the cost adding up. There is no way a little bit of admin work is enough to pay for all that. Add in the fact that Reid was basically on the clock 24/7. I couldn't understand why they were willing to do any of this for me. Thinking about it made me anxious, so Reid redirected the conversation to lighter topics when our food came.

I let Reid take my hand as we leave the diner, Tina shouting out that he'd better call his mother or else as the door closes behind us.

He opens the door to the truck and helps me in—something that isn't necessary, but I kind of like the feeling of being taken care of. No one has ever opened my car door before. I'm not one to insist on traditional gender roles, but in this moment, the simple gesture feels nice. I smile shyly at him as he closes the door with a firm click.

The ride to his house is quiet, and while not completely comfortable, my mind isn't screaming at me to escape. He drives through a relatively normal suburban neighborhood with homes that have a distinct charm, each one with unique features. The houses here aren't the cookie-cutter developments I'm used to, where every home looks almost identical, with just a handful of floor plans to choose from. Back there, everything felt so rigid, from the identical lawns to the strict HOA rules that required Halloween decorations to be taken down by noon on November 1st and Christmas lights put away by New Year's. I could have sworn one of the HOA board members once measured my neighbor's grass.

Here, it's a different world. Each house has its own character—mid-century ranch houses mixed with charming bungalows and even a stately colonial with faded brick and blue shutters. It feels alive, like a neighborhood where people could truly be themselves.

Reid pulls up to a two-story Craftsman-style house with a wide porch, complete with a cozy porch swing. I can imagine myself curled up there with a book and a glass of lemonade. The shingles are a soft blue-gray, not too bright but enough to stand out. The yard is large, with trees that practically beg for a treehouse or at least a lazy afternoon spent climbing them. A brick-paved path leads from the driveway to the front steps, adding a touch of old-fashioned charm.

Reid seems almost nervous as he unlocks the dark blue front door, and for a moment, I wonder why. I half-expect a big dog to come bounding out to greet us, but instead, I'm met with a dainty meow.

"You have a cat!" I breathe, immediately crouching and extending my hand to let the little tabby inspect me. Within seconds, the cat is purring, rubbing its head against my hand and claiming my attention.

"That's Ham," Reid says, smiling down at me as I fuss over the cat. "Her brother's around here somewhere. Probably in the kitchen waiting for the food timer to go off."

"Ham?" I ask, cradling the cat in my arms.

"Yeah, short for Hamburger," he admits with a slight wince. "Don't judge. I didn't name them. Vaughn's little girl did. She found a stray in the back yard. Well more like the stray adopted her. She brought the cat inside and, well... the next day, the cat had kittens."

I snort, imagining the scene. "I bet Vaughn was thrilled."

"Oh, he was," Reid laughs. "Especially when the cat decided his bed was the perfect place to have her kittens."

"No! Right on his bed?" I'm grinning now, barely holding back laughter.

"Yep. He went to work with one stray he planned to take to the shelter, and came back to seven more cats all cozied up on his bed."

I'm nearly wiping away tears from laughing. "So what did he do?"

"Oh, he complained non-stop for weeks. Swore he'd rehome every last one of them, but he ended up keeping the mama cat—Dinner—because his daughter had already fallen in love with her."

"Dinner?"

"Yeah, she was 3 so she named them after food. By the time we all got roped into adopting the kittens, the names had stuck."

"What's Ham's brother called?"

"Dog," he says, grinning at my incredulous expression.

"Let me guess—short for Hotdog?"

"Bingo."

I shake my head, chuckling. "Who'd have thought big, scary Reid would have two adorable cats named Ham and Dog."

"Ham is adorable," he corrects. "Dog thinks he's a dog, has the appetite of a bear, and the energy level of a sloth."

I laugh again, and he seems happy to see me so relaxed in his home.

I look around and see the staircase immediately off the entryway, bisecting the house. To the right, it opens to the living room; to the left, a hallway. The living room is clean but comfortable—not obsessively spotless or sterile like Jordan's house, but not cluttered. The few decorations are tasteful and carefully chosen. Black-and-white photos hang on one wall, and dark drapes frame the windows on the other, balancing the room.

The furniture is as inviting as it is stylish. A dark blue couch sits in the center of the living room, the kind you could fall asleep on during a movie marathon. Matching armchairs flank it, with a low coffee table made from reclaimed wood in front of them. A woven throw is draped over the back of the couch, adding a cozy touch.

"So... you did all this?" I ask, raising a skeptical eyebrow as my gaze sweeps over a ceramic vase filled with dried wildflowers, a patterned rug under the coffee table, and a trio of well-placed candles.

Reid chuckles, shaking his head. "Not exactly. My cousin Emily helped. She runs a furniture store in town, and I gave her free rein with the place... within limits, of course."

"Well, she has great taste," I laugh.

He points out the guest bathroom and the door to his home office. "I don't keep anything confidential at home, so feel free to come in if you need anything. You can log into the guest account on the computer, or I can set you up with your own. Behind the stairs is one of the doors to the backyard—the other is in the kitchen."

Upstairs, he leads me past a few closed doors. "This is my room," he says, gesturing to a door at the end of the hall. "If you need anything, I'm just next door. This is the hall bathroom, but your room has its own." He opens the door to the guest room beside his.

"I've never really had guests, other than the guys crashing on the couch or something," he admits, looking a little sheepish. "But I asked my mom to swing by and put on fresh sheets while we were at the office."

I run a hand over the soft duvet, feeling Reid's warmth and care in making me feel welcome. I haven't felt this at ease or safe in so long.

"Feel free to settle in and make it your own while you're here. This is your space," he says, a touch of humor in his voice. "I promise I won't come in unless invited... or there's an emergency."

"Thank you," I murmur, glancing up at him.

Back downstairs, he takes me down the hallway we initially passed, which leads to a dining room with a sturdy table that could seat six, illuminated by a simple pendant light, and then into the kitchen.

Just as he'd predicted, a very round cat sits in front of a bowl connected to an automatic feeder. The cat lets out an indignant meow, casting Reid a scathing look as he ruffles the fur on its head. Just then, the feeder clicks, releasing a small portion of kibble, and the cat immediately dives in, scarfing down his food. Ham trots over from the living room and daintily eats her share.

The kitchen is spacious and beautiful, with stainless steel appliances, dark wood cabinets, and pale granite countertops. A breakfast bar with three stools upholstered in dark blue sits opposite the main counter, and the same dark wood flooring continues from the living room.

A sliding glass door opens to a large backyard. Unlike the dining room, which has an almost formal feel, the patio and yard seem well-used and loved. A large grill stands in one corner, and a sturdy patio set with an umbrella dominates the space. Nearby, a small firepit is surrounded by chairs, as if they'd just been left out from a recent gathering.

Returning to the living room, Reid stops me, gently taking my hand. "This is your space too, for as long as you're here," he says earnestly. "Don't be afraid to use it. I want you to feel comfortable—not as a guest, but like it's your home too."

His words are sincere, and somehow, despite having only been here a short time, I already feel more at ease in his home than I ever had in the place I'd shared with Jordan.

"I'm going to get some paperwork finished in the office. You're welcome to join me, or you could watch something on TV," Reid says, his tone light, hands in his pockets as he looks at me.

My chest constricts, and my next breath stutters in my lungs. I turn from him to look at the TV. The idea of having to make a choice leaves me frozen in place. It feels like a test, one of those no-win situations Jordan used to set up, where every choice seems to lead to anger. My eyes dart from him to the living room, landing momentarily on the small bookshelf in the corner. What if he wants me in the office? Will he think I am lazy if I choose to watch TV instead? It has been so long since I've felt free to simply... relax.

"You could read a book too," Reid adds from behind me, his voice casual, "or I've got some video games if that's more your thing."

Too many choices. I feel my panic rising, my heartbeat thudding in my chest, drowning out his words. My vision blurs as memories collide with the present, making me feel like I am back in that other house, trapped in one of Jordan's "tests," where any wrong move can lead to pain.

Reid notices something is wrong because he is suddenly at my back. I tense, every muscle locking up as a rush of fear shoots through me. I am not in Reid's house for a moment anymore, and the man behind me is not Reid. I cannot catch my breath. I can almost feel a cruel hand gripping my shoulder, bruising my skin. I hold my breath, waiting for the strike that never comes.

"Hey, it's okay, Sage," a far-off voice murmurs. "Can you tell me five things you can see?"

See? I cannot see past the blinding panic. I am trapped in my mind, lost in the fear of making the wrong choice.

"Sage, look at me," the voice says again, softer this time. Slowly, I force my gaze up, my eyes locking onto a pair of warm, hazel eyes.

He chuckles gently, the sound anchoring me. "I've never thought of my eyes as pretty, but thank you for the compliment." His tone is calm and familiar, pulling me out of the memory.

"Huh?" I manage, startled by his lighthearted comment.

"Alright, give me four more things you can see," he says, his voice steady, as though grounding me is the most natural thing in the world.

I blink, realizing he is on his knees in front of me, so I look down at him. It is deliberate, I realize, his way of making himself smaller, letting me hold the power in this moment. "Uh… your hair…" I scan the room, my voice becoming steadier. "the pictures on the wall."

"Good, good," he encourages, his tone soothing. "Two more things."

My gaze darts back to him. "Your face," he gives me a small chuckle, and my eyes dart away again, "and the coffee table." I feel more centered, my breathing slowing as I follow his lead.

"Perfect," he says softly. "Now, can you tell me four things you can hear?"

"Um… your voice, the fan, the clock ticking and the… cats' toy."

"Great job, Bunny. Now, give me three things you can feel."

He continues guiding me through the grounding exercise, his patience unwavering as I name things, one by one. By the time we finish, I am calm again, my hands still wrapped in his. I look down, noticing the gentleness in his expression and the slight tension he cannot quite mask.

"Can you tell me what I did to trigger that, Bunny?" he asks gently, his voice filled with concern. I can see the guilt in his eyes, the way he is silently berating himself. I need him to understand that it is not his fault.

"It was stupid… I don't know what happened. I was fine and

then... I was not," I whisper, my voice thick with frustration.

"Hey, it's okay, baby. Can you think back to what made the panic start? I just need to know so I can avoid it in the future."

Silence stretches between us, and I search his face for any hint of anger or impatience. All I see is kindness and worry. It is so different from what I am used to. No resentment, no irritation... just understanding.

"It felt like a test," I admit softly.

His brow furrows as he nods, piecing it together.

"I gave you too many options," he murmurs, almost to himself.

"But I don't get it," I say, exasperation seeping into my tone. "I get mad when I don't have choices, but then when you give them to me, I panic. Who does that?"

"Someone who's been dealt a shitty hand," he replies as if it is the most obvious thing in the world. "We just need to find the balance, that's all."

"But... that is not all," I whisper, embarrassed.

He waits patiently, focusing solely on me, encouraging me to continue.

"You walked up behind me, and... it reminded me of... before."

He nods again, his gaze steady and understanding. "Okay. I'll be more mindful of that."

"That's ridiculous," I argue, shaking my head. "You can't just avoid walking up behind me forever."

He smirks, a hint of humor lightening his expression. "I can sure as hell try."

He gently squeezes my hands, his voice dropping into that warm, reassuring tone. "Alright, here's what's going to happen. I'm going to get some paperwork done in the office, and you'll pick out a book and spend some time reading. I noticed you eyeing the bookshelf a few times." He pauses, studying my face. "Then, when I'm finished, we can find something to watch on TV together. How does that sound?"

I feel the tension in my shoulders ease as I process his words. It is a simple plan that gives me enough guidance to feel safe but does not trap me. "I can work with that," I say, offering a tentative smile.

"Good." With my hands still in his, he uses gentle pressure to steer me toward the bookshelf, letting go only when I take a few steps.

When I am a few paces away, he heads into the office, leaving the door open in case I need anything. I am touched by the careful way he handles me, aware of my needs without making me feel fragile.

The idea of feeling breakable does not sit well with me, but today... I feel as if the slightest nudge might shatter me. Tomorrow, I promise myself, I will be stronger. But tonight, I allow myself to breathe.

I run my hand along the spines of the books, noticing the mixture of mysteries and sci-fi novels. A small smile tugs at my lips as I spot a well-worn copy of Darth Bane. So, he's a fan of the old Star Wars lore, I muse, feeling a strange sense of comfort in the familiarity of the title.

Settling onto the couch, I start reading, the words drawing me in and giving my mind a much-needed break. A little while later, Reid joins me, sitting on the opposite end of the couch. He turns on the TV, flipping through channels until he lands on a cooking game show where contestants must cook under ridiculous conditions. Ham hops onto the couch with a soft meow, rubbing her head against Reid's thigh. Reid ran his fingers absentmindedly through her fur.

My book forgotten, I find myself laughing as the contestants scramble to adapt to the bizarre challenges. The host plays the role of the "evil" mastermind perfectly, adding new, diabolical twists to each round. I cannot hold back a snort of laughter when he makes the contestants switch baskets of ingredients, forcing them to throw out their plans and think on their feet.

"Why would anyone go on this show?" I ask, my smile widening as I watch the chefs struggle.

"Money," Reid replies with a grin.

"But they bid it all away!"

"Maybe they just want to say they won. Looks like fun, though," he says, casting me a sideways smile.

I chuckle, leaning back on the couch. "I guess that's a good reason."

Eventually, as the sun starts to dip below the horizon, Reid gets up and switches on a lamp, casting a warm glow over the room. "Do you have any dinner preferences?" he asks as he heads toward the kitchen.

I glance between him and the TV, where the cooking show is still playing. "Not really, just... nothing made in a coffee pot, unless it's coffee," I say, unable to keep the playful note out of my voice.

He snorts with laughter. "Yeah, I'm not a bad cook, but I'm

definitely not creative enough to make some of those situations palatable."

Not wanting to be left alone, I follow Reid into the kitchen, where he is already pulling ingredients out of the fridge, Ham weaving around his feet. "How about a stir fry?" he asks, looking to me for real input, as though my opinion matters.

Surprised by the question, I consider the mix of ingredients on the counter. "Chicken stir fry sounds good. Anything I can help with?"

"You can keep me company, maybe keep this one occupied," he says, tilting his head toward the breakfast bar in an invitation to sit, picking up Ham, and plopping her gently into my arms. I fully expect her to dart away, but she happily settles against me, purring her little heart out as I stroke her fur. "I'll let you in on a little secret, though." He leans forward conspiratorially, and I cannot help the grin that creeps onto my face.

"Oh? What's the secret?"

"I cheat," he says with a snicker, pulling out a bag of pre-chopped vegetables and holding it up like a prize. "See? Already chopped and mixed—cabbage, carrots, snap peas, broccoli, and a few other things."

"You can do that?" I ask, incredulous. The idea of not having to spend ages chopping vegetables feels almost like a revelation. Jordan would have lectured me for being lazy and wasteful. I give myself an internal shake as if I could erase him like an etch-a-sketch.

"Yep. Learned a long time ago that if I bought everything separately, it would just sit in the fridge and go bad. All that chopping and cleaning... way too much work for one guy."

"That makes sense," I admit, settling onto the stool.

I watch him pull out a red cutting board and start slicing up the chicken. I cannot help but notice that other cutting boards are tucked in the cupboard, each a different color—blue, green, white, and wood.

"Are your cutting boards... color-coded?" I ask, amused.

Reid glances down, his ears tinged with a hint of red. "My mom worked in a kitchen for years and drilled food safety habits into me, same with Aunt Tina. Certain things stick. Last thing I want is food poisoning."

"You've got a point," I reply, charmed by the care he takes in the kitchen.

It is relaxing to watch him cook. He moves efficiently, not wasting any motion. Though he is not trying to make anything look fancy, the meal comes together beautifully. When he places a bowl of perfectly cooked stir fry and fluffy rice in front of me, I am surprised by how delicious it looks—and even more so by how good it tastes.

I gently place Ham on the ground where her food awaits her.

We eat at the breakfast bar, enjoying the easy conversation that flows without effort.

Later, he pulls out his gaming system. I manage to whoop his butt on a racing game but lose miserably in a first-person shooter. The lighthearted competition and laughter feel like a balm after such a difficult day; before long, it is time to call it a night.

Upstairs, I change into a threadbare pair of sweats, brush my teeth, and slide under the covers. I notice my phone on the nightstand, having left it there earlier. Part of me wants to leave it alone, afraid of what I might see, but the urge to see if maybe Juniper sent me a message is too strong.

My heart sinks at the sight of new messages, none from Juniper. The first is clearly a phishing scam with a suspicious link, which I delete immediately. The second is some sort of coupon for a random sports store, maybe the phone's previous owner signed up for a mailing list. But the third is from an unknown number again, with the cryptic message, "Home is where the heart is."

I clench my jaw, feeling a shiver of dread crawl up my spine. Maybe, just maybe, the person will lose interest if I continue to ignore the messages. I hope so, at least. It's not like I can even respond when the number is blocked. Placing the phone face down, I try to push the unsettling thoughts away.

After the emotionally draining day, I fall asleep quicker than I expect. But my dreams are plagued by faceless shadows, twisted and dark, with an ever-present feeling of fear chasing me through the night.

The first time I wake up, my heart pounds in my chest. I hold my breath, listening intently to the silence, relieved to realize I have not cried out. The last thing I want is to disturb Reid.

I lie back down with a sigh, but the darkness of the room feels oppressive. I pad over to the bathroom, turn on the light, and leave the door cracked, allowing a sliver of soft light to seep into the room. That helps. Just enough to take the edge off the fear.

Though I do not check the phone—I do not want to see if there are more messages—I guess it is somewhere after midnight. I take a deep breath, settling under the covers, hoping for a few more hours of rest.

After waking up from nightmares three more times, I notice the first light of dawn creeping over the horizon. I decide it is as good a time as any to get up, maybe make breakfast as a small gesture of thanks.

Barefoot, I make my way downstairs, only to be surprised by the sight of Reid already in the kitchen. He stands by the coffee pot, shirtless, wearing running shorts, a thin sheen of sweat covering his well-toned body. I stop in my tracks, watching as he lifts his shirt to wipe his face, revealing a ripple of muscles beneath his skin.

The light patter of my footsteps catches his attention, and he turns around, clearly not one to be snuck up on. "Morning, Sage," he greets, his voice warm. "I hope I didn't wake you."

I shake my head, feeling a blush creep up my cheeks. "Did you go out for a run?"

"Nah," he replies with a grin. "I've got a mini gym set up in the garage. Haven't set up a secure perimeter to run outside yet."

I walk over to one of the bar stools, trying—and mostly failing—not to stare at his very fit physique. I catch the hint of a smirk on his face as he pours coffee, and I know he notices me checking him out.

"How do you take your coffee?" he asks over his shoulder, pulling down two mugs.

"Just a little cream, no sugar," I reply, forcing myself to keep my gaze on the countertop instead of on him.

He nods, grabbing a small jug of cream from the fridge and fixing my coffee just the way I asked. When he places the steaming mug in front of me, I cannot help but feel a pang of gratitude—and a flicker of something warmer, something more profound, that I am not quite ready to examine.

We sip our coffee in comfortable silence, the morning light filtering through the window, casting a soft glow over the kitchen.

CHAPTER TWELVE

Reid

I finish my coffee and make us breakfast before leaving Sage to curl up with her book in the living room. After a quick shower, I glance at myself in the mirror, assessing my build. I am not vain, but I know I am solidly built—functional muscle rather than showy bulk, necessary in my line of work. I smirk slightly, recalling Sage's occasional glances at me. Some women prefer the lean, runner types, but she does not seem to mind my more rugged frame.

I head downstairs, letting her know I'd be in my office if she needs anything. She glances up from her book, giving me a small nod before diving back into her reading.

Once in my office, I settle into my chair, checking emails and touching base with a few of my guys in the field. Just as I am about to stop for lunch, my phone buzzes with a message.

Vaughn: Call me ASAP

Instinctively, I feel a knot form in my stomach. I tell myself to keep calm; this is routine, but somehow, with Sage involved, it does not feel routine.

The line barely rings once before Vaughn answers. "Is Sage in the room with you?"

I frown. "No, is everything okay? Do you want me to get her?"

"No," Vaughn replies, his tone tense. "It's probably best if she doesn't hear this."

I feel my jaw tighten. "What's going on?"

74

Vaughn takes a deep breath. "I read over the forms she filled out."

"Good. Are they in the system yet? I'd like to review them."

A long pause. "Reid, I don't think you should read everything just yet."

My tone hardens. "Excuse me?"

"Some of the stuff in there... I know we've seen some rough cases, but this one..." Vaughn hesitates, as if choosing his words carefully. "Look, Rhett started a background check, and some things seemed off, so he dug deeper. She's right to want to disappear."

My stomach churns. "I can't protect her if I don't know what I'm dealing with, Vaughn."

"I get that, man. I'm not saying go in blind. I'm sending you everything on him, but I think it's better if she tells you some details of her past herself. Too much, too soon, could ruin any trust you're building."

I clench my jaw, feeling my patience fray. "I don't need you playing matchmaker, Vaughn."

"I'm not. But you like her, yeah?"

I am silent.

"I haven't seen you take an interest in anyone since Rosemary. Finding out everything about her from a file could set you back with her. You need to tread carefully, Reid. It is better if she trusts you with her secrets rather than taking them."

"Secrets you already know?"

"I'm not someone she has to interact with every day."

I sigh, rubbing a hand over my face. "I'll prioritize her safety over any chance at... anything else. She's not looking for that anyway."

There is a pause and then a sigh, "All right. I'll send over the essentials."

"I want all of it, Vaughn."

I open the secure folder as soon as Vaughn hangs up, steeling myself. The first thing I see is a photo of a younger Sage, eyes haunted, in the arms of a man in a tailored suit and an expensive watch. Something about the man's face sparks a memory, a flash of familiarity, but I can't quite place it. He is well-dressed and good-looking in an oily way—maybe a politician or a CEO type—but the way he holds Sage sends a chill down my spine.

His hand digs possessively into her shoulder, her body subtly turned away, a demure smile that doesn't reach her empty eyes as if she has trained herself not to react. Her floor-length silver gown hugs her body perfectly, make-up expertly applied, and the jewels sparkling around her neck could purchase a small island. She looks polished and poised. I'd been to enough galas as security to recognize the type of event this photo was taken at.

I click through to the next file. Rhett's notes tell me it's a buried police file. Nobody asks Rhett how he gets the information that he does, plausible deniability and all that. The hospital she was at reported it, but the police dismissed the case. The officer who started the case is not the one who closed it. It's clear when the other office took over. It went from a DV case to someone having a mental breakdown. The conclusion is that the injuries were self-inflicted.

I can't look at the photos for more than a moment. How anyone could think it's self-inflicted is beyond me. Someone brutalized her.

Then there are medical files. Multiple reports declared her mentally unwell. Prone to self-harm, lies, delusions of grandeur, paranoia. All signed off by the same doctor.

He discredited her. I draw in a slow and steady breath, trying to press down the rage that is simmering just below the surface. I need to keep my emotions under control if I am to get through this file.

I clicked through more files, following the timeline Rhett built. He must have spent the entire night working on this. Bank statements, images, emails, text messages. It all painted a bleak picture of her life with him. Financial abuse. Physical abuse. Emotional abuse. My heart stops at a graphic group thread.

He trafficked her. Drugged her and... I click to the next file, and my stomach threatens to revolt. How could anyone do that to their partner?

A sharp gasp breaks my concentration. I look back to see Sage standing in the doorway; her face pale as she stares at the screen, transfixed, as if seeing a ghost. In a way, I suppose, she is. I minimize the screen. She doesn't need to see that.

"Sage," I whisper, the calm tone contrasting my racing pulse and the unwanted spike of guilt I try to smother. It is necessary for me to know about her past.

I turn and stand slowly, watching Sage's reactions. I move

carefully, closing the distance but keeping my stance non-threatening.

"Bunny?" I ask softly, my voice coaxing, gentle.

Her eyes do not move from the screen even though it's a benign desktop photo now. "How did you get those photos?" Her voice is small, hollow, and distant; her mind a million miles away. I recognize the signs of dissociation. Fuck.

"It was part of the briefing, Sage," I reply, kneeling slightly to meet her gaze at eye level, trying to draw her back. "Just some background information. I need to know what I'm up against to keep you safe."

She nods, but it is mechanical, her focus still far away. "Briefing?" She repeats in a whisper, as if testing the word on her tongue.

I gently take her hand, giving it a reassuring squeeze. "Let's go to the kitchen, grab something to drink, and I can explain." I don't know whether the lack of panic is a good thing or not. In her state, probably not.

Wordlessly, she lets me lead her to the stool she claimed earlier at the breakfast bar. I fill a glass with ice and water and pass it across the counter to her, hoping the cold sensation will help ground her. She takes it, her fingers tightening around the glass, the chill seeming to bring a touch of awareness back into her eyes, but she doesn't drink.

"Sage," I say, "Vaughn sent me the preliminary case file so I could understand who we're dealing with. I need to know who this man is, what he's capable of. This is not a reflection of you."

She stares down at her hands gripping the glass. I watch as something passes over her face, and it hardens, as if she's coming to a painful decision. "He's a monster," she says finally, her voice bitter, edged with anger and pain. "He'd probably watch his own mother's house burn down and proudly hold the match."

My gut twists, but I remain silent, letting her speak at her own pace.

"His family protects him," she continues, the anger in her eyes strengthening her, her words dripping with vitriol. "His father and brother are in politics. Dad's a senator; the brother works in PR, cleaning up the images of messy politicians. They get him out of every mess he makes." She looks up at me, her gaze sharp, filled with venom. "He cleans up their messes, too. They have a problem, they go to him, and it just... disappears." She makes a poof motion with her hand to illustrate the point.

"His father is Senator Beltran?" I ask, realizing the man in the image is a carbon copy of the older man I'd seen on TV far too many times because of his controversial views.

She nods, a bitter smile twisting her lips. "The one and only." She stands abruptly, her hands braced on the counter as she leans forward, her voice growing more intense. "Jordan runs clubs, not that any of them are under his name. On the surface, they seem fine, bars catering to different crowds. But some of them... some of them you have to know people to get in, be invited, vetted. Not to see if you are safe but if you are the right clientele. Those aren't even about money either."

I nod, silent but absorbing every word, my mind piecing together the web she describes.

"Those clubs," she continues, "are where people go to get whatever they want. And I mean anything. It doesn't matter how dark or twisted—it's available if you have enough cash or a juicy secret. Maybe trade a favor or two. He can get his hands on anything they want." She turns to me, eyes flashing. "And the cops? They don't do a damn thing. Some of them go to his clubs. And in exchange, they look the other way. He's untouchable."

Sage's fury turns to despair as she looks back at me, her shoulders sagging. "And I've put you all in danger," she whispers, her voice raw with guilt.

I straighten, moving to her side and resting a steady hand on her shoulder. "Sage, you didn't put us in danger. I've dealt with men like him before. We can handle this."

She shakes her head; her gaze unfocused, distant again. "He's... he's different, Reid. He has money, power, connections. You don't understand—he can ruin lives with a phone call."

I tighten my grip, grounding her with my presence. "Then we'll be prepared. Vaughn and I, the entire team—this isn't our first high-stakes case. We know how to keep you safe."

She looks up at me, searching my face, her vulnerability laid bare. "But you're all at risk because of me. I can't... I can't live with that."

My voice softens as I lean in, my hand resting reassuringly on her shoulder. "Sage, listen to me. You're not alone in this. We're here because we choose to be. Vaughn, me, everyone—we're here because we want to protect you, because no one should face that kind of danger alone."

Her eyes glisten with unshed tears, and for a moment, she looks like she is about to break. Then, she takes a shaky breath and nods, the slightest hint of relief breaking through the fear.

I squeeze her shoulder gently. "Now, let's focus on getting you through this, one step at a time. You don't have to shoulder this alone. Trust me, trust us."

Sage looks down, brushing a tear from her cheek. When she looks back up, there is a flicker of determination in her gaze. "Okay," she whispers. "One step at a time."

I smile softly. "That's all we need."

I watch as she gathers herself, a new tension filling the room. When she finally speaks, her voice is soft but laced with pain.

"Did you... did you read all the file?" she asks, her eyes fixed on me with a sudden urgency. Her gaze is guarded, but I can see the flicker of vulnerability there, like she has just realized exactly how much of her life she has laid bare on those forms Vaughn asked her to fill out.

"Not yet," I reply gently, hoping my tone will reassure her. Fuck, maybe Vaughn was right? "Is there something...is there something you don't want me to see?"

She bites her lip, uncertainty etched on her face. "It's not... it's not what you'll read that scares me," she admits. "It's what you'll think."

My heart twists. "Oh, Bunny," I say softly, shaking my head, "I could never blame you. None of this is your fault."

She cuts me off before I can say more. "You don't understand." Her voice is desperate, pleading. "I went to one of his clubs, Reid." Her eyes lock onto mine, almost as if daring me to judge her. "I went there willingly."

My brow furrows in confusion, not sure how going to a club could condemn her, but I stay silent, sensing she needs to get this out.

"That's where I met him, you know," she continues, her voice barely a whisper. "It was one of his clubs." She pauses, swallowing hard, and the words seem to drag out of her like they have been buried deep within her. "It was... it was a BDSM club."

She spits the word out as if it is something dirty, her gaze flicking to my face, searching for any sign of disgust or scorn. I remain steady, keeping my expression soft and open. There is nothing wrong with a BDSM club; hell I'm a member of the one in the next town over, even if

I haven't been in a few months. She probably thought it was a safe place to explore. It should have been a safe place.

"I'd gone there with a friend, one of his public-facing clubs, and it seemed safe," she continues, her voice picking up speed as though it is a relief to finally release the words. "We went a few times a month, but I never did anything serious. Just… watching, you know? And she had a partner she'd do scenes with, and I'd always had a red wristband so no one ever approached even though I was on my own." I nod; the color wristband system is standard in a lot of clubs; even the local one uses it. "And then one night, and he was there. Jordan." Her eyes grow distant, reliving the memory. "He was charming, Reid. He was so charming. We talked for hours after he bought me a drink. He didn't brag or try to impress me like most guys do. He asked about me. About my life, my dreams, my family… I didn't even care that he ignored the red wristband and talked to me first because he didn't ask to play. We just talked, and that was safe, right? And it was so fast — gifts and dates and he said all the right things and fixed all my problems and he was always there."

Her voice breaks, and she looks at me with tear-filled eyes. "And I lapped it up, Reid. Like some… some pathetic, needy girl."

"Hey," I interrupt gently, reaching out to place a hand over hers to stop her from digging her nails into her arms. "Don't call yourself names."

"But I was," she insists, her voice cracking, a tear slipping down her cheek. "I was so stupid. I didn't see through him. I let him manipulate me. I ignored all the red flags that are so obvious now. Made excuses when he got mad."

"No," I say firmly. "He manipulated you. He love-bombed you, Sage."

"Love-bombed?" She looks up, the term foreign to her.

I nod, my voice soft but resolute. "He showered you with attention, moved the relationship at lightning speed. How long did it take for things to change? For him to stop listening, to stop saying and doing the nice things?"

She looks away, her face clouded as she recalls. "A few months… maybe not even that long. It was like once I moved in with him… he was like Jekyll and Hyde."

I give a decisive nod, my hand tightening slightly on hers. "That's what abusers do, Sage. They create a mask, a version of themselves tailored just for you. They make you believe in something that doesn't exist."

She stares at me, shock mingling with a strange sort of relief, as though my words are starting to untangle a knot she has been carrying for years.

"Were you close to your family?" I ask quietly.

Her expression darkens. "My mom died when I was young. I lived with my aunt after that, but my dad was... in and out. Then he left for good when I was sixteen." She looks down, shame creeping into her voice. "I guess... no, not really."

My heart breaks a little more. "He targeted you," I say softly. "He saw that vulnerability. He knew no one would step in when things got bad."

She nods, almost imperceptibly, and then her gaze drops to her lap. "But I stayed," she whispers, her voice thick with self-recrimination.

"Sage," I say, my tone gentle but unyielding, "do you know what trauma bonding is? Or the cycle of abuse?" I was going to have to buy Tessa a gift basket for her damn classes. Younger me, stupider me would have wondered why she stayed.

"A little," she murmurs, her voice barely audible.

"Abuse... it rewires your brain, Bunny. It's designed to make it hard to leave. Good times followed by bad times followed by good times again. It creates a cycle that leaves you convinced that if you can just do or be the right thing, he'll go back to being who he was. That's hard to get away from. But you did. You found a way out."

Her face crumples, her hands clenching in her lap. "But it took years, Reid. He did so many horrible things, and I stayed."

I take her hand in both of mine, squeezing gently. "He stole your power. He manipulated you. It wasn't your fault."

She lets out a shaky breath, looking up at me with haunted eyes. "The first time... the night I moved in, that's when he changed. He took me to the club, saying he wanted to celebrate. I was so excited. We'd done a lot of scenes, and he told me he had a surprise planned."

I watch as she drifts into the memory, her face growing pale. "He asked if he could... gag me. I trusted him, so I said yes. Everyone in the room heard me agree. But then..." She shudders, wrapping her arms around herself. "He let others... join." Hearing her say it, even knowing the horrific things that happened to her, made me want to hunt him down. "He told them it was part of the scene. I couldn't use my safeword because I was gagged, and I couldn't get away because he'd tied my arms. When we got home, he twisted my words, told me it was what I wanted, that I'd talked about fantasies like that before."

She looks at me, eyes wide and glassy. "And he was so convincing. He had all these details, and eventually... I started believing him. I thought I'd asked for it."

I clench my jaw, my own anger simmering beneath the surface. "Sage, that's gaslighting. What he did was a violation of your consent. A true Dom would have made sure you had a non-verbal safeword. He would've given you an out, checked in. There should have been detailed negotiations, safety checks, aftercare, hell, a debrief of what you liked or didn't like for next time. Did he talk about any of that?"

She shakes her head slowly. "No... there was no aftercare. He just... took me home."

"Oh, Bunny," I murmur, pulling her into my arms. I hold her as she trembles, my hand stroking her hair. "That was abuse. That wasn't BDSM. That was him violating every rule there is. None of that was your fault."

"But I stayed with him," she whispers, her voice small. "I didn't leave, even after that night. Even went back to that club with him."

I pull back slightly, my gaze locking with hers. "You stayed because he made you think you had no other choice. He manipulated you into believing that was normal. That's not on you."

We sit in silence for a moment, her head against my chest, my fingers gently running through her hair. After a while, she tilts her face up to look at me. "You... you know about BDSM?" she asks, her voice laced with curiosity and a hint of apprehension.

I chuckle softly, rubbing the back of my neck. "Yeah, it's been a while, but I've been to a club here and there. There's one I go to occasionally. The guy who runs it? He's strict about safety. A scene like the one you just described..." I pause, choosing my words carefully. "It never would have happened there. They'd stop it before it even began if it weren't fully consensual."

She shakes her head, a bitter smile twisting her lips. "But it's his club. Who's going to tell him no?"

My expression hardens. "In any well-run club, the DM—Dungeon Monitor—will step in, no matter who's involved if something seems off. They don't care about status or who owns the place. Safety is the top priority."

She sighs, a distant look in her eyes. "That sounds... nice." The wistfulness in her voice is painful, and I feel a surge of protectiveness flare within me.

I reach out, tucking a loose strand of hair behind her ear, and hold her gaze. "You deserve that, Sage. You deserve a place where you can feel safe, where your boundaries are respected. None of what happened was your fault. It was all on him."

She gives a slight nod, a contemplative look in her eyes—a glimmer of hope, perhaps. I'm determined to protect it, to protect her. I will do everything in my power to ensure that she never feels powerless again.

CHAPTER THIRTEEN

Sage

I teeter on the bottom step, debating between sneaking back upstairs and locking myself in my room again with the book I pilfered from the bookshelf, or daring to go into the kitchen to get a snack. I picked at my meals the last few days, my nerves turning my stomach into a twisted tangle of knots that made every bite, as delicious as it was, stick in my throat.

Now I am paying the price.

After my word vomit the other day, where I laid my deepest shames at his feet, I feel like an exposed nerve. I practically stripped off every piece of armor I had and showed him some of my worst scars, demanding him to pass judgment. The entire time I was internally screaming at myself to shut up. I never wanted to give anyone the tools to hurt me again, and yet, seeing those images, the words came tumbling out.

All I want to do now is hide away and rebuild all my walls.

It doesn't matter that he insists that it wasn't my fault; he could be a priest offering me ablution, and I'd still carry the guilt of my inaction. I am not sure how to act around Reid. He told me to make myself at home, yet I can not help but worry that I am intruding in his space. I oscillate between wanting to snap at him for treating me like spun glass and terrified that if I say the wrong thing he'll toss me to the wolves.

And can I blame him for being so careful? I float around the house like a ghost. I can't tell if it's because I am waiting for the tides to turn or I am ashamed of what I confessed. Maybe both?

He says the right things. Made me feel safe each time my world was falling apart. Swooped in and insisted on helping when my car broke down, navigating each panic attack with ease and now insists on protecting me. I am dependent on him right now. How is any of that different from Jordan? Is this love bombing too?

I am unsure whether I should stay in my room or hang out in the common areas. He's invited me to join him multiple times, but knowing he knows about my worst mistakes makes it hard to accept the invitation.

We've gone backwards. Within days of meeting him, I feel stripped bare, certain that even if I can think of a quippy one-liner, he'll see through my mask to the terrified girl behind it.

He has no problem talking during mealtime and doesn't seem bothered by my one-word replies. It is me. I just feel tongue-tied and scared. I can't find the prickly self-assurance I had when I first met him. I am so out of practice that I do not feel like a normal human. Normal people know how to have a back-and-forth conversation.

Normal people do not agonize over every minor decision.

My eyes dart to his closed office door and the path that leads to the kitchen. All I have to do is walk to the kitchen. But what if there is a 'no snacking' rule? Jordan had one. I could not eat outside of designated mealtimes and only foods he approved. He once came home and found crumbs from the graham crackers I had eaten in the kitchen—crumbs I was sure I had cleaned up—and he spent an hour lecturing me about wasting food and unhealthy habits.

He made me feel like a disobedient child.

The silence of the house worries me. Will he hear my footsteps? What if I eat something that is meant for a recipe?

The twisted grumbling in my stomach decides for me.

I hasten to the kitchen, careful not to make any noise. I look around the pristine counters and feel lost. What can I eat that will not make a mess or be missed? A piece of fruit, maybe? Fruit is healthy. I dare not open the fridge. It might as well be Fort Knox. The fridge is off-limits.

I spot a fruit basket tucked in the corner full of apples. I reach for one and then hesitate. Maybe they are all already spoken for. Jordan was precise in what he bought. Exactly enough berries, carefully portioned out for each workday. None for me, of course.

I pull my hand back, clasping my hands together, wringing them in front of my chest. But I am hungry. Ugh, I feel like a thief. Maybe I can pitch in for groceries?

I reach out again, pause, before snatching the apple from the basket. I feel triumphant. And guilty. I should wait for dinner. I put the apple back on the counter. No, I do not deserve to eat.

Wait, no. That is not true. That is not my voice. That is him.

I grab the apple and take a bite. The crunch is so loud I flinch, worried he can hear me. The crisp juice floods my taste buds with sweetness, overshadowing the noise.

Maybe I should have waited until I was in my room. But no, that could bring bugs.

I freeze as I stare at the apple, realizing a core will remain. I cannot hide that. Maybe I can bury it in the trash?

"You should have some peanut butter with that apple," Reid says from behind me.

I whirl around with a shriek, and the apple, to my horror, flies out of my hand and lands hard on the floor. I freeze momentarily, staring at the mess, before launching myself for the paper towels.

"I'm s-s-sorry," I stammer. "I'm so sorry. I didn't mean to waste food, and I won't steal food again. I just wanted a snack, and, and..." The apple in one hand, the other rubbing the floor, cleaning a nonexistent spot. "I should... I could mop. I have to clean this up, and —"

Reid takes the paper towel and apple from me and puts them in the trash. I am trying hard to control my breathing, trying not to cry, when Reid gently takes my hands, pulling me up and guiding me to a stool at the counter. The same one I sat at when I confessed how stupid I was for staying with Jordan.

"Do you like peanut butter on apples?" he asks, his back to me as he selects another apple and pulls out a cutting board. The random question stalls my spiraling thoughts. The rhythmic chopping distracts me. What was his question?

"Um, I liked it when I was a kid," I mumble.

He gives a nod of his head. "You haven't eaten much today. A little protein would be good for you," he says more to himself than me.

I watch silently as he cuts the apple, pulls out a jar of peanut butter, and plates my snack. The entire time, I am frozen in fear and waiting. Waiting for the lecture. Waiting for him to yell.

But he sets the plate in front of me, apples neatly sliced, with a dollop of peanut butter on the side. "I figured you could dip your apple slices and see if you still liked it." He steals a slice off my plate and dips it in the peanut butter before taking a bite. He smiles at me before returning to the cutting board and cleaning up the remnants of the food prep.

"You're not... mad?" I ask, my voice scarcely a whisper.

"For what?" he asks, his tone conversational, the water from the sink running over the cutting board.

"I wasted food."

"Bunny," he says, turning to look at me, "I'm pretty sure that was my fault. I should have made more noise or something. I'm sorry about that. Scaring you again, I mean." He gives a rueful smile. "I promise I didn't mean to."

"You're... apologizing. To me?" I ask incredulously.

He turns off the water and sets the dishes in the dish rack.

"Am I forgiven?" he asks, brows raised. "Should I do something to make amends?" he teases.

"I... you're forgiven?"

"Good." He claps his hands together. "Now, since you're down here, what were you thinking for dinner? I could make chicken, or..." He opens the fridge and looks inside. "Chicken." He smiles at his poor joke. "We had that yesterday." He muses, "Do you mind?"

I give a slight nod, then realizing that he might think I mind, I shake my head. My voice seems to have deserted me. I feel off balance. Like I am on the edge of a precipice, waiting for the ground to fall out beneath me. Am I being lured into a false sense of security? I want to trust this, but it feels too perfect.

"I'll order groceries tomorrow. Add the snacks you like to the list." He points at the list on the fridge behind him. "I try to stick to fruits and veggies, but if you want anything in particular, you'll have to tell me."

I say nothing. It feels too presumptuous to ask for anything more. He already does too much.

I watch Reid move around the kitchen, cataloging his body language. Each movement fluid and relaxed, with no ticking jaw or balled fists. No flash of an angry sneer telling me I can expect retribution later. Bit by bit, the tension leaves my shoulders.

"Could we maybe go to the store instead of ordering?" I ask long after the conversation about groceries was over.

But the blinding smile Reid sends me makes butterflies tap dance in my stomach. "I'll check with Vaughn tomorrow."

"I'm sorry, Bunny, but we can't go to the store today."

"Why?"

His eyes dart to the side as he rubs the back of his neck, his mouth twisted in a grimace. "Vaughn wants to get confirmation of Jordan's location before we go anywhere."

"What does that mean?"

"It means that in the few days you have been here we've had no luck locating him."

"Can't you just call his assistant and pretend to set up a meeting or something? She always knows where he is."

"You'd make a great PI," Reid laughs. "Rhett did that. Pretended to be an investor. He made some other calls before he found a chatty sales executive who complained that Jordan had been frequently absent from the office for months, then unexpectedly took a vacation and hasn't been seen in weeks.

"That's... not like him." Jordan is a workaholic. Long hours, bringing his clients home, his fingers in everything, always on call for those 'special' clients of his. "But it's not like he knows I am here, and he never goes to grocery stores."

"That may be, but Vaughn wants us to stay put for a bit, and I agree."

Stupid Vaughn. I don't even like Vaughn. "He doesn't know I am here!" I can hear an edge of a whine in my voice. Panic tinged with anger. I leap onto the anger. I don't need to fall apart in front of him again.

"Sage..."

"I could wear a hat and sunglasses." My words are tumbling over themselves. Where is that anger? "Hide my hair and… and he doesn't know I am here!"

Reid's expression is calm and sympathetic. "Sage the tracker would have led him to this town." His words match his expression. Pity.

I step back, deflated. A flash of rage slices through me. I hate Jordan so much. I turn on my heel and storm upstairs like a petulant child. "You should have mailed the damn tracker to Alaska."

I swear I hear a muffled chuckle just before I close my door.

I spent the rest of the morning hiding after my outburst. At lunch, Reid offers me a boon; Vaughn has some work I can start doing remotely. It's data entry, mostly processing incident reports into spreadsheets, but I feel better about Heartwood Security and, by extension, Reid offering me protection now that it doesn't feel so much of a handout.

The next few days settle into an easy routine between us. We work in his office in the mornings, him on his ridiculous four-screen setup and me on a desktop he claims he just happened to have tucked away.

While I had been upstairs sulking, he had set up a workstation for me, complete with a huge monitor to make it easier to look over the scanned incident reports and enter them into a spreadsheet without constantly flipping through windows. A warm feeling I can't identify fills my chest, soothing my volatile emotions.

The afternoons are relaxed. We have similar tastes in movies and shows, and he's coaxed me into coming out of hiding with video games. It is a tentative calm.

But by the end of the week, I can feel restlessness creeping in, gnawing at me. My broken sleep doesn't help with managing my emotions. I want to trust Reid, but something holds me back.

No updates on Jordan, and even weirder, no more strange texts. I can't help the growing worry that something is going to happen soon. A part of me wonders if it has all been a fluke or some prank and I read too much into those cryptic words. I should tell Reid about it, but there is also relief that they have stopped, and I don't want to think about it anymore.

"Is my car fixed yet?" I ask over breakfast, catching Reid off guard. He pauses, fork halfway to his mouth, the morning sunlight streaming through the kitchen window casting him in a warm glow.

"Uh, maybe," he replies, furrowing his brow. "I'll have to call Maddox and see."

I nod, taking another bite of my food. Reid watches me thoughtfully for a moment before asking, "Why? You planning on going somewhere?"

"Oh, um..." I hesitate, suddenly unsure how to explain the surge of need I feel for my car. "I... no? I just... want to have my car back. In case... In case I need it."

"If you really need to go somewhere, we can figure something out. I know we've been lying low, but it will not be forever."

"Yeah, I know, but it's my car," I reply, the words coming out weaker than I intend. How can I explain that having my car feels like having an escape plan? The feeling is irrational, maybe even paranoid. I do not want to leave. Reid's home feels safer than anywhere I have been in years, and he is kind, steady, direct but never harsh. And yet, a piece of me cannot shake the need to know I have a way out. Just in case.

Reid's gaze softens as he seems to sense my inner conflict. "I'll call Maddox after breakfast. Chances are, it's already fixed up. But in the meantime, the keys to the truck are over there," he points to the hook by the garage door where several sets of keys hang. "If there's ever an emergency, we can take my truck."

I chew on my bottom lip, not fully comforted. "What if you're not here?"

Reid leans forward, his voice reassuring. "Until we're sure you're safe, there won't be a time when I, or someone from my team, isn't nearby. And if you want to drive, that's fine too. I'm not about to lose my man card if I end up riding shotgun." He flashes me a grin, trying to lighten the mood, and I cannot help but giggle.

"Could we go somewhere today?" I ask, my tone tinged with hope.

"That depends, where to?" he asks, leaning back in his chair.

I shrug, frustrated. "I don't know—anywhere that's not here. The coffee shop, the bookstore..." The store, but I do not voice that one out loud. "Just out. Juniper wants to hang out."

He seems to consider it before nodding slowly. "I'll see what I can arrange. If we can create an environment I can secure, then perhaps," he says, his answer feeling too vague for my liking, but I let it go.

After finishing breakfast, he takes his plate to the sink and heads toward his office. I stay behind, pushing my food around on my plate, my appetite gone. I am not sure why I feel so out of sorts, my mind spinning with restlessness. I feel... trapped. The realization hits me like a punch to the gut. It is the same feeling I get when I stay in one place too long on the road. The urge to run gnaws at me, my body thrumming with a desire to escape.

I clench my fist, the metal fork pressing into my palm as I take a shaky breath, trying to steady myself. But the tension only grows, bubbling under my skin, making my pulse race. I abruptly stand, dumping my half-eaten breakfast into the trash and placing my dishes in the dishwasher. My heart is pounding, and I am struck with a sudden, overwhelming need for fresh air.

My eyes dart to the back door. Yes, outside. That will help.

I slip out quietly, grateful the sliding glass door opens easily and closes behind me without a sound. I step past the patio set and into the grass, standing in the middle of the yard and tilting my face to the sky. It is cloudy, which is not surprising for Washington, but the breeze is gentle, rustling my hair, and the grass is cool and damp under my bare feet. The privacy fence with its tall hedges makes me feel safe, hidden, as I take deep, steadying breaths. Slowly, my heartbeat calms, my panic easing into something manageable.

But then the sliding glass door opens behind me, the sudden sound shattering my calm. "Sage!" Reid's voice cuts through the quiet, the tension in his tone jolting me. I turn to see him standing in the doorway, his face a mix of worry and frustration, one hand gripping the door frame as if he is bracing himself.

"What are you doing?" His voice is sharp, and I flinch, dropping my gaze. I feel the familiar fear of having messed up twisting in my gut. He is angry. I really messed up this time. Will he tell me I am too much trouble? Send me away?

He moves closer, but I step back. He slows his steps, hands up and cautious. I freeze, shoulders bunched up. I close my eyes, bracing. "Sage?" His voice no longer has a sharp, angry edge. Was it even there? "Bunny?" I keep my eyes shut. Waiting. This is the part he tells me I messed up. That I deserve what he does next. "Look at me,

Bunny," he murmurs, coaxing me to meet his gaze. "I'm not mad. I was just scared."

"I'm sorry," I whisper, my voice trembling. "I didn't mean to scare you... I just needed to be outside."

He reaches out, gently tipping my chin so I cannot look away. "I'm sorry I raised my voice," he says, looking contrite. "I shouldn't have done that. I just... I came out and didn't see you. You never take too long to join me in the office, and you didn't answer when I called, and I couldn't find you anywhere in the house, so I thought maybe something had happened."

My shoulders slump, shame eclipsing the fear. "I'm sorry," I stammer. "I didn't think... I should have told you where I was going, and I..."

"Shhh," he soothes, squeezing my hand gently. "It's okay." But I am shaking my head, my voice rising, panicked.

"I won't go outside again," I say, my tone frantic. "I didn't mean to worry you. I'll stay inside."

"No, no, baby," he reassures me, shaking his head. "You're not a prisoner. I'm not trying to stop you from doing anything. I just need to know where you are to keep you safe. You can go outside anytime you want—just let me know, okay?"

I look at him, my brow furrowing at his words. "So... I'm not trapped inside?"

"No, not at all," he replies, holding my gaze. "If you need space, I can give you space. But I can't do my job if I don't know where you are."

The word job hangs in the air between us, a reminder of why he is here, of why he is being so careful with me. I try to ignore the sting of it, reminding myself that I am, after all, just a job. That is the reality.

Reid seems to sense my discomfort and changes the subject gently. "I called Maddox when I was in the office. He said your car is fixed, but he'd like to hold on to it for a little longer."

My eyes widen. "What? Why? If it's fixed, I want it back," I demand, a hitch of panic in my voice. The car represents my independence, my escape.

"It's a safety thing," he explains, but I cut him off, frustration spilling over.

"What safety thing? You just said I'm not a prisoner," I retort, my voice sharpening.

"Sage," he says, his tone firm but calm, "listen to me, and I'll explain." I fall silent, my jaw tight as I look at him, waiting.

He takes a breath, meeting my gaze steadily. "Rhett found a tracker in your car, remember?"

I nod, my stomach tightening.

"Jordan—or whoever put that tracker there—has the last location of your car," he continues. "But they don't know where you are right now."

"We could leave the tracker there," I mumble, more to myself than to him.

"We could," he agrees. "But Rhett already disabled it, and Maddox offered to hold on to the car in case someone's watching it. If someone's looking for you, they'll be looking for that car first. I think that is a good idea."

I nod slowly, realizing he is right, even if I hate it.

"Besides," he adds, his tone lighter, "you can use my truck. You're not trapped, but for now we need to limit where we go to places we can control. Consider me your personal chauffeur. I arranged for us to go see Juniper at the bookstore. She has some book club thing going on. Or we can take a quieter trip somewhere else if that's what you need."

I look down, processing his words, the tension gradually draining from me. "Okay," I murmur, feeling the flutter of hope that maybe things might be okay.

CHAPTER FOURTEEN

Sage

Nervous excitement has me practically bouncing as we arrive at the bookstore. After a week of texting with Juniper, I am finally going to see her in person again. She invited me to her book club days ago, and Reid, being overly cautious, arranged everything with his team to ensure the bookstore is safe. I find his diligence endearing, though unwarranted. After all, I am certain that, despite Jordan knowing my general location, he will not be lurking in a random bookstore.

Reid holds the door open for me as we step into the cozy shop. I inhale deeply, savoring the comforting scent of paper and the sight of shelves stacked high with books. Two displays flank the entrance. The first one, on my left, showcases an eclectic selection of romance novels: everything from sweet, clean romance, to old-school bodice rippers, to contemporary covers with shirtless models, a few reverse harems, and even a selection of darker romance with masked men brooding on the cover. My heart skips a beat at the display. I devour romance novels—any trope is fair game for me. Cowboys who call the heroine "darling", unrealistic billionaire workplace romances, even blue-skinned aliens from space—I love them all. The escapism, where women get a happy ending with a man who adores them, is exactly what I need sometimes.

On the right is a display of all things bridal. There are wedding planning journals, the latest issues of bridal magazines, flower catalogs, and DIY centerpiece kits, all arranged in a charmingly coordinated chaos. I chuckle, guessing that romance and weddings naturally go hand-in-hand here.

Reid guides me through the rows of books toward the back of the store with an arm wrapped around my lower back, where a cozy seating area is set up. There, I see Juniper, who is chatting animatedly with three other women: one in a long black dress that looks like it has been lifted straight from Morticia Addams' wardrobe, another with bubblegum pink hair piled on her head in a messy bun, and the last one dressed in a sharp, intimidating pantsuit that practically screams "lawyer". Sitting to the side, looking bored, is Maddox, who gives me a chin lift in greeting.

The moment Juniper spots me, she jumps up with an excited grin, her eyes flicking to the way Reid's arm is wrapped securely around me. Her smile turns conspiratorial, and she bounces over, looping her arm through mine and whisking me toward the couches. "Don't worry, Reid," Juniper calls back over her shoulder, "we'll take good care of her. You go stand somewhere and look scary. Maddox, you go with him." She tells her brother, making shooing motions with her hands.

A chuckle escapes me as I am unceremoniously plopped onto a couch. I glance back at Reid, but he is already moving back towards the front of the shop, talking to Maddox. Juniper settles into the armchair across from me, leaning forward with hands clasped on her knees, her face earnest and her eyes sparkling. Her dark hair catches the light, and I cannot help but admire the perfectly applied cat-eye makeup, as well as the bracelets and necklaces that jingle with every move.

"So," Juniper starts, letting the word hang in the air with a mischievous grin. "How was it?"

"What?" I blink, caught off guard by the sudden attention and the keen, almost predatory glint in Juniper's eyes. I glance at the other women, who are all watching me with equally amused expressions.

"She means, how was he in bed," the woman with the pink hair says bluntly, leaning forward.

My cheeks flame red, and I nearly choke on my spit. "What? I... We haven't... I...!" I stammer, feeling the heat rise to my face.

"Really?" Juniper asks, snickering. "You said he is hot, and he's gone all daddy dom on you." I stifle a groan. I should not have spilled to

Juniper about the apple incident. I was lamenting how stupid I'd been to panic, and all she got out of it was Reid cutting up a snack for me.

"Why not?" asks the Morticia look-alike, her head tilted as if genuinely puzzled by the concept.

I stumble over my words. "Well, it's just... I mean..." My gaze darts up to where Reid is standing, eternally grateful he seems to be out of earshot.

"He likes you," the pink-haired woman interrupts, as direct and unfiltered as before. "He opened the door for you, had his arm around you."

I stammer, "He's... he's guarding me. It's not —"

Juniper jumps in, grinning. "I promise you, he doesn't need to be that close just to guard you. Reid's in love," she singsongs with a laugh.

"Well, I don't think..." I try to protest, but I am immediately cut off as the woman in the power suit joins in with a dreamy smile, her soft expression a contrast to the fierce, professional image she projects. "He hasn't dated anyone in so long. It's nice to see him happy," she says wistfully. For a brief moment, I wonder if she is interested in Reid romantically, and I have to squish down the unwanted spark of jealousy.

Reid and I are not dating.

"You saw us together for like... 30 seconds and...but... we're not dating," I insist, my voice slightly higher with exasperation.

"Are you sure?" Pink Hair chimes in, giving me a challenging look. "All the evidence suggests otherwise. We know Reid; he's clearly into you. If you don't like him, you should tell him. He'll respect your boundaries." Her tone is firm, matter-of-fact.

I shake my head, looking at Juniper. "I don't even know any of you," I say, a little exasperated. "I thought we were going to talk about books."

"Oh, right!" Juniper exclaims, springing to her feet. "I forgot to introduce everyone. We all know each other so well, and I just sort of assumed... I mean, the only new faces around here are usually tourists for a wedding, and they're gone by the end of the week." She takes a deep breath. "And book club is what we call our hangout time. I mean, we do read, but we talk about other things too." She hastily explains, "Sage, this is Lyra," pointing to the pink-haired woman,

"Elowyn," gesturing to the power-suited woman, who waves slightly, "and this is Sunshine." She nods to the woman in black.

I raise an eyebrow at the name, and Sunshine shrugs, rolling her eyes. "My parents were hippies. I got off light compared to my siblings."

I grin. "Dare I ask what their names are?"

"Let's see... Saffron, Bodhi Tree, Harmony Song, Flower Petal, Echo, Indigo Summer, and uh, Sparrow. I think. I haven't met the youngest yet."

My jaw drops. "You have six siblings?"

"Seven, actually. I might have some half-siblings out there, but no one has shown up yet," Sunshine says. "Mom might even be pregnant again. Poor kid will probably end up named something like Mountain Range."

I cannot hold back a laugh. "Are your parents still together?"

"Oh yeah," Sunshine replies casually. "They have a... well, an 'open' relationship, I guess. So who knows how many siblings I might actually have." She shrugs as if this is the most natural thing in the world.

I shake my head, grinning. "I don't even know what to say to all that."

Sunshine shrugs again. "Enough about me—what's going on with you and Reid?"

I shift, looking at each face in turn. "Honestly... I really don't know. He found out about some... stuff going on with me and sort of... took over."

"Yeah, the men here have that tendency," Lyra chimes in with a smirk. "Sometimes you've got to tell them to back off. It's nice sometimes, but other times..." She trails off, clearly thinking of her own experience.

The others nod in agreement, murmuring in commiseration.

I find myself nodding too. "It's actually been kind of nice," I admit, my voice softening. "I... didn't have the best experience with my last..." I hesitate, searching for the right word. "Partner," I finish weakly. "But Reid's been really... careful. And understanding."

Lyra's face softens. "Was your last boyfriend... mean?"

I look away, my voice barely a whisper. "Understatement of the century."

A heavy silence settles over the group before Juniper clears her throat, steering the conversation back to lighter territory. "Well, do you like Reid?"

My cheeks flush as I try to find the right words. "He's... nice."

"Nice?" Juniper snickers. "He's hot as hell, has a stable job, loves his mom but isn't a mama's boy, has his life together, and he's a Dom. That man is a catch!" She gives me a knowing look. "Not that I'd want to be with him—he's too much like a brother. But I want to see him happy with someone he likes."

I raise an eyebrow, skeptical. "How do you know I'm that person?"

Juniper leans in, her eyes twinkling. "Because Reid needs someone to take care of, and you need someone to take care of you."

"That's not... I'm not taking advantage of him," I begin, but Juniper cuts me off.

"Let me put it this way," Juniper says gently. "He wants someone who could take care of herself but trusts him enough to let him help."

"And you think that's me?" I ask, my voice barely above a whisper.

"Uh, yeah," Juniper replies, nodding emphatically. "Only a strong, kick-ass woman could survive what you have. If you needed to, you could take care of yourself. Hell, you have been taking care of yourself. But letting him take care of you? That fulfills a need he has. It's that Dom-sub thing, you know."

My face turns red. "But I'm not one anymore."

"A sub?" Juniper raises a brow. "Sage, that's not something you can turn on or off," she says kindly.

I look down. "Juniper, I told you my experience with... BDSM hasn't exactly been the best."

"That's why Reid is perfect for you," she presses. "He is so by the book."

"You're really insistent, you know that?" I mutter, half-smiling, looking up at Reid, catching his eye before darting my gaze back to Juniper, who grins back unrepentant.

"I know. I'm the best matchmaker around. Haven't failed yet."

"Ahem," Elowyn interjects, rolling her eyes.

"That was a fluke!" Juniper protests, laughing. "And I stand by it— it'll work out!"

Elowyn shakes her head, but her gaze softens as she looks at me. "Look, Reid's a good guy, Sage. And from what I can see, the two of you are good together. I don't know the whole story about your ex, but I promise... you can take a chance on Reid."

I am grateful when the conversation shifts to gossiping about their own lives. Sunshine has some issues with a boss at work, and Elowyn had three disastrous first dates in a row and is convinced she is cursed to only date assholes.

"Can you believe the last one brought up me quitting my job as soon as we get married? I didn't work my ass off in law school only to give up a job I love to play Susie homemaker. What was it he said? Something about 'This law thing is just to fill your time until you have a family. I mean, you will not be able to take care of me and our kids if you have to go to court.' There are lots of women who would love to be stay at home wives. That's not me." We all nod as she continues her tirade. "Like Vicky. Remember her?" She asks, not that she gives anyone time to answer. "She always wanted to be a mom. That girl loves kids, even had a backup plan in case she couldn't have one on her own or didn't meet Mr. Right." I don't know this Vicky, but Elowyn's rant is rather entertaining. "I swear every man I date is worried about how much I make or wants me to eventually quit." She gives out a long-suffering sigh. "I should date women."

"Or Benji," Juniper teases.

Elowyn sends her a venomous look. I lean over to Lyra. "Is Benji an ex?" I whisper.

"Nope," she whispers back. "You know Vaughn?" I nod. "His oldest brother and Elowyn's rival since preschool. I am pretty sure if they'd stop bickering for five minutes they'd realize they are perfect for each other."

"Benji is an idiot," Elowyn states firmly. "I thought we were actually going to talk about books this time." I can't help laughing along with the other women at the poor attempt to change the subject. But Juniper pulls out a copy of the book they've been reading and hands it to me, along with a list of the next few books they plan to read.

I meet Reid at the door when book club is over, bouncing on my toes, the book list clutched in my hand.

"Juniper said the register is already cashed out for the night, but can we come back later to get some books?"

He gives me an indulgent smile before handing over a black canvas bag with the bookshop's name on the front that I hadn't realized he was holding. Peeking inside, I see every book on the list.

"Reid," I say, looking up at him, my voice cracking a little.

"Come on, let's head home." He wraps his arm around my shoulders, leading me outside into the night. I look back and spot Juniper sporting a huge grin, and a 'I told you so' expression on her face.

In the truck, I clutch the bag of books to my chest.

"Thank you, Reid," my words still choked up. He just flashes a smile before putting the truck in gear and taking us home.

CHAPTER FIFTEEN

Reid

"Ugh," Sage groans, "Kane's handwriting is also so hard to read. Does that look like a P? Could be a T? Maybe it's a 9?" I silence a laugh as I listen to her musings. "Reid," she calls, her voice elongating the middle part of my name, "can you tell what letter that is?"

I turn to see her leaning forward in her chair, eyes inches from the screen, zoomed in on an incident report. The distorted text looks more like a child's scribble than a word.

"Huh, I got nothing," I reply. "There is no way those are words. I think you are going to have to email him, Bunny."

She gives a dramatic, exasperated sigh, and I have to curb the smile that threatens to spread. It's cute when she gets upset. Not that I am stupid enough to say that aloud to her. Again.

"Fine, I'm going to tell him he has to type his reports too from now on," she mutters as she aggressively taps away on the keyboard.

Working with her is highly entertaining. After the initial few days where she was scared to make noise, afraid she'd distract me, she began to relax. The more she relaxes, the more I get to see her little quirks, like how she talks to herself, little things like figuring out what someone wrote, but also random commentary, sometimes insulting the handwriting of one of my — well, I suppose our coworkers now — or making random remarks about some of the incident reports.

I don't think I've ever enjoyed being behind a computer this much. Normally, I am itching to get out into the field. It doesn't matter the job, whether it's long-term requiring travel or just a local gig playing bouncer at a wedding. But lately, I've actually been okay with the paperwork and planning. All because I get to spend more time with her.

"I'm going to make us some lunch," Sage says, the undercurrent of annoyance still in her tone. I guess she is still irritated about Kane's handwriting. Honestly, I am pretty sure that's why this task gets so backlogged—half the guys have shit handwriting and detest paperwork. It has to be done, but none of us wants to do it, so either they rush through it, making it indecipherable, or they put it off until they've almost forgotten the details. Makes logging everything a pain in the ass.

She stomps out of the office, but despite the aggression in her steps, she doesn't slam the door. Hmm, maybe not as angry as she's pretending to be. I let out the chuckle I had been stifling. Aside from deciphering horrible handwriting, she seems to like the job.

Lena is supposed to handle this task, but she hates it, so she leaves it until she has nothing else that needs to be done, causing it to pile up. I have to give Vaughn credit; I was worried he'd invent some busywork just to placate Sage, but no, he found her a task that actually contributes.

I can't help but imagine us a few years from now, both still working in this office. Wait, no. I am getting ahead of myself. This is temporary, just until we ensure her safety. She is going to move on, get her own place, start her own life—one where she won't have constant reminders of this terrible time when she was essentially on the run. She won't want me around then. I'll be a living reminder, and I don't want to be that to her. I scrub my hand over my face, the longing heavy in my chest.

Despite what I told Vaughn about keeping everything totally professional, he is right: I do want her. But I'm not going to act on it. It wouldn't be right. She depends on me for her safety. She lives in my house. Hell, the number of panic attacks I've talked her through already creates a power imbalance. While I eventually want whatever long-term relationship I have to become an ongoing D/s dynamic, that kind of submission has to be earned and freely given. A gift. It can't be taken or coerced. Acting on this attraction now would be incredibly unethical.

Right?

Maybe this would be easier if the attraction were one-sided. If I hadn't caught those looks she gave me at the bookstore when Juniper and the girls were clearly talking about me or felt the spark when our hands brushed. Before that, I had been operating in blissful ignorance. There was always a maybe, a flicker of possibility, but no confirmation. The lack of certainty made keeping things professional much easier.

No. Friends. That's what she needs right now. A friend.

Besides, her last relationship was shit, and her experience with the BDSM community was worse than tarnished—it was weaponized against her. No one protected her when she needed it; she was assaulted and gaslit into thinking it was her fault. There is no way she would ever willingly step back into a submissive role after that. And a club is out of the question.

I'd be fine never going to a club. Nope. Not the point.

She needs control now. Not control over someone else, but absolute control over herself and her choices. She won't be able to cede that control, not really, not to me. The little moments where I take care of her, while fulfilling on some level, aren't enough for what I ultimately need in a relationship. I need to be more than a caretaker. And she wouldn't want the kind of dynamic I crave—the deep trust, the power exchange, the rules designed to be tested, the carefully negotiated scenes exploring sensation, both pleasure and pain...

Get those thoughts out of your head, Reid.

The last person I had anything long-term with didn't end well. She claimed she wanted the same things I did, the same dynamic, but after a while, she admitted she'd only agreed to make me happy. We met at a club; she acted experienced but later confessed she only went there hoping to run into me. I was gutted. It forced me to rethink every scene and interaction, wondering if I'd missed some sign or hesitation behind her enthusiastic 'yes.' Had it all been reluctant compliance? It destroyed the trust essential for our dynamic. I couldn't be sure if she genuinely wanted something or was just people-pleasing. If I couldn't trust her to safeword honestly, I couldn't trust myself to push any boundaries, to play with any real intensity. Soon, we were limited to vanilla sex. She seemed content, but I felt like a core part of myself was missing. She wanted the stability I represented, an idea of me, but not all of me—not the part that needs to care for a partner through dominance, not the part that finds connection in exploring sensation, both pain and pleasure. I don't think we lasted a month after her revelation. I tried, but the end was inevitable.

I know I can't give up that part of myself, not long-term. But maybe for Sage I could? No, that would only lead to resentment and harm us both in the long run.

I try to refocus on work. Sage will call me for lunch when she's ready. Her cooking was another surprise, insisting we take turns. I like seeing her grow more comfortable here, taking the initiative. She's still jumpy, though. A few weeks of safety is nowhere near enough to erase years of trauma; I know that. She has a long road ahead—eventually, she'll need to talk to a professional, process everything, and rebuild her life. But in the meantime, watching her start to bloom, even a little, in the safety of my home has been...

No. Focus. You have a job to do.

My phone chimes with an incoming text. I whip it out, desperate for anything that will pull me from the thoughts of Sage. One glance tells me I'm out of luck.

Blake: Call me as soon as you are alone.

Fuck. That is not good. Blake was assigned to look into Jordan after Rhetts cursory check revealed he'd been missing from his home and work for a while. He was supposed to do a deeper dive and see if Jordan was just lying low. Wishful thinking, of course. I know better, but still, I had hoped.

Blake answers on the first ring.

He doesn't waste time on pleasantries. Not Blake. "He's in the wind, Reid. You need to be on guard; he may be close," his voice is calm and even, belying the frustration I know he's masking. Blake is our top PI; when we need to catch a skip, he's the one who finds them. He prides himself on being able to find anyone. Honestly, I'm not sure how he does it, and half the time, like Rhett, I suspect it's not entirely legal, but I don't ask. It isn't like anyone other than Rhett or Asher would understand the technical jargon.

"What do you mean by 'in the wind' exactly?"

"Hasn't touched his bank accounts or credit cards. Phone's at home, car's in the garage, house is empty. No digital footprint, no physical trail. Like the man vanished."

"Sage mentioned his business isn't exactly legitimate. Maybe a rival...?"

"No, his foot soldiers are keeping things running smoothly, like they've got long-term orders. Looks like he planned to go off-grid. But aside from confirming standing orders for his managers and getting a vague 'he's on vacation' from his assistant, I've got nothing solid."

"That's never stopped you before," I point out. "You found Marshal Grady holed up in some random fucking cave in Colorado."

"Yeah, well, Grady left crumbs. This guy's a ghost."

My stomach tightens. "What does this mean for Sage?"

"She needs to stay locked down, I guess." My jaw clenches at his cavalier tone. I know Blake doesn't care about Sage personally—she's just a client—but this news will crush her. And I have to be the one to tell her. She's already going stir-crazy again, desperate for another trip out. The last one was a little more than a week ago.

"I'll keep digging. I'll find the asshole. But stay sharp, Reid."

"Fine. Thanks for the heads-up."

Click. Goddamn asshole. Not even a goodbye.

I lean back in my chair, rubbing my face with my hands. Fuck.

"Something wrong?" Sage asks from behind me. I whip around. She's standing in the open doorway. Shit, how long has she been there?

"Maybe. Think we can talk about it after lunch?" I ask, trying to buy time. I have to tell her, but she needs to eat first.

She shrugs. "If it has to do with me, I'd rather know now, or I'll just spiral."

Fuck. Fair point. As much as I want to shield her, I can't protect her by hiding things. "I just got off the phone with Blake," I begin. Her confused expression confirms how much I haven't kept her updated. "He's the PI Vaughn sent to locate Jordan." No reaction. "The asshole from the garage?"

She nods, her body stiffening slightly. I can see her brace for impact. I hate that this reaction is instinctive for her now. I quickly fill her in on the few details Blake provided, watching her face closely for any sign of panic, ready to ground her if needed.

"Okay," she says slowly, mouth pursed. "So, we don't know where he is, I need to keep lying low, and Blake is going to keep investigating?"

"Essentially, yes," I confirm.

"Okay," she says, giving her head a decisive nod.

"Okay?" I ask, surprised by her composure.

She looks up, brows drawn. "Yeah. It would have been nice to know he was back home, moving on. But I always knew he'd try to find me. This just means nothing has changed, really."

I'm shocked at her calm assessment, but I suppose she's right. For her, nothing truly has changed.

"Lunch?" she prompts, her expression shifting into a smile, though I can still see the tension behind her eyes.

"Yeah, lunch," I reply, following her toward the kitchen.

"Booooo!" Sage yells at the TV as the contestant she was rooting for is eliminated in the first round. "That was rigged, I tell you!"

"Aww, poor Bunny. I told you my chef was better. It's the hat." I laugh because the hat in question is ridiculous and has no bearing on culinary skill, and the way she rolls her eyes tells me she doesn't believe my reasoning any more than I do.

"Fine, well, I still say your guy will not win." She grabs another piece of popcorn and pops it into her mouth. I just chuckle and lean back on the couch, relishing how close she is sitting. A far cry from the first time we sat on this couch, where she practically glued herself to the opposite armrest. Now, she's sitting cross-legged, bowl of popcorn in her lap, her knee occasionally brushing against my thigh. It's such a small thing, maybe even accidental, but that she doesn't immediately recoil makes me feel like a teenager with his first crush. Relishing the contact, yet terrified that acknowledging it will make her pull away. I'm acutely aware of her every movement: her expression as she watches the contestants, the quick smiles she flashes my way when we cheer for people who can't hear us.

It's almost perfect. But beneath the surface, I worry about what is going on in her head. Sage says she's okay with the update about Jordan—or lack thereof—but I wonder if it's all a facade. She seems outwardly unfazed by not knowing where he is, honestly handling the uncertainty better than I am. But I can't shake the feeling she's putting on a brave face so I won't worry. Not that it's working. Especially after three more days pass with no updates from Blake, settling us deeper into this tense routine.

If I weren't watching her so closely, I might miss it—the little cracks in her armor. An anxious glance toward the window, followed by a hasty look at the door. There's a flicker of relief in me that she is feeling something, that she isn't completely repressing it, but guilt immediately swamps that relief. I hate that she carries this worry, and there's frustratingly little I can do to alleviate it beyond what I'm already doing. Blake is hunting Jordan, the local team is keeping watch for sighting of him in town, and her immediate physical safety is secure with me. She's in a controlled environment, and I'll gladly stand between her and any demons—job or no job.

She turns back to the TV, the moment forgotten. If I hadn't been watching, I would have missed the way she expertly smoothed the anxiety from her features, the serene smile sliding back into place.

As the days wear on, her anxiety becomes more pronounced, harder for her to mask. I notice her staring out the window longer, her eyes darting to the doors more frequently. The restless tapping fingers, the low hum of jittery energy that radiates from her. It reminds me too much of the day I found her outside, face turned to the sun. She'd been jittery then, too, edgy, looking for escape. Hell, she'd asked about her car—if that wasn't a sign she felt trapped, I don't know what is.

I still feel guilty for startling her that day, never mind my own spike of panic when I couldn't find her anywhere in the house. I don't want a repeat performance.

I don't think she'll ask to leave, not until she's completely overwhelmed by the need to run. I need to head that off. Maybe take her into town? Shopping? There are some nice boutiques, though most cater to the wedding crowd. Do I want to spend all day navigating shops and calculating security risks with so many unknowns? Probably not. The logistics would be a nightmare on short notice.

Maybe just one location, like the bookstore again? No. A date in town risks an ambush by Juniper and her crew, or maybe even one of the guys, asking questions I'm not ready to answer. Wait... date? Not a date. Getting ahead of myself. Yes, I want to spend time with her, preferably alone, but it's not a date.

Friends, remember?

Besides, we've both been confined indoors for too long. Home is safe, but she needs fresh air. Needs to be outside. Maybe the falls? It's remote, not well-known beyond locals, and the trail is short and easy. We could make a day of it. Have a picnic.

I check the weather app. Tomorrow: clear skies, warm. Midweek, so the trail should be quiet—bonus. A plan starts to form, and by dinner, I'm ready to propose. The outing. Just the outing.

Except I do not know how to ask without sounding like an awkward teenager asking out his crush. Ugh. Focus. Not a date, remember. Just a hike. With a friend. To a scenic waterfall. For a picnic. Totally platonic. Right. I can just imagine Vaughn giving me shit over this later, telling me to just put my cards on the table. But I've already decided not to pursue her. Mostly. Shit.

She's quiet at dinner, lost in thought. Have I waited too long to suggest getting out? Her mental state is as critical as her physical safety right now, and the last thing I want is for her to feel trapped here. Maybe she needs space from me and wants to see Juniper instead?

"What do you think about getting out of the house tomorrow?" I ask, aiming for casual. There. Neutral enough. Ball's in her court.

"I... yeah, that would be nice, but..." she pauses, searching for the words, brows furrowed. "I'm just not sure I have the energy for... people... right now?" The admission brings a blush to her cheeks. "I know Juniper wants to hang out again," she adds hastily, "and I do too, but I don't think I can handle being 'on' around a group." She trails off, gaze distant, then snaps back to me as the silence stretches. "But not... not you. You're not 'others.' And..." Her blush deepens.

"It's okay, I get it," I say, relief and something warmer flooding through me. Part of me is doing a silent victory lap that I don't fall into the 'draining people' category for her. Not that Juniper is draining, exactly, but for Sage to make that distinction—it feels significant. The other part hates that her hypervigilance has worn her down this much. I should have suggested this sooner.

"So, how about we do something tomorrow? Just us. Outside, away from people?" I suggest.

"Like what?" she asks, tone laced with suspicion, though a small smile softens the edge.

"It's a surprise," I reply, aiming for mysterious, probably landing on awkward.

She considers this for a moment. "Okay. As long as it's peaceful," she concedes, narrowing her eyes playfully. "Nothing loud. No crowds."

"Your conditions are noted," I grin, feeling ridiculously pleased. "Finish your dinner, and maybe there's ice cream later."

She gives me a mocking salute and a dry "Yes, sir." I bite back a grin. Yeah, these feelings are definitely getting dangerous.

CHAPTER SIXTEEN

Sage

The scenery blurs as I stare out the window, trees whipping by, sunlight flickering through their branches in rhythmic flashes. My hand hangs out the window, rising and falling with the air current. My hair is a windswept mess, but I don't care. Despite Reid insisting I could drive, I declined. I don't know where we are going, and there is something comforting about letting him take the wheel. After months of being on the road, always the one in control, it is nice to sit back and watch the world pass by.

I glance over at Reid, catching his eye as he looks my way, and give him a small smile. His short dark hair remains utterly unaffected by the wild wind rushing through the open windows. He returns my smile with a warm one before focusing back on the road.

I have been texting with Juniper over the past few days, planning another visit, but today I wanted something quieter. I told Reid I needed a place to clear my mind, somewhere peaceful, and let him decide where to go. Eventually, we pull into a small dirt lot. Though 'lot' is perhaps too grand a term—it is just a small patch of gravel and packed earth surrounded by dense forest. A sign at the trailhead marks the beginning of several paths leading into the woods.

"Hiking?" I ask, glancing at him dubiously as I stay seated in the car. "I'm not sure what about me screams 'hiker,' but I can assure you I'm not."

Reid, already out of the truck and rummaging through a bag in the backseat, lets out a hearty laugh. I feel a spark of pride at making him laugh like that, even if it is a little at my expense.

"Bunny," he says, still chuckling as he pulls out a couple of backpacks, "I promise it's not a long hike. A half mile at most, I swear. The view will be worth it."

I raise an eyebrow. "I don't know... that sounds like a lot of walking," I mutter, feigning reluctance.

He snickers, shaking his head as he slings one of the bags over his shoulder and hands me the smaller one. I take it reluctantly, giving it a suspicious look.

"You said it wasn't a long hike," I point out.

"It isn't," he replies, grinning. "But you never go into the woods unprepared."

I snort, shouldering the bag. "You were a Boy Scout, weren't you?"

"Surprisingly, no." His answer catches me off guard, and I glance at him curiously. "I, uh... got into a fight, and the scoutmaster didn't want me back."

This time, I burst out laughing. The idea that calm, collected Reid could be the type to get into fights seems absurd, and yet there is an edge of nervousness in my laughter. Is Reid capable of violence? "Why do I feel like there's more to that story?"

He smirks, ignorant of my conflicting thoughts, leading me toward the trailhead. "Go on this little hike with me to the most beautiful spot in the world, and maybe I'll tell you."

"Fine," I sigh, adjusting the backpack. "What's in here anyway?"

"Just the basics—emergency kit and a few supplies. I may not have been a Boy Scout, but I still know how to be prepared."

"Whatever, lead the way," I say, rolling my eyes but feeling a strange thrill of excitement that far outweighs my apprehension. Reid hasn't done anything yet to make me distrust him.

He reaches out, gently takes my hand, and we start down the trail together. As we walk, I notice various paths branching off, each marked with signs indicating different trail lengths: five miles, a 7.8-mile loop, and even one that boasts a 22-mile trek. I shake my head at the idea of hiking that far; they must be out of their minds. But Reid ignores all the branching paths, guiding me forward with confident steps.

Neither of us fills the silence between us with chatter. Nature makes its own cornucopia of sound. Leaves rustling, animals darting into the brush, the crunching of our feet on the packed earth. Each step away from the car left me feeling lighter. A heavy weight in my chest I didn't even realize was there began to loosen. In the distance, I can hear the trickle of water.

We walk in silence for perhaps 10 minutes when the sound of water becomes even more pronounced, a steady, rushing noise mingling with the softer rustle of leaves. We step out of the shaded path into a clearing, and I gasp, speechless as I take in the scene before me.

We're at the base of a beautiful waterfall, its water tumbling into a shallow, crystal-clear pool stretching out before us. The water does not look deep, maybe a foot at its deepest, and I can see all the way down to the sandy bottom, where tiny fish dart around. Moss drapes the rocks and trees surrounding the area, giving the entire scene an ethereal, almost otherworldly quality. Behind the waterfall, I glimpse a small cave, partially hidden by the cascading water.

I turn back to Reid, a huge grin lighting up my face. He does not say, "I told you so," but the smug look on his face is enough. I roll my eyes and walk to the water's edge, peering into the clear pool. A rustling sound draws my attention, and I hold my breath as a deer steps out of the trees, only a dozen paces away. I stand as still as I can, watching as it lowers its head to take a drink.

The deer's ears twitch at the snap of a twig, and it bounds off, disappearing into the underbrush. I let out a soft breath, feeling a thrill at witnessing such a quiet, beautiful moment. I glance around, catching sight of birds flitting between the trees, their songs filling the air. A squirrel scurries up the trunk of a nearby tree, pausing to look at me before darting away.

When I turn back to Reid, he is setting up a red-and-black plaid blanket on the ground. He pulls a few containers and a thermos from his bag, arranging them neatly. It finally dawns on me—he packed us a picnic. He thought ahead, found this beautiful spot, and planned everything out. Warmth settles in my chest as I watch him, my heart swelling with gratitude. He looks up, catches my gaze, and smiles, not with any cocky pride but with a simple, genuine warmth that melts me.

I walk over to him, my footsteps crunching softly on the sandy bank, and settle down on the blanket, running my hand over the soft fabric. I glance shyly at him, feeling a blush creep up my cheeks as I busy myself with the snacks he laid out.

"So," I say, trying to break the comfortable silence, "you promised to tell me what happened with the scouts."

He laughs, shaking his head. "It honestly wasn't that deep," he begins, grabbing a container of green grapes and popping one into his mouth before offering it to me. "There was this kid, Peter, whose dad ran the troop. We'd never really gotten along."

I take a grape, nodding for him to continue.

"One day, Peter started running his mouth like always. We've clashed before, but this time, he said some... things about my mom and cousin." He hesitates, his jaw tightening briefly. "Things I won't repeat. But my mom and Aunt Tina were single moms, so they raised us together, and we were all really close."

I feel a pang of sympathy as I watch him, seeing a flicker of anger and hurt in his eyes.

"I tried to ignore it, let him get a few insults in... but this time he wouldn't stop. Followed me when I tried to walk away, and eventually, I just lost it. I took a few shots. It was over quick. And despite his bloody nose, he seemed rather pleased with himself." He looks down, embarrassed by the memory. "Not my proudest moment." He is silent for a moment, his eyes dart to my face before looking down again. "His dad was furious—didn't even bother to ask what started it. Just acted like I was the problem. Wanted to get the cops involved." He shrugs, popping another grape into his mouth, still avoiding my gaze. "The assistant troop leader heard the whole thing, made Peter apologize for his part, but it was so half-assed that I refused it."

"What did your mom say?" I ask softly, my voice filled with understanding.

"She wasn't happy, that's for sure." He chuckles, shaking his head. "She said it didn't matter what anyone said; I had to keep my cool. But by then, it was too late. Peter's dad made it clear I wasn't welcome back. He couldn't officially do anything since it would mean his own son would be in trouble too, but his dad had no problems throwing his power around to make it clear I wasn't welcome. I got assigned the worst jobs, left out of events, told the achievement I'd worked on didn't count so he wouldn't sign off on them."

"That doesn't seem fair, now his dad was bullying you?" I grumble, indignation in my tone.

Reid shrugs, a faint smile on his lips. "It worked out in the end. My mom put me in boxing. I learned a lot from it, like how to control my temper, channel my emotions. And not long after, I met Vaughn and his brothers. They were a few years older, already working for their dad, planning to take over the company. They must've seen something in me because they took me under their wing."

I nod, my eyes softening as I look at him. "I'm glad they did," I say, my voice barely above a whisper.

He meets my gaze, his eyes warm and steady. "Me too, Bunny. Me too."

The rest of the afternoon is bliss. We snacked on the goodies Reid packed, laughing and swapping stories about our youth—nothing heavy or serious, just the kind of light-hearted anecdotes that have us smiling until our cheeks hurt. After his story about why he was kicked out of scouts, I want something less intense, something that will keep this easy feeling between us.

Still, my mind keeps returning to his confession about his childhood temper and how much it shaped him. I suppose it could be a red flag— a possible warning that he could be dangerous. I know part of me is searching for those signs, something to justify pulling back, a guilt-free reason to leave because I am scared of what I am feeling. I like him. As more than a friend, that is terrifying after what happened with Jordan. But he wasn't proud of his past; he admitted his mistakes honestly and clearly worked hard to channel that part of himself into something constructive. Now, he uses his strength and skills to protect rather than harm. Instead of adding distance between us, that admission makes me feel safer.

As the day goes on, I find myself leaning into him, letting my hand linger a little longer than necessary whenever he passes me something. It feels nice, natural even. Safe.

Maybe the fear I am feeling isn't the kind of fear one experiences when facing down a gun but rather the fear just before the roller coaster drops. Terrifying. Exhilarating. But oh, so worth it.

After we eat our fill, Reid packs up the leftover food, and we wander down to the creek's edge. I cannot resist the urge to slip off my shoes and socks and roll up my pants to wade in. I let out a small gasp at the chill of the water but muscle through, savoring the feeling of cool sand and smooth pebbles underfoot. I wade carefully, picking my way past rocks and driftwood, my toes curling against the creek's sandy bottom.

A loud splash behind me makes me turn just in time to see Reid trying to steady himself after knocking over a large rock that splashed water onto his pants. I giggle, and he flashes me a sheepish grin, shrugging as if to say, What can you do?

Feeling like a kid again, I crouch down in a shallow spot where the water barely covers my feet. It tickles as it rushes by, and I watch, fascinated, at the tiny ecosystem unfolding around my toes. Small, nearly translucent shrimp skitter around, while long-legged creatures, like waterborne daddy-long-legs, skim the surface. Little silver fish dart by, their scales catching the light in quick flashes.

"What's this?" I call out, my tone filled with wonder as I look up at Reid before glancing back at the miniature world beneath me. "I can sort of see through these things!" I giggle, my gaze dancing with excitement.

Reid steps closer, studying the water with me. "Amphipods, I think," he replies, sounding unsure.

"How do you know that?" I ask with a grin, impressed.

"One of Vaughn's brothers used to bring me here," he explains, a fondness in his voice. "He's... well, he's a little different from most people. Loves to info-dump about whatever he's currently fascinated with. For a while, it was all the critters you could find in this creek. Every time we came here, he'd share some new fact about them."

I smile at that, my grin widening. "Do you remember any more? What else do you know?"

He chuckles, scratching his head. "A little. I'll do my best, but I don't have the kind of memory E does."

"E?" I ask.

"Short for Edward," he replies with a smile. "He doesn't like being called Ed or Eddie, so E it is."

I nod, my interest piqued. "So, what about those spider-looking things?"

"Those, I do know for sure," he says, crouching beside me. "Water striders. Not spiders at all."

I wrinkle my nose, looking dubious. "Water spiders would've been cooler."

He grins, pointing at the tiny insect. "See? Four legs, not eight. No spider here."

I follow as he moves from one area to another, showing me different spots in the creek and doing his best to answer my endless stream of questions, though he admits he is not sure about many of them. It is peaceful, a gentle connection in sharing this quiet moment.

As we near the waterfall, he warns me, "Careful, Bunny. The rocks are slippery here."

But his warning comes just a moment too late. My foot slips on a mossy stone, and I fall, landing with a splash in the chilly water. The spot is just deep enough that my head dips under for a split second before I come up sputtering, water streaming down my face as I sit there, looking up at Reid with a shocked grin. He laughs, loud and unabashed, which only makes me narrow my eyes at him in mock annoyance.

When he reaches out to help me up, I seize the opportunity. With a quick tug, I pull him down into the water beside me, sending up a large splash. For a moment, he sits there, wide-eyed in disbelief, and then a look of mischief spreads across his face. I squeal and scramble to my feet, trying to run, my waterlogged jeans weighing me down as I splash through the shallows, laughing the whole time.

Reid catches up easily, wrapping his arms around me from behind. "Oh, now you're in for it!" he threatens, laughter in his voice. Without warning, he drags us both back under the gentle cascade of the waterfall.

We tumble together into the water, but he makes sure to position himself beneath me so I will not go too deep or get hurt on any of the rocks. We lie there for a moment, giggling and catching our breath, hidden from the world in the misty cover of the waterfall. The rush of water muffles all other sounds, creating a bubble of intimacy.

As I look down at him, my laughter softens, my gaze meeting his.

Reid reaches up, gently brushing a stray, damp strand of hair from my face, his fingertips lingering as they trace the line of my cheek. The air between us grows thick, charged with unspoken things. I am not sure who leans in first, but our lips meet in a tentative, feather-light kiss. I pull back, just a breath away, searching his eyes, and then lean in again, this time with more certainty. His hand tangles in my hair, pulling me closer as he deepens the kiss, his touch firm and sure.

When we finally break apart, he looks at me with a tenderness that makes my heart ache, his hands cradling my cheeks like I am something precious.

We eventually climb out from behind the waterfall, drenched and laughing at our soaked state. Reid packs up the blanket while I slip my shoes back on. The afternoon sun is no match for the evening chill, and I shiver as we start walking back. Reid lets go of my hand long enough to pull out the picnic blanket and wrap it around me before retaking my hand. I give him a soft smile before holding tight to his hand. Despite how uncomfortable I am in my wet clothes, I wouldn't change anything about this day.

When we return to the parking lot, I feel a pang of guilt about his truck seats getting wet, but he just shrugs and hands me a towel he pulls from the back seat before turning to rummage some more.

"Should've known you'd be prepared," I mutter, rolling my eyes but grateful, nonetheless.

Before I can say anything more, he leans in and gives me a quick kiss, then hands me a dry set of clothes, turning his back to provide me with a bit of privacy while I change. His clothes hang off my frame, and the drawstring of his sweatpants is the only thing keeping them from slipping down. When I finish changing, I turn to find him standing there, having changed into his own dry clothes. I cannot help but notice how good he looks in gray sweatpants, the kind of sight that will make any girl weak in the knees.

As he drives us home, I reach out to hold his hand. Grateful for this afternoon, for this place, and for him.

When we return to Reid's house, I feel like I am floating. The day has been exactly what I needed, dispelling the trapped, panicky feeling that has clung to me over the last few days. I feel lighter, almost free.

In the bathroom, I relax under the spray of warm water, letting the last remnants of creek water wash from my skin, my body wash filling the small room with a crisp, citrusy scent. After stepping out of the shower, steam billowing around me and fogging the mirror, I wrap myself in a plush blue towel.

I hesitate, then use the corner of the towel to wipe away some of the steam from the mirror. I rarely look at myself for more than a few seconds, preferring to keep my self-care tasks quick and practical. Jordan chipped away at my confidence until I struggled to find anything about myself to like. He picked apart each feature—the color of my eyes, the faint wave in my hair, even the tiny scar above my nose that can only be seen if someone leaned in close.

But for the first time in ages, I don't see haunted, fearful eyes. I don't catalog each flaw and how I need to fix it. I just am.

Back in my room, I slip into a comfy T-shirt and a pair of black yoga pants, clipping my damp hair up so it is away from my face. Downstairs, the comforting aroma of dinner drifts toward me as Reid finishes cooking. We eat at the breakfast bar, exchanging bits of conversation, but not feeling the need to fill every moment with chatter. It is rare to find someone you can just exist with.

After we clear the dishes together, we settle on the couch, Reid taking his usual spot on one side. I hesitate, glancing at the space beside him, feeling the familiar pull of my internal debate. Should I keep the safe distance I kept the previous nights? But today has been good—a reminder that maybe, just maybe, something real and safe can grow here. Taking a steadying breath, I sit beside him, letting my leg brush against his before leaning into him.

Reid seems to sense my hesitancy but, without missing a beat, wraps his arm over my shoulders, gently pulling me back against his chest. He reaches up, unclipping my hair, letting the damp strands fall freely.

I squirm, a soft protest escaping me. "I'll leave a wet spot on your shirt," I murmur, only to realize the unintended double meaning. My face turns crimson, and I hide my face in his chest, mortified.

He chuckles softly, his fingers tangling in my hair and brushing through it in slow, soothing strokes. Soon, I feel myself relaxing against him, melting into his warmth. I lose track of time, my mind slipping into a blissful haze, barely aware of the TV playing in the background.

All too soon, bedtime arrives, and the sense of comfort fades as we rise to part for the night. A part of me wants to crawl into his bed with him. Just to sleep, but I know it is smart to take things slow; my relationship with Jordan was a whirlwind, and I do not want to make the same mistakes. If this is going to be real, it has to be different. Slow.

In my room, I go through my nighttime routine—washing my face, brushing my teeth, a dab of lotion—then turn off all the lights, even the one I usually leave on in the bathroom. Tonight, I feel calm and safe, maybe even brave.

I climb into bed, the blankets warm and soft against my legs. My phone rests on the nightstand where I left it, and I pick it up, thinking that Juniper might have messaged me. I feel recharged enough that a hangout with her and the others doesn't seem so daunting. Plus, I need someone to talk to about this new development. Maybe reassurance that I am not making a terrible decision by exploring things with Reid.

But when I open it, my stomach drops. There are messages. But the top one isn't from Juniper.

Unknown Number: Deliverance, what a funny name. Do you think he can keep you from me? YOU ARE MINE.

My heart hammers as I stare at the message; my vision flickers as black spots dance in front of my eyes. It's been more than two weeks of silence. I thought they had given up. My pulse roars in my ears, drowning out rational thought. Part of me wants to delete it, pretend it is not there, but I can't. Not anymore.

The phone slips from my fingers, bouncing off the bed and landing on the carpet with a soft thud. The screen glows momentarily before it dims, casting my room back into darkness.

My first thought is to tell Reid. I know I should. But my body is paralyzed, frozen in place. It is him. There is no question in my mind. This confirms it. I can't deny the cryptic texts are from him any longer. But how did he find my number? I did everything to stay hidden, down to using a fake name and paying cash when I bought the phone.

My thoughts spiral. The tracker in my car, finding my number even when it isn't in my name. Has he been just a few steps behind me this entire time? I clutch the blankets, my heart racing as my mind spins in panicked circles, unable to break free from the suffocating grip of fear. I try to take a deep breath, but I can't get enough air into my lungs.

Darkness presses in from every corner of the room, every shadow alive and menacing. I want to move, to call out for Reid, but the terror holds me rooted to the bed, muscles locked. My vision blurs, and it is only then that I realize I am silently crying, hot tears sliding down my cheeks and dripping onto my hands.

I hate he still has this power over me. Even from miles away, he can reduce me to a trembling mess, hiding under the covers like a frightened child.

Hours pass, each one feeling like a lifetime. Exhaustion takes over, and I drift off into a fitful, restless sleep, haunted by nightmares of shadows that loom too close, and his voice echoes in my mind, repeating, 'You are mine' over and over.

CHAPTER SEVENTEEN

Reid

A piercing scream shatters the night, jolting me awake from a deep sleep. Instinct kicks in, and I am on my feet in seconds, blankets pooling on the floor as I race from my room. The automatic night lights in the hallway flick on, the soft glow just bright enough to guide me without entirely disrupting my night vision.

I burst into Sage's room, heart pounding, expecting to find her fighting off an intruder.

Instead, I find her tangled in the sheets, thrashing and crying out in terror, her voice choked with desperate pleas. "No, please... no, I promise I'll be good. I won't do it again. Let me go!" The anguish in her voice guts me.

I flick on the bedside lamp, squinting against the sudden light as I decide the best way to approach the scene. She is still trapped in her nightmare, flailing and whimpering, utterly unaware of my presence. I hesitate, knowing I cannot just leave her like this, but also wary of startling her. The last thing I want is for her to wake up and find me looming over her.

I crouch beside the bed so she will see me at eye level when she wakes. Gently, I reach out and shake her shoulders, calling her name, trying to rouse her without frightening her further. She flinches under my touch, pulling away as if it is painful, her face wet with tears, her voice reduced to soft, broken apologies. "I'm sorry, I'm sorry..."

"Come on, Sage," I mutter under my breath, shaking her a little more firmly, my voice louder. "It's just a dream Bunny, wake up for me."

When she does not wake, I consider my next move, feeling hesitant. I have kept my Dom side in check around her, always careful about my tone, sensing she needs gentleness more than authority. But she remains lost in the terror of her dream, and I'm rapidly depleting my options.

With a steadying breath, I let the command slip into my voice, deep and firm. "Open your eyes, Bunny."

As if the words hold magic, her eyes snap open, locking onto mine, her body stiff, braced for an attack. I hold her gaze, whispering now, my tone soothing and reassuring. "Shhh, it's okay, Sage. I'm right here. You're safe."

She is panting, her eyes wide and glazed with lingering panic. I keep my voice low and calm. "Just breathe with me, alright? In and out, nice and slow. That's it... there you go. It was just a bad dream. You're safe here, in my house. No one can get to you. I won't let anyone hurt you."

I brush the damp hair from her sweaty forehead as her breathing evens out. "There you go, Bunny," I murmur, my voice as soft as my touch. "Do you want to talk about it? My ma used to make me tell her my bad dreams. She said bringing them into the light made them smaller."

She shakes her head, her wide eyes glistening with tears. Guilt flickers in her expression; she seems worried I'll be disappointed she doesn't want to talk.

"That's okay, baby," I reassure her, my hand moving through her hair, untangling the strands she twisted in her thrashing. "You don't have to say a word if you're not ready."

She clings to my hand as I make to pull away, a soft, panicked sound escaping her throat. I pause, my eyebrows raised, waiting for her to tell me what she needs, but she doesn't fill the silence. The rising panic on her face forces me to act.

"Want me to stay?" I coax. If she can't ask for what she needs right now, then I can give her options. She nods vehemently, her grip tightening around my hand.

"You tell me what you need, Bunny, and I'll do everything I can to give it to you," I whisper, watching her face closely. Her mouth opens, but she hesitates, then closes it again, looking down. I notice the vulnerability in her expression and the way her shoulders curl inward, as if she is afraid to ask for comfort.

"Not able to talk right now?" I guess. I've never played with a sub that goes nonverbal, but a buddy of mine, his partner, does. This is not play, but I think back to what he told me about how heightened emotions, both bad and good, would overwhelm her, and she'd be unable to speak. He'd take charge, provide stability, give her other ways to communicate, until she could regain her voice.

Sage shakes her head, looking so lost that my chest aches for her. Without another word, she shifts over on the bed and pats the space beside her, inviting me in. Okay, that's a good sign. She is finding other ways to communicate her needs.

I take the hint, sliding onto the bed beside her and staying above the covers. She curls up against me, resting her head on my lap and pulling my hand to her hair, wanting me to continue the soothing touch.

I chuckle faintly, feeling a flicker of warmth. I feel ten feet tall that even in such a vulnerable state, she feels safe enough to demand what she needs from me, even without words. *That is a good sign.* It means she trusts me, even after everything she has been through.

With the bedside lamp casting a soft glow over the room, I run my fingers lightly through her hair, the repetitive motion grounding for both of us. As I stare up at the ceiling, I think about all I know —and do not know—about the depths of her trauma. I want her to tell me everything that's happened to her. I want to wash all her terrible memories away, convince her I will keep her safe. I hate that I do not have all the answers, that I cannot protect her from the nightmares, but I will be damned if I ever leave her feeling alone in her fear again.

I look down and find her watching me, her eyes wide and still a little glassy, but calmer now. She reaches up and taps my mouth, frowning slightly, as though trying to pull me from my thoughts.

"Just thinking, Bunny," I answer softly, offering a reassuring smile.

She narrows her eyes, gives me a skeptical look, and taps my mouth again, her frown deepening.

I chuckle, surprised by her persistence. "So, I'm supposed to share now, huh?" She gives me a slight nod, her lips quirking into a faint smile. The sight makes my heart twist in a way I do not quite understand.

"How about I tell you a story?" I offer, feeling a sudden urge to keep her grounded in this moment. I don't want to tell her I am thinking of all she must have gone through and how much I wish I could get rid of all her demons. A story is much safer. She nods again, snuggling closer, her trust an unspoken warmth between us.

I lean back, one hand still gently combing through her hair as I begin a quiet story, my steady voice masking the turmoil I feel.

CHAPTER EIGHTEEN

Sage

I blink momentarily disoriented before realizing I am curled up against a hard, warm chest. Reid. My face flushes, and I quickly wipe at my mouth, relieved to find my face drool-free.

My movement must have awoken him, or perhaps he has not slept at all, because when I look up, his eyes are already open, watching me intently. His gaze softens as our eyes meet.

"I... um... I'm sorry about last night," I mumble, my cheeks burning with mortification. I push up, trying to create distance between us. "I'm sorry I woke you up, and you had to stay with me."

"Shhh," he soothes, trailing a gentle finger down my cheek, stopping my backward retreat. "There's nothing to apologize for." He pauses, studying me. "Did you want to talk about it now that it's daylight?"

"Not really," I admit, looking away.

"Do you know what triggered it?" he presses, his brows drawing together. "Was it..." He trails off, and I know he wonders if the kiss during our hike somehow unsettled me.

Desperately wanting to put his mind at ease, I shake my head emphatically and sit up to face him directly. My gaze briefly lands on his bare chest before I glance back up, trying to ignore the heat creeping up my face. "No, it's... well, I have nightmares every night," I confess.

"But never this bad," he points out. "I would've come to you if

I'd heard."

I nod, sighing. "Yeah, well, this one was... pretty bad. I think..." I tense. Not sure if I am bracing to take a hit or getting ready to run. I withheld information, not exactly deliberately, but in my experience, that never goes well. "I think Jordan texting me might have triggered it."

His body goes still, his expression darkening as he processes my words. This is it. The point where he is done with me. "He texted you last night," he says, more to himself, his brows drawn down, "But you said this was a burner phone. Is it registered under your name?"

"Um, no. The woman at the phone store put it under a fake name when I told her I was... she just put a random name when I asked and I used that name for anything I needed to create an account. I paid cash and didn't use an ID. There is nothing that connects to my old life." I'm rambling now.

"Can you show me?" he asks, his voice calm but laced with a hint of urgency.

I jump out of bed and retrieve my phone from the floor. Relief washes over me as I see the only new message is from Juniper. I swipe to the thread with the unknown number and hand the phone to Reid, who is now sitting up, his legs planted on the floor. I stand awkwardly in front of him, back ramrod straight, and fidget with my hands. My eyes dart around the room. The door is on the other side of the bed.

He reads through the message, his jaw tightening. "Is this the first time?"

I look away. "There were some messages a few weeks ago, all from different numbers that I blocked. I thought someone was playing a joke." His fingers dance over the screen. A low curse slips from his lips, and I flinch. His gaze flicks up to meet mine, and I am taken aback to see the hurt mingling with the concern in his eyes.

"Why didn't you tell me about this?" he asks. His voice is calm, but I can tell he is upset. "We could have gotten you a new phone."

I look down, feeling ashamed and needing to explain myself. "I... I didn't think it was him at first," I stammer. "It was weird, but I just sort of talked myself out of thinking it meant anything. I thought it was the wrong number." I bite my lip, my fingers fidgeting nervously. "I wanted it to be a wrong number," I confess. "Then...

after the second-to-last message, I meant to tell you, but... I got distracted. But then they stopped, and I thought it was done," I finish weakly, glancing off to the side.

He stays silent, waiting for me to continue, his expression unreadable.

"When the message came last night... I..." I swallow, feeling tears prick at the corners of my eyes. "I froze. I wanted to tell you, but I couldn't... I couldn't move, couldn't do anything. I felt trapped in my body. I'm sorry," I whisper, my voice rough with guilt.

He reaches out, grasping my hands to stop my frantic hand-wringing, and I freeze. Waiting. But his voice is full of understanding, and there is no hint of the anger I expect. "I'm so sorry you felt you couldn't come to me." He pulls me forward so I am standing between his thighs.

I shake my head. "That's not it. I wanted to. I really did," I sob, "I just... I couldn't do anything. I felt... trapped. It was the worst feeling."

"Oh, Bunny," he murmurs, pulling me into his chest, arms wrapping around me. He holds me close, gently rocking me as he runs his hand up and down my back in slow, soothing strokes. I can slowly feel the fear leech from my body. I lay my head on his shoulder, letting him take a little more of my weight. "I'm so sorry I wasn't there when you needed me."

"But you came," I counter, wanting to absolve him of any guilt he might feel. "You came."

"I'll always come when you need me," he replies with certainty. A small part of me wants to hold on to the hope his words stir within me, to let that feeling bloom. But another part cautions me to be careful, to guard my heart. Still, I cannot help but lean into the warmth of his embrace, if only for a moment.

After a while, he pulls back slightly, brushing a stray hair from my face. "After breakfast, we should go to the office, so Rhett can look at this and see if he can trace anything."

I stiffen at the mention of the office. Reid notices immediately. Of course he does. His brows knit together as he scans my face. "Or... I could have Rhett come here to pick up the phone if you don't feel safe enough to leave."

"It's not that," hating how vulnerable I sound. "It's just...

will there be a lot of guys there?"

"Possibly," he admits. "But I promise, they might look big and scary, but they'd never hurt you."

We arrive at Heartwood Security mid-morning. I follow Reid down the hallway, anxious to get to Rhett's office and sort out my phone issue.

Offices line the right side of the hallway, each door fitted with a keypad lock and framed with heavy, black windows. I recognize Vaughn's office from my previous visit, with its leather chairs and tasteful setup. We pass two more offices: one dark and unoccupied, and another with windows that are opaque. I pause in front of it, puzzled. Now that I look closely, each room along this hallway has windows with various levels of opacity.

Reid notices my curiosity and chuckles. "Remember my cousin, the interior designer who decorated my house?" he asks, grinning when I nod. "When Vaughn and his brother inherited this place, it looked... let's just say it wasn't exactly client-friendly."

"So they hired her, and when my cousin saw the place, she put in these enormous glass windows for all the offices on this floor. Vaughn and his brother nearly had a heart attack. They complained you couldn't have confidential meetings when anyone walking by could see you. They started demanding blinds or something to cover the windows."

"So what happened?" I ask, amused.

"She was so insulted by the idea of blinds, said it would ruin the atmosphere." He makes little air quotes with his fingers, "So she pulled out a remote and, with a click, turned the windows dark. They stopped complaining after that." He smirks, gesturing from Vaughn's office to the opaque windows in front of us. "All the executive offices are on this floor. We don't want clients wandering off to other areas."

We continue down the hallway, passing a large conference room and an elevator. Reid leads me to a stairwell, gesturing to the stairs as he explains, "Downstairs is the gym. There's another set of stairs in the front, so you can get there without coming down this hallway since we have self-defense and other classes available to the public. But those stairs don't connect to the upper offices. You already saw one of the safe rooms."

He nods toward the stairs, indicating we will go up. We climb to the next floor and stop in front of a door with a keypad lock. "We would've taken the elevator, but you need a key card, and I left mine in the office," he admits with a sheepish grin. "My office is up here."

He types in a code, and we enter another hallway, this one more utilitarian than the one downstairs. Though it retains the exposed brick and pipes, it lacks the warmth and charm of the lower level. The atmosphere here is more serious, almost secretive, with no nameplates on the doors, and an air of mystery.

Reid stops before a nondescript door and knocks, waving up at a small camera above it. After a moment, we hear the click of a lock, and Reid opens the door to a blast of cool air and walls lined with monitors. The soft hum of computer fans fills the room, which is unmistakably a surveillance hub.

Rhett and another guy sit at the center of the room, surrounded by screens showing multiple locations. My eyes widen as I realize some monitors display people's homes or businesses. Each monitor displays several camera angles, labeled with their monitoring locations.

Reid notices my gaze and leans over to explain, "Some clients pay for 24-hour surveillance. Some of these are active cases, for... other things." He points to a wall with a row of black towers. "Those are for clients who only need recordings. We pull the tapes for review upon request."

"That's... a lot," I say after a moment, absorbing the magnitude of their operation.

"It's boring, is what it is," Rhett says with a smirk. He looks over his shoulder at the other guy. "You got this covered?"

The other man nods. "Yeah, I'll call Alex or E to take over for you. Take your time."

We follow Rhett into another room filled with computer equipment and other gadgets, though thankfully without the wall of monitors. Reid hands over my phone, and Rhett gives it a once-over before handing it to me.

"Mind taking the passcode off?" he asks. "I could break it, but I'd rather not take the time if I don't have to." I fumble through the settings, acutely aware of the men waiting silently. "Thanks, doll." He says with a flirty grin when I hand him the phone.

Reid lets out a low growl, and Rhett smirks, clearly enjoying the reaction.

"Give me a little time, and I'll tell you exactly where this asshole is texting from," Rhett says, plugging the phone in to a computer.

"Is that... even possible?" I ask, my eyebrows raised. "It's throw away numbers. Wouldn't you have to hack..." I trail off.

Rhett rubs the side of his nose, giving me a little wink. "Falls into a gray area," he says with a mischievous smile.

I narrow my eyes, trying to figure out if he is teasing.

Reid cuts in, his voice firm. "There are things we don't ask Rhett to explain. Come on, we're getting you a new phone."

"What? No, that's okay, I don't need a phone," I protest.

Reid rolls his eyes. "You need a phone. You can't use this one anymore. So, new phone it is."

"But I can't afford to just buy a new phone!" I argue, crossing my arms stubbornly; a part of me is not even sure why I am protesting, but a louder part demands I not continue to take and take from Reid.

"Who said you were buying it?" He tosses over his shoulder, already on his way out of the small office.

"No," I say indigently, "You can't just buy me a phone. You already do too much!"

"Give me three reasons," Reid challenges, facing me with his arms folded over his chest.

"You're already guarding me, and..." I fumble, unable to find more reasons.

"Seems like that's an argument for getting a new phone. I'm guarding you. My job is to keep you safe, and you need a new phone."

"But you can't pay for it."

Rhett, who has been watching our back-and-forth with growing amusement, finally speaks up. "As entertaining as this is," he says, holding back a chuckle, "I agree with Reid. You can't use this one anymore, and you need a new phone. Now go argue in the hall." He grins and makes shooing motions with his hands.

Blushing, I follow Reid into the hallway. Once the door closes behind us, I look down, my shoulders rounded. I let my hair fall over my face like it's a shield. "I'm sorry," I say stiffly. "I don't know what came over me. I'll try not to embarrass you again."

Reid shakes his head, reaching out to tip my chin up. "Sage, no. You couldn't embarrass me."

"But I argued with you," I mutter, still not meeting his gaze, my eyes looking off to the side.

"And I'm glad you feel safe enough with me to argue, even if I think you're wrong about this one."

I peek up at him through my hair, searching him for any signs of anger or frustration. With Jordan, he could give off an air of calm to others, but I knew his tells. Clenched fists, tight jaws, and the subtle arched angles of his brows hinted at his simmering anger and the punishment I could expect. But with Reid, there is none of that. He is calm, his body relaxed and open.

"I just... I don't want you to buy me a phone. It would feel..." I struggle to find the words. "It would feel like I owe you. Even more than I already do. You are doing so much and I...I'm not."

Reid briefly considers my words before replying, "What if we took the cost out of the DV fund? Heartwood would cover it, and later, when you're ready, you can take over the plan."

I hesitate, weighing the idea.

"That's what the fund is for, Sage," he reminds me gently.

After a pause, I nod. "I should probably talk to Vaughn about doing more work."

"You already do enough with the reports."

"But if it helps me feel more..." I trail off, searching for the right word. "In control?"

He sighs but nods, clearly understanding. "Working to regain some control is a much better reason than feeling like you owe me or anyone here. You don't. You are not indebted to me. No one is keeping score."

He turns, leading me down the hallway toward the stairs. Before we get far, I hesitate, glancing back. "Where's your office?"

"You are going to be disappointed," but leads me to another unmarked door. He types in a code and opens it, standing to the side to let me pass.

I step inside and wrinkle my nose. Four metal desks are clustered together, facing each other, like an elementary school classroom; each has a computer and minimal decoration.

"It's... boring," I say, eying the lack of office decor and the gray filing cabinets against the walls.

He chuckles. "Emily only had free rein downstairs in areas clients might see. Me and the other guys who use this space spend a lot of time in the field, so we don't put much into decorating."

"You didn't put anything into decorating," I snark.

He smiles but ignores my comment. "Let's go get you that phone."

The aroma of cinnamon and sugar envelops me as soon as we step onto the sidewalk outside Heartwood Security.

"What is that?" I ask, my gaze sweeping the street to find the source of the delicious scent.

"That is Sugar 'n Spice. Best bakery in town," Reid supplies, a hint of pride in his voice. "Dezzie, Rhett's little sister, has been running it for the last year or two and really transformed it.

"It smells amazing." I inhale deeply. "We should get something for lunch." I am already turning towards the bakery, eager to indulge. And perhaps skip the new phone shopping.

"Whoa, hold up, little Bunny." Reid chuckles, easily catching my hand. "You're going the wrong way, and we need to get a phone first."

I pout playfully. "How about cinnamon bun then phone?" I plead, giving him a wide-eyed, hopeful look. The earlier tension gone.

He chuckles and gently boops my nose. "Phone with no argument, lunch," he pauses and raises a single brow to emphasize the point, "then cinnamon bun," he counters, lacing his fingers through mine and giving me a gentle tug in the other direction.

"Are you bribing me with sugar so I won't get mad when you insist on a stupidly expensive phone?" I ask, walking beside him, enjoying the warmth of his hand enveloping mine. I focus on the shop windows, not wanting him to see me blush or the too-wide grin on my face. "I don't think I even need a phone."

He shrugs with a playful smirk. "Perhaps. But how are you going to text Juniper or your other friends?" He asks. The word friends makes me smile more. He has a good point.

We stroll in comfortable silence, my attention drawn to the various shops. A bridal boutique overflowing with white gowns, sparkling beads, and tulle, a photography studio with a disproportionate wall of wedding portraits, a flower shop bursting with colorful bouquets and sample centerpieces.

Glancing across the street, I notice more wedding-themed businesses. "I'm sensing a theme with this street. Isn't it odd having a security company in the middle of the wedding district?"

Reid throws his head back and laughs. "You'll find that the whole town is basically a wedding district." He points ahead. "That street over there has two more dress shops, four wedding planners, and a caterer who only does weddings. And on the other side of that street is a stationery shop and a place for suits."

"The town is not big enough to need any of that!" I exclaim. "Honestly, I'm surprised you have even one dress shop."

"There are like a dozen wedding venues here. A while back, some celebrity got married here, and it's become a status thing for certain people. Add in another influencer who caused another surge two years back, and well, half the businesses here have some tie to the wedding industry. There is a girl who does marketing for the town that somehow keeps us relevant in the wedding market."

"You know a lot about the wedding stuff."

"Yeah, well, being the only security company in town has its perks."

"What do you mean?"

"The high-profile weddings need security. Sometimes they bring their own, but most of the time, they hire us for the night. Even small weddings need a bouncer or a security guard. Depending on the wedding, it's surprisingly fun."

"You like weddings that much?"

"Eh, the reception, mostly. It's usually pretty easy. Stay in the background, keep people out of areas they shouldn't be in, and if people get drunk, you often get a funny story. One of venues hires us just to keep drunk people out of the koi pond." He chuckles. "We are pretty good at reading a room and intervene before things escalate. People tend to follow patterns, so you start to notice the common tells. Plus, if the bride is chill, you get cake."

He directs me toward a phone store. "Hey, Frank," he greets a middle-aged man at the counter. "Need to add a new phone line."

I let go of Reid's hand and wander around the store, looking at the sample phones on display. The price tag for each one makes my stomach churn, but I say nothing. I am going to get my cinnamon bun.

"Find one you like," Frank asks, startling me. I turn with a yelp. Both he and Reid are right behind me. Heart racing from the surprise, I point to the cheapest phone on the display I'm in front of.

Reid scowls down at my selection and shakes his head. "That thing has no storage and is going to be really slow. You need something better."

Frank grins and begins to talk specs, pointing to a far more expensive option. I flash a panicked look at Reid, my eyes wide, heart pounding in my chest. 'You decide,' I mouth to Reid. He smoothly takes over the conversation, and I escape to the far side of the store where Frank can't ask me more questions, and I don't have to think about the cost. Reid can handle things.

Leaving the store with a new phone in hand, I give Reid a triumphant grin. "Okay, I didn't complain, even though it took forever to set it up. Cinnamon bun time now, please."

Reid shakes his head. "That's a complaint," he jokes, "and lunch first."

"Sage!" a familiar voice calls out, coupled with the sound of running footsteps. Juniper skids to a halt in front of us. She squeals and does a little happy dance when she sees me holding Reid's hand before pulling me into a tight hug. "I knew it," she sings, swaying me back and forth in excitement. I take a step back when she releases me, feeling a little discombobulated at her whirlwind appearance.

"What are you two up to?" she asks, bouncing with energy. "I just finished at the coffee shop and I've got some time before my shift at the bookstore."

"New phone," I sigh, looking less than impressed at the shiny new device in my hand.

"Cool, let me put in my number." I unlock the phone, hand it over, and watch as she effortlessly saves her number before calling her own phone. "I'll make sure the girls get the new number."

"We are about to get lunch. Do you want to join?" Reid asks Juniper.

"Sure," she replies.

"But...my cinnamon bun," I protest with a pout.

"Oh, did you get ensnared by Sugar 'n Spice?" Juniper teases.

"Yep, she's been trying to get me to go there since we left the office," Reid confirms with a smile.

"Dessert first?" I ask, hoping to get her to join my cause. "And then we won't have to double back here," I reason, since we'd have to drive to the other side of town to get to the diner Reid wants to go to.

"Oh, that's a good idea!" Juniper agrees, hooking her arm with mine and starting towards the bakery.

Reid quickly intercepts us, wrapping an arm around my shoulders and steering us towards his truck. "Food first, then I'll get you both cinnamon buns."

"Don't believe him," I stage-whisper to Juniper as we climb into the cab, though my smile betrays my amusement. "He said we'd get one after the phone."

"I said lunch first."

Juniper rolls her eyes. "Don't worry, we'll get your cinnamon bun if it's the last thing we do today."

Tina's Diner hums with the sound of conversations and the clatter of dishes. I still feel a slight flush at the attention we draw when we walk in, but no one seems to focus on us. Tina, busy taking an order, nods towards the booth we sat in last time, and Reid leads the way.

"How is this table empty?" I whisper to Juniper. "This place is busy."

"This is Reid's table." Juniper shrugs. "Or anyone from our group, really. Growing up, we hung out here, so Tina keeps a spot open for us."

The worn vinyl of the booth squeaks as I slide in, my fingers tracing the menu Reid places in front of me. Once again, he doesn't need one.

Tina ambles over, notepad in hand. "I see you haven't scared this one off," she says to Reid, her tone dry. She nods at me, "Nice to see you again, hun."

"So, Sage, are you coming to the farmer's market this weekend?" Juniper asks once Tina has left with our order.

"I don't know. I didn't know there was one," I reply, glancing at Reid.

"You have to! It's got the most stereotypical farmer's market vibe, what with all the tourists, but honestly, it's so cute. Sunshine has a booth there, and I can introduce you to a few others I know. I think you'd like it."

I look up at Reid. "Can we?"

Reid pauses, his gaze running over my hopeful expression, his face drawn in a contemplative look. "It's a little short notice, but I'll let Vaughn know so we can arrange a team to keep an eye out in the crowd, since we don't have a location for Jordan."

"Oh," my voice drops, right, more security. "I... I don't want to be a bother if it's going to require all that." I look at Juniper, "It's too dangerous, my ex knows I'm here and we don't know where he is.." I try to make it clear that I have a good reason.

"Whoa, hey, no. You are not a prisoner. You can go out and do things, you are allowed to have a life. He doesn't get to take that away from you. It's my job to make sure the things you want to do are safe or figure out how to make them safe. Until I get confirmation that Jordan is far away from here, we'll be cautious. Fair?"

"All things considered," Juniper pipes in, "compared to some of the other people he's had to guard, you make things easy." She turns to Reid. "Remember the rapper's daughter? What was her name? Diamond?"

Reid groans, shaking his head. "Don't remind me." He winces. "Hardest assignment I've ever been on."

Juniper bounces in her seat. "Yeah, she wanted to go to all these clubs and didn't seem to care that she had some crazy fan stalking her. And her daddy let her do anything and got mad if Reid tried to stop her, so she'd go out partying every night."

"How do you know this?" I ask, curious.

"Because Diamond posted pictures on her social media. Vaughn made her take them down, something about a contract, I'm sure, but I saved them. Want to see?"

"Of course," I say, smiling as I reach for the phone Juniper offers. Reid groans and leans his head back as if he was seeking aid from the heavens. Sure enough, there is Reid, a stoic figure amidst a sea of dancing bodies, glaring at anyone who dares to get too close to a tall, beautiful woman in a sparkling dress. I can't help but laugh at his pissed-off expression. So that's what he looks like mad. Even angry, I don't see the same undercurrent of violence that always surrounded Jordan when he was mad.

"There's more," Juniper prompts.

I scroll through a few more pictures, then freeze. I know that club. My breath stutters out of me, and I close my eyes, willing myself to stay calm.

"Sage?" Juniper asks, concerned. I look up and realize that both Reid and Juniper are staring at me with worry. "Is everything okay?"

"Umm, yes, just... I know that club. It... my ex owns it. I mean, he probably owns all the clubs she went to, but that one I recognize. And there's..." I pause, unsure if I should say anything. But it probably doesn't matter. "That guy," I say, zooming in on someone in the crowd staring at Reid's charge with predatory intensity. "If you ever see him, run. He is not a good man."

Reid's concern deepens. "Did he do anything to you, Sage?" he asks softly.

"Not...not directly," I reply, my voice quiet. "But I overheard some stuff about him I wasn't supposed to, and it didn't really go well for me." I freeze, thinking of that night. I'd made a noise of shock during their conversation. I was supposed to be serving drinks, not eavesdropping. The memory threatens to pull me down. The pain of the blows, the way Jordan snarled that he would let that man take me if I ever fucked up again. The guilt that I didn't try to report him, even though it would have been pointless. Jordan has so many cops in his pockets.

Reid's warmth penetrates the icy fear slithering through my body, keeping me grounded. I shake myself as if I am ridding myself of the memory. "I kind of learned to be..." I pause, searching for the right word, "empty when my ex had people over. I'd put on this perfect hostess mask and go on autopilot. It was safer to exist in my head." I shake my head. "My memories from that time are patchy, but I remember him. He was... creepy." I pause, not sure if I should continue, "I think he might have been a pimp or something like that." I look up at Juniper's stricken expression and try to give her a reassuring smile. "But it's okay, I'm not there anymore," false brightness in my tone. Reid looks concerned, but he didn't need to talk me down from my panic this time. I feel a kernel of pride in managing my own feelings.

Juniper seems unsure how to react, and I feel a pang of guilt for dampening the mood. Luckily, Tina arrives with our food, and we busy ourselves with eating.

"So," Juniper begins, dragging a French fry through a blob of ketchup, "Have you finished reading the book for Book Club? The next meeting is soon."

I roll my eyes. "Last time, we didn't even talk much about the book."

"That's cuz you're more interesting. But do you have any suggestions for adding to the book list?"

I laugh, "Yeah, I have a few I want to add." I give a sideways glance at Reid, a blush staining my cheeks. "One by Penny Lee," I mumble.

Juniper grins before throwing her head back with a laugh. "I knew you'd be a fan of her books. Have you read them all?"

"I don't think I have anything by her in the house." Reid muses. I bury my face in my hands, partly embarrassed and partly amused at the idea that Reid would add a romance author to his library of sci-fi books.

"I don't think her books are your type," Juniper snickers, "The covers always have some shirtless guy and the sex scenes," She waggles her brows and pretends to fan herself, "so hot!" We share a glance and burst into laughter.

By the end of lunch, the last tendrils of the fear the memory ignited had slipped away. Juniper kept me occupied with random questions about books we like and stories from when they were kids. I glanced at Reid a few times, hoping he wasn't bothered by Juniper and me pretty much ignoring him, but he seemed content to watch us, a small, satisfied smile on his face. Reid takes care of the bill, and we head back to the bakery.

Sugar 'n Spice is a pretty little bakery with a bright yellow awning and window boxes overflowing with flowers. The huge windows show off the crowd inside, so I am not surprised when we have to wait a few minutes to order. Inside, the air is warm and fragrant with the sweet scent of vanilla, cinnamon, and freshly baked bread. Rows of cupcakes with elaborate frosting, giant cookies with colorful sprinkles, and flaky croissants piled high fill the display case. And there, in the middle row, are the cinnamon buns.

A woman rushing around in the back gives Juniper and Reid a

wave, but she doesn't stop. That must be Rhett's sister.

After the teenager manning the counter takes our order, we settle on a bistro table outside, eagerly digging into our cinnamon buns. I moan with delight at the first bite, the pastry melting in my mouth. It tastes even better than it smells. "This is so good," I declare between bites.

Reid, who opted not to get a bun, leans closer. "Let me have a piece."

I playfully glare at him, hugging the container to my chest. "No. Mine. You go get your own."

He laughs and turns his attention to the street, feigning indifference. Deciding to be generous, I cut a small piece and offer it to him on my fork. "Here," I say. "One bite."

"Oh, so generous of you," he says with mock gratitude, accepting the offering.

I laugh. "You're supposed to say 'thank you, oh generous one.'" I giggle at my silliness. I

"You two are too cute," Juniper declares, leaning forward with her chin resting on her hand. She takes another bite before closing the lid of the box the buns came in. "Too bad I need to head to work." She bounces up and gives both of us a hug. "Remember, this Saturday at 9am!" she calls over her shoulder. "I'll text you both to remind you!".

The rest of the afternoon drifts by in relative peace. My nightmare and Jordan's threatening text messages feel like they'd happened in another lifetime and not just last night.

But when it's time for bed, I grip Reid's hand tight. I don't want to sleep alone.

CHAPTER NINETEEN

Reid

I relax on the couch, Sage's warm body pressed into me, the throw wrapped around her. Ham and Dog snuggled up close to her side. I loathe to leave, but she's nodded off a few times, and by the third time she jerks awake, shaking her head slightly to clear it, I know we both should head up to bed. It's been a long day, and neither of us had the best night's sleep last night.

"Come on, sleepy Bunny, time for bed," I whisper, turning off the TV.

"No," she protests, "another one." But there is no conviction behind her protest, and she reluctantly stands up. I watch her stretch, the throw falling to the floor at her feet. I stand momentarily lost as she raises her clasped hands above her head and leans back slightly, her back bowing as she stretches, eyes closed. A satisfied moan slips from her mouth. Her eyes snap open, catching me staring, and she gives me a cheeky smile before bending to pick up the throw at her feet.

Fuck.

We head upstairs, her hand gripping mine tight, and I give in to temptation in the hall. I cup her face with my free hand, fingertips grazing the soft skin of her neck, and my thumb runs over her lips. They part with a small gasp, and I lean down, swallowing her gasp with my mouth and taking full advantage of her parted lips to tease her tongue with mine. The kiss is over far too quickly, and she lets out a mewl of protest. Just a tease. But I want her to want me as fiercely as

I want her. If heady kisses that are enough to tease but not satisfy are the way to go, then so be it.

Delayed gratification can be so satisfying in the end.

I kiss the tip of her nose, then her forehead. "Good night, Bunny," I whisper. Pulling away to head to my room, her hand tightens on mine. I look back, expecting a playful grin and a request for more, but she looks apprehensive.

I blanch. *Nice going, Reid. She had a rough day, and you just rushed things.* I am an idiot for moving too fast, but I take a moment to study her. Her wide eyes look from her door to me and back again. She opens her mouth to speak, but nothing comes out.

Oh.

"Do you need me to stay with you again tonight?"

She nods, then immediately shakes her head no, conflicted, letting me go abruptly and taking a step back.

Okay? I step back, seeing if she wants space, but her whimper has me closing the distance and pulling her into my arms in a tight hug. "It's okay, Bunny," I murmur into her hair. "I'll stay with you. I'll keep you safe."

I debate momentarily and decide she isn't ready to spend the night in my room. Her space would be safer. Maybe.

In her room, I overthink. Should I sleep on the floor? On the bed, above the covers, like I had the other night? What would make her more comfortable? She still isn't talking, but her body language is much calmer.

Shit, I need to change.

"I'm going to change," I begin, before her vehement head shake interrupts me.

"I'm sleeping here, Bunny," I insist, needing her to listen. "But I need to get ready for bed. Go brush your teeth, and I'll be back in a few minutes."

In record time, I change into sweats and an old t-shirt and finish reading for bed. I still wasn't quick enough, because when I return she is sitting on the bed wringing her hands in the blankets, her body tense. She visibly relaxes when she sees me but gives my shirt a disgusted look. She probably already realized after last night that I don't normally sleep with a shirt.

She rolls her eyes and pats the bed beside her, the covers already pulled down, ending my internal debate about where I should sleep.

With the bedroom lights off, she snuggles into me. Her ass settles perfectly against my groin. *Think unsexy thoughts. Think unsexy thoughts.* But it doesn't work.

She wiggles and makes a squeak of surprise.

"Ignore him. I do," I say, my voice full of chagrin.

She just giggles and settles into my arms, her body slowly relaxing as her weight settles against me, and I fall asleep holding my world in my arms.

The days settle into a pattern: coffee and breakfast together before spending the morning working in my—our?—office, taking turns cooking, watching TV, or playing video games in the evening. It was all so domestic. It was increasingly difficult to avoid thinking of us as a unit. Having her in my space felt natural. In my house. She made it feel like home. I want her to see this as home, too. To not think of herself as a guest.

Time. It would take time. I could already see her becoming more comfortable. Moving around the house with ease. The casual touches. Brief hints of her presence settling into the house: her sweater draped over the couch, her current book sitting on the coffee table, the lingering scent of her shampoo.

My phone rings, breaking the silence of the office. I glance at the caller ID before looking over at Sage, who is pretending not to eavesdrop. I consider taking the call in the other room, but it's probably about her phone, and I'll have to tell her anyway.

"Hey, man." I say, answering it.

"So, I've got news," Rhett begins, hesitating.

Well, that doesn't sound promising.

"All the phone numbers used to contact her belong to a Dirk Johnson, who lives in Seattle. He is a real person, but he has no ties to Jordan."

That's odd. I give a noncommittal hum.

Rhett continues, "Jordan may have spoofed the numbers, or she has a different stalker, but I looked into this guy. He isn't a saint, but nothing about him screams stalker. By all accounts, he is pretty boring."

"Any new messages?"

"Yeah, a handful. I'm glad I have the phone instead of her. She doesn't need to see any of this shit."

"What do they say?"

"Creepy things. A mix of threats and promises that life will be great if she comes back. Weird cryptic things as if they are still together. I don't like any of it. It seems like he is unraveling."

I don't like the sound of that either.

"Are we sure it isn't the Dirk person?" I press. "Hang on."

I turn to look at Sage, who is openly staring at me, any pretense of not eavesdropping long gone.

"Do you know a Dirk Johnson?" I ask, and her brows draw down in confusion.

"No, the name isn't familiar."

My phone pings with an incoming text message. A quick glance tells me it's a photo from Rhett. I have to give the guy props for multitasking.

I turn the phone to face her.

"Do you recognize him?" Rhett wasn't far off the mark with his description. The man is average. An everyman who'd probably blend into a crowd. Mid-30s maybe, brown hair, no distinguishing marks.

Sage shakes her head.

"Never seen him? Around your ex, maybe? Perhaps you ran into him while you were traveling?" I prompt.

She shakes her head again. "No, if I did, I don't remember him."

"Did you catch that?" I ask Rhett, putting the phone back to my ear.

He sighs. "Yeah. I'll keep looking. I don't like that he keeps sending messages."

I set the phone down after the call and rub my forehead.

"How tech savvy is your ex?" I ask, eventually.

"Not very, but he is smart and knows people."

I nod at her reply; none of this bodes well. We are supposed to go to the farmers market on Saturday. It's one of the month's busiest days, with many people from out of town. Many from Seattle. Sorting out the logistics of Sage's safety when we don't have any clue about

Jordan's whereabouts will be hard. It's doable, I'll admit. I've had to work in significantly worse situations before. But I've never been this personally invested. Never been so concerned about a client's happiness or mental health. My sole focus has always been their physical safety. But with Sage, I'm trying to balance giving her safety and freedom, all while building a relationship with her.

That's what this is, after all. No point in denying it, even to myself. We haven't talked about the future, but I know I want her to stay. Stay in this town. In this house. In my bed.

Twice so far, she's attempted to cancel. Insisting it wasn't worth the extra resources. Had she been someone else, I probably would have let her. Instead, I reminded her she should be able to spend time with her friends and do normal things and that I would make sure she could.

That last time, tears had been involved. She called herself a burden and not worth it. I hate this situation is so hard for her. I'm not so naïve to think that she won't need therapy to process everything, but perhaps I should suggest we look for someone sooner rather than later.

I'm lost in thought, so I am surprised when she wraps her arms around me from behind, but I quickly relax at the feel of her pressed against me, despite the hardback of my office chair in between. She drops a kiss on the side of my head.

"Sandwiches okay for lunch?" she asks.

"Sounds perfect, Bunny," I reply, missing her touch as soon as she leaves the office.

My phone pings with a text message. I flip it over and see it's from Juniper.

"Don't forget about Saturday! Sage says she is looking forward to it!!"

I groan. I need to call Vaughn again and make sure everything is ready to go.

I make two more phone calls before leaving the office. Vaughn gave me some shit about being right about Sage, but he approved the extra guards for Saturday. Like there was any risk of that request being denied. The second call was to Blake, but he didn't answer, so I left a voicemail. It's been a while since he gave me a report. I am hoping no news is good news.

Sage is humming to herself in the kitchen as she plates our lunch.

Grilled cheese and apple slices. I can't help but smile at the simplicity of the moment. I lean against the door frame, watching her as she navigates around Ham, dancing underfoot. Dog is waiting by his food dish, per usual. She looks up and smiles when she catches me watching her.

This. I need more of her smiles. I push aside my lingering worry about the potential safety risk. Her happiness is worth the extra work.

Night is its own form of torture.

Each night we go to bed, I follow Sage's lead. So far, she hasn't asked me to give her space; if anything, she's done her best to eliminate it. Sleeping as close as possible, head on my chest, and when I wake up, she is wrapped around me like a little koala. Maybe I should start calling her that instead of Bunny.

So far, she hasn't had any nightmares where she woke up screaming. The one time I tried to give her space, wanting to avoid crowding her, led to her crying out in her sleep. As soon as she felt my touch, she settled down. Like I am her personal stuffy. A few times, she's woken me up with small whimpers that I easily soothe away without her waking up.

Each night, with her wrapped in my arms, tests my self-restraint. I have to remind myself to keep my hands in safe places, not let them wander, and not lean down and kiss her. I feel like I am walking a fine line, so afraid to push her too fast, too soon. I don't want to be the asshole that takes advantage of her in this situation. She is seeking comfort, not sex. But I also don't want to risk her feeling rejected if she perceives my restraint as disinterest.

"Do you normally sleep with a shirt?" she asks when I return to her room wearing sweats and a t-shirt.

Well, fuck.

For a moment, I contemplate lying and saying yes. It would end the conversation, but it is such an unnecessary thing to lie about. It would break trust for no reason. Besides, that first night, I didn't have a shirt on. We had the blanket between us. The shirt is just a flimsy attempt at keeping distance. Not that it is working.

I give a sheepish shake of my head.

"So why now?"

"To... um... make you more comfortable?" But it comes out as a question. I give an awkward cough and scratch the back of my neck. "I didn't want to make you uncomfortable by pushing you into something you may not be ready for," I try to explain my reasoning.

She just smiles, as if I am being ridiculous. "You don't need to keep your shirt on. I am comfortable with you. I trust you."

Those words make me feel 1000 feet tall. I want to ask if she is sure and question her until I feel sure, but I don't want to undermine the confidence that she is showing. If I keep asking if she is sure, she may take it as me questioning her judgment, and she needs to know that I trust her as well. That I trust what she says the first time she says it.

I climb into bed with her, sans my shirt, and she doesn't hesitate to snuggle up next to me, just like she has every night so far. I feel the tension leaves her body, as she draws random patterns on my chest with her fingertips. The touch feather-light.

The only thing that would make this better is if we were in my room, my bed. The desire to have her in my space is almost as great as my desire for her touch.

"Reid," Sage hesitantly asks, "when all this is over, will you still want me?" The darkness makes her brave.

I know why she is asking. The assumption is that I have a savior complex. Juniper seems to think so. While my job is meant to protect others, I never get this close to a client.

This is a conversation we both need to have, even if the timing is a little abrupt.

"I wanted you before I knew you needed help."

She scoffs. "Well, aside from the car trouble." I amend with a smile. "I figured I'd swoop in and save the day by either fixing your car or calling in Maddox, and maybe give you my number after asking you to dinner."

"But then?" she prompts.

"You clearly didn't want me around, and were terrified by me, so I figured the attraction was one-sided and accepted that. Wasn't going to stop me from helping you. But then I saw the cut belt, and well, it doesn't take a genius to add two and two together to realize your trouble went beyond a broken-down car. But the longer I am around you, the more I dread and hope for the day he is no longer a threat to you. I want you safe, but I like having you here. I didn't realize how empty my home was. I want you to stay here and..." I pause, wondering if I am exposing too much. I don't want her to feel like I am pressuring her or moving too fast. "I worry that you'll want to forget about this town. Forget... me. I'd get it if you needed to." I give a rueful laugh. "I like you, in case you couldn't tell."

I feel the quick exhale of her breath on my chest as she lets a gasp.

"I like you too," she whispers. "I think," she pauses, carefully weighing her words, "that when this is over, I want to stay here. In this town." She hesitates. "With you. I could get my own place; it doesn't have to be here here," she rambles. Her words speeding up. "Get a full-time job, and..."

I turn so I am facing her. I reach out to cup her cheek; the darkness makes her features hard to see. "We can sort the logistics of that after. But I like you in my space." The unsaid implications of my words hang in the air.

I feel rather than see her nod her head.

I press my lips to hers, just a quick kiss, tasting the mint of her toothpaste. I don't deepen it, despite her protest when I pull back. My self-restraint is only so good.

"Go to sleep, Bunny," I whisper, pulling her closer and tucking her head under my chin. "I've got you."

CHAPTER TWENTY

Sage

I am feeling bold this morning. For nearly a week now, I've shared a bed with Reid, and he's been nothing but a gentleman. We went from having a blanket between us that first night—when he came charging into my room looking like he was going to fight my demons with his bare hands—to now cuddling together entirely under the covers.

I may have insisted on it. At first, it was because I felt safer. But gradually, I have grown accustomed to sleeping wrapped up in his arms. I haven't slept so deeply in years. Sure, he keeps the worst of the nightmares away, but it is more than that.

Despite him being shirtless that first night, every night after—much to my disappointment—he's had a shirt on, and he's never pressed for more than a kiss. To be honest, I am not sure if that is a green flag or not, but the slow pace is annoying me. It would be fine if he was setting the slow pace for himself. I wouldn't want to pressure anyone, but the careful, controlled way he is when he touches me tells me all I need to know. He is waiting for the okay. Hell, I had to encourage him to take his shirt off because, clearly, that's not how he normally sleeps.

Last night, it was easy to be brave in the dark. To talk about a potential future.

Feelings.

My cheek pressed against his skin, and the steady thump of his heartbeat—all of it made me realize I wanted more from him. More than just whatever this is.

I take a deep breath, his clean, masculine scent filling my nose, and sink into the relaxed, languid feeling of his body against mine. I don't want to get up just yet. The warmth of his body is comfortable, with one of his arms wrapped around my back; I feel safe in this little bubble we have created. I drag my fingers up over his chest, tracing a random pattern, oh so gently, on his skin. Tracing over scars and tattoos, and creating my own pattern of swirls.

Looking up, I expect to still see him asleep. But despite his calm, even breathing, his eyes are open, his gaze steadily watching me, an unreadable expression on his face. I smile and stretch, pressing closer to his body.

At the feel of his hard-on, I can't help the smirk that lights my face.

"Sorry," he says, the first words to break the silence of the morning.

That feels wrong.

I don't want him to be upset by his reaction to me. It's flattering. To be seen as desirable. To want someone. For so long, I thought I was broken. That *he* broke me. But the warmth coursing through my body and the low throb that makes me want to press even closer, tells me that my body is working fine.

I pepper kisses over his chest. I can't say the words just yet, but maybe my actions will be enough. I don't want his apologies. I don't want him holding back.

My tongue darts out, tasting his skin on the next few kisses.

"Sage," Reid groans, his voice strained.

I look up; his eyes are closed. He is trying to hold back. I don't want that.

"I should get up," he whispers.

"Hmm... No," I murmur, pressing closer, moving my mouth up to his neck. Smooth skin giving way to morning stubble. He groans briefly, as if in pain—or maybe pleasure? Any question of what I was doing is long gone.

"Bunny, my control is only so strong." His voice is strained. I smile against his skin. The arm not wrapped around me is fisted at his side. I want him to lose control.

"That's too bad," I reply, my poor attempt at flirting, but I push ahead anyway. "Maybe I don't want you to be in control. Well, maybe a certain kind of control is good," I smile at the thought. I never thought I'd ever want to dip my toe into BDSM again, and yet I am already thinking of how willing I am to cede control to this man who has done nothing but take care of me. I can only imagine how wild, calm, and controlled Reid will be when he finally lets go.

I push up on the bed so that I am looking down at him as he lies against the mattress. I take a moment to admire the gorgeous picture he makes. His body is perfection. He isn't lean, nor overly muscular, but fit. His muscles tense in an effort to hold himself back, the strain making the veins prominent on his arms.

That won't do. It's been weeks of dancing around each other, the tension simmering under the surface. Even if things do not go further than a heavy make-out session, I wasn't about to let this moment slip through my hands.

I want this.

I lean over him, pressing my lips to his, before nipping at his bottom lip. And as if a rubber band snapped, his control is gone.

I let out a squeal as I am flipped over, our positions reversed, and I am the one with my back to the bed while he looms over me.

I arch my back, trying to get closer, but he has my hair gripped in one hand and the other holding both my hands above my head. Now, when did that happen? I muse with a chuckle, perfectly happy with my current predicament.

He looks down at me, eyes filled with dark intent, the hand in my hair moving to stroke down the side of my neck. "Tell me to stop, and I will. 'Stop,' 'red,' 'No,' a few taps—and I'll stop. No hesitation, no hard feelings. Promise."

I nod and lean my head up—the only part of my upper body I can move at the moment—and give another nip.

He is still holding on to that control.

He growls and slants his mouth over mine, his tongue thrusting into my mouth. This is so different from how he's kissed me all the other times. This Reid is aggressive, almost angry, and feral in how he handles me, his hands possessive.

He trails sucking kisses down my neck while one of his legs forces mine open, his hard thigh pressing into my center, causing me to moan. I can feel his lips tip into a smile against my neck before he does it again. His teeth gently bite down, the pain mixing with the pleasure. Maybe he'll leave a mark.

I want that.

Fuck, I like this version of Reid. The opposite of his calm and control. Wild, aggressive.

I can feel how wet I am becoming, and a distant part of my brain wonders if he can feel it through my yoga pants. A tiny part feels embarrassed at how quickly I've become aroused, and another part, a stronger part, likes the idea of leaving a mark. A visual claim that he is mine.

I thrust my hips up, seeking more friction, panting into his mouth as he returns to mine, his tongue demanding entrance, sliding to tangle with mine. I want to touch him. Run my hands through his hair, his body, pull him closer, but the more I tug against his hold, the more he presses my hands down into the bed.

He moves more on top of me, just enough of his weight to be acutely aware of him, but not suffocating. I spread my legs, cradling him in the juncture of my thighs, his hard, cloth-covered cock pressing against my core, exactly where I want it. He rolls his hips, and I close my eyes, falling into the sensation, another moan tears from my throat as he does it again.

And then he is pulling away. I let out a mewl of disappointment as he lets go of my hands and pulls me into a sitting position, but rather than stopping as I feared, he is pulling up my shirt. I rush to help him tug it off, scarcely noticing when he tosses it into a random part of the room.

"So fucken beautiful," he says on a breath before pressing me back down and climbing on top, his legs straddling my thighs.

When I reach out to touch him, he captures my arms and presses them back above my head. "Keep them here or I'll stop," he says sternly.

"But I want to touch," I reply, pressing a little, testing his hold.

"You got your chance to play. I am in charge now," he trails his hands down my arms, his touch light and teasing. I want to move, but a bigger part wants to obey him.

"Yes, sir," I say with a teasing smirk.

He smirks down at me, "Good girl, when we are like this, I am sir to you," he growls, and warmth fills me. A tiny part wonders if we are going too fast, but a bigger part screams that this is right. This is how it is supposed to feel. Safe. Exciting. Any desire to disobey him disappears. He rewards my good behavior by reaching down and pinching my pebbled nipple, the shock of pain a surprise that he quickly soothes with his tongue. He wraps his lips around the nub and sucks, his other finger rolling and kneading my other breast.

I look down, watching him play with my body, his eyes intent on my face, watching my reactions, cataloging the noises I make, the way I move, learning what makes me writhe under him. He switches breasts, and his fingers pinch my damp nipple, nothing to soothe away the pain. Fuck, I like that.

I like that after weeks of being careful, he isn't anymore. It's clear that I like what he is doing, and he rewards each of my responses with more pleasure.

He moves over to lie on his side next to me while I am on my back. One arm bent, cradling his head in his hand, watching me while his other hand moves down over my body. That wildness has given into controlled arousal. I wonder if this is the Dom side taking over. The utter control of himself turned on me. I can easily see him mastering my body. Owning my pleasure. I close my eyes as I feel his fingers move down my sternum, over my tummy, lower and lower still until they pause at the top of my yoga pants. I look up, his eyes intent on me, silently asking permission. "Please," I whimper, wanting more.

His fingers dip into my pants and push into my underwear, fingers rubbing against my clit. I arch into his touch, pressing myself into his hands.

"Ah, ah, ah," he says, "you take what I give you, Baby Girl." Oh, that's new. I like that. I groan in protest, but I still move my hips.

"Good Girl," he whispers, and I preen under the praise.

His fingers circle my clit, his touch light.

"Please Sir, I need more."

"You are so wet, Bunny" his fingers dip down, just enough for a taste, before pulling away to swirl more slickness to my clit. "Is this all for me?"

I'm nodding my head. Maybe. At least, I think I am. I feel out of control and on fire and it is just his fingers. I am fighting not to move. To stay still and be his good girl. The more out of control I become, the more in control he becomes. How does he seem so unaffected? If it wasn't for his cock pressed into my side, he could be mistaken as almost bored. But the slight rhythmic press against my side betrays how he feels. I like the way he teases.

His fingers dip inside again, rubbing against a spot that has me seeing stars, and I close my eyes again, head thrown back as I moan.

"No, eyes on me, Bunny. Watch me as I make you come, so there is no doubt who controls your pleasure. It's my fingers in your cunt making you feel good."

If my mind was working, I'd blush at the crassness of his words, but my mind is mush, riding the waves of pleasure, getting closer and closer to that edge. He pushes another finger into me, stretching me. I groan at the slight stretch, but if I ever want him to fuck me, I know I'll need to take more than that.

His thumb strokes my clit, and he presses a third finger into me. I can feel myself tighten on his fingers.

"You're going to come soon, aren't you, baby?" but it isn't a question. An air of arrogance cloaks him. He knows what he is doing to my body. He knows he is making me fall apart. My thighs tremble, so close. "There are some days I am going to make you ask for your pleasure. Make you wait. Edge you until you are a mindless mess."

Why is he talking? How is he so calm? I can barely think. "But I think today I will reward you. You can come whenever you want." I want to snark at him. Tell him how magnanimous of him, but my mouth isn't working. I can't form any sentences, just gasps and moans and desperate, please, please, please!

I fall over the edge, struggling to keep my eyes on him as I get lost in the pleasure, but the utter satisfaction on his face makes it worth it. He slows his trusting, letting me ride out of my orgasm before slowly winding me up again.

I shake my head, "I can't again," I gasp out, even though my body is rising to the demand.

"I think you can. Because it will please me. And I know you want to please me." He pumps faster, adding more pressure to my clit. "I enjoy watching you come." His tone is almost conversational, as if he is still unaffected. "You are so pretty when you come. You wouldn't deny me, would you, Bunny? Don't you want to be my good girl?" I can only whimper in response, so close once again.

How the hell did he bring me right back to the edge so fast?

"I think this is my new favorite thing. The sounds you make, the way you cry out, the wet sound of your cunt. The feel of you wrapped around my fingers. I can't wait to sink my cock into you." His words are undoing me. I love the mouth on this man, and he clearly knows it. "You are so perfect. I love the way your body responds to mine. That's it, baby," he encourages, "just like that. Come for me. Be a good girl and come all over my fingers. I want your thighs to be soaked. Yes, that's it."

I am falling again. He leans down and captures my mouth, stifling my cry as I scream. The orgasm is not as powerful, but no less intense. He holds my gaze as he slows his fingers, once again working me through the end of my orgasm and letting me come down. I am breathing hard as he gathers me into his arms.

He licks his fingers clean. "Delicious," he mutters before giving me a heated kiss, the taste of myself on his tongue. He holds me, murmuring sweet words as he rubs circles on my back.

"I want to touch you," I finally say, reaching for him, but he stops me.

"No, this morning was all for you."

"But what did you get out of it?" I ask, worrying my lip.

"Everything, Bunny. Your surrender. Your pleasure. Your trust." He peppers each one with a kiss. "Let me take care of you," he murmurs, rubbing his hands over my body, his touch soothing rather than sexual.

We lie together, enjoying the afterglow, until I am suddenly aware of the need to pee. I wiggle, trying to detangle myself from Reid's hold.

"Hmm, no, let me hold you longer," he murmurs into my hair.

"But I have to pee," I say with a laugh. A part of me can't believe I just blurted that out.

He just laughs and opens his arms, letting me free. "Go, and then time for a shower."

"Together?" I ask.

He shakes his head. "Not yet. I won't be able to keep my hands to myself if we are both naked and wet." He chuckles at my pout. "We will get there, Bunny," he says with a smile. "Come on, we don't have much time left to get ready."

CHAPTER TWENTY-ONE

Reid

The sound of the shower fills the room, and I groan, palming my erection. What I would give to join her like she asked. But I wasn't lying when I told her I wouldn't be able to keep my hands to myself. It was hard enough holding onto the sliver of control that I did, but it was worth it to see her come apart. I wonder if her any of her previous partners ever focused on her pleasure. I bet her ex was the sort to just take and take.

I lie on the bed a moment longer, remembering the feel of her skin against mine. Maybe I could join her in the shower.

No. It is almost time to go, and we both need to get ready.

In my room, far away from temptation—though not far enough—reality creeps in. Did I cross a line? Take advantage of her? I am supposed to be keeping her safe. Safe from her ex. Safe from her nightmares. Should I be keeping her safe from myself?

I wait for the guilt, the self-recrimination to creep up. The self-loathing for taking advantage of a client. But it doesn't come. No, I can only remember the way she begged me for more. Took what she wanted. Gave me the control I need. And all I can feel is satisfaction.

This feels right. Regardless of protocol.

If one of Vaughn's brothers was heading her case, I'd probably have something to worry about, but as it stands, Vaughn is in charge at the moment—and this is what the meddling asshole wanted, anyway.

In the shower, I take care of my problem while I imagine myself sinking into her welcoming body. I finish preparing for the day, strategically placing weapons for easy access, yet concealed from the public eye.

I greet her in the kitchen with a searing kiss. The taste of coffee on her lips.

I make us a quick breakfast, acutely aware of how everything has shifted.

We are washing the breakfast dishes when my phone rings. I tense when the caller ID says Blake.

"Go, I'll finish up here," Sage says, pressing me out of the way of the sink.

I kiss her quickly on the top of her head before snatching my phone up and hurrying to my office.

"Tell me you have good news," I say, in lieu of a greeting. Blake isn't one to observe pleasantries, so there is no point in wasting time on empty hellos.

"I can confirm he is in Washington."

I freeze on those words before reminding myself that we are already operating as if he is nearby.

"I was able to pull some security footage that places him in Seattle two days ago."

"You didn't think to tell me two days ago?" I snap.

"I'm telling you now."

I suppress the urge to roll my eyes. Fucking Blake.

"Where is he now? Do you have eyes on him?"

"Not entirely sure. I've been staking out the place he was last at, but he hasn't returned."

"You think he is here?"

"There is nothing showing he has gone anywhere else, but I figured you should know. He might be there. I'll keep looking." Blake ends the call, and I am left reeling.

Fuck. I suppress the desire to throw my phone. That won't solve anything.

I sit down heavily in my office chair, rubbing my eyes with the heel of my hand. Fuck. What do I tell Sage? Tell her we need to cancel today? Keep her locked up inside, just in case? Move her to a safe house?

No, I am getting ahead of myself.

The number of tourists from Seattle and the surrounding areas is high. Can I keep her safe? I try to think about this logically. Remove my desire to wrap her in bubble wrap and hide her from the world.

How would we proceed if she were any other high-profile client with a planned event? We'd have a guard on the client. In this case, me. Check. Guards in the crowd close by. Check. An exit plan, established and discussed with the client. Check. I know the area. I'll have men in the crowd. Hell, half the local guys will be around at some point, and they know that I am guarding someone.

It'll be fine, I tell myself.

It. Will. Be. Fine.

Sage is putting on her shoes at the door when I leave the office. She flashes me a huge smile, practically bouncing in excitement. It's a far cry from earlier in the week when she worried about being a burden.

Her tears had angered me. Not that she was crying, but that she even had a reason to cry. The words I was going to say die in my throat. I don't want to dim her smile. She deserves a peaceful day out. She doesn't need to be looking over her shoulder every five minutes. I need to be the one to carry that burden.

"Ready?" I ask, gathering my keys and holding out my hand.

"Yeah, let's go!"

CHAPTER TWENTY-TWO
Sage

I am a bundle of nerves. The good kind, mostly. I've been looking forward to today since Juniper mentioned it last week in the diner and dreading it in equal measure. I know Reid already ensured everything would be safe. He is insistent that coordinating something with his team isn't an issue and that he is certain it will be low-key enough that I won't even notice the extra security.

I've tried to cancel a few times, culminating in a moment where I burst into tears about being a burden. At first, it seemed as if Reid was angry at me when that happened. It took me a moment to realize that he was angry for me. Angry that someone had made me feel like a burden, angry that someone was causing so much chaos in my life that I couldn't even do everyday things like go to the farmers market with a friend without worrying about potential dangers. It was... nice to have someone care so much.

That only caused a torrent of more tears. These left him a little baffled, and I tried and failed to explain that I was happy at his anger. Here he was, angry and ready to fight the world, and for some reason, he was convinced that I deserved that kind of devotion. This only sparked disbelief from Reid, who swore he would do something about my skewed world perception.

Reid parks his truck a few streets from the farmer's market. He gives me a stern look, which has me rolling my eyes, but I stay in place, knowing that he wants to ensure it is safe before he opens my door. While I pretend that his insistence to play the gentleman is on the annoying, over-the-top, treating-me-like-a-damsel side, I secretly like that he holds his hand out to help me from the vehicle and holds me close as we walk down the street together. The tiny smile on my face betrays my enjoyment of the treatment, and Reid isn't deterred by my fake show of annoyance.

"Wow," I breathe out when we turn the corner. Easy-up awnings in various colors have taken over the entire town square and surrounding streets, each selling something new. The air buzzes with the hum of voices overlapping so much that I can't really make out what anyone is saying, but the general hum is happy.

I speed up, eager to see what everyone has for sale. "Reid," I say when he doesn't match my quickening steps, "hurry up!" He just laughs and gives my hand a tug, causing me to collide with his side, and he lets go of my hand to wrap his arm around my shoulder, tucking me more securely into his side.

"I promise it isn't going anywhere. We have plenty of time. No one will be cleaning up until around 4 pm. We have hours, I promise."

I grumble in protest but don't pull away again, savoring the warmth of his body as a consolation prize.

When we get closer, I am not even sure where to start. The town square is a large square park in the middle of downtown, with a large gazebo in the middle. The booths are arranged in a square, with a large square of booths on the far side of the street near the businesses, the next slightly smaller square on the side of the street flanking the park, and two increasingly smaller squares in the park itself, with the gazebo in the center currently occupied by a violinist and rows of chairs in front for people to enjoy the performance.

"Oh wow," I say again, my gaze torn. I look left, then right, trying to decide which way to go. Maybe I can go with the flow of traffic? No, that won't work. There isn't a discernible flow, as everyone walks in every direction. Should I start in the center and work my way out? From the outside in?

Decisions, decisions.

The rows of fresh produce catch my eye—vegetables in bright pops of color and a variety of sizes and even some shapes that never would pass quality control for a supermarket.

"Is that a purple carrot?" I ask, pointing with a laugh. "And a red one? I didn't know carrots can come in different colors. Can we get some?" Pleading with Reid, before I catch sight of something else over his shoulder, forgetting all about the carrots. "Ooh, what's that?" I dart around him, spying a booth full of pretty soaps.

Only the soaps on the table in front don't look like boring bars of soap. These are made to look like layered cake slices. The sign above says 'Slices of Suds' with hand-painted little cake slices and soap bubbles. It is such an odd combination that I am absolutely charmed by it. And the smells wafting from the booth—lavender, honeysuckle, citrus, eucalyptus!

As I get closer, tugging Reid along the way, I can see wooden crates stacked on their sides, used like shelves. These have a sign that says 'For When You Are Not in the Mood for Cake' showing beautiful bars of soap with what looks like flowers and herbs inside, bottles of lotions, and rows of bath bombs.

A little sign boasts 'All Natural Ingredients, Ethically Sourced, and Safe for Pets.'

Next to the soaps is a booth bursting with cut flowers, perfectly complementing the wonderful smells coming from the soap booth. I turn and see a booth across the street with colorful scarves on display.

Reid laughs before giving my hand another little tug to get my attention. "Let's go down this way." He points, showing the direction. "Juniper said she'd meet us at Sunshine's booth, and she always sets up shop over there."

I let him lead me for about thirty seconds before I am distracted again and tug him to another booth, this one with handmade paper. Some are woven into hand-bound journals, others tied in sets of ten with brown twine. Some boast seeds in the paper, saying, 'Send a letter and instruct the person to plant after reading and to wait for wildflowers to grow.' Next to the seed paper is a basket with little balls labeled 'seed bombs,' the tag saying to toss them wherever you find a clear area of dirt. 'They explode on impact, sending native wildflower seeds around.' Next to that is paper with pressed flowers, some with pretty leaves, and others infused with wonderful scents.

"Reid!" A feminine voice calls out and Reid turns to the sound, a huge smile on his face. He lets go of my hand as a tall, dark-haired woman launches herself at him. A hot flush of hurt and anger bubbles up at the laugh Reid lets out. Before I can say anything, the woman pulls away from Reid and turns to me and gives me just as enthusiastic hug. "Oh, mom was right! She said she was way too pretty for you."

"Emily," Reid groans. Over her shoulder, I see him rub a hand over his face in exasperation. Emily? The cousin?

"You must be his cousin." I say hesitantly.

"Yep, and you're Sage. It's so nice to meet you. Reid won't tell me anything, but Juniper has lots of nice things to say." She sends Reid a mock glare. "I can't wait to get to know you more. Sorry I can't stick around, I have a booth to man, but come visit me!" And as quickly as she appeared, she is off, disappearing into the crowd.

"So that was Emily," Reid says after a beat and I can't help the burst of laughter.

We continue on, passing a booth selling dried meats, and another offering honey. People surround the beekeeper as she explains how the honey is harvested.

I lose interest halfway through; there seem to be a few people so enraptured by her explanation that she doesn't notice us moving on to the next booth.

A few booths down from the honey booth, we find Juniper behind a table with Sunshine.

Juniper jumps up to greet me, pulling me into a tight hug. "Something is different," she says, pulling back and inspecting me with a critical eye. Her gaze lands on my neck, and she gives a gasp. "Reid Mathews, did you give poor innocent Sage a hickey?" she squeals.

I duck my head in embarrassment, my cheeks flushing, and a smile forms on my lips. I am not ashamed of the mark, but I am acutely aware of the attention Juniper has called to us, and I feel a prickle on the back of my neck as if I am being watched.

"We are going to talk about this latest development," she continues. Luckily, Sunshine rescues me from Juniper's grasp, giving me a slight reprieve.

Sunshine's booth is a polar opposite to the bright, almost bohemian vibe the rest of the market has going for it. Instead, her wares are dark and moody; everything reflects a gothic aesthetic: paintings in a Tim Burton-esque style, moody landscapes, bats and castles, and other spooky elements. She also offers little charms with sigils and stones, pendants with moons and stars, and small, hand-decorated 'potion' bottles, so detailed they seem to be from a fairy tale.

"Wow, did you make these?" I ask Sunshine, picking up a shocking purple bottle. Upon closer look, I can see that the purple liquid has something silver in it as well, causing it to appear to swirl around, giving it a magical air. The top is corked and sealed with wax artfully dripped around it, a cute little ribbon with small amethyst stones, and a label with the words 'Elixir of Fortune' in beautiful calligraphy.

"This is so cute," I say, smiling at Sunshine, who beams with pride.

"How do you make it swirl?" I ask, looking at all the different bottles —a pale pink labeled 'Love Potion Number 9,' a green and red bottle labeled 'Christmas Cheer'—all with the same swirling liquid inside in various colors.

"Oh, it's rheoscopic fluid."

"What?"

"It's particles that let you see the flow of the current."

"But how?"

"Normal people terms," Juniper calls from the sidelines. "Sunshine works in a lab all day doing cool science things that us normal people wouldn't understand, and she makes all this"—Juniper spreads her arms to indicate everything in her booth—"as an escape from the boring, mundane world and into one of magic."

Sunshine flushes a little. "Uh, sorry, um, mica powder, usually, for most of them. Pretty cool, huh?"

"Very."

"How are you enjoying Deliverance's monthly farmers market so far?" Juniper asks. "I didn't lie about the turnout, huh?"

"There is no way all these booths are people from this town."

"Oh no, a lot of the vendors come from other towns, some as far as Tacoma or Seattle. Creates even more buzz with the tourists. Plus, if you go to that row all the way on the other side," she motions to the other side of the square, "it's pretty much a bridal fair over there, and a lot of the vendors get booked out for months."

"For a small town, you sure are popular," I remark.

"Our one-woman marketing team is top-notch," Juniper says, laughing.

"Katie isn't doing the town's marketing anymore," Sunshine says, the comment shifting the mood.

"What? Did she finally start her consulting business?"

"I'm not sure," Sunshine replies with a shrug. "Convince her to join our next book club, and we can find out what's going on with her."

I say goodbye to Sunshine, leaving her to run her booth while Juniper and I venture off to explore the rest of the farmer's market. Juniper bounces beside me, her energy matching mine, enthusiastically pointing out who is who—whether they run a business in town or are just here for the market.

I had felt invisible the last time I had been at a fair. Strangers' gazes passed over me as if I didn't exist, their focus solely on the vendors and their wares. People chatted amongst themselves, their voices overlapping and blending with the shrieks of children on rides and the shouts of vendors advertising their goods. I remember the sun beating down on me, my skin reddening as it burned because Jordan had "forgotten" to pack the sunscreen I was certain I had placed in the bag before we left. The air had been thick with the cloying mix of burned popcorn, cotton candy, sweat, and overflowing trash cans. It sours my stomach just thinking about it.

Here, though, it is different. Juniper pulls me along with an infectious energy, waving and calling out greetings to people who are still strangers to me. Yet, I can't help but return the smiles cast my way. The midmorning sun is warm on my face, stretching my shadow long in front of me. It isn't overly hot, but even if it were, I still wouldn't need to worry about sunburn, as Reid insisted on sunscreen this morning. Just another way he takes care of me.

The market buzzes with life, the hum of countless conversations blending into a lively symphony. Occasionally, a violin's faint, sweet sound rises above the din. Each stall we pass is bursting with color and character—knitted clothes and plushies, hand-carved wooden toys, dried herbs filling the air with their soothing, earthy aromas.

A gentle breeze ruffles my hair, carrying the tantalizing scent of chocolate. I spin, searching for its source. I pause, seeing a man in the distance, his eyes on me and Juniper. He looks familiar and for a moment he reminds me of Jordan in build, but Jordan only wears suits. This man has a baseball cap pulled low over his face and is wearing jeans and a dark henley. This must be one of Reid's guys.

I grab Juniper's arm and drag her toward a stall featuring an array of beautifully crafted chocolates.

"This is Mr. Peterson," Juniper says, gesturing to the man behind the booth. "He doesn't live here, but we forgive him because he has the best chocolate shop in the city."

Mr. Peterson is an older gentleman with salt-and-pepper hair, wearing a tan apron embroidered with the words Chocolate Fixes Everything.

"Maybe when I retire, June dear," he says, his voice warm, before he turns to help the next person in line.

Juniper doesn't miss a beat, pointing out someone else. "Oh, that's Amy. She works at the bank."

I laugh, shaking my head. "Juniper, I can't remember all this!" I say, grinning as she rattles off another tidbit of information.

"How do you guys know so much about everyone?"

Juniper shrugs with a playful smile. "That's what happens when you live in a small town. Everyone knows everyone."

I glance over my shoulder at Reid, who is trailing us at a respectful distance, close enough to keep an eye on things but far enough not to intrude. "Is that true?" I ask.

Reid smiles faintly and shakes his head. "I don't know most of the people here. Juniper, though, she knows everyone."

Juniper beams at the praise, throwing her arm around my shoulders. "See? I'm the town's unofficial ambassador. Stick with me, and you'll know everyone, too."

I just shake my head. I don't think I'll ever be as extroverted as Juniper. We walk around for another hour or two before stopping for lunch. Reid buys us chicken strips and lemonade from a vendor, and we return to Sunshine so we can all eat together.

Reid touches base with some of his guys before sending them back into the crowd. I wonder if the guy watching us earlier has already finished his shift since he never checks in with Reid, and I don't see him anymore.

So far, everything is fine.

But just as I think that, I get that prickle at the back of my neck again. I look around, trying to see if I spot anyone. Aside from the extra guards, no one else seems to pay any mind to me. I try to shrug off the feeling of being watched. This is all part of the deal to keep me safe. I don't have to like it, but this is how it is until Jordan is gone.

Before we head out again, Reid insists on more sunscreen. I squeeze my face up in disgust, but I don't put up a fight as he sprays the aerosol sunscreen over my skin. It's better than the lotion kind. Or burning.

We walk past more booths, and I am surprised to see a few of them unmanned. One had a little box saying to place payment for items there, and another had a "Return in 10 Minutes" sign on the table.

"Isn't someone afraid that someone will steal their stuff?" I ask Juniper, pointing to one of the empty booths.

"Nah, their neighbor will keep an eye on things. That's more than enough. They probably just left to get food or a bathroom break."

I shake my head at the trust people have.

We meander towards the center of the square. In the center of the square, the violinist playing in the gazebo is gone and teenagers are setting up their equipment. Throughout the day, different musical numbers have cycled through, keeping the fair alight with a variety of live music.

When the teen band plays, I am a little surprised at how good they sound. Juniper must have noticed my look because she bumps my shoulder.

"Just watch. Someday they are going to make it big. Well, those three," she gestures to the drummer, lead guitarist, and the singer. "The bassist doesn't really have the drive for music. Pretty sure he is going to go into accounting or something."

"How do you know that?"

"I know everyone, remember?"

I laugh and shake my head.

We stand on the edge of the audience, watching the band play a mix of punk rock covers and a few original pieces that actually sound fantastic when there is a loud squeal from the speaker. I cover my ears, flinching at the deafening sound. The noise abruptly stops, but then a song begins to play. Everyone looks around in puzzlement; even the poor teenagers on the stage are confused, having paused their music in the middle to stare at each other in confusion.

A jaunty tune is coming from the speakers, an old-timey song from the 50s, perhaps, with a man singing about rabbit pie day. But then a second voice joins, and I freeze. Something about it is setting off alarm bells in my head. "Run, rabbit, run, rabbit, run, run, run." I shake my head. No, that's a weird coincidence. I know Reid calls me Bunny, but there is no way Jordan would know that. Like, this screams psychological torture, one of his specialties, but it's not him. "Bang, bang, bang, bang goes the farmer's gun." My breath is coming out choppy. I feel myself flinch with each "bang."

The crowd is equally confused, but they don't seem as bothered by the song's words, just how loud it is playing. There are technicians on the gazebo-turned-stage, talking into walkie-talkies, pressing buttons on the sound system, and shaking their heads in puzzlement.

I turn to Reid and tug on his shirt, feeling like a little kid. "Can we leave?"

He looks down and takes in my stricken face before wrapping an arm around me and motioning for Juniper to follow. We head back toward Sunshine's booth. The creepy song still playing. The lyrics tell the rabbit not to give the farmer his fun.

I feel like the rabbit. Running from danger. If Jordan gets me, he will eat me up until there is nothing left but a shell of a person. I shake my head again. No, he isn't here. This is just a weird problem with the sound system. A prank.

Bang! Bang! Bang!

That wasn't the song, I instantly realize. My mind feels slow and sluggish, as if my thoughts are fighting through a current. People scream and start running. I freeze, but Reid doesn't; he presses me down behind a tree, putting his body over mine. The pops continue for what feels like forever, but are probably only a few seconds. The people stampeding don't help. It takes me a split second to realize Juniper has someone else covering her. And Reid is barking orders, but my ears are not working. The jaunty tune is still playing loops in my head. "Run, rabbit, run, rabbit, run, run, run."

Reid says something to me, but I give him a blank look. He wraps an arm around me and powers through the crowd. I feel numb. My body is on autopilot, and I follow the direction that Reid leads.

We move from grass to sidewalk, to street, back to sidewalk, and I still float outside my body. I don't know how long we walk, but I am surprised when we don't go to Reid's truck. Instead, he opens the door to a shop and ushers me inside, pushing me towards the back of the store. He is on the phone. I don't know who he is talking to.

I can feel parts of my body again. My fingers and toes are tingling. I'm shivering. Why am I so cold?

I look around and realize we are in a bar, not a shop. People crowded around, everyone talking—a steady hum tinged with anxiety and excitement. Suddenly, the world fast-forwards, and it's like whatever put my brain in slow mode has gone, and I can think again.

I see Juniper, but no Sunshine.

"Sunshine?" I ask, but no one pays any attention to me. Is my voice even working?

"Where is Sunshine?" I try again. My voice is ringing with an air of hysteria. "Did someone get Sunshine?" I look from Reid to Juniper to the unnamed guard. I see tears sliding down Juniper's face and my heart stutters.

"I have a man on her," Reid interrupts. "She is fine."

I nod, momentarily placated. I try to wade through what happened. The snippets from other people start to penetrate. "Fireworks"... "weird song"... "No shit? Marly's booth?"

Juniper takes my arm and leads me to an open chair.

Was this Jordan? It had to be, right? That song? The fireworks? But it could have been a prank? Teenagers being stupid. Bored teenagers get into trouble, right? Besides, no one knows where Jordan is; he can't be here.

I stay locked in my head, thinking for who knows how long. Eventually, Reid is satisfied with whatever information he has sorted out and concludes it is safe for us to leave our temporary base. I follow as he leads us to the car, and to my surprise, it appears that some people are returning to the market. Like everything is fine.

Is everything fine? I'm not sure. I watch Reid navigate the busy downtown streets before pulling up in front of Heartwood.

Hmm, maybe everything isn't fine.

CHAPTER TWENTY-THREE

Reid

I worry about Sage the entire time we are at the office. She doesn't respond much, spending most of the time in a state of shock. I know I need to get her home so she can relax. We need to talk about what happened. I need to tell her that one or both disturbances might have involved Jordan. I need her to be aware and prepared.

I give Vaughn's hand a firm shake and a tip of the chin before leaving his office. Sage and Juniper are in one of the safe rooms watching a movie. One of my guys helped Sunshine pack up her booth since the market would be shutting down soon, anyway.

No one saw who threw the fireworks. The local sheriff has been in contact with us, and so far, all we have is a vague description of a guy in a dark hoodie and nothing else from witnesses. Not a single one of our cameras caught anything, and neither had one of my men. I think we are all beating ourselves up about it.

We should have noticed a suspicious person wearing a hoodie on a sunny day. Admittedly, I only had eyes on Sage, preoccupied with watching her spiral and feeling helpless about how to help her.

That song really upset her.

She follows me to my truck without a complaint, and we are quiet on the way home. Me, because I don't know what to say to get anything other than one-word answers from her, and her... well, she is focused on the scenery, stuck in her head.

Once we get home, she scoops up Ham, holding the kitty close to her chest, and stalks over to the couch; she grabs the throw and curls into a ball.

Poor Sage.

I say nothing when I scoop her up—cat, blanket, and all—and put her on my lap, wrapping her in my arms, hoping she can draw comfort from them.

"I'm sorry today ended on such a bad note."

She nods but doesn't talk.

"Can you tell me where your head is at?"

The silence feels heavy.

"Do you think any of that was Jordan?" she eventually asks.

I don't want to lie to her. "It is possible."

"But we don't know where he is," she says, more to herself.

I tense.

She must feel the sudden tension in my body, because she twists around to face me.

Ham gives an indignant meow at being squished and scampers away.

"What do you know?" The emptiness is gone from her voice, her eyes narrowed at me, a spark of anger. Okay, anger is good. I can work with anger. That's better than the emotionless shell.

"Blake spotted him in Seattle two days ago, and while he doesn't have a sure location on him, he thinks he might be within a hundred-mile radius of the city."

She stares at me in disbelief. We are within those parameters. I can see her thoughts whirling behind her eyes, and by the narrowing of her eyes, I don't think I like the conclusion she has come to.

"How long have you known? Did Vaughn tell you this during the debriefing?"

I wince, knowing she was essentially giving me an out, hoping that was the case. Alas, that wasn't the truth.

"Since Blake's call this morning."

"This morning?" she repeats as if tasting the words on her tongue, her eyes down as she processes. "That means..." she leaps out of my arms, her movements forceful and jerky, and I don't dare hold her still. "You knew," she says quietly, pacing, the blanket falling to her feet forgotten. "You had confirmation he could be in the area, and you didn't tell me?"

"I didn't want to worry you; knowing wouldn't have changed anything about today."

"Except that wasn't your choice to make. I might have been more aware and paid better attention." She snaps back, her voice rising, "You can't keep things from me when it involves my safety! I need to be able to protect myself." She stops, hands balled into fists, an angry flush on her cheeks. "That wasn't okay... I'm... I'm... angry at you, Reid," she spits out.

I don't know who is more surprised at the outburst, her or me. She opens her mouth again, but closes it again before saying anything. She turns and stomps upstairs. I half expect to hear her door slam shut, but I should know better; she isn't one for theatrics.

I sit in silence. Thinking.

She is right. While it wouldn't have changed anything, I withheld information that wasn't mine to withhold. I was being selfish, wanting to shield her from everything, wanting to see her smile. I have been trying to give her the agency she needed, to show her I was different, that I wouldn't control her in any way she didn't consent to. In one poor decision, I knocked that trust down.

I lean forward, elbows on my knees, hands over my face. *Fuck. I need to apologize.* As I think that, another thing niggles at me. Something I can do to show that I want to give her the tools to protect herself.

I give her a few more minutes before I climb the stairs. I half expect her to ignore me when I knock, but the door is wrenched open, as if she was waiting on the other side. Her face is a riot of emotions, but the most dominant one is fear.

"I'm sorry," she rushes out. "I shouldn't have yelled..."

I hold a hand up, pausing her. "No, I'm sorry. You are right. It wasn't fair of me to withhold information. I should have told you right away instead of waiting."

Her expression turns to disbelief.

"I will do my best in the future to not withhold important information when it comes to your safety."

"So you'll tell me everything?" she asks, skeptical.

"I will tell you when I know something, and when it is speculation. Sometimes, in this field, you have to make decisions when you don't have all the information." I pause, thinking how to word this next part. "There will be times when I am not able to tell you stuff; I will be honest when that is the case." She scowls at that. "There will be things related to my job that I can't talk about," I hastily point out. "I will be upfront with that as well."

"I can work with that."

I rush into the next part: "I think it would be a good idea for you to start self-defense lessons, and maybe learn how to shoot." I watch her expression to gauge her reaction. Her wide grin and excited embrace are not what I expect.

I rock back a moment before wrapping my arms around her, grateful we got through our first little spat with little issue.

"Can we start today?" she asks, looking up at me. Behind the excitement, I see an edge of desperation. I imagine that after today, she feels particularly vulnerable, and the reassurance of being able to throw a punch could go a long way toward helping her self-confidence.

"Sure, Bunny. I can teach you a few things tonight, and we can see about setting up some lessons with Tessa. She's in charge of managing everyone's training schedules and teaches most of the classes."

Sage nods, but then her expression drops. "I really am sorry for yelling at you," she whispers, her body coiling tight.

I shake my head. "No, Bunny. I told you I was the one in the wrong. You can always be honest about your feelings with me. I'm going to be an overbearing dick sometimes, or I'll do something that annoys you; that's part of being in a relationship. As long as we can talk things out, we'll be fine."

She doesn't look like she believes me.

"I used to make Jordan mad." She whispers, like she is sharing a secret. "If I talked back or disagreed..." she shudders. "Eventually, I stopped. There was no point in arguing."

"I know it is going to take a while before you fully trust that you can be honest with me, but I swear, all your feelings are welcome. You are allowed to be mad at me. There may be times I am upset..." I hate the way she flinches at that. "But I promise we will talk things out. We will use our words. Civilly." I watch her smile a little at the clarification. "Okay?" I ask.

"Okay."

"How about that first lesson?" I ask later that evening.

I lead her to the garage. A treadmill, weights, and a punching bag make up this tiny makeshift gym.

"First, your goal will always be to create an opportunity to run," I explain. She screws up her face in distaste at the thought.

"Is it Tessa's goal to create an opportunity to run?" she sasses.

I raise a brow at her. "Tessa is a former professional fighter with years of training under her belt. Start training with her regularly, and maybe someday your goal will turn from running away to incapacitate."

"I think I want to meet this Tessa," she replies.

I laugh. "You will. She's a much better teacher than me when it comes to self-defense and fighting." I lead her over to the mat. "Let's start with weak points."

I point out the areas of the body that cause the most pain or damage with the least amount of effort.

"Wait," she says, eyebrows furrowed. "Isn't kicking someone in the groin fighting dirty?"

"Bunny, when it comes to life or death, you fight as dirty as you need to. Throw sand in their eyes, hit them with a weapon—do anything you need to get away."

We practice a few more moves, and I go over how to escape a few holds before calling it a day.

"We'll keep practicing those moves over and over until it becomes muscle memory."

"Won't that get boring?"

"Yep, practice can get boring. But when you are in a dangerous situation—not that I am going to allow that—it becomes hard to think. Your body will fall back on a move you've practiced a thousand times, and that could be the difference in getting out alive."

"We'll add condition to your day."

She scowls at me. I hold my hands up, "You agreed to learning self defense. This is part of it."

"Exercising is dumb," she mumbles under her breath as we head upstairs to shower.

I'm just glad to see her spark back.

Tucked up in bed later that night, Sage's head on my bare chest, her fingers drawing those feather-light patterns of hers, she asks me about being a Dom.

"You once told me you've been to clubs before. What did you do there?"

"That's a very broad question." I pause to think of a tactful way to explain without scaring her away. "Like you, I first went with a friend. I tried almost everything there at least once—both as a bottom and a top—to get a feel for what I liked and disliked."

"You're a switch?"

"No," I chuckle. "Get any ideas about topping me out of your head, little Bunny. But a good Dom should know what an implement feels like before using it on a sub."

"That's okay. I don't think I could be in charge. It's exhausting for me. What did you like the most?"

I let the question hang, worried that if I am honest, it will scare her away. "I like... being completely in control. To have a sub completely submit to me. To tie them up and decide if they will feel pleasure or pain. Sensory deprivation, the sense of anticipation. Sometimes, that control is more mundane: a day where I make every decision and care for every one of their needs. Knowing they trust me to take care of them." I take a breath, wondering if I am revealing too much, but if I am going to be all in, I must be upfront. "I like... when you let me take care of you."

She is silent. Taking in my words. Her hand trails down to mine, interlocking our fingers.

"What if I can't let you tie me up?" she asks.

"Then I never tie you up," I say as a matter of fact as I can. "Is that a hard limit?" I hedge.

"I don't know," she admits. "I'd want to be able to get out if I need to."

"There are certain knots that you could undo on your own. But, Bunny, we decide what we do together, and if bondage is a limit, then that is okay."

"I don't want him to take away the things I liked. I am not even sure what I like anymore."

"That's okay. We can explore together. We can always add or change limits."

"So if one day I say I never want impact play..." the question hangs.

"Then no impact play."

She nods.

"Did you like what we did this morning?" The morning in question felt like ages ago, not just half a day.

"Yeah, it was good." Even though I couldn't see her in the dark, she ducked her head, pressing her face to my chest as if trying to hide.

"How do you feel about honorifics?"

"I liked calling you Sir, but I am not sure that is an all-the-time thing."

"We can keep our dynamic to the bedroom. What else did you like?"

"Reid," she says in protest.

"Bunny, if you don't tell me what you want and like, then I can't give it to you."

"I liked you telling me what to do and making me stay put," though it comes out more as a rushed mumble.

"Is there anything you want to try with me soon?"

"What do you mean?"

"Well, we can talk about options for a small scene."

"I don't want to go to a club," she whispers.

"We don't need to go to a club to play. We can play anywhere you feel safe."

"Okay, but I can't think of anything I want to try."

"How about this: what did you like most about BDSM before you met him?"

"I liked not having to think. To have all the decisions taken from me for a little bit. I think I got to subspace maybe a handful of times, and it was amazing, but eventually I couldn't. But when I did, it was always because of impact."

"I can give you a safe place to turn your brain off for a bit. How about I list a few things we can try, and you tell me if it is a limit or not?"

I feel her head nod.

"Blindfold?"

"Yes, that's okay."

"Toys, like vibrators or dildos?"

"Yeah."

"Sensation play?"

"I think so, yes."

"What about pain?"

"Maybe. I used to like it, so maybe we could try?"

The more we talk, the more she opens up until she admits to a handful of fantasies that leave my cock aching. God damn my insistence that we take things slow.

"There was one scene," she says, her voice tiny as if she can hide away in the dark. "I think it was the very first time I was at the club with my friend. There was this woman, and she was so fidgety, and she looked nervous. The person she was with was talking to someone, not even paying attention to her, but then he turned to her and told her to kneel. It was like this light switch flipped, and all that anxious energy disappeared. She was so graceful sinking to her knees."

Her voice takes on a dreamy quality, like she is reliving the memory, wishing she was there in that sub's place. "He was still talking, and sub knelt at his side, and she just looked so at peace, and how he looked at her before telling her to stand... It was like, yes, she was lower than him, and there was that visual representation of her submission, but it was clear he adored her. I remember watching when they did a scene. He was so rough with her, but I don't know; there was like this bond," she sighs.

"Later, after the scene was over and the aftercare was done and they came back and were socializing, she looked tired. He told her to kneel again and lean her head against his thigh. He played with her hair, and she just looked so blissed out. I wanted that so much," she admits. "That level of adoration and softness, but at the same time, he was so rough."

"What did he do to her?" I ask, elated she was revealing so much about her wants.

"He.. He put her on a spanking bench and tied her down, and he used so many toys on her." She wiggles a bit, trying to get comfortable.

"It started gently with these floggers, and the longer the scene went, the harder the hits became. Her ass and thighs were covered in marks, welts and bruises. It was beautiful," she presses against me.

I don't even think she realizes the way she rolls her hips, seeking friction; my hand lowers, teasing the waistband of her pj bottoms. I bet if I reach in, I will find her soaking wet. "Then he spanked her... her... cunt." She whispers the word, and I hold in a chuckle. But if my cock hadn't been hard already, the way she said cunt would have done it. "And she liked it. Like she screamed, but then she started chanting that she was close." Her breath hitches as I turn us and press my thigh between her legs, applying much-needed pressure at the apex of her thighs.

"Keep going, Bunny," I say, my hands on her hips, encouraging her to use me to get herself off.

"He thrust his fingers into her, and he must have pinched her clit or something, but she was coming so hard. Then he untied her and pushed her down to her knees. Her eyes were glassy, and she had this huge smile, and opened her mouth wide. He... he fucked her face. It was forceful, but so hot. His hands in her hair, his cock down her throat. It was like he was using her."

She moaned, pressing her panting mouth against my chest. "Did he fuck her, Bunny?" I ask.

"What?" she was grinding harder on me.

"Did he come in her mouth, or did he fuck her?" I ask, my voice sounding composed enough, though I was anything but.

"He.. he came in her mouth," she gasps out. She gives a mewl of protest when I pull my leg away, but as soon as I put my hand down her pants, my fingers finding her slick wetness, it turns into a frantic "yes, Reid. More!"

My fingers push inside, pumping. "Then what happened?" I prompt.

"He.. He made her clean him up with her.. Oh god... her tongue. Please, Sir, may I come. I am so close," she whines.

"Come for me, Bunny," I growl, feeling her walls flutter around my fingers, the gush of wetness before she screams her release. I slow my fingers before pulling them out and bringing them to my mouth. I lick them clean, savoring the taste. Soon, I will taste her at the source. I barely notice where her hands are going until her fingers grasp my hard cock through my sweatpants. I stifle a moan of my own.

"Did I tell you that you could touch me, Bunny?" I growl.

"No, but please. I want to make you feel good. I need to make you feel good." She insists, an edge of desperation in her tone. The need to please. "Please, Sir!"

"Okay, Bunny," I compile. I am far too soft on her, giving her whatever she wants. "You may explore as much as you want, as long as you want," I say that knowing damn well she could be a devious brat and edge me. But I wouldn't push her. Tonight.

"Thank you, Sir," she says, her fingers already pushing my sweats down and pulling out my cock. I help her before laying back with my hands behind my head. My relaxed posture is a complete facade. I groan as her hand strokes over my cock, her thumb swirling over the precum at the head. I am counting backward in my head, willing myself to last, and oh fuck, she licks me from root to tip in one long swipe. Fuck.

"You don't" I try to grasp out, but she ignores me, her warm, wet mouth sucking in the head of my cock, her tongue swirling around and licking up my precum. The words I was going to say die on my lips.

"Fuck, baby!" There is no way I am going to last. I look down and can see her head bobbing in the dark, her eyes closed; she seems lost in the act.

She takes me deeper, her hand at the base moving in sync with her mouth, and no amount of counting can hold back my orgasm. "Bunny, I'm going to," I don't finish as she increases her enthusiasm, her mouth like a vacuum; I moan, my cum shooting into her mouth, feeling as she swallows me down.

I lay back, panting as she delicately licks me clean, the way she described in her story. I look down, and she is watching me, a proud little smile on her face. She giggles. "Did you like it?"

I just stare in disbelief, unable to form words. "Fuck, Bunny," I eventually say, tugging her up to lie next to me. I kiss her gently, parting her lips with my tongue, and taste myself on her tongue. Her taste still lingers in my mouth, and I like the thought of us combined. I pull away to look at her.

Fuck, I think I am gone for her. It's not the sex. It's just her. Everything about her is perfect.

CHAPTER TWENTY-FOUR

Sage

"What's this?" I ask, holding up an envelope with my name on it.

Reid glances at it briefly before returning to his work. "Vaughn dropped it off this morning. Probably your paycheck," he says distractedly, his attention returning to the scheduling conflict he is trying to sort out. With him being out of the field, he's taken over coordinating who does what job.

"But I'm... not..." My brow furrows. "It's an exchange," I trail off.

"Vaughn probably deducted a payment from your check."

I open the envelope, and there it is: a check signed by Vaughn with an invoice for services rendered as an Administrative Contractor.

"I thought I was lying low."

Reid glances back over, his eyes briefly taking in the invoice in my hand with the Heartwood logo on top. "Yeah, he paid you as if you're a contractor. Contractors and venders are paid monthly. No W-2, since you said he's got friends in high places, it's not exactly under the table, per se. When you are ready, we can get you your own account. In the meantime, we can go to the bank and cash it. He may have agreed to let you 'hire' Heartwood, but he wouldn't take it all at once."

I'm not sure how I feel about this. A part of me wants to rip the check up. Insist that all my labor is to pay off the security detail, but another part likes having my own money. Jordan demanded joint bank accounts, and when he made me quit my job, he took away my access to even that, saying he would handle everything. If it weren't for his ridiculous 'apology gifts' from the first few years of our relationship, which I pawned, I never would have had any money to escape.

"It makes this feel like a real job," I murmur.

Reid scoffs. "It is a real job. It needs to get done, and no one wants to do it. No way Vaughn is going to let you quit. We are almost up to date on our documentation. His brothers are demanding he hire you permanently. If you want that..." Reid rubs the back of his neck. "I mean, I don't know what field you were in before, but you're good at data entry and getting the guys to correct their reports when they mess up and calling them out when they slack off, and..." he trails off.

I have to smile. He isn't hiding the fact that he is trying to give me as many reasons as possible to stay here, to entwine my life as much as possible with his.

"I'll think about it," I say, but in truth, I have already made my decision.

There is a loud crash and a squeal of tires from outside. I freeze.

"Stay here!" barks Reid. He reaches into his desk with his left hand and pulls up his outside camera feed with his right. Then he is up and out of his seat in seconds. A flash of metal tells me he left with a gun.

I stare at his monitor. Each entry point to the house is monitored, but there looks to be nothing out of the ordinary on the screen. I watch as he opens the front door and makes his way off-screen. My stomach is tripping over itself with worry, and I have to sit on my hands to stop biting my nails.

He is back just as quickly, already tucking away his gun.

I stand in the room, anxiously wringing my hands.

"Well?!" I demand when he returns.

"Someone ran into the mailbox." He glances at the computer screen. "Literally the one spot I don't have a camera, since the mailbox is in the neighbor's yard." He shakes his head. "I'm going to have to talk to him and see how he want to fix it. Bet he is going to regret not letting me set up my cameras now."

"Do you think it was him?" I whisper.

"It is possible, but I don't think so," He replies as he moves to the monitor and enlarges one of the camera feeds—the one that catches part of the road—and types something on his keyboard. We both watch as a beat-up old red car with tinted windows comes barreling down the sidewalk. You can't see the driver.

"Seems like an asshole wasn't paying attention," Reid murmurs.

"Jordan wouldn't be caught dead in a car like that," I say, more to myself.

"No, I am pretty sure I know who that car belongs to. I am going to have to have words with his dad."

I sigh in relief. Okay, just a dumb teenager.

A week later, as we are leaving another exhausting training session —I'm working with Tessa and Reid, sparring with one of the other guys in a boxing ring that's set up on the far side of the gym—Reid pauses and makes an about-face, and leads us both back inside. I want to demand what is going on, but I've come to read his body language, and I trust him to do what needs to be done and fill me in on everything as soon as it is safe. He sends a quick text, and in seconds, Vaughn and one of his brothers I haven't met yet stride from the back and leave with Reid.

Reid leaves me with a stern, "Stay here." I look around, my fingers drumming on my thighs, feeling untethered.

Lana isn't here. It's technically after business hours, but lots of classes are held in the evenings, though, and some of the guys stop by to use the gym. Between the team that monitors the security feeds and the unconventional hours of many of the staff, there's always someone at Heartwood. Yet I feel alone in the empty waiting room.

I can't sit. I consider going downstairs to hang out with Tessa, but she's probably getting ready to go home. And I don't want to worry Reid if he comes back and finds me gone.

The door opens, and I jump, turning to watch the three men stride inside, expressions pensive.

"—think that motherfucker did it." I catch the middle of their conversation, and my mind whirls.

"Camera damaged and tires slashed," the unknown man says. "Seems pretty damn likely to me. I'll go through our other feeds, maybe tap into the local business and see what I can find."

"Thanks, E. Sorry to make you work so late," Reid says, clapping him on the back.

"It's fine. I'll call Asher in, and we'll sort it out. Take my car." He fishes keys from his pocket and hands them to Reid. "Asher can take me home when we finish here, and I have my bike."

The door to the gym stairs opens, halting the conversation, and Tessa walks out, a bag slung over her shoulders.

She pauses when she sees the men talking in a huddle, then her gaze flicks to me, standing off to the side. Her eyes narrow, but she doesn't say anything about it. I can almost guarantee the next training session will include a plethora of questions.

"Night, guys," she calls over her shoulder, and E turns to watch her retreating form, turning back to the other men only when the door closes behind her.

His eyes fall on Vaughn, who is grinning. "Not a fucking word from you, asshole," he growls before stalking away and heading to the door that leads to the offices.

I slowly walk over to Vaughn and Reid. "What happened?" I tentatively ask, feeling braver now that it's just them.

Reid sighs. There is a shimmer of anger behind his eyes. "Someone slashed the truck's tires, and whoever did it took out the camera facing the truck." I nod, having already pieced that together, but glad that Reid wasn't hiding anything in order to spare me. "Don't worry, Maddox will tow it in the morning, and we have E's car until we get the truck back."

"It was him, wasn't it?" I ask, the guilt bubbling up.

They share a look before Reid answers me. "Yeah, we think so. Maddox is going to do a full inspection to make sure nothing else was done." My stomach twists. What if there is permanent damage that can't be fixed, and Reid has to get a new car? Or maybe Jordan cut the brakes or rigged it to explode. My breath comes in a gasp. This is all my fault.

"Don't worry, Bunny," Reid says, pulling me into a tight hug, grounding me. "I'll keep you safe."

"But this is my fault," I cry.

"No," Vaughn says sharply, cutting in before I can continue. "It is his fault, his choices." I turn my head to look at him, Reid's arms still around me.

"Do you understand?" he asks.

I give a little nod, but Vaughn shakes his head. "Not good enough.

Say the words." I glance up at Reid, who returns my look with a raised brow.

"This is not my fault," I whisper.

"Again. With conviction," Reid demands. I roll my eyes but try again. "This is not my fault."

"Good," Vaughn says, starting to back away. His gaze turns to Reid. "You make sure to fix that," he demands. I am pretty sure I can guess what Vaughn demands to be fixed.

He starts to say something else before his pocket vibrates. He pulls out his phone, and whatever he sees causes his expression to morph into anger, and it feels like the temperature of the room drops 10 degrees. I tighten my hold on Reid. This is not calm, collected, and charming Vaughn.

"Vaughn," Reid prompts.

Vaughn looks up, and I see the full force of his anger. For a moment, it reminds me of Jordan. The way the charming façade falls away. But unlike Jordan, I see no violence swirling in his expression. Rather, his anger is tinged with sadness, concern, and resignation.

"That was my neighbor," he explains. "It seems Jessica left our daughter to take care of the baby. And after an hour of nonstop crying, the neighbor stopped by to see if she could help. I need to go." He stalks out of the building, leaving us alone.

My mind flashes to the picture of the toddler on Vaughn's desk and the story of the cats. "I thought Vaughn's daughter was little," I whisper, looking up at Reid.

His expression is equal parts concern and anger. "She is. She's 4."

I gasp. "Where is her mom?" I demand.

"Come on," Reid replies, leading me to the door. "Let's head home, and I can tell you a little bit of what is going on."

Once we are in the car, a newer model black SUV, I give Reid an expectant look. My own feelings are forgotten in the pursuit of knowing what was going on with Vaughn. "Well, long story short, Vaughn's daughter was a surprise. Jessica was a one-night stand and demanded he make an honest woman of her, and it's been a struggle. He was filing for divorce when she said she was pregnant again. I think she thought it was going to delay things. Their prenup protected Heartwood and his trust. But he let her stay in the house—in a separate room—because the kids are really little and she'd only be able to afford a small apartment." Reid pauses, then continues, "I think he'll be going for full custody now. He's been trying to give her chances,"— he shakes his head—"She isn't a good mom. I don't even think she likes their daughter, but full custody means no child support."

I try to puzzle out the story. "Don't they live together? Why would she be getting support now?"

Reid lets out a humorless laugh. "Yep, live together, technically 50/50 custody. He pays for everything. She still demanded support before she'd sign anything. He could have fought it, but he's trying to keep things civil." There is a long moment of silence before he adds in a low voice, "I don't think things will be civil after this."

We are almost home when I voice my concern. She may be a horrible mom, but his anger worried me. I don't want to be worried about her, but I can't help it. "What will he do when she comes back from wherever she went?"

"Serve her an official eviction notice and blackmail her into leaving," Reid answers without hesitation.

"What?"

"He'll want to avoid a fight in front of the kids. She'll escalate the situation." He gives a sideways glance at me. "I've seen her pick fights out of nothing. It's not pretty." I shiver at that because it reminds me of how Jordan would do that. "So he'll tell her he won't call the cops for child endangerment if she leaves. That, or bribe her."

"But why wouldn't he report that?"

"Oh, he will. He'll use it in the custody case. He's been considering it for a while. Building up a case. I think he hoped to make a happy family for his kids, the kind of home he had."

We arrive home, and I am lost in thought as we go inside. Too many things are tangled up. My anxiety about my own situation. Worry for Vaughn and his kids. I need a way to quiet my mind.

I let Reid pull me down onto his lap, and both of us snuggled on the couch. We watch another cooking competition show. This one is not as absurd as the one with the silly challenges, and my fingers stroke the fur of Ham when she comes to join us.

I am still locked in my head at bedtime. We've fallen into a routine, and I love it. We work together, train a few days a week at the office, and he even arranges security so I can spend time with the girls at the bookstore. If it weren't for the lingering shadow of Jordan, life would be perfect. I still had my moments with triggers, but I am working through those. Even my physical relationship with Reid is progressing. Each night we go to sleep—his bed now, though Reid calls it *our* room—our hands explore, pushing a little more. Our dynamic is developing more and more each day.

In some ways, we are still in the early stages of exploring our sexual relationship. We haven't progressed past oral sex yet, but that isn't necessarily a bad thing. Both of us need a D/s relationship, and that takes trust. Juniper was right when she said that wasn't an aspect I could just turn off, and now that I have it back, it is empowering. Liberating.

But it is more than that. When I feel completely out of control, I can hand over all my fears to Reid and just exist, knowing he is taking care of everything, and I can just be. That relationship I coveted the first time I went to that club is here. It isn't the same, of course, but it's mine. Ours. A dominant partner who also adores me and gives me the space I need to feel secure rather than trapped.

I set the toothbrush down, lost in thought as I watch Reid from the bathroom mirror, both of us preparing for bed. He's been holding back. I know he has. Going slow, for my sake. But I want more. I need more. I look at my reflection; the person staring back at me is a far cry from who I was just two months ago. My eyes are less haunted, and the bags under my eyes are almost gone. I looked healthier. I feel stronger.

Ask for what you want, Sage, I think to myself. I take a deep breath. This catches Reid's attention, and his concerned gaze meets mine in the mirror. Probably worried about my head after another instance where Jordan tried to destroy my sense of safety.

"I'd like to try one of the scenes we talked about." I pause, then add "Sir" for good measure. I wait for him to ask if I am sure, to maybe tell me I am not ready for him. But I need this. I need him to take control of everything, and I am pretty sure he needs this, too.

Instead, his eyes darken. I feel a thrill go through me. "All right, Bunny, did you have a specific one in mind?"

"The one where you blindfold me, Sir."

"Good girl for telling me what you want." I shiver at the praise.

"Finish getting ready, then meet me in our room."

Ten minutes later, I am standing by our bed, bare feet digging into the carpet. He is methodically lining up toys on the dresser. Some meant for pain, others intended for pleasure.

"Come here Bunny, are there any here that are yellow or red?" I look over the spread and hesitate on the cuffs and ropes. "There is no punishment for taking something off the table." He reminds me gently when he spots my hesitation.

"I don't want to be restrained if we use a blindfold, Sir." He presses a kiss to the side of my head before returning the cuffs and ropes to his toy bag.

"Good girl. Thank you for telling me your limits. Is everything else green?" I nod, "Words Bunny."

"Everything else is green, Sir."

"Good, I want you to strip and lie down face up on the bed."

I am shaking with anticipation as I lie down on the thick comforter. I don't wait long before he comes over and places a blindfold over my eyes.

"You will keep your hands by your side unless you need to signa. Do you understand, Baby Girl?"

"Yes, Sir."

"Show me your signal."

I raise my hand up in a fist. "Thank you, Bunny," he murmurs, kissing me.

He starts with slow, gentle touches. Teases that leave me aching for more. His hands roam everywhere but where I want them. My breast and pussy woefully untouched.

"From here on out, all your orgasms are mine." He whispers as his fingers gently brush over my clit, startling me. "You don't get to touch this cunt without permission," I whine in protest.

"But Sir," I start to say.

"If you want to come and I am not here to give you an orgasm, then you will need to ask me." I shudder. Orgasm control. We discussed this, but I thought it would be a while before he claimed them all. Maybe he realized what I was doing in the shower. "And if I catch you playing with this pretty pussy in the shower, I'll have to spank this ass until it is red and hot" Well shit, I guess I wasn't as quiet as I thought I was.

He circles my clit with more pressure. "Yes, Sir," I gasp

Something clicks, and a buzzing fills the room. His fingers are replaced with something vibrating, and my body tenses.

"Remember, no coming without permission, Baby Girl." I can only whimper.

His hands return to their tantalizing game; sometimes, it's his fingers, and sometimes, it's a toy. My body is on edge. I don't know what will happen next. I gasp as his wet mouth envelops my aching breast before switching to the other side.

"Please, Sir!" I cry, "May I come?"

"No," I want to cry at the refusal. My body is tense; I don't know how long I can hold it off.

I am hanging on by a thread when he removes the vibration. I cry out in both relief and disappointment. The disappointment doesn't last long because he takes a long lick of my cunt, bringing me right back to the edge. "Oh, Sir."

I am trembling, trying to hold on. "Please Sir, Please"

"You may come as much as you want, Bunny," he says before returning to my pussy, his tongue lapping at my flesh while his fingers push inside me.

"Oh, god."

I'd been teetering on the edge for so long that I fell over right away, my body bucking as moans spill from my lips. He doesn't let me come down, driving me to another orgasm on the heels of the last one. I lose track of time. I am panting by the time he moves away, but instead of taking my blindfold off, he climbs up my body, "Arms above your head, Baby Girl," he says, pushing my arms up because my brain is struggling to make sense of the instructions, before straddling my chest, his bare legs warm against my sides.

"Green, Bunny?" he asks, his cock centimeters from my mouth.

"So green," I whimper, lifting my head slightly to lick the head. Tasting the salty taste of his precum.

"Ahh ahh, I didn't say you could taste me yet."

"I'm sorry, Sir."

"Maybe I shouldn't reward you with my cock," his tone is musing. I hate how much I love that. How in control he sounds when I am falling apart.

"No, please, I'll be good," I cry.

He chuckles but presses forward, his cock sinking into my mouth. "Tap my thigh three times if you need me to stop, Baby Girl." He uses my mouth, taking his pleasure, chasing his orgasm, and I love it.

He thrusts faster, deeper. Making me gag. Spit drips from my mouth. It is obscene. I feel so helpless under him, but at the same time, I feel powerful, like I can do anything because I make this man lose control.

He thrusts deep, so deep that when he comes, I can do nothing but swallow.

I pant as he takes off the blindfold, and I have to close my eyes as the dim light is still too bright. He gently wipes my face and helps me snuggle under the covers.

"I am going to get you something to drink, and then we can snuggle," He murmurs. When he returns, he pulls me into his body, gently rubbing his hands up and down my body, helping me come back down. I fall asleep as he whispers praises, interspersed with chaste kisses, a stark contrast to how he was just using my body.

CHAPTER TWENTY-FIVE

Sage

I pull a hoodie over my head and tie my long brown hair into a ponytail, giving my appearance a cursory glance in the bathroom mirror.

In another lifetime, I would have done a full face of makeup, layering on the cover-up and foundation to hide any flaws—the dark circles, the fading bruises. Even if it was just a trip to the grocery store. Not that Jordan Beltran or his girlfriend would ever have set foot in a grocery store. No, that was far too common a place for the likes of them. I scoff at the thought.

My old life seems like a hundred years ago. Maybe I'll get some mascara or something simple. I miss the ritual of makeup but don't miss the heavy feeling of it on my skin, the way it felt like I was donning a mask to hide myself from the rest of the world. To hide my true self. But a little would be nice. That wouldn't feel like I am trying to erase who I am with every stroke of the makeup brush.

I give my reflection one last lingering look before bounding down the stairs, my quick footsteps announcing my presence to Reid at the bottom. In my excitement, I miss a step. Quick as a flash, Reid moves, catching me in his arms before I can crash to the floor.

I giggle, partly in relief and partly in surprise that he can—or will—move that fast to catch me. But he doesn't return my happiness. Instead, he scowls as he sets me down.

"I think I'm going to insist on a 'no running down the stairs' rule."

"What?" I exclaim. "Rules! I Don't need rules!"

"Bunny, you took nearly ten years off my life. What if I'm not here the next time you tumble down the stairs because you were running?" he says sternly.

I roll my eyes and give a very exaggerated huff. "Fine," I mumble, scowling back, his stern gaze not frightening me in the least.

I can see that he is fighting a losing battle with a smile, but he quickly schools his expression.

"So, let's review the rules for this trip."

"It's just the grocery store. It'll be fine. We've done it before." That last part is said under my breath.

"Bunny," he says, exasperated. I know he needs the comfort of routine and structure, but I don't feel like making it easy on him.

I give another huff. I am acting like a brat, and part of me doesn't understand where this behavior is coming from. After all, he is keeping me safe from someone I know from experience is resourceful. But another part, a bigger part, is thrilled at the idea of pushing back. I want to see his reaction when he runs out of patience.

"Stay close to me." Long dramatic pause, "At *all* times."

Another roll of my eyes. "I'll stick to you like glue, Captain." I give a mocking salute. "Can we go now?"

"If you see anything at all, you tell me. You don't approach or engage."

"Like I'd be stupid enough to do that." I tug on his hand. "Let's goooo!" I practically whine. "I want ice cream and fruit roll-ups, and oh! Can we get Goldfish?" My eyes are alight with excitement as I list off snacks. We need more junk food in the house.

"Brat," Reid says in a warning voice.

"Oh no, what are you going to do about it, Sir," I sass right back before freezing. That is a different element of our dynamic that we haven't talked about yet. Sure, I call him "Sir" when we play or do scenes together, but that keeps everything tucked away in a neat little box. This pulls the dynamic out of the bedroom. I was the one who set that boundary, and here I am, breaking it.

I blush and mumble an apology, my shoulders scrunching up. I can't meet his gaze. I can't believe I slipped into a bratty headspace so easily. I hadn't even noticed it. Come to think of it, that is probably where the behavior is stemming from—the need to test my Dom. Jordan had hated that element of me, made me squish it down, and told me that no sub of his would behave so childishly. My job was to serve him without question, not to play games.

But when I really think about it, aren't the lines blurred already? Everything Reid does is that of a caregiver. Do I want to label it? Add more to it? Let my bratty side take the reins once in a while and play?

"Bunny," he asks tentatively, watching me closely, but there is no judgment on his face. "Do you want to renegotiate our dynamic?" I pause as I think about his question. Analyzing his tone, the words for any subtext, but the question feels genuine.

"I... maybe? If you want that too, then I guess?" I hedge.

"That's not how this works, Bunny. I need words that it is what you want."

My gaze darts up to him before flashing back down to the floor.

"I..." I look off to the side; that is safer. Maybe if I explain... "He... didn't like that side of me. It's okay if you don't like it either. It's... I don't need it." I trail off, trying to laugh, but it comes out hollow. My eyes are hot, tears threatening to fall, but I won't let them.

Why is this so hard?

His fingers stroke the side of my cheek before sliding to my chin and forcing my gaze up to him. "I take my role as your Dom seriously, and we will need to negotiate our rules and expectations when we have a quiet moment, but I would very much like to expand our play to outside the bedroom if that is what you want as well."

"You would?" I ask, my traitorous heart swelling with hope. A stray tear falls before I hastily wipe it away.

"Very much so," he replies softly.

"You like it when I brat and tease you?" My question is tentative.

He chuckles, pulling me into his arms and tucking my head under his chin. His hands run soothing circles down my back. "Oh yes. It reminds me of when I met you, and you were so prickly."

"I was a bitch." My voice deadpan.

"You were protecting yourself," he corrects, "But I liked your spark then. And I love your fire now."

A warm glow rises from my stomach from his words, and I can feel my mouth stretching into a huge grin. I press my face against his chest, touched and overwhelmed.

"Okay," my voice no more than a breath. I pull back to look up at him and continue in a stronger voice, "Okay, I'd like to expand our play to outside the bedroom. I like playing with you. Besides, you already take care of me like a daddy dom."

He gives me a sheepish look. "I know we agreed that certain D/s elements are for the bedroom only, but the caregiver aspect of being a Dom, well, it can extend to every part of our relationship. I've been working on reining it in, but—"

"You like taking care of me," I finish for him, "I sort of noticed. I thought at first you were just being really nice because of, well, everything from before, but you didn't treat it like a chore."

"Taking care of you is not a chore; it is a privilege," he cuts in, his voice fierce.

"I.. as long as you don't try to control me, you can take care of me."

He drops a kiss on the top of my head. "Come on," he says, taking my hand and leading me outside to the borrowed SUV. "We can talk a little about what we want to change on the way to the store."

I hop out of the SUV, a shy smile gracing my lips as Reid takes my hand. The fine mist clinging to my skin does nothing to dampen my spirits. We've held hands plenty of times before, but something has shifted between us.

Reid has been caring for me in those small, subtle ways. Ensuring I ate, comforting me after nightmares, and patiently guiding me through trauma triggers. Sure, those are things any decent partner would do, but it feels like it means so much more with him.

The clatter of metal echoes as Reid effortlessly maneuvers a shopping cart one-handed, leading us into the brightly lit grocery store. The sudden onslaught of colors and sounds leaves me momentarily disoriented after the gloom of the Pacific Northwest. I am grateful for the grounding presence of Reid's hand in mine.

He steers us towards the produce section, and the aroma of cilantro wafts through the air as we pass a selection of herbs.

"Oh, cherries!" I exclaim, my eyes lighting up at the sight of the ruby-red fruit. Reid immediately guides the cart towards the display, searching for the best bag. My smile falters when I see the price. "No, it's too much, Reid."

"Do you like cherries?" he asks casually.

"Yeah, I like all fruit, but cherries and berries and mangoes are the best," I admit.

He chuckles. "My Bunny has expensive taste," he says, placing the bag in the cart.

"But..." I start, a wave of shame washing over me. I don't want him to think I am taking advantage.

As if sensing my discomfort, Reid reassures me, "Bunny, it's just cherries. I promise it'll be fine."

I nod, unsure how to reconcile the conflicting emotions swirling within me. Part of me revels in his care, while another worries I am using him up.

We continue through the store, methodically navigating each aisle.

Reid is comparing two different pasta sauce brands when I catch a glimpse of someone I desperately hope never to see again. A flicker of movement out of the corner of my eye. I turn for a better look, but it is just a man with the same dark hair as Jordan reaching for something on the top shelf. Confusion clouds my vision. For a split second, I'd been so sure...

Shaking my head to dispel the unsettling thought, I turn back to Reid. "This one is good," I say, pointing. "I like the one with basil." He smiles, places my choice in the cart, and we continue down the aisles.

Twice more, I think I see him out of the corner of my eye, only to find it is nothing. A cardboard cutout, then just another stranger. I can't shake the growing feeling of being watched. Worry gnaws at me. Am I losing my mind? The happy feelings from earlier are slipping away, replaced by an increasing sense of vulnerability and dread. I inch closer and closer to Reid.

And then I see him. A profile, turning a corner that could only belong to Jordan.

"Bunny?" Reid asks, his brows drawn down in confusion as my body freezes and my breaths come out in pants. I fight down the panic.

"That was him," I breathe.

"What?" he starts, but I am done talking. I walk in the direction the man had gone.

"Sage!" Reid's voice is a sharp command, but I am not listening. I am compelled forward. I need to know for sure. Breaking into a run, my footsteps echo on the linoleum floor as I burst into the next aisle, frantically searching. But he is gone.

"Sage." The steel in Reid's voice halts my search. I look back at him, almost flinching at his expression.

"What is the rule?" he asks, his voice flat and dangerously calm.

"Don't run off," I mumble.

"Don't run into danger!" His eyes flash, and his jaw clenches.

"But he was here." I pause, feeling my face flush, a sinking feeling growing in my stomach. "I... I thought it was him. It... I know what he looks like and... and I was..." But did I? I've been wrong multiple times already. Was this just paranoia? PTSD? I worry my lip, wondering what Reid must think of me now. Would he still want me if I am seeing things?

But Reid isn't treating me like I am crazy. He is pulling out his phone, typing furiously, his jaw still tight. He pulls me close, and for a moment, I am surprised. But the frantic beating of his heart against me betrays his fear. Beneath that calm facade, I have scared him. I sink into the comfort he offers. Guilt threatens to come up in the form of tears, and I have to fight them back.

"Rhett will pull the tapes from here right now, since he is already in the office. He will go over every angle. Rhett will find him if he is here," Reid says, pocketing his phone. He scans our surroundings before taking my hand and leading me back to our abandoned cart.

"You... believe me?" I ask hesitantly. He takes my hand and places it on the side of the cart. His look makes it clear that he wants me to hold it. I feel like a disobedient child being punished.

He pushes the cart, but his gaze isn't on the shelves. He is in protector mode, his eyes scanning our surroundings.

"Of course," he says smoothly, not looking down at my stunned face.

"And you can get the camera footage just like that?" I ask, keeping pace as he steers us towards the checkout. Luckily, there isn't a line, and I hurriedly help him place our items on the conveyor belt.

"Considering we handle security for most of the town," he gives me a smirk, "yeah, just like that."

The beep of the scanner seems distant as I consider the situation. "And what if I was wrong? What if I'm just seeing things?"

He turns back to me, reassuringly squeezing my hand before resuming his scan of our surroundings. "To be honest," he starts, a slight wince on his face, "I do hope you are wrong." The look he gives me is apologetic. "It's normal to think you might see someone that hurt you. Your brain is hypervigilant right now, and that's to protect you. But until we have proof that he wasn't here, we treat the situation with the gravity it deserves."

He pays for the groceries, thanks the cashier, and we leave the store.

The damp drizzle outside raises goosebumps on my skin. Fitting that the weather should mirror my mood. I hold on to the side of the cart like a child as we walk to the car. The hairs on my neck prickle, and I glance back at the store. The tinted windows reflect only a distorted image of the parking lot, but I can't shake the eerie feeling of being watched.

"I'm sorry," I say, helping Reid load the groceries.

"For what?" he asks, startled by the sudden apology.

"For ruining the shopping trip with my paranoia."

"No, none of that. Your gut was telling you something, and it's best to listen to it. Just because I hope you were wrong doesn't mean I'm discounting what you said. I just don't want him to be close to you." He opens my door and helps me in, then gives me a stern look. "What you should be sorry for is ignoring protocol and running after him. We'll work on that." He closes my door and rounds the hood.

"My job is to protect you. Your job is to let me."

A yucky feeling starts to grow in my stomach. Guilt, maybe. I lower my head. "I'm sorry, it's just... I kept seeing something out of the corner of my eye. It was like he was toying with me, and I was getting frustrated."

His brows furrow. "Why didn't you say something the first time?"

"When I turned, it was always something normal. Another person, a cutout." I shake my head. "I don't know."

"We'll sort this out. I promise. In the meantime, breaking the rules has earned you a punishment."

"What kind?" I ask hesitantly.

"I haven't decided yet. I could edge you for hours and not let you come. Maybe have you write 'I will not run into danger' 100 times." He glances sideways at me; I am shaking my head. That all sounds terrible. "I could spank your ass." I freeze, feeling a warmth spread through my body. I don't hate the idea. He chuckles at whatever he sees on my face. "We'll sort out your punishment later tonight before bed."

Reid gets a text while we are putting away the groceries at home.

"Do you feel up to a meeting with Vaughn and Rhett, or do you need time to relax? I can summerize everything for you." I take a moment to assess where my head is at; the lingering panic is humming under my skin. I don't think I can stand to see Jordan in the footage. But I also can't stand the idea of being wrong.

"I.. uh… do you promise to tell me everything later?" I ask.

"I will," he says with a decisive nod. "You watch some TV and try to relax. It shouldn't be too long."

Time slows to a crawl as I wait for Reid to come out of his office and tell me something.

We've been back from the grocery store for an hour already, and there is no word yet whether I have been seeing things or if Jordan really was that close. Maybe it is a bad idea to let Reid handle it all, because I am left to wrestle with my own spiraling anxiety.

I stare at the TV, my eyes not registering the images on the screen. The sound, playing at a low volume, might as well be muted for all the attention I pay it.

Every few seconds, my eyes dart from the screen to the closed door of Reid's office. I can't hear anything from him in there, but I know he is busy. I shouldn't interrupt him. I am fine. The meeting is important.

I was fine when he left me. The balm of him believing me soothed a jagged edge I didn't even know I had. So I curled up on the couch and turned on a random movie to distract myself from everything, but my mind can't settle. My thoughts spin and tumble, each one more distressing than the last.

I should be part of the conversation, right?

On the one hand, I want to have a bigger part in keeping myself safe. On the other hand, I am just so tired. My emotions are ragged and frayed. Reid's absence has stripped away all calm reprieve. The longer I sit by myself, the more fragile I feel.

I can't help them. What could I offer, anyway? I lack the resources, the experience, the strength to contribute.

The scene on the TV flickers and shifts to something dark and ominous. Even without paying attention, I know I need to change it. Darkness is unbearable, a suffocating weight. Even light feels oppressive, a harsh reminder of my vulnerability.

I turn the TV off, and the following silence is somehow worse. It pulses with a suffocating, heavy presence. How can silence feel so loud? I stand abruptly, pace a few steps, then retreat back to the couch. My hand hovers near the remote before curling into a fist and dropping to my side.

I stand again and move to the office door before pausing. I growl softly under my breath and run my hands through my hair, tangling my fingers in the messy strands. Frustrated, I let my arms drop and begin pacing the room.

What to do?

I need to know, but I don't want to know. Don't want to see him on the security feed. I don't want confirmation that he was there. And if he isn't there? If I am just losing my mind, would that be worse?

But not knowing? That is eating away at my insides. My stomach twists in knots, doing somersaults and backflips, and for the first time, I am grateful we hadn't eaten lunch yet; I would have surely thrown it all up.

My mind is spiraling. I can feel it. Distantly. I can recognize what is happening, but it is like my thoughts are falling through my fingers and are just so far out of reach. I might as well be a fly on the wall of my mind.

This is so like Jordan. The mind games. So subtle, so insidious. Tiny petty acts, seemingly insignificant on their own, but cumulatively devastating. He'd eroded my sense of reality, made me doubt my sanity, and then gaslighted me and blamed me for the chaos he created.

Was Jordan really following us around the store? That can't be possible. He didn't know I was staying with Reid, right? The tracker would have led him to the garage across town. Nothing to lead him to

Reid's house.

And for him to be at the store when I was there with Reid? At the same time? Coincidence?

No. I know better. Know Jordan better.

He is the sort to play with his food. He'd have no qualms about following me around a store and staying just out of sight. Make me think I was losing my mind. It is one of his many favorite games to play with me. Memories flood back of all the little ways he would toy with my mind. Random things going missing. My food tasting off, by just a little bit. Sounds he'd deny hearing. Telling me things and then insisting we'd never talked about it. Putting me in no-win situations so he'd have a reason to punish me.

This just screams Jordan.

But... but maybe I am just paranoid. Perhaps it is nothing. That would be better, right? Better to be losing my mind than to be on his radar.

But if it is nothing, I am wasting resources and everyone's time. I am not worth all this. I am not worth the trouble.

Back and forth, I pace; the sounds of my footsteps do nothing to ground me. My hands twist together, the thought circling endlessly in my head: Not worth it. A waste of time.

"Bunny?" a voice calls, but it is so far away, like it is coming through water. I keep pacing back and forth and back and forth, my eyes not seeing the room.

Not worth it. Not worth it. The words stick on repeat.

I come to an abrupt halt when I collide with a solid chest, hands reaching out to wrap me in warm arms before I lose my balance. "Sage," the voice calls again. It is right there, and yet it is still so far away.

I don't pull away from the person holding me. The arms are familiar. Safe. I recognize the scent but can't remember the name of it. Just that it is home. And he is swaying with me and rubbing my back. Saying something. But what? His words make no sense to me, but the tone is so calming. I cling to him, a buoy in the middle of a turbulent ocean.

Gradually, the storm in my mind recedes. A soft meow is the first thing my mind registers, and the feel of a small, warm ball of fluff rubbing itself on my legs. Reid is still holding me, his arms solid and tight, better than any weighted blanket, anchoring me.

"It's okay, Bunny," Reid is saying, his voice a steady anchor. "I have you. I will keep you safe."

"I'm sorry," I croak, my voice thin and reedy.

"Shh," he hums, tucking my head under his chin. "Nothing to be sorry for. I shouldn't have left you alone for so long after everything."

"But," my voice cracks with a sob. "I should be stronger than this. I shouldn't be falling apart at just the idea of him." I spit the word out in disgust; the venom, though, is meant for me. "I'm so weak."

"No, Bunny, you are processing trauma in a less-than-ideal situation."

"But I freaked out over nothing." I sniff, acutely aware of the damp spot I had created on his shirt. "I've wasted everyone's time. We didn't even finish shopping, and I ran off and..."

I trail off when I notice how tight his jaw is.

"Are you mad at me?" I ask tentatively, my voice sinking into a whisper as my body tenses, and I duck my head as if to make myself smaller.

"Oh, no, Bunny." His face softens, and he pulls me closer. "I just... I don't know how to tell you this without making you panic."

I feel my stomach plummet. In a way, being right about Jordan toying with me is so much worse than being wrong.

"He was really there, wasn't he?" I ask, bracing myself for the blow.

After a pause, Reid lets out a breath of air before nodding. "Yeah, Bunny, he was following us." He swallows his expression, a mask of barely restrained anger. "I am so sorry, baby. I'm sorry I let him get that close to you."

My spiraling thoughts come to a sudden halt. Now that my panic is gone, I can see Reid is the one who needs comfort. He is blaming himself. The anger he carries isn't directed at me—it is at himself. I know that feeling all too well.

"You can't blame yourself," I say, tightening my hold on him. "He's incredibly smart. That's what makes him dangerous. Now that we know he knows where I am, we'll be more prepared."

Reid chuckles. "I'm pretty sure that is my line." He gestures to the couch. "Come on, we can watch a movie and relax."

I gladly take the reprieve, but try as I might, I can't focus on the movie. The panicked feeling is gone, but I still have a heavy pit in my stomach. My muscles are tense, and I keep darting glances at Reid, just waiting. We talked about punishments within the dynamic, and from my perspective, I did something that deserves a punishment, but this waiting will drive me crazy.

"Are you okay, Bunny?" Reid asks, his face full of concern.

Be brave, Sage. "Are you... are you going to punish me, Sir?" I ask, sitting on my hands so I don't fidget with them. "I... I didn't listen in the store, and that's a safety rule, right?"

Reid studies me carefully. "I am not sure a punishment right now is a good idea so soon after a panic attack."

"Does that mean no punishment?" I ask, and the bolt of disappointment surprises me. I don't like the idea of being let off the hook. That feels wrong.

"No, we will save it for later when you are in a better headspace."

I shake my head. "I don't think it would be good to wait. I'll keep thinking about it, and I..." I pause, taking a deep breath. "I need to get the bad feelings out."

He studies my face and I hope he can see how much I need this. I need to wipe the slate clean. It needs to be now, not later.

"Okay Bunny, upstairs to the guest room, clothes off." I pause and give him a quizzical look. "Our room will never be used for punishment. Any pain we play with in there is strictly for fun. It will always be a safe place."

Nodding, I bolt upstairs, knowing he is right behind me. I strip my clothes, folding them carefully and placing them on the dresser. Already slipping into a submissive headspace, and the need to please is taking hold.

Reid enters the room and sits on the bed, a paddle in his hand.

Oh, this is going to hurt. "Over my lap, Bunny," his voice calm yet stern. I hastily comply, acutely aware of how vulnerable I feel that I am naked and he is fully dressed. The texture of his pants just reinforces that difference.

He rubs my bare butt with the flat of the paddle before letting it rest there. "What is your safeword, Bunny?" he asks.

"It's red, Sir."

"Good girl. It will be 10 with the paddle. There will not be a warmup and then I will have you write lines. Do you know why you are being punished, Bunny?"

"Because I didn't stay with you in the store."

"Yes, I can't keep you safe if you run off, and you certainly do not run head first into danger."

"Yes, Sir, I'm sorry, Sir."

He rubs my butt again, and then the paddle is gone, and I tense for the first strike. The paddle whistles through the air, and the loud thwack of it hitting my flesh fills the room. For a moment, I don't register anything but the sound, but the pain follows swiftly, and I scarcely settle into the pain when another strike comes.

I cry out with this one and struggle to stay still, to not cover my ass with my hands or kick my feet. No, I need to purge this feeling. Once the punishment is done, I will have nothing to feel guilty about.

The blows keep coming, and my ass is on fire, tears streaming down my face. I don't even register that he has stopped and twisted me around to snuggle me in his arms, running his hands down my back.

The tears are cathartic.

"You took that so well," he whispers. We stay like that for a while before he leads me downstairs, still naked, to the rarely used dining room where he sets a paper and pencil down. I flinch as my hot bottom touches the chair, but I grit through it.

"100 times, 'I will not put myself in danger,'" I nod. My hand hurts when I am done, but the pit in my stomach is gone. Reid dresses me in one of his t-shirts and a soft pair of pj bottoms before pulling me onto his lap on the couch.

I tuck my head under his and relax, finally able to actually pay attention to the movie.

CHAPTER TWENTY-SIX

Reid

I stare at Blake's latest report. Between him and Rhett, all we know for sure is that Jordan is in Deliverance, but so far, nothing else. Two weeks and no sightings. No leads on him or his car. No idea how he knew we were in the grocery store that day. Watching the footage was heartbreaking. How could I not have noticed Sage's growing agitation as he toyed with her? It's plain as day on the monitors.

Since then, we've returned to ordering groceries and limiting trips to places I can control. However, I don't know how long we can continue this without Sage breaking down. She deserves to live a life without jumping at every shadow or wondering if he is in the background. She should be able to make plans to see her friends without a whole security detail needing to be part of the equation.

With Jordan somehow getting so close, my own paranoia has ratcheted up. I made a special order with Rhett, and a few days later, he sent me a pretty necklace with a tracker embedded inside. I would have been no better than Jordan had I just given it to her with no explanation.

Instead, I prefaced the gift with a monologue, justifying my reasons, promising she could take it off when the threat was gone, praying the entire time that she'd agree it was a necessary precaution. In the end, the monologue was unnecessary. She'd readily agreed. Admitting the idea actually made her feel safer.

I lean back in my chair, the spreadsheet in front of me blurring, and

I run my hands through my hair, tipping my head back to stare at the ceiling. I should call it quits for today. Maybe see what Sage is up to. Just the thought of her curled up on the couch with Ham snuggled into her lap, perhaps reading a book, helps unravel the knot in my chest. Maybe we can put on a movie. Something light.

Even with Jordan trying to terrorize her, she's blossomed so much from that terrified woman I met on the side of the road. Proving every day just how brave and resilient she is. She laughs easily, teases me without fearing my anger, and unapologetically asks for what she wants. Her trust in me is an absolute gift.

My phone beeps with a notification, and I tilt my head to the side to glare at it. Then, another notification on the heels of the last one. I sigh and try to muster up the energy to see what it is now. Probably Vaughn letting me know we picked up more contracts and expecting me to sort out who goes where. I can't wait until I can go back into the field.

That thought draws me up short. The field might mean jobs far away. Days, weeks, even months of travel. I shake my head; no, I'll have to talk to Vaughn, but when I do go back, local jobs only. The idea of leaving Sage for an extended period leaves a bad taste in my mouth.

Local jobs don't come with a large bonus, but my savings are solid and expenses manageable. My priorities have shifted and solidified into a single, unwavering point: her. I can't help imagining our future. Marriage someday. Perhaps kids if she wants them, too.

We just need to remove this threat against her.

My phone pings again. I grab it, only for it to ring in my hand. Blake's name flashes on the caller ID, and I quickly answer it, a jolt of adrenaline sharpening my senses.

"Blake."

"Nice of you to respond. I have a lock on Beltran's location." Blake's voice is flat, devoid of inflection as always, but the words hit me like a punch.

"Well?" I demand, my knuckles white as I grip the phone.

The silence that comes from the phone makes my stomach drop. Blake isn't one for softening the blow on anything, but this pause feels loaded.

"I sent a link for a video call." Click.

"Fucken Blake," I mutter, slamming the phone down harder than intended. I turn to my computer, hands flying across the keyboard to join the video conference. The screen flickers to life, and the faces of Blake, Vaughn, and Rhett snap into view. Their presence, expressions grim, does not bode well for me. For Sage.

The next hour is a descent into a carefully controlled rage I haven't felt in years. Blake, true to form, lays out the facts with clinical detachment. Rhett chimes in with corroborating evidence—pings from burner phones, low-level Wi-Fi captures, grainy security footage from a neighbor's Ring camera showing a shadowy figure. It all points to one horrifying conclusion.

"He's in your neighborhood, Reid," Vaughn says, his voice carefully neutral, but I can see the concern in his eyes. "An empty house, one street over from you. That ugly one that's been on the market for a year."

One street over. The words echo in my head, each one a hammer blow. He's been that close. Watching? Waiting? The thought of my Sage laughing in the kitchen or reading on the porch swing, unaware of the predator lurking practically on our doorstep, makes bile rise in my throat. My hands clench into fists under the desk.

"How long has he been there?" My voice is dangerously low.

"We think he's been camping out for a month. Possible longer," Blake states. "The place is supposed to be empty, ready to sell. But they have it listed at that ridiculous asking price that no one even bothers to tour it anymore. Easy enough to slip in, especially for someone with his resources."

"When did you figure this out?" My question is a trap, and Vaughn knows it.

Vaughn meets my gaze unflinchingly. "Blake brought it to me late yesterday. I wanted to verify before bringing it to you. This is too personal. I didn't want to risk you charging over there half-cocked before we had a solid plan."

Fucken Vaughn. He should know me better than that. The patronizing logic of it, the implication that I can't control myself when it comes to Sage, grates on every nerve.

I would never endanger her.

"So, he's been practically in my backyard for a month now, and no one thought to at least warn me? How the hell did we miss this?"

"Blake discreetly set up surveillance," Rhett interjects, trying to smooth things over. "We have eyes on him and he hasn't left the property."

"And the plan?" I bite out, the word tasting like ash. "What's the goddamn plan, Vaughn? And don't even think of the possibility of keeping me on the sidelines."

Vaughn outlines it, his voice calm, measured. Confirm his location. Serve Jordan with the Order of Protection we've had drafted and ready, the one that's been sitting waiting until he could be located. Vaughn would do that part by acting in an official capacity as a process server.

"And then what?" I demand. "We serve him a piece of paper and just hope he fucking goes away? This is Jordan Beltran we're talking about! A protection order is toilet paper to a man like him! He needs to be arrested for stalking."

Vaughn had to talk me down twice from confronting the motherfucker myself during that call. He reminded me of protocol, of the legalities, of the risk of escalation if we go in too hard, too fast, without irrefutable proof of current wrongdoing beyond trespassing in an empty house. He spoke of optics, of not wanting to give his father, Senator Beltran, an excuse to bring his political weight down on us, on Sage. Not to mention the favors Jordan has amassed. He has friends in high places.

I don't give a fuck about politics.

But he's right, damn him. On some level, I know he's right. Every protective instinct in my body screams at me to eliminate the threat, to drag Jordan out of that house and make sure he can never get near Sage again.

Fucken Vaughn, making Blake sit on the information for a day. How the hell am I supposed to protect Sage if the danger is practically breathing down our necks?

I finally end the video conference, the anger leaving me seething, an icy knot of dread tightening in my chest.

I debate what to tell Sage. Every fiber of my being wants to shield her, to keep this fresh horror from touching the fragile peace she's found. She asked me to always be honest so that she can protect herself. Considering how upset I am over Vaughn keeping me in the dark, even for a day, I can't do that to her. She needs to know. She has a right to know.

We have the bones of a plan. Confirm he is there and serve him with the order of protection. And what? Hope he goes away? Our plan is shit. It feels reactive, not proactive. Insufficient. A piece of paper will not deter Jordan. He's playing a different game, a long game, and this feels like another move on his twisted chessboard.

I let out a deep breath, trying to quail the fury simmering below the surface. I needed to talk to Sage before Vaughn and I finalize the plan. We have another call scheduled for later. For 'when I've cooled down a bit.'

I need to be calm when I tell her. I must present this to her in a way that empowers her, not terrifies her. Another deep breath.

Fuck. Here goes nothing.

CHAPTER TWENTY-SEVEN

Sage

I look up from my book as Reid comes out of his office, his face drawn and his shoulders tense. The smile falls from my face. He looks upset. Instinctively, I glance at his hands and brows, searching for any sign that his distress masks anger directed at me.

I know it is silly; Reid has done nothing to harm me, but all the habits I'd learned from years with Jordan will take more than a few months with Reid to break. Countless times Jordan would come out of his office with a mild expression, only to fly into a rage moments later and take it out on me. I'd learned to look for the smallest signs, ready to make myself invisible or stay out of his way when he was in any mood.

Deep breath, I whisper to myself. It's just Reid. You can trust him.

"Is everything okay?" I ask tentatively. I must not have managed as neutral an expression as I'd hoped because he winces, quickly offering me a reassuring smile.

"Yeah," he replies before sighing and changing his mind. "No. I just got out of a meeting with Vaughn, Blake, and Rhett. We have a new lead on where Jordan might be hiding."

"That's good, right?" I ask, squinting at him in confusion. The sooner they find him, the sooner they can make him go away. I know the plan is to serve him with a restraining order first—for all the good that would do, I think with an internal scoff. But to do that, they need to know where he is.

Reid rubs the back of his neck, looking torn. Is he planning on lying to me? I feel myself brace for a half-truth.

"Blake thinks he's been hiding out in a vacant house in this neighborhood."

I feel my blood run cold, my heart speeding up. "That... that close?" I whisper.

Reid quickly closes the distance between us, sitting on the couch beside me and drawing me into the warmth of his embrace. I try to take comfort in his arms, but inside, I feel so cold.

"Shh, it'll be okay," he whispers, running his hands gently over my arms. I belatedly notice that I am shaking. "I was worried about telling you this, but I didn't want to lie—not about your safety."

"No," I say, shaking my head, my voice weak. "No... I... I need you to be honest with me. I need to know these things even if... even if it feels so... so violating," I finish, my voice growing louder. "He... just... I didn't think he'd be so close to home, you know?"

"I know, babe. You tell me when you're ready to hear more."

"Just... give me a minute."

He nods, sitting quietly with me while I process.

My mind races through all the places Jordan might be. I haven't been living with Reid long enough to know the neighborhood well. I didn't know anyone here, so it's not like I'd know which houses are empty. Maybe if we'd been able to take walks, I would've noticed something. No, I give myself an internal shake. They'd kept my movements limited to a few select areas. Walking around without more security wouldn't have been safe, anyway. I take a deep breath, calming myself. Jordan doesn't get to disrupt the peace I have found here.

"Okay, what's the plan?" I ask when I feel steadier, pulling away from Reid just enough to sit up and face him directly.

"We have surveillance on the house, and Vaughn and I are going to check out the address tonight."

"Okay." I nod, my brow furrowing. "Is someone coming here to stay with me, or..." I trail off, uncertain.

"I think it would be better if you were somewhere a little farther away."

"Maybe I could go to Juniper's house? She was asking when we could have our next girls' night."

"That could work."

A quick exchange of texts with Juniper, and in less than 10 minutes, she has a girls' night planned.

"So," I say with a smile, though it feels a little forced, "Juniper says to meet her and the girls at the bookstore at six. And to bring snacks," I add, snickering.

"It would be nice to make some cookies to bring," I muse out loud as I think about what snack I could bring to girls' night. "Or brownies."

"Oooh, brownies," Reid's eyes light up. "I love brownies. You can make either. Or both. I'm pretty sure we already have everything you need." The way he says we never fails to make me melt.

"Yeah? You think?" I ask, the undercurrent of excitement already bubbling up as I run through which recipes to make.

"Sure, I can even help if you'll let me. I just have to finish planning things with Vaughn first."

"You can help if you really want to."

"Perfect, then it's a date. You get started, and I promise as soon as I am done with Vaughn, I'll come and help. He and I need to have a chat." The last part is said with an edge, and I am glad I won't be around for that conversation.

I give him a quick kiss before turning to bound off to the kitchen, but Reid grabs my arm and spins me back, cupping my face in one hand and pulling me close to him with his other, giving me a searing kiss before letting go. I am a little breathless as Reid smirks at me. "Now you can go," he says before heading to his office.

I am almost done with the brownies by the time Reid joins me. I spy him watching me from the hall, leaning against the wall and a smile on his face.

"You said you'd help me make brownies," I admonish from the kitchen, a wooden spoon dripping with chocolate batter held aloft in one hand. "Are you breaking your promise?" I ask, a mock seriousness in my tone.

Reid laughs, walking into the kitchen, and I feel the weight of the last hour slide off my shoulders. Upbeat music plays softly from my phone. My hair is up in a messy bun, a flour-dusted apron over my clothes, my face free of makeup and smudged with a bit of flour. I glance at the pan of brownies and the two plates of cookies on the counter.

"Looks like you accomplished your goal without me, Bunny," Reid says, snatching a cookie and taking a bite.

I give him a fake scowl, my hands on my hips. "Hey! Those are not for you."

"No?" He raises an eyebrow, chewing thoughtfully. "They taste like they're made for me," he teases, reaching for another.

I dart around the counter, blocking him, my arms crossed in an X and the spoon still coated in chocolate batter, held high in one hand. "Nope, you have to make some with me if you want some." I stick my tongue out and hand him the spoon. "You can mix the dry ingredients."

He leans in and gives me a quick kiss on the nose before heading to the bowl I'd set out. As he gently mixes the ingredients, he watches me measure the wet ingredients, humming under my breath and dancing around the kitchen, darting from one thing to another.

Reid, when he cooked, was methodical—he gathered everything at once, kept it within arm's reach, and cleaned as he went. I am like a little tornado. Used dishes pile up in the sink, ingredients scattered across the counters.

Catching him watching me, I blush. "What?" I ask bashfully, looking away.

"Nothing," he replies, smiling. "Just... I like that you're happy."

"Oh, well, I like baking." I smile, though it falters as my shoulders slump slightly. "He never let me bake. Said I didn't need the carbs," I mutter darkly, mentioning my ex casting a brief shadow over the light moment.

"Good thing he has no say in your life now," Reid says, giving me a reassuring smile. "You bake whatever you want. Just add whatever we need to the grocery list, and we'll get it next time."

I beam at him, then give him a gentle hip check, nudging him away from the bowl.

"Hey, I wasn't done," he laughs, but he steps back, leaning against the counter and watching as I mix the bowls together, pour the batter into a floured pan, and slide it into the oven. I grab my phone and set a timer. "There. Timer set."

"That didn't look like cookies to me," he grumbles.

"Nope," I reply, popping the "p" for emphasis. "You get brownies. The cookies are for girls' night."

"Did you have any more baking to do?" he asks, eyeing the flour-strewn kitchen.

"No, I should..." I trail off, looking around as if seeing the kitchen's chaotic state for the first time. My shoulders slump. "Oh god, I'm so sorry, Reid. I promise I'll clean it up."

The carefree feeling vanishes, replaced by a strong wave of panic. I wring my hands, my gaze darting around frantically.

Reid's relaxed posture shifts to concern as I spiral. He keeps his tone calm and matter-of-fact as he steps forward. "Let's put away all the ingredients and clear off the counters," he suggests.

"What?" I freeze, my gaze unfocused as it flits around the kitchen.

He grabs the eggs and butter I'd left out and turns to the fridge. He crouches to place them on the shelf and speaks with his back to me. "Do you want to use Ziploc bags or clips for the flour and sugar?" He glances over his shoulder at me. "My mom always used clips, but Aunt Tina likes to use Ziploc bags. You're the baker of the house, so you tell me. I've got both."

"Um... Ziploc bags," I murmur, my voice uncertain. What is going on?

He smiles. "They're in that drawer," he gestures, rising to his feet and keeping his tone casual as he continues to clean up. Slowly, I start moving again, joining him in putting things away, my earlier panic fading like it had never happened.

After clearing the counters and sweeping the floor, only the dishes remain. "I wash, you dry?" he asks, already filling the sink with soapy water.

"Yeah, I can dry," I reply, "I'm sorr.."

"Nope," he says, cutting me off, "Sometimes random shit will trigger you when you least expect it and you do not owe anyone an apology because of it." He doesn't give me a chance to reply before changing the subject to girls' night, asking me mundane questions and teasing me about my plan to leave the bookstore with a dozen new romances.

Halfway through the dishes, without looking up, I whisper, "Thank you."

He glances down at me, catching the slight blush on my face, and smiles. I know he understands exactly what I am thanking him for.

Just as we finish the last dish, the timer goes off.

"Brownies are ready!" I announce with a grin.

Reid moans as he takes a bite of the chocolaty goodness. I can't hide the pleased smile at his evident enjoyment. We may have made them together, but it was my recipe.

"Absolute perfection, Bunny," he says before grabbing another.

"Yeah?"

"You could probably rival Dezzie. Hell, give her one of these, and I bet she'll want to hire you on the spot."

I flush at the thought. I know he is probably just exaggerating, but that he is singing my praises feels really good. Jordan had always found something to criticize me for. Didn't matter if the dish I made was technically perfect. He'd find some flaw, real or imagined. Thinking back on it, even before his mask fell, he would find subtle ways to critique me, all under the guise of 'helping' me.

Reid builds me up. He makes me feel good about myself and reminds me I am strong and capable, just as I am.

I take a bite of my brownie and moan my own sounds of satisfaction as the still-warm chocolate taste fills my senses. Reid grabs a third piece, and I hide my mouth behind my hand as I fail to suppress a chuckle. At this rate, he might just eat the whole pan. Not that I can blame him. It was the perfect balance of chocolate, and the texture was perfect.

I finish my brownie and wipe off my hands. "You have something right here." I look up, and he brushes his thumb over the side of my lip. The gesture is so soft, and my breath catches as his thumb lingers. The mood in the room shifts.

His lips replace his thumb in a bruising kiss, a frantic edge to the need that hadn't been there a moment before but now burned, urging me to meet his aggression with eager kisses of my own. My fingers thread through his hair, the short, silky strands weaving through my fingers.

His tongue slides along the seam of my lips, asking, no demanding entry, and the slight sting of his hands in my hair made me gasp. He takes immediate advantage of it, his tongue diving in, stroking along my own. I can taste the chocolate of the brownie and something that is uniquely Reid. A flavor I don't think I will ever get enough of.

His hands run down my sides until they come to rest on my thighs. Another gasp as he lifts me and sets me on the counter. He pulls away from the kiss just long enough to slide my shirt up over my head, tossing it across the room before retaking my mouth. His hands move over my skin, his fingers kneading my flesh before trailing up my back to unclasp my bra. That article joining the shirt in some distant part of the room.

He cups my bared breasts, squeezing and kneading before pinching my nipples, eliciting another gasp at the sudden sharp pain that instantly warms into pleasure. I feel him smirk. My own hands find their way under his shirt. It isn't enough. The shirt is in the way. I tug, making it clear what I want, and sighing when the offending fabric is gone and I can freely run my hands over his skin.

His fingers continue to dance over my skin, alternating between sensual strokes and little bites of pain. The kind of pain I am starting to crave.

"Sir," I gasp, "Sir, please! I need... I need," but I can't form the words I need.

"Hmm?" he murmurs as his trails kisses down my neck and, finding a particularly sensitive spot, stops to suck gently.

"Sir!" I cry on a gasp, my eyes practically rolling back in my head. God, that feels good. Too soon, he pulls away, and I can't help the sound of disappointment that only causes him to chuckle. The sadist. He likes to do this, leaving me on the edge. Make me beg. Find all the little places that give me pleasure and pull away before I've had enough.

But then his hot mouth envelops my nipple, and I forget all about the sensitive spot on my neck in favor of the way his tongue swirls around the tight nub.

More. I need more.

I wrap my arms around his head, holding him close to my chest, my heart beating so hard it's a wonder he can't hear it. My cunt throbs in time to my heart, the empty feeling so hard to ignore right now. I can't stop the desperate way my hips cant trying to rub my pussy against him.

"Does my greedy girl want more" he whispers as he pulls away from one breast and moves to the other. I can only let out a whine as he sucks on the other nipple, and his fingers pinch and tweak the other.

"Please Reid, I want you to fuck me."

His teeth nip my nipple sharply in a warning.

"I'm sorry Sir," I gasp, "Please, I need you."

He pulls away from my breast, his lust-filled gaze meeting my eyes, and whatever he was looking for, he must have found because he grips me under my thighs and lifts me with ease. I don't worry about how he navigates the house as I press desperate kisses up his chest and neck. My tongue glides over his skin before nipping. That earns me a swat to my ass, and I giggle because that is not a deterrent, so I nip again.

"Behave, or you won't get what you want," he growls.

I can't help the pout that forms on my face or the spark of defiance giving me wicked ideas and whispering that maybe I don't want to be a good girl. I nip again, this time a little harder.

"Oh Bunny, you'll regret that," his voice full of dark promise.

"Promises, promises," I sing song, a little surprised at the wild, playful energy thrumming through me.

He slides me down his body, keeping the movement extra slow to tease me. I can feel his straining cock through his pants, and the need that shoots through me makes my knees weak. He steps back, and I whine at the sudden loss of contact. But he just takes another step back. "Ah ah ah, Bunny. Naughty girls don't get rewards." His tone teased before taking on a dark edge. "Now strip for me."

I shiver at the command but deftly unbutton my jeans and shimmy them down my legs, adding my underwear to the small pile of clothes at my feet. I stand naked in the living room. The only thing on my body is the necklace he'd given me with the tracker. The one I promised never to take off.

He is still wearing his pants, much to my disappointment. Still, the impressive bulge causes me to lick my lips in anticipation as I admire his toned body. He circles me, causing the anticipation to rise. I keep my hands at my sides, fighting the urge to cover myself. With him admiring my ass, I gave it a little wiggle, the playful energy still in charge. I am rewarded with another series of sharp slaps, the burn that comes with warming my skin only adding to the growing fire.

"Are you going to be my good girl?" he asks. "Or..."

I don't let him finish the sentence, turning to face him and putting a finger to my face in a mock thinking face. "I don't know if I want to," I say in a sassy voice.

"Someone really wants a punishment." He growls, but the hint of a smile on his lips tells me he is enjoying this as much as I am. I just laugh before turning to dart away. Before I can get even two steps, his arm bands around my waist, hauling me to his body, and he carries me over to the couch. He tips me over his thighs, so I have to put my hands on the ground.

"Such a pretty little ass. Too bad it's going to be so sore. What is your safe word, Bunny?" he asks.

The words I'm in danger flit through my mind, and I giggle again. "It's red, sir."

"and what color are you," he asks

"green, so damn green."

He peppers my ass and thighs with stinging blows, and I felt myself sink into the pain. Losing myself, my mind quiet, focused only on this. The feel of his hand, the feel of his legs. Nothing but him and me in this moment.

He rubs my ass now in a soothing circle. "so pretty, I love this shade of red on you, Bunny; you did so well. You are my good girl, aren't you?" he coos, but I'm not in a state to respond; I only nod.

Slowly, he helps me off his lap.

"Kneel."

His commanding voice wraps around me, and I can feel myself slipping deeper into a submissive headspace. The playful brat pushed back to the back of my mind and the good girl taking her place. I drop gracefully to my knees, looking up at him with what I am sure is a look of adoration.

"Unbuckle my pants and take my cock out," he orders. I shiver in anticipation; this is one of my favorite ways to serve my Dom.

Eagerly, I comply. My greedy hands desperate to take his cock in hand. I make short work of his pants and pull out his long, thick cock, the head already wet with precum.

I stare at my prize, desperate to taste him. I reach out to stroke him.

"Did I say you could touch, Bunny?" The reprimand coupled with a raised brow.

I give a disappointed whine but bring my hands down.

"You can't be topping from the bottom now," he chides. "Open your mouth."

Oh, this was good. This was better, actually.

I open my mouth and wait, knowing I don't have permission to take him into my mouth just yet.

"Such a good girl. See, I knew you had it in you." He presses forward,

"Lick."

I lean forward, my eager tongue lapping him up, his taste exploding on my tongue.

"Suck."

I suck the head of his cock into my mouth, my tongue swirling around the head before taking more in, my body leaning forward just slightly to close the gap between us, desperate for more. I hollow out my cheeks, bobbing on his cock, my hands behind my back, knowing I'm not to use them. His hands came up to my head, one on the back and the other cupping my cheek gently.

"Look at me, Bunny."

My eyes peek up at him, his cock still in my mouth.

"Show me your safe word when I have you like this," he demands. I tap his thigh twice before putting my hand behind my back again.

"Good girl. Use it if you need it. I'm going to fuck your face now." His eyes are dark and possessive.

I. Loved. It.

Love the way I make him so full of lust that he lets himself go with me. He presses closer, pushing his cock deeper into my mouth; I relax my jaw, breathing through my nose. Closing my eyes, I give him control. I trust him to take care of me. Even when he uses my body in dirty and depraved ways, I trust he will honor my safe word always.

"Watch me," he orders

My eyes snap open, and my gaze focuses on him.

He uses my mouth, fucking my face, pushing his cock deeper and deeper until my face is pressed flush to his crotch, his neatly trimmed pubic hair tickling my cheek. He holds me there for a beat before pulling back and letting me take a breath through my nose before pushing deep once again, repeating that until I lose count of the number of times I am choking on his cock before returning to fucking my mouth. My eyes are streaming, my vision blurry, but I am a good girl and keep my eyes focused on him and the twisted pleasure on his face, the look of satisfaction as he uses my mouth for his own needs. I want to touch myself; I can feel how wet I am, can feel it drip down my thighs. But I am a good girl; I don't dare to even rub my thighs together.

Not until he says I can.

He murmurs praises; the words telling me how good I am, how my mouth feels like heaven, how I am so perfect for him, his perfect good girl.

He pulls out, breathing hard, and I give a cry of protest, eyes utterly lost to him.

He kneels down and pulls me to him, hand on my throat, controlling me, kissing me deeply, not caring that the taste of his precum is still in my mouth.

"My perfect girl," he murmurs again, his lips whispering against mine.

"I should reward my perfect girl, huh?"

I just gaze at him, telling him silently that I am his to do as he pleases.

He trails his hand down until he is cupping my cunt, my wetness obvious and soaking his fingers.

"Hmmm, did fucking your face make you hot, baby girl?"

He strokes the tips of his fingers over my slit, just enough that I can feel it, but not enough to give me the pleasure that I am so desperately craving.

"Hmm, answer me, Bunny. Did you like sucking my cock? Do you like it when I take control and fuck your face? Stuff my cock so deep down your throat you can't breathe?" /his fingers still so gentle. I whine.

"Oh, but I need words, Bunny. do you like it when I use you?"

"Yes, Sir. So much, Sir," I gasp out, the words coming from a place so deep inside.

"Should I reward you?"

"If it pleases you, Sir," I whisper, eyes on Reid

I am rewarded with two fingers pushing inside my soaked channel. The stretch of the sudden intrusion feels so good.

I have to fight to keep my eyes open. He trusts roughly, the harsh movements so different from the gentle feather light touches from just a moment ago.

I want to cry out for more, but I am his good girl. I will take what he gives me.

He pulls his fingers out and licks them clean, eyes still on me.

"I need more. Lay back," he commands.

I lay back on the carpet, and he swipes his tongue over my cunt in a long lick, causing me to moan. Then he feasts, licking up all my juice and coaxing more from me.

I can feel my orgasm quickly approaching. So close to the edge already. I want more, more, more. I am teetering on the edge; it is right there. But he pulls away. I cried out in dissatisfaction, but he smiles down at me.

"Not today, Bunny. Today you come on my cock and nowhere else." He crawls up my body and then positions himself over me, using his cock to tease me some more before pushing inside. I moan at the stretch. His cock is so much bigger than his fingers, and it feels so good.

I cant my hips to meet his thrust; his lips captured mine. Our bodies slick with sweat. The orgasm he had denied me rushes up to meet me, and I scream my release, my cunt pulsing around his pistoning cock; he rides me through my orgasm before pulling out and flipping me over and pressing into me again, fucking me even harder. His large body, draped over mine, feels so good. The wet sounds of my cunt, our heavy breathing, and the slapping of skin, a symphony to my ears.

He pulls out just as I can feel another orgasm building, and I cry out in frustration.

"Oh no, Bunny, we are not done." He gathers me up and sits with me on the couch, positioning me over his cock. "Ride me, baby." I sink onto his cock, moaning at the feel. My knees on either side of him, rocking on him, rubbing my clit just right.

His hands grab my hips, pressing me harder into him and grinding me down on him, and I cry out again. He has a dark smile on his face as he watches me fall apart, leaving me boneless in his arms. He pulls my hands behind my back and holds them in one hand, causing me to thrust my chest out and throw my head back before he thrusts hard up into me over and over again until he came with a moan, spilling himself inside me.

A deep sense of satisfaction fills me as we sit there, catching our breath. I am content, wrapped in his arm, his cock still inside my cunt. He gently runs his hands over my body, his touch soothing as we both slowly came down. He holds my face tenderly as he gave me a soft kiss before pulling me back to his chest to enjoy the afterglow.

His fingers run through my hair. "Such a good girl," he murmurs. "That was amazing, Bunny." I gave a soft hum of agreement and nuzzle my cheek into his chest.

"How do you feel, Bunny? Do you need anything?" he asks, his voice gentle, the complete opposite of his commanding tone from minutes ago.

I shake my head. "Just cuddles," I murmur, snuggling deeper, tucking my head under his chin and breathing him in.

CHAPTER TWENTY-EIGHT

Reid

I tighten my hold on Sage. Her body sated and relaxed. Sex with Sage is amazing. Transformative. I've never met someone that matched me perfectly. But this, this quiet afterward, these soft moments where her walls are down, and I just get to hold her, well, I'd burn the world down to have more moments like this.

I think I love this woman. I stroke the side of her face; she looks so peaceful. No. I know I love this woman. A smile tugs at my lips, and I kiss the top of her head. I twist a little to lie on the couch, pulling Sage down on me. Awkwardly, I pull the throw that's always on the back of the sofa over us both and just relax into the stillness, my hands still running up and down her body.

"I love you," I murmur into the silence, and her body stiffens.

Oh, that isn't the reaction I was hoping for; my breath catches in my throat. Her face tips up, her expression serious as she studies me. "It's ok if you are not there yet, but I love you, Bunny." Tears shimmer in her eyes, and she tightly wraps her arms around me, her body relaxing into mine.

"I love you too, Reid."

The relief that she loves me too fills me with so much happiness that it overshadows the darkness we are up against.

Almost.

We shower together, and I show her again how much I love her, and then we get ready to go. Her donning comfy clothes to hang out with the girls, and I don my battle armor. Weapons strapped in strategic locations just in case things get out of hand. Bulletproof vest under my shit.

The drive into town is quiet. Neither of us knows what to say to fill the silence. Instead, we hold hands over the center console.

My truck, back from the shop, with a clean bill of health and no tracker to be found, is a small comfort. Outside of slashing my tires, he didn't try anything else. Makes me wonder what else he has been doing if he's been this close all along.

The closed sign is on the bookstore door, and one of my men in plain clothes sits on a bench nearby, newspaper in hand. It's a little on the nose, but not so apparent that a person making a cursory glance at the shop would realize that a guard is stationed by the door. A quick knock, and Rhett unlocks the door and ushers us inside. Sage leans in to give me a kiss and a tight hug. "Be safe," she says, her voice serious.

"I will. Stay inside until I get back. If you need anything, Rhett is here. So is Maddox. We'll have a guard at the front and back." I kiss her again before watching her head to the couches in the back and greet her friends. She looks happy, but I can see the tension in her shoulders. Hopefully, when I return, this will be the start of putting her past completely behind us, and she can have a future free of Jordan's reach.

"Ready?" Vaughn asks, his hand on my shoulder. I nod before looking at Rhett and Maddox.

"Keep her safe."

"With my life," Rhett replies. Maddox gives me a decisive nod.

I can't shake the increasing dread as Vaughn and I drive back to my neighborhood. Something isn't right. My gut twists with a raw, urgent need to get back to Sage. I can't explain it, but the feeling gnaws at me, intensifying with each passing second we get closer to where Jordan is supposedly hiding out.

I try to shake off the impending doom. She is safe with Juniper and the other girls. Rhett, Maddox, and two other men watching over her mean she is safe. Rhett may be one of our IT specialists, but he is more than capable of guarding Sage. I keep telling myself I must trust her to stay inside and be safe.

This feeling in my chest—it is ridiculous. Paranoid, even.

The rest of our team is watching the house. So far, no movement. This lead we are following could be the break we need. Enough evidence to build a case to prove he is stalking Sage. I need to figure this out if Sage is ever going to be free. As much as I would gladly spend the rest of my life as her shadow, protecting her, I know she deserves to feel safe without me always hovering nearby. She should be able to go out, visit friends, and work without planning every detail around her security. She should never have to worry about her safety again. I am determined to make that her reality.

My phone rings through the Bluetooth system, and I answer it immediately.

"Update," I bark.

"He is on the move. Heading out of town in a black sedan. I ran the plates. Stolen." Of course, it is. All the better for building our case.

"Follow him." Vaughn cuts in.

The phone cuts out. Goddamn Blake.

"Plan B?" I ask Vaughn. We'll never catch up to him; this is our chance to check out where he has been staying.

We have a key, after all.

Vaughn, always the strategic one, managed to get permission from the owners by spinning a tale about teenage vandals hitting empty properties in the neighborhood.

It was really a dumbass teen driving recklessly that smashed the cluster mailbox in my neighbor's yard when he was at work. But they didn't ask for details. He'd called on behalf of Heartwood Security, offering to check on the house and give a free security assessment. Vaughn's words have a way of nudging people in the right direction without ever outright lying. He could charm the Fae from one of those fantasy novels Sage loved.

Vaughn and I are in a small house in my neighborhood. It is supposed to be empty, listed for sale for a ridiculous price that the stubborn owners refuse to lower despite it sitting on the market for over a year. They own a handful of properties in town, so I guess this one isn't really a priority for them.

The idea of that man lurking so close to Sage makes my blood run cold. How long had Jordan been there, watching? Pretty sure you can see my house from the 2nd story window.

A part of me hopes we won't find anything. I want proof that Jordan hadn't watched her every move from this close. But a larger part—the part that wants justice, even vengeance—wants Jordan to be here. I want to put an end to this nightmare myself.

I force myself to tamp down that urge, reminding myself we have to stay within the bounds of the law, even if we are skirting around a gray area tonight.

My phone pings with a notification, and I glance at it.

Blake: He clocked my tail and gunned it, heading west on Pine Crest.

Fuck.

"That's towards the freeway," Vaughn muses, reading over my shoulder. "Unless the asshole magically doubles back without passing Blake, we should be clear to search the house."

I ignore the dread in my stomach. This is our chance.

The door opens without resistance, and we step inside. The silence is thick, and the darkness presses down on us. I curse the lack of any kind of lighting. Empty house and all.

Luckily, we'd come prepared. We both pull on night vision goggles, a recent purchase Rhett had been particularly proud of. We'd all ragged on him for the waste of funds, but now I am grateful for his panache for high-tech toys. The built-in IR illuminator casts an invisible light, allowing us to see in grainy shades of gray.

Let the search begin.

CHAPTER TWENTY-NINE

Sage

I pretend to be engaged. Fake it till you make it, but my mind is firmly on Reid and Jordan. I pray Jordan doesn't hurt him. I don't know what I would do if something happened. Reid has become such an essential part of my life that I don't think I can exist without him. And Jordan is a monster that can't let things go.

I worry my lip before grabbing a cookie, hoping eating something will distract me.

My stomach revolts after one bite and I excuse myself to go to the bathroom. It's through a door and down a narrow hallway that ends at a back exit. Rhett follows, but thankfully has the decency to stay in the hall. I splash water on my face and startle when the door opens, and Juniper strides in.

"You okay?" She asks.

I nod before shaking my head. Not able to lie. She doesn't fill the silence with false promises that everything will be fine. Just pulls me into a hug. "It's okay to not be okay," she says, pulling back to look at me. "We are all worried. I know not as much as you, but we'll keep you distracted until he is back. Come on, you can tell us all the status of you and Reid. Have you finally progressed past hand-holding" she teases. I muster a tiny smile, but my blush gives me away. She knows darn well that we've gone past that. Though I haven't told her, we both said the L word today. My tiny smile tips into a full grin. "Oh girl, we need deets!" she exclaims.

A muffled knock startles me. "Oh, that must be Clark. He said he had a late delivery for the shop." She says. "Finish up in here, and when you get back, we can go through the newest box of books and you can fill us in on all the dirty detail." A pause, "well maybe not all of them. Reid is too much like a brother." She laughs and opens the door, heading left down the hallway towards the back exit rather than right towards the front.

I take a fortifying breath and give myself a little pep talk.

Everything will be okay. Vaughn will serve the paperwork. Jordan will be forced to face me in court, and even if a judge doesn't make the temporary order permanent, there will be a clear record I want him gone from life. It isn't perfect, but it is a start.

Ugg, that does little to quail the building dread.

Raised voices that I can't make out. A crash. A loud bang. Followed by a thud. My body freezes for a moment. But the thought of Juniper in trouble has me opening the bathroom door.

I see Rhett lying on the floor of the hallway, a pool of blood around his head, and I look up just in time to see Jordan pulling Juniper through the back door, a gun pointed at her head.

"Help," I scream, "Rhett is hurt, call 911." I don't know if any of the girls hear me because I am already bursting out the back door, the loud boom of the metal door slamming against the wall from the force of my push, chasing after my monster. My breath stutters at the sight of two more bodies. The younger one must be the delivery boy. I don't have time to process the surrounding carnage.

I catch up with them in the alley, my breath coming out in pants as I gulp in air.

I tremble as I stare at Jordan, but I fight to keep my voice steady, forcing myself to appear brave despite the terror coursing through my veins. I can't show weakness, not now. Juniper's life is on the line.

"You come with me willingly, or she dies," Jordan snarls, pressing the barrel of the gun against Juniper's temple. His other arm wraps tightly around her, holding her in a brutal grip I remember far too well.

Juniper whimpers, her eyes wide and pleading, tears slipping down her cheeks in silent terror.

"Okay," I manage, my voice level even as my body betrays me, shaking with fear. "I'll go with you, just... just let her go. She hasn't done anything wrong."

"No!" Juniper's cry is cut off by Jordan's furious snarl.

"Nothing wrong?" he spits, his face twisted in a mask of rage. "This little bitch lied about your whereabouts. Told me you weren't here tonight. Just for that, she deserves to be punished. Don't you think, Sage?" His voice drops to an eerily calm tone, his face adopting a placid facade, one I know means he is close to doing something sadistic. Jordan's fury simmers just below the surface, like water about to boil over. I'd seen this look countless times, and I know just how dangerous he is in this state.

I swallow hard, forcing myself to keep my focus. I have to get Juniper away from him, have to turn his attention to me. "I know," I say, keeping my voice as calm as I can. "But, she didn't know, Jordan. She didn't know that she could tell you, or she would have. It's me you're mad at, not her."

"Isn't that right Juniper, you would have told him?" I lock eyes with her, willing her to understand that she needs to go along with my lie. Safer to play along with his delusion.

His eyes narrow, seeing right through my attempt to shift his focus. "Maybe I'll take you both," he sneers. "That asshole you hitched yourself to seems to care about her. Let's see how he feels when I take two women away from him. Maybe I'll gift-wrap her body and leave it on his front porch."

Another cold wave of terror washes over me, freezing my blood in my veins. No. I can't let this happen. I won't let this happen.

"What do you want me to do, Jordan?" I ask, my hands up in a gesture of submission, my mind racing through every self-defense tactic I've ever learned. Maybe if I play along, I can distract him long enough for Juniper to escape. My heart hammers so hard it drowns out nearly everything else, pounding in my ears like a war drum. Focus, Sage. Keep him focused on you.

"Walk to the car," he orders, using his head to indicate the direction, the gun still pressed to Juniper's head.

I take a deep breath and obey, stepping carefully through the dark alley, the stench of garbage thick in the air. Each step feels impossibly loud against the wet concrete, echoing through the narrow space. I strain to listen for his footsteps behind me but find it hard to hear over the sound of my own thundering heart.

I try to glance back, needing to see Juniper's face to know she is okay.

"Keep walking," he snaps, his voice closer than I expected, and I have to suppress the instinctual flinch.

A black sedan is parked just beyond the shadows at the end of the alley. It sits there like a waiting predator, sleek and ominous, its tinted windows hiding whatever fate he has planned. If we both get into that car, it will be the end. Tessa's voice flits through my mind, 'Never let them take you to a secondary location. The statistics of getting out alive after that are grim.'

Why hasn't anyone come from the store yet? It feels like time is crawling. Surely, someone heard something.

"What are you waiting for? Get the fuck in," he barks, his voice sharp with impatience.

I reach for the handle, relieved to find it locked. A small kernel of hope blooms inside me. I turn to him, keeping my voice as calm as possible. "Can you unlock it for me?" I ask, my body angled toward him, watching for any sign of an opening.

Jordan's grip on Juniper shifts, the gun still loosely trained on her, but the arm he had caged around her is now busy as he fumbles in his pocket for the keys; he mutters under his breath, insults I'd once let chip away at my self-worth. But not anymore. His words are empty. I know my worth now.

He has power over me only because he has a gun, I remind myself. Without it, he's nothing.

The keys jingle as he finally pulls them out, his gaze flicking down to find the unlock button. Just as he presses it, the car's lights flash and the gun dips away from Juniper's head for a split second. That is all I need.

I throw myself at him, my arms grabbing for the hand with the gun, pushing it upwards as I use my weight to knock him off balance. Jordan stumbles, and we all topple to the ground. I struggle to keep Jordan's arm pinned.

The gunshot shatters the stillness of the alley, echoing off the brick walls like a clap of thunder. My ears ring, but I don't let go.

"Run!" I scream at Juniper, my voice raw and desperate. I see Juniper stumble to her feet, her face pale, her eyes wide with terror.

"Sage!" Juniper gasps, but I cut her off, my voice rising in a snarl.

"Run!" I shriek again, putting everything I have into the command. "Get help!"

Juniper's footsteps recede, pounding down the alley. I let myself breathe a small sigh of relief, though I know my struggle is far from over.

Distracted by Juniper's escape, I don't see Jordan's fist coming until it is too late. His punch sends me sprawling off him, my head slamming against the pavement with a sickening thunk. Pain explodes behind my eyes, and my vision blurs, two of him swaying above me as I try to shake off the dizziness.

Through the haze, I see him raise the gun, aiming at Juniper's retreating form. No. No, he can't—I won't let him.

With every ounce of strength left in my battered body, I lurch up, throwing myself at him once more. My weight knocks him off balance, and his shot goes wide, ricocheting harmlessly off the alley wall.

I hear Juniper's scream, sharp and frightened but unhurt. Relief washes over me as I look up at Jordan, my lips curling into a defiant smirk. I'd beaten him, if only for a moment, and I will hold on to that victory. *If I'm going to die tonight, I'll die as the strong, defiant woman I fought to become—not the cowering girl he tried to turn me into.*

I brace for him to raise the gun again, but instead, he drives his knee into my stomach, knocking the air from my lungs. I double over, gasping, barely able to process the pain before he strikes me again, slamming his fist against the side of my head. Darkness crashes over me like a wave, and I sink into it.

CHAPTER THIRTY

Reid

We move cautiously through the house, guns drawn, our ears straining for the faintest sound. But the house feels oppressively empty, every corner filled only with silence. Each cleared room heightens my mixed emotions—relief that maybe Jordan hadn't been so close since there is no evidence of him living here and disappointment because it means we don't have enough evidence. That is until Vaughn's voice comes crackling through the earpiece.

"Reid... get in here. Now."

My pulse spikes as I follow Vaughn's voice to the laundry room—one without windows and a single bare bulb as the light source. I remove my goggles and blink, squinting as my eyes adjust to the low light.

"Fuck..." The word leaves me in a harsh whisper as I take in the room.

Photos cover the walls. Every inch of wall space plastered with images of Sage. Some include me standing with her or in the background. In many of the pictures, Sage's face—or both of our faces—had been scratched out, dark jagged lines carved across her features. Some are defaced with ink; others are scored with something sharp. Each mark is a testament to Jordan's unraveling.

I move closer, studying the collage of obsession and hatred. Some photos are older, taken before she'd ever arrived at Deliverance. A few look like stills from security footage—shots of her in motels, fast-food places, the phone store. My blood runs cold at the ones from rest stops. The progression is chilling. A distant shot of her car in an empty parking lot. Another closer, as he approached her car. The next, even closer, shows her asleep in the back seat. The final photo in that series, taken right at her window.

It is as if he is mocking her, toying with her. Taunting her with the closeness she had never realized.

"He was following her the entire time," I say, my voice thick with barely restrained fury. "Stalking her every move."

Vaughn nods, his face set in a grim mask. "This guy's obsession is off the charts. He wasn't just stalking her—he was playing some sick mind game." He pulls out his phone and starts snapping photos, the camera's soft clicks filling the heavy silence. "Think he planned on showing her all this?"

I clench my jaw, my hands itching to tear down the photos. "Maybe. Or maybe he wanted her to feel like she could never escape. This is sick."

My gaze shifts to a cluster of photos on one side of the wall. Some have words scrawled across them in jagged capital letters: "MINE," "RUN, RUN, RUN, AS FAST AS YOU CAN," "YOU CAN'T OUTRUN ME." "RUN RABBIT RAN."

My stomach twists as I see a clear timeline laid out on the wall, an eerie chronology of her journey. Bruised and battered images of Sage stare back at me, some from the time she first left Jordan. She's looking over her shoulder in many of them as if sensing someone watching.

She probably had.

"This is twisted," Vaughn murmurs, his voice soft, like he is afraid of disturbing the warped shrine. "Look."

My gaze follows Vaughn's gesture. The earlier photos from when she first arrived to town show passive, almost pleading words scrawled over them, words like "I'LL SAVE YOU FROM HIM" and "HE CAN'T HAVE YOU." But as I move along the timeline, the writing grows harsher, more venomous. My face is slashed out in many of the photos, replaced with phrases like "I'LL MAKE YOU PURE AGAIN" and "BETRAYER." Toward the end, the words are outright hateful. "WHORE." "WORTHLESS." "DIE"

"Oh, shit..." Vaughn curses softly.

"What?" I demand, my pulse thundering in my ears. I turn from the photos to take in the contents scattered on a folding table. More photos, old school composition notebooks, a closed laptop connected to a high-quality printer, reams of photo paper, and refills of ink. He planned to be here for a while.

"The ramblings of a delusional man..." Vaughn breathes, sifting through papers on the table. He pulls out a notebook, then another. All three look worn, their pages crinkled from frequent use. "Look at this, Reid... it's a detailed log of her every move. When she got somewhere, when she left, every little detail from long before she even got here." Vaughn thumbs through, his face going pale. "Pages filled with delusional rants. One moment, he's begging her to come back, calling her his soulmate. The next, he's spewing hate. There's a... a eulogy in here, and then a list of vile names."

My eyes narrow, the sickening realization settling in as I glimpse the last few pages, where Jordan's handwriting shifted to a frightening calm, the letters precise and deliberate. Vaughn studies them, going pale.

"We need to get her out of here. Now," Vaughn says, his voice cracking with urgency. "The two of you are going to a safe house tonight."

"What's in there?" I demand, snatching the notebook from Vaughn's hands.

The final pages outline a detailed plan, each word like a ticking time bomb. It lays out how he will isolate her, how he'll lure her away from everyone else, leading to a list of horrific things he intends to do. An address for where he will take her. The words "SHE WILL DIE" are underlined multiple times, each stroke more forceful than the last.

"Fuck... let's go." My voice is a low growl as I turn on my heel. Vaughn grabs the other two notebooks and laptop, and we leave the house in grim silence.

Outside, Vaughn pauses, casting a wary glance at the house. "How do we know this isn't a trap?" he asks, gesturing toward the sinister plan in his hands.

"I don't care if it is. I'm getting Sage out of here before he can even think about touching her," I snap, already racing toward my truck. We'd parked down the street to avoid suspicion, but now I couldn't care less about caution. I need to get back to Sage.

As I climb in, I pull out my phone and immediately dial Rhett. The phone connects to my truck's Bluetooth, and I speed out of the neighborhood. Vaughn is already on the phone with the sheriff.

"The walls are covered in photos," Vaughn says urgently. "He's been stalking her for months."

The phone rings, and I clench the steering wheel, my heart pounding.

"Sir, with all due respect, this is an emergency," Vaughn continues. "This man is spiraling. He has a detailed plan to hurt her. This is serious."

The call goes to voicemail. I try again, my worry mounting. Rhett never misses a call on duty unless he is incapacitated.

My stomach drops, and I call Blake. No answer.

"Call the girls," I bark at Vaughn, dialing Sage's number with shaky hands. Each unanswered ring heightening my dread.

"I got Sunshine," Vaughn says beside me, his voice tense.

I exhale, clinging to the hope that Sunshine will explain everything, that Rhett's phone had simply died. It is just a coincidence.

"Breathe, Sunshine," Vaughn says, his face going pale as he listens. My hope shatters. "What? Is he alive? Have you already called an ambulance? Where... No. Stay there. Where's Maddox and the other guards? We're on our way."

Vaughn hangs up, staring grimly ahead, his voice devoid of inflection. "Sunshine found Rhett unconscious in the hallway by the bathrooms. Two more bodies outside the backdoor. Juniper and Sage... they're missing."

My hands tighten on the steering wheel, my knuckles white as the sickening realization takes hold.

We are too late.

CHAPTER THIRTY-ONE

Sage

When I come to, pain is the first thing I register — a dull, throbbing ache at the back of my skull and a sharp taste of copper in my mouth. My entire body hurts, every movement sending fresh bolts of agony through my limbs. I fight back a whimper, clenching my teeth. This isn't the safe, comfortable bedroom I share with Reid. Maybe I'd gotten really drunk with Juniper and was just sleeping off a killer hangover... but what kind of hangover makes you feel like you'd lost a fight with a semi-truck?

Wait. Juniper.

Memories flood back. The fight in the alleyway. The gun pressed to Juniper's head. Juniper running for help. Was that last night? An hour ago? Days? I can't be certain. How much time has passed? Did Jordan drug me? I wouldn't put it past him. Thoughts of 'secondary locations' mock me. I hadn't willingly gotten into the car, but he'd taken me, nonetheless.

I force myself to stay still, to keep my breathing slow and even. I am not sure where I am or if he is still watching me. *Stay calm, stay silent.* If he thinks I am still unconscious, I might have a chance to figure out my next move. I am alive, at least. That much is certain. But I don't know for how long.

Until I can assess my surroundings and my body's condition, it is best to pretend I am still unconscious. I keep my breathing even and slow.

My hands lie at my sides, and I resist the urge to wrap my arms around myself. I know the impulse is instinctual, a need to protect myself, but I can't let him know I am awake. I take stock of my surroundings: the surface beneath me isn't as brutal and unforgiving as the ground, but it isn't comfortable either. It is lumpy and stiff, with a slight give. I carefully press down with the tip of my finger, feeling the rough texture. Fabric? A bed, maybe? The chill that racks my body tells me no blanket is covering me, so maybe it is a couch.

Even with my eyes closed, I can sense light in the room.

Is he here? I strain my ears, listening for any sound. In the distance, I hear a steady drip, drip, drip of a leaky faucet, each drop like the relentless ticking of a clock, reminding me of my limited time.

A shuffle opposite the dripping faucet makes me flinch. I force my face to remain passive, suppressing any grimace of pain.

"Wakey, wakey, my lovely little Sage," a voice I wished I'd never hear again teases in a chillingly light tone, belying the danger I know I am in.

There is no use pretending to be asleep anymore. I crack an eye open; the brightness stabbing my senses like a razor blade, forcing me to close it again before trying once more.

"That's a good girl," he murmurs, his voice sickeningly sweet. I internally shudder at his use of those words. He doesn't get to call me that.

I turn my head toward the direction of his voice; the movement sending a jarring pain through me. My vision is blurry. Do I have a concussion? I am almost certain of it. Though I can barely make out his figure, the blurred outline suffices. I would recognize his shape in a crowd.

Blinking again, I try to make the room stop spinning.

"You thought you could get away from me?" he chuckles, standing across the room, his features unreadable.

"Baby," he whispers, his voice almost tender, like it had been in the beginning. "Don't you know you're mine?"

I sit up slowly, noting I am on a couch. My body feels ancient, every movement a monumental effort. I shake my head, trying to clear it, but he must have taken it as a refusal.

"You are mine!" he roars, his body moving with jerky intensity as he grabs an object and hurls it in my direction. It shatters against the wall beside me, and I can't stifle the whimper of fear that escapes.

He's just trying to intimidate me, I remind myself. Trying to scare me into submission.

My hands reach up to the pendant that has become my worry stone since Reid gave it to me. But my fingers grasp nothing.

"Did you think I'd let you keep any souvenirs from that asshole?" his voice is mocking. I know better than to answer.

There is no chance of anyone finding me now. No phone. No necklace with the embedded tracker that I'd promised Reid I would never take off while Jordan was still a threat. The bleak dark of hopelessness threatens to consume me, dragging me down into the depths of despair.

No. I am stronger than that now. I have to think. But damn, the pounding in my head makes it so hard to focus. I have to push past the pain.

His voice softens again, laced with sickly sweetness. "It was so cute, the way you thought you could leave me." He chuckles softly, taking a step forward, his tone turning menacing. "I let you go, you know? Let you think you could escape me."

My vision is finally clearing, and the room comes into focus. I stifle another whimper as I take in my surroundings, realizing with dread that I recognize nothing. Honey-brown wooden planks line the walls, decorated with kitschy cabin decor. This must be a rental cabin. Nothing about this place screams Jordan. The couch I am on is a worn brown fabric, trying and failing to look like leather. Two wooden rocking chairs flank me, one with a cute autumn-leaf-patterned throw. A well-worn red and blue rug covers the wood floor, the same honey-brown as the walls. Across from me is a brick fireplace, the mantle lined with knickknacks.

I search the room for anything I can use as a weapon or a possible escape route.

"When we get back home," he says, his voice filled with mock affection, "you should wear that sunflower dress you bought in Lexington."

My body locks. What? How did he...? I'd bought that dress miles away from him, in a small thrift shop where I hadn't lingered.

"You twirled around, letting it flare out," he continues, his tone nostalgic, tainting the memory I'd cherished as one of my first acts of independence. My heart sinks. He is stripping that moment of its joy, turning it into something sinister.

My face betrays my shock as I stare at him. He smirks, fully aware of the effect his words are having.

"You thought you were free of me, but Sage, baby, I've always been with you. Keeping you safe. I knew all about your plans." He gestures to himself, pride evident in his stance. "I kept you safe on your travels."

He paces in front of the fireplace. "The motel in Oakland had such scratchy sheets. You should've let me find us a better place." He is mocking me, taunting me. I remember that motel with pay-by-the-hour rates and a bed I scarcely wanted to touch.

He hadn't been days behind me. He'd been with me, step by step, watching, lurking.

"I let you spread your wings and fly," he continues, his smile turning predatory as he walks closer. "It makes it all the more satisfying when I clip them." He reaches out, running a finger down my cheek. I lock my muscles, refusing to flinch, even as my stomach churns. His caress turns into a slap, sharp and mocking rather than painful, but it leaves me reeling.

"Poor, careless Sage," he says, circling behind the couch like a vulture. I feel like prey, trapped, unable to escape his circling. "Sleeping at truck stops, at rest stops..." He trails off as if savoring the memories of each place I'd thought I was safe. Then, his fingers trail up from my shoulder to my neck, his breath hot against my skin.

"I wonder if you would've screamed if you'd woken up to see me standing there, just the glass between us." His chuckle is dark, and his hand tightens around my jaw, forcing my head to turn so our eyes meet. "You looked so precious."

I feel dirty, violated. He'd watched me sleep. I'd thought I was alone and safe from him, only to find he'd been mere inches away, toying with me.

"But then," his voice drops, shifting in tone, his body language shifting, volatile, "you had to ruin everything!" He leans down, towering over me, his face twisted in rage. "I had a plan, and you ruined it!" His hand comes down, barely missing my face, but I cower, my arms instinctively shielding myself. "You and that... that thief," he spits, his eyes wild, his face close enough that I can see the madness flickering there. "He stole you from me. He thought he had a right to you. He touched you without MY permission. YOU. ARE. MINE."

I shrink back, pressing myself into the couch, desperate to create distance.

Abruptly, his demeanor shifts again, like he'd flipped a switch. He straightens, adjusting his tie, brushing off his shirt as if we were about to discuss a business deal. He looks every bit the polished man I'd once believed he was. If it weren't for the red stain on his pristine white shirt, he could've been getting ready for work.

A small flicker of contempt stirs within me. He wants to break me, but I won't let him. I take a deep breath, steady myself, and force my face into an emotionless mask. If he can wear a mask, then so can I. I match his gaze with a calm, detached look, my heart pounding but my posture poised. I tell myself that this is just a business meeting with a difficult client. I can fake it.

"For a moment, I thought I'd lost you," he says casually, as if we were sharing coffee. "I was going to swoop in and save the day, rescue you from the side of the road. Remind you why we're meant to be together."

My mind flashes back to a distant memory from when we first started dating. I'd tried to set boundaries, asked for space, but my car had broken down the very next night. I remember standing by the side of the road, watching cars pass, and then there he was, his black sedan pulling up behind me. He'd made it sound like fate, rescuing me and then taking me to his place. I hadn't wanted to be ungrateful, even though I told him just a day before that I didn't know him well enough to go to his house. Even then, he'd been manipulating me, planting seeds of dependence.

"Did you... did you do something to my car?" I whisper, barely able to get the words out. I am not asking about my most recent car troubles.

He smirks, ignoring my question, his gaze drifting to the window. Outside, darkness has settled.

"You must be hungry, Sage," he says, his tone laced with something sinister.

"I... maybe a little, but I... I need to use the bathroom first," I stammer, my voice shaking.

His smirk widens, and he makes a magnanimous gesture to a closed door near him.

I hesitate, testing my aching body as I stand and walk carefully toward the door he indicates. Passing far too close to him for comfort.

Inside, the fluorescent light makes me look ghostly pale in the mirror, a bruise already darkening my cheek. I hadn't lied; I did need to use the bathroom. As I sit on the toilet, I assess the room, my gaze falling on a small window. Maybe…

I flush the toilet and turn on the sink, hoping the sound will mask my actions. My heart hammering, I try to open the window. It moves with ease. I can't miss this chance. Closing the window quietly, I take a breath and open the door a crack.

"Would it be okay if I took a shower before we eat?" I ask, forcing my voice to sound soft, submissive.

"You have ten minutes," he snaps, his voice coming from somewhere in the cabin.

Quickly, I close and lock the bathroom door, turning the shower on as I reopen the window. I slip out, my bare feet hitting the cold ground. Every muscle in my body protests, but I ignore it, adrenaline propelling me forward. I have no choice.

I take a deep, shuddering breath and sprint toward the tree line, my lungs burning. Ten feet. Five. I am so close. But then, from behind me, comes the sound of rapid footsteps.

No. No, no, no.

I am so close.

He tackles me from behind, his arms locking around my legs, sending us both crashing to the ground. His laughter is dark, triumphant.

"Did you really think I'd make it that easy?" he sneers, tightening his grip on me as I struggle. "Tut, tut, you failed my little test."

I fight, kicking out wildly, and land a solid hit. But the victory is short-lived. He yanks me to my feet, his hand clamping around my neck, cutting off my air. Desperately, I claw at his grip, my vision dimming as he drags me back to the cabin, my hope dying with every step.

CHAPTER THIRTY-TWO

Reid

The word "gone" echoes in my head, each reverberation colder and more final than the last. The car is silent after Vaughn dropped that bombshell. Gone. She can't be gone. I was supposed to take her to a safe house. How could we be too late?

The app. I'd given her a tracker embedded in the necklace. I'd sworn never to use it unless it was an emergency, and this is the goddamn definition of an emergency. My hands tremble as I navigate to the tracking app on my phone, steering one-handed. It will tell me where she is. It has to.

The app takes an eternity to load, each second stretching into agonizing infinity. When her location finally pings, relief surges through me. "The tracker says she's near the bookstore," I manage, my voice thick with desperation. I thrust the phone at Vaughn, needing him to see it, to confirm it.

Vaughn studies the map and quickly calls Maddox. I strain to hear, clinging to every word like a lifeline.

"She has to be there... She has to be okay..." The words loop in my mind, a desperate mantra as I grip the wheel, my teeth clenched. Why did I have to live so far from downtown? Twenty minutes might as well be twenty hours.

"Juniper's back?" I hear Vaughn ask, and my heart stutters with hope. If Juniper is safe, maybe Sage is, too. "And Sage? There should be a necklace..."

No, not the necklace, I think, my mind a mess of frantic thoughts. *Look for Sage. Sage is wearing the necklace.*

"Yeah?" Vaughn says, his tone dropping. "Okay... no, you did good. We'll find her."

"Well?" I snap when Vaughn hangs up, barely able to breathe.

Vaughn looks grim. "He must've known the necklace was a tracker. He took it off her before he took her."

The words hit me like a punch, the buzzing in my head amplifying into a roar of denial. No. No. NO!

"Maddox found it on the ground," Vaughn finishes, his voice heavy.

I don't respond. I pull my car into a no-parking zone outside the bookstore, skidding to a stop without a second thought. The fine doesn't matter. Nothing matters but finding her.

I bolt from the car, racing inside, barely aware of the shocked stares from passersby. My heart hammers in my chest, pounding out a rhythm of dread as I beeline for the seating area where the girls usually gather. Part of me clings to the absurd hope that this is all a dream, that I'd find her sitting there, looking up at me with confusion, maybe annoyed that I'd interrupted girl time so early.

But the scene that greets me is one of raw pain. Juniper is slumped in a chair, her face red and blotchy, mascara streaking down her cheeks like black rivers. She is surrounded by her friends, who try to console her, but she is inconsolable, sobbing, and broken. I scan the room, desperate to find Sage among them, but each face I see drives a deeper nail into my heart. She isn't there.

My gaze locks onto Sage's necklace clutched in Maddox's hand. A part of me had clung to the hope that Vaughn was wrong, that it had been some cruel mistake. But now, seeing that necklace, the truth hits me in full force. She is gone. And it is my fault.

I should have insisted she go to the safe room at Heartwood.

"What... what happened?" I choke out, my voice cracked and raw. Just getting the words out feels like trying to breathe through shattered glass.

Juniper looks up, her tear-streaked face contorted with guilt and sorrow. She breaks into fresh tears, her sobs mingling with fractured sentences. "I'm sorry... I'm so sorry..."

I fight to hold back my anguish, swallowing it down to focus.

"Juniper, please," I urge, my voice a strained whisper. "Just... tell me what happened."

"I tried... I really tried," she sobs, each word punctuated by desperate gasps for air. "He... he had a gun, Reid. I didn't mean to leave her... she told me to get help... I thought I was doing the right thing. I... I'm so sorry! It's all my fault!"

Her words come out in a torrent of grief and shame, and I can see the torment in her eyes. I've never seen Juniper cry. Always optimistic and bubbly in every situation—hell, I'd seen her break an arm without shedding a tear—but now she is utterly devastated, haunted by the guilt of leaving Sage behind.

"It's not your fault, Juniper," I say, though the words feel hollow, forced. My mind is screaming for more. I can't wait for her to calm down. "Please... tell me what you remember. Anything. Everything."

She shakes her head, her hands trembling as she swipes at her face, trying to compose herself. "I thought... I thought it was just Clark. Sometimes, he makes deliveries at the back door. I swear, Reid, I thought it was him. He texted me to give me a heads up since I told him we were closing early," she cries, her voice pitching higher. "I would never have opened the door if I'd known!"

The other girls try to soothe her, murmuring words of comfort, but I can see it is no use. The trauma is too fresh, too raw, and Juniper is crumbling under the weight of her guilt.

Maddox appears, his expression stricken as he moves through the shelves and wraps Juniper in a tight hug, rocking her gently. "It's okay, Junebug. I'm here," he murmurs softly, trying to ground her.

I clench my fists, forcing myself to remain still. I feel my patience thinning, my desperation mounting. "Find out what you can," I say to Maddox, my voice low and urgent. I know my presence is only adding to Juniper's distress. Right now, she needs Maddox, not me.

I head down the narrow hallway that leads to the restroom and the back door of the building. There is parking out back, but this door is usually locked and treated as an emergency exit. I knew they sometimes brought deliveries through it to avoid walking around to the front. So far, all I knew was that Juniper had opened this back door, but that didn't explain how Jordan had managed to get Sage outside. I need answers.

At the end of the hallway, I find the back door ajar, its dull metal frame silhouetted against the flashing red lights of an ambulance. I quicken my pace, breaking into a jog as I take the last few steps and reach the scene outside.

Rhett is being loaded onto a stretcher, his limp form secured by straps as two EMTs maneuver him carefully into the ambulance. Vaughn stands nearby, his hands on his hips, looking tense and worn, worry etched into his usually composed face.

"Any update?" I ask, my voice rough.

Vaughn doesn't look up immediately. "He took a pretty bad hit to the head," he says, his jaw clenched. "Hasn't woken up. They're worried about brain swelling. They're gonna check him out Deliverance Medical, but they are already talking about possible medevac to Seattle, but they want to stabilize him first."

"Fuck," I mutter, the word a heavy sigh of frustration and dread.

"Yeah." Vaughn's eyes flick to me, and momentarily, I see a crack in his stoic façade. Vaughn is worried, too—a rare display of emotion from the man who is a rock for everyone else.

"What about Peter?" I ask, "And the delivery boy, Clark?"

Vaughn doesn't answer, but his expression is enough.

"Blake?" I hesitate to ask.

"Declan found his car shot to hell and wrapped around a tree." I brace myself; I can't handle much more. "He was unconscious, but otherwise, okay." Vaughn finishes.

"We need to see the security footage," I say, a hard edge to my voice.

Vaughn nods. "I already have one of the guys trying to retrieve it for us. Alex and E are both out of town and it's a closed system. He isn't as efficient as Rhett," he adds in a softer tone. His warning is that this is going to take some time.

"We've got nothing, Vaughn," I hiss, my fists clenching. "No leads, no tracker, Rhett's out, Juniper's too traumatized to tell us anything. Sage is in danger now. We need to get to her now!"

"I know, man."

"You don't fucking know!" I explode, my breath coming in short, furious pants. The rage simmering inside me boils over, a volatile mix of frustration and guilt. I wanted to blame someone—anyone—but there was no one responsible but me. I hadn't been there when she needed me, and that was on me.

"She's... I can't... I can't lose her. She is everything," I say, the anger giving way to something rawer. This desperation turns my voice into a pleading rasp. "I promised I'd protect her. I swore she'd be safe, and now that sick son of a bitch has her."

"We'll find her, Reid. It's what we do," Vaughn says, his tone steady but carrying an undercurrent of urgency.

"Hey, uh..." One of the EMTs steps forward, clearing his throat. His face is grave, his eyes shifting between Vaughn and me. "They're taking him to the hospital now," he says, gesturing to the ambulance leaving with Rhett. "Another ambulance is on its way, but I need to check on the girl now."

Without waiting for confirmation, the EMT turns and strides back into the bookstore. Behind them, the ambulance doors slam shut, and the vehicle pulls away, its sirens wailing, lights flashing against the darkened street.

Vaughn checks his phone, his mouth set in a grim line. "Mark says we should have the footage in fifteen."

"Fifteen? We need it now!" My frustration flares up again, and I struggle to keep my voice steady. "How do we not have the tapes?!" My fists clench, my knuckles white.

"It's not our system, Reid," Vaughn replies, his own patience fraying. "The owner's in New York, and we can't reach him for the logins." There is an edge in Vaughn's voice that tells me exactly how Mark was going about obtaining the footage.

"How fucking secure does a security system need to be in a goddamn bookstore that it takes one of our guys fifteen minutes to get in?" My voice is laced with bitterness. Any other time, it might have been a darkly funny comment, but right now, with Sage's life on the line, it only highlights the unbearable weight pressing down on me.

Together, we head back inside, where the EMT carefully checks Juniper's vitals. My heart twists at the sight of her, shaking and hunched over as if she were trying to shield herself from some unseen horror. Her breathing is ragged, and she clutches at her arms, her fingers digging into her own skin as if to ground herself.

Maddox is beside her, speaking softly, his voice barely above a murmur. The other girls stand huddled a few steps away, their expressions a mixture of fear and concern.

"We need to get them home," Vaughn murmurs, glancing over at me.

I shoot him a sidelong look, my expression fierce and determined. "You handle that." Without waiting for a response, I walk over to Juniper, my footsteps measured but purposeful.

"June?" I coax gently, trying to keep my voice steady. If I can put on a calm mask, maybe she'd be able to answer some questions. Perhaps she'd remember something—anything—that could point me in the right direction.

"I'm sorry, Reid," she chokes out, fresh tears spilling down her face. I flinch, worried she is about to spiral again.

"It's okay, Juniper," I say, my voice even, soothing, though inside I am cursing Jordan for everything he's done. I struggle to keep my composure when I am vibrating with anger and fear, but I need a distraction from the agonizing wait for Mark to retrieve the video footage. I need something to focus on, some small step forward.

"Just walk me through what happened, okay? Step by step."

"But... but I left her," Juniper's voice cracks, her words thick with guilt and shame. I fight to keep my frustration in check; she isn't trying to be difficult. She is as much a victim as Sage right now.

"You did the right thing," I say softly, fighting the urge to scream. "You put on your own oxygen mask first, June. You had no choice." Inside, I am raging, but I know that if she hadn't run, Jordan would have both of them now—or worse, maybe Jordan would have killed Juniper to get to Sage. The thought is too sickening to dwell on.

Juniper takes a shuddering breath, trying to steady herself. "I... I opened the back door, thinking it was a delivery. Clark sent me a message saying that he'd gotten here," she whispered, her voice breaking. "Rhett was behind me... he warned me, but I didn't hear him in time."

She gasps, her eyes wide with fresh horror. "Oh my God, Rhett!" Another loud sob escapes her, and I feel my insides twist.

"He'll be okay," I lie gently, forcing myself to sound certain even though I had no idea how bad Rhett's injuries were. I couldn't tell her the truth, not when she was barely holding it together as it was.

Juniper clutches her hands together, her fingers trembling. "He... he hit Rhett, and... and Sage came out of the bathroom. And... oh God." She takes in a shaky breath, barely able to speak through the sobs building in her throat. "She... she tried to protect me. She told me to run. But he had a gun... I thought... I thought I was going to die."

She breaks down completely, her body wracked with sobs as she whispers, "She saved me... and I ran. I left her."

Frustration wells up in me like a storm, and I run my hands through my hair, trying to contain the fury simmering beneath my skin. Any semblance of calm that Maddox had coaxed out of her is gone now, washed away in the flood of guilt and terror.

I pace back and forth, checking my phone for the time, the seconds ticking at an agonizing crawl. I feel useless. Helpless. There is nothing I can do at this moment for Sage, who is out there somewhere, alone, in danger. The pit in my stomach gnaws at me, reminding me again and again that this is my fault. If only I'd called tonight off. If only I'd insisted she stay home or found a different kind of tracker or taken her to a safe house. Every decision I made feels wrong now; every choice was a step closer to this waking nightmare we are living.

I can't just stand here doing nothing.

Without another word, I stalk out the back door and into the dark parking lot. The cold air is biting against my skin but barely registers. I scan the area, my gaze tracing over the empty asphalt, the box on its side, the spilled books, with some of the pages flapping in the wind. The faint outline of a road that runs along the far side. It connects to the alleyway where the attack must have happened. My heart pounds as I walk slowly through the narrow, shadowed passage, my eyes straining for any sign, any clue. I ignore the police tape. The offices combing the crime scene. I've worked with many of them before, so they don't stop me.

The rancid smell of garbage from the nearby dumpster hits me, sharp and pungent. I ignore it, stepping past empty pallets stacked against the wall, my eyes scanning every inch of the ground, every shadowed corner. There are no footsteps, tire marks, or anything that will help me at this moment, but I am still searching.

I just need one thing. One clue to show me where Jordan had taken her.

I clench my fists, feeling the raw scrape of frustration clawing at my throat. I growl under my breath, my fists tight, before turning and heading back inside.

"Got it," a voice calls out as I enter the hallway.

I race alongside Vaughn into the small office, where Mark is hunched over a computer. We cluster around the screen as grainy black-and-white footage flickers to life, showing four camera angles: the parking lot, part of the alleyway from the parking lot side, the other side of the alleyway from the sidewalk, and the front of the store.

Mark taps a few keys, beginning what feels like the worst silent film I have ever seen.

The footage shows a man in a delivery uniform with a box. Clark. He jokes with the guard we have stationed there before he raises his arm to knock on the door when a man in a well-tailored suit walks up behind them. The guard notices too late because the man in the suit pulls out a gun and, in quick succession, shoots them both. The box tumbles to the ground, and the contents spill out. He drags both bodies to the side, just out of view of anyone who opens the door. He returns to the back door, straightening his jacket on the way and knocking with a calm precision that belies the horror of his intentions.

The audacity, I think bitterly, my fists clenching as I watch. The door opens just a crack, and in that brief instant, the man—Jordan—wrenches it open the rest of the way, flinging Juniper aside with chilling ease.

Mark presses more keys, switching to a different angle, showing the bookstore's narrow hallway. My gut twists as I recognize Jordan's face, wearing a mask of civility as if this is a casual visit.

Rhett barely has time to react before Jordan strikes him on the side of the head with what looks like the butt of the gun. Rhett crumples to the floor like a sack of bricks, out cold. Jordan seizes Juniper before she can get away, pressing the gun into the side of her head. Then, the bathroom door opens, and Sage steps out, freezing when she sees Jordan.

Jordan says something we can't hear. She must have replied, but I can't see her face. He just smiles, a big, polished Hollywood smile that twists my insides with rage. *This man is a sick fuck*, watching in helpless horror as Jordan steps back, dragging Juniper outside.

Sage immediately ran after them.

No, Bunny, you should have called for help. But she can't hear me, and I feel a helplessness that claws at me, suffocating.

Mark switches the camera feedback to the street view, and my heart sinks as I watch Sage dart after them. Another switch and it is the alley next to the bookstore. But then, a flash of pride surges through me as I see her launch herself at Jordan, pushing the gun aside and shouting something at Juniper, likely telling her to run. Juniper bolts, and for a second, hope flickers.

But then I wince as Jordan turns his fury on Sage. The screen is a silent witness to the violence—Jordan striking her, Sage collapsing in a heap, limp and vulnerable. In seconds, Jordan tosses her into the backseat of his car as though she is nothing more than a bag of groceries. He leans over her prone body before pulling back and throwing something. Her necklace, most likely. Then, just as the guard station in the front rounds the corner, he drives off.

I stare, horrified, at the scene that had just unfolded before my eyes. Less than five minutes. It took less than five minutes for him to breach our defenses and take Sage. The need to rescue her surges within me like a storm, raw and unrelenting, but we still don't know where Jordan has taken her.

Behind me, I can hear Vaughn speaking on the phone, his voice tense but focused. My thoughts moving in a muddled haze, half racing, half weighed down by the sheer horror of what I'd witnessed.

I feel numb. Every nerve seems dulled, every emotion stretched too thin, barely containing the roiling rage within.

Vaughn's voice cuts through my haze. "The sheriff's putting out an APB on the car. The rest of the team is already out looking. We'll find them, Reid."

Ignoring Vaughn, I turn and storm back outside, my steps heavy and unsteady. I make my way to the middle of the alleyway, where the memory of that terrible footage seems burned into the shadows around me.

The reality of it finally hits, crashing down on me like a wave. I let out a raw, guttural bellow of rage that echoes off the walls, filling the night with the sound of my anguish.

Breathing heavily, I stare down at my hands, feeling lost. But then I remember—the notebooks. Jordan's sick, meticulously detailed plan.

I know where she is. Or at least where she could be. I have to take a chance. I know I should go to Vaughn, know protocol demands I follow proper procedures, but if I do, Vaughn will insist on taking things slow, doing things by the book. At any other time, I would have insisted on the same. But this is Sage. My gut screams at me to go now, to save her before it is too late.

Without hesitation, I race down the alley toward the sidewalk, my feet pounding the pavement with desperation, and jump into my car, still parked in the no-parking zone. With trembling hands, I take a quick picture of the plan in the notebook, sending it to Vaughn before peeling away into the darkness.

In my rear view mirror, I see Vaughn burst out of the bookstore, standing on the sidewalk, staring after me. I am too far away to make out his expression, but I can imagine Vaughn's frustration and worry.

My phone rings immediately. I answer without a second thought, Vaughn's voice sharp on the other end. "What are you doing, Reid?"

"I know where he took her," I reply, my voice strained. "It's in his plan."

"You can't just run off half-cocked, Reid. What if it's a trap?"

"Don't care," I growl. "I need to get to her. I can't wait."

I hang up before Vaughn can respond, ignoring the phone as it starts ringing again. My focus narrows, my world reduced to the road ahead and the relentless drive pounding in my chest. The town streets give way to the winding roads of the forest, shadows stretching long and dark around me. I know I am driving too fast, know the curves of these roads could send me careening into the trees if I am not careful, but I can't bring myself to care. My hands grip the steering wheel so tightly that my knuckles are white, and I lean hard into the turns, once nearly flipping the truck as I take a corner too sharply.

As I near the cabin, I turn off my headlights, hoping to minimize my presence. I know the engine's sound will give me away, but at least my approach won't be visible in the dark. The trees close in on either side of me, towering and oppressive, but then they break, revealing a clearing—and the cabin.

There she is.

My heart seizes in my chest. Jordan is dragging her toward the door, and she is fighting him every step of the way, her body resisting, her spirit fierce. But she isn't gaining any ground, her struggles barely slowing him down.

I don't even bother to turn off the car. I throw it into park and leap out, sprinting toward her, my feet pounding the dirt as I close the distance.

I'll save you, Sage. The words burn in my mind, a fierce, unbreakable promise.

CHAPTER THIRTY-THREE

Sage

Jordan uses my hair like a leash, dragging me back toward the cabin. I thrash, twisting and turning, trying to break free from his grip, my screams echoing through the trees. The fear I felt earlier has hardened into fury, burning away my last remnants of terror.

I know I will die tonight. My one chance at freedom was just stripped away as easily as he had taken everything else from me over the years.

We reach the porch past the stairs. Closer to the cabin's open doorway, each step dragging me nearer to a fate I'd accepted but refuse to meet passively. He pulls me through the threshold, flinging me to the floor as he slams the heavy wooden door shut behind us, the bolt sliding into place with a final, ominous click.

I sit on the floor, propped up on my arms, panting as I try to steady the storm raging inside me. Fear coils tight in my gut but laced with an overwhelming sense of defiance. Anger for everything he'd put me through. Sadness that I'll never get to see Reid again. And pride—pride that I hadn't fallen apart in front of him, that I am still holding onto my strength, that I hadn't let him break my spirit.

My gaze flickers over Jordan with satisfaction. His suit jacket gone, his white shirt torn and stained with blood, his normally pristine appearance is in tatters. Even his hair, which he always kept so meticulously styled, is disheveled. I can't help the smirk that tugs at my lips.

Jordan catches the smirk and snarls, striding forward to backhand me, his palm cracking against my cheek with enough force to make my ears ring and my skin burn. I close my eyes briefly, steadying myself and collecting my composure. It doesn't matter. The gratification of seeing him unravel, of watching him lose control, is worth the pain. I won't go down begging for mercy. Not this time. Not ever again.

Slowly, I rise to my feet, eyes fixed on him with unwavering contempt. I stand tall, my gaze sharp, my expression carrying the weight of every wrong he had ever committed against me.

"You bitch," he spits, his voice rising with frustration. "You ruined it all. Again. That's all you're good for. Ruining things." He paces in tight circles, his hands clenched into fists. "You ungrateful, worthless waste of space!"

I blink at him, my expression calm and steady. Those words— words that once made me shrink, words that had me apologizing and pleading to do better—now bounce off me. They mean nothing.

"I gave you a good life!" he rants, pacing quickening. "I gave you everything, rescued you from your pathetic, lonely existence! What were you before me? Nothing. You were trash. Your daddy didn't love you, but I..." He trails off, panting, his eyes scanning me up and down with a twisted mix of anger and something darker. "Well, you had a purpose with me."

I raise an eyebrow, unimpressed. So he's going with the 'I never loved you' tactic. It's not exactly groundbreaking. I wonder if he is aware of how pitiful he looks, ranting and raving, while I stand, calm and unshaken.

My lack of reaction only fuels his anger. He lunges at me, and I brace, half-expecting a shove or a slap, but I keep my posture composed, refusing to flinch. I know he wants to see me cower, wants me to look fearful and defensive. But I won't give him that pleasure. Never again. I'd found my strength, and nothing he does will strip that from me.

He looms over me, trying to use his size to intimidate me, to push me back into submission. "You are nothing!" he screams, spittle flying from his mouth and landing on my face. I grimace slightly, disgusted, but otherwise remain impassive, staring back at him with an empty, almost bored expression. It's reckless. I'm daring him to kill me. To give me a quick death out of anger.

He takes a step back, clearly thrown off by my reaction—or lack thereof. None of this is going the way he planned. I can see it in his eyes, in the way his movements falter. This wasn't supposed to happen. I was supposed to beg, to grovel, to play my part. But I am done playing. I am done being a part of his twisted narrative.

"I am not yours," I say, my voice steady and clear, each word enunciated with quiet power. "You never loved me. You liked the power you had over me. Even now, you see me as nothing more than a thing. But I am not a thing. And you don't scare me anymore."

A cold fury flashes across his face. I recognize the subtle signs of his rage, the twitch of his eyebrow, the tightening of his jaw, the way his fists clench at his sides. I know he is about to hit me. A distant part of me wonders if this is how I am going to die. Beaten to death.

A sudden pounding on the door startles me, but what shocks me more is Jordan's lack of reaction. He doesn't even flinch; he expected this. The twisted smile on his face confirms it.

"Sage!" My name, my lifeline, the one voice I long to hear—and the one voice I fear for most. Reid had come for me; of course, he did. I almost wish he hadn't, that he would have stayed safe. But I know him.

My Reid will always come for me.

Jordan's smile sharpens, a mocking edge twisting his features. "That's fine," he sneers, his voice dripping with venom. "You don't have to come back with me." I tense, but I don't let my expression betray my fear. I can hear Reid slamming against the door, desperate to break through.

Jordan's eyes gleam with sadistic delight as he continues, his voice taking on a sickeningly sweet, mocking tone. "It's so unfortunate," he says, feigning sadness, "that my darling little Sage got into a tragic accident while hiking in the wild Washington forests. So sad." His hand slips to a side table, and when it returns, he is holding a gun aimed directly at my chest. "I think I'll let him find your body before I kill him, too."

I stand tall, my head held high. There is no escape, no way to dodge a bullet from this close. But if this is the end, I'll face it on my terms without giving him the satisfaction of seeing me cower.

As Jordan's finger tightens on the trigger, the door bursts open, crashing to the floor. Reid stands in the doorway, silhouetted in the moonlight, his own gun drawn and aimed, his face hard with determination.

Jordan whips around, his gun now directed at Reid, both men locked in a silent standoff. I watch, frozen, my heart racing. These two men—my past and my future—stand toe-to-toe, one drenched in twisted obsession, the other in fierce resolve.

Jordan's lips curl into a sneer. "You really think you can take her from me?" His voice is filled with deranged confidence. "She's mine. She'll always be mine. You'll never have her. I'll make sure of it."

"You've already lost, Jordan," Reid says, his tone steady, unshaken. "The cops are on their way. Put the gun down."

Jordan laughs, a chilling, hollow sound. "Oh, I don't think I will. Plenty of time for me to take care of the both of you before they arrive. I've got friends who will make this all disappear."

But it is my voice that cuts through his bravado. "You've lost, Jordan." I smirk, refusing to look away, my gaze steely. The simple statement strips him of his last shred of control.

That one sentence snaps something in him. His face twists, flushed with fury. He whirls, his gun swinging back toward me, his eyes wild with rage.

Before he could pull the trigger, Reid fires. The shot echoes through the cabin, a sharp crack slicing the night. Jordan's body jerks, the gun falling, his hand dropping to his side as he stumbles backward, pressing the other hand to his chest. His eyes go wide, staring down at his bloodstained fingers, disbelief etched into every line of his face.

He sinks to his knees, his gaze fixed on me, as if unable to comprehend that I am standing there, free of his grip, free of his control. Then he pitches forward, collapsing face-first onto the floor, his life draining away.

Reid doesn't waste a second. He strides forward, kicking Jordan's gun out of reach and kneeling down to check for a pulse, his own gun still at the ready. His eyes close briefly, relief mingling with something darker when he finds none.

Rising, he turns to me, his voice gentle, filled with concern. "Are you alright?"

I feel a rush of relief at the sound of his voice, but my body is numb, my mind struggling to process what had just happened. I stare down at Jordan's body.

"I... I..." My words falter, barely audible. I have seen too much death tonight.

"Baby," Reid whispers, taking slow, careful steps toward me, his gaze never leaving mine. He hesitates as if worried I might shy away, and I realize he is afraid that I am afraid of him now. But I am not. Not him. Never him.

He moves closer, his gun holstered, his hands tentative. "Where are you hurt, Bunny?" he asks, his eyes scanning me for injuries, cataloging each bruise already forming on my skin. "I don't want to cause you any more pain."

A tear slips down my cheek, and I lean into him, needing the warmth and solidity of his presence to ground me. "I... I... you came?" I whisper, my voice thick with tears.

His arms come around me, pulling me close, gentle but strong. "I will always come for you, Little Bunny. Nothing would've stopped me from finding you and bringing you home." He holds me, his voice a quiet promise against my hair. "We need to get you to a hospital so they can check you for injuries."

"I'm... I'm okay," I stammer, my voice shaky. "Are you... are you okay? You had to..." I trail off, unable to say the words.

Reid's arms tighten around me, a fierce protectiveness in his embrace. "I will do anything to keep you safe, Bunny. I'm just so glad you're okay."

I nod, the weight of what almost happened pressing down on me. If he had been just a few moments later... if he hadn't come... I shudder, pushing the thought away.

"Come on, Bunny," he whispers, guiding me gently out of the cabin. "Let's get you outside."

I let him guide me to the porch, where we stand together in each other's arms, trying to process everything that had just happened. The chilly night air feels surreal against my skin, grounding me yet making me feel even more distant from reality, as if I am floating outside my body.

In the distance, I can hear sirens growing louder. I watch, almost in a daze, as police cruisers spill into the clearing, their lights flashing, followed by a few unmarked SUVs. Reid's team pours out of the vehicles. In moments, the stillness of the clearing is consumed by the commotion as law enforcement officers take stock of the situation.

I feel detached in the crowd, like I am watching a scene unfold in a movie. A cop is grilling Reid about what had happened, and I try to focus, but everything sounds muffled like I am underwater. My mind drifts, unable to hold on to the present.

Then Vaughn appears beside me, holding out a phone with the game Tetris open on the screen. "Here," he says, his voice gentle but firm.

"What?" I blink, looking between the phone and Vaughn, confused. This hardly seems like the time for games.

"You've been through a traumatic event," Vaughn explains. "Research suggests that playing a game like Tetris right after can reduce the effects of PTSD. If you don't like Tetris, I can find something else."

I take the phone, still feeling detached, and glance down at the bright blocks falling on the screen. I am unsure why Vaughn thinks this will help, but why not if he insists? I tap the screen, moving the pieces into place. The simple, repetitive motion feels comforting, pulling me back into myself, one level at a time.

I am on level 8 when Reid gently takes the phone from my hand. "It's time to go to the hospital, baby," he says softly, nodding toward the waiting ambulance and the EMT standing nearby.

"Are you... are you going to come with me?" I ask, a trace of vulnerability in my voice.

"If you want me to," he replies.

"Of course I do. You need to be checked out, too. You broke down a door, for crying out loud." I realize I feel more grounded after playing the game, but I brush the thought aside and focus on Reid.

"Bunny, you're the one he hurt," he reminds me gently.

I wrinkle my nose, a small laugh escaping me. "I'm fine. You should've seen his face when I told him off." Pride blooms in my chest as I recall the moment.

Reid chuckles, his eyes soft with admiration as he looks down at me. "I am so proud of you, baby. You did so good standing up for yourself."

He leads me to the ambulance, where an EMT welcomes me with a warm, reassuring smile. Her tone is soft, and she explains each thing before doing it.

At the hospital, I am growing more frustrated by the minute. "When can I go home?" I ask, for what feels like the seventh time.

"When the doctor says you can," Reid replies patiently, seated in a chair he'd pulled close to my bed.

"Why didn't they make you stay in the hospital?" I grumble, crossing my arms.

"Because I don't have a concussion they need to monitor," he replies, still calm.

"But the bed's uncomfortable, and there's nothing to watch, and—"

Reid takes a deep breath, cutting me off gently. "What's really bothering you, Sage?"

I stop, surprised by his question, then look down, feeling a bit silly. "It's stupid," I mumble.

"Nothing you need is stupid," he says, touching my hand.

I hesitate before finally looking up at him, my cheeks flushed. "I just... I want to go home so we can cuddle on the couch," I admit, embarrassed by my vulnerability.

I almost look away, but I stop myself, watching as the most beautiful smile spreads across his face. Without a word, he shifts onto the bed beside me, pulling me gently into his arms, careful of the cords attached to me.

"Better?" he asks, his voice low and comforting.

I just nod, resting my head against his chest, finally letting myself relax. With him holding me, everything feels right. For the first time in a long time, I feel truly safe. No longer is there a distant cloud tainting that safety. Everything is going to be all right.

Epilogue

Ten months Later

"Alright, Sage, we'll talk again next week."

"See you next week, Helen," I say before logging off the telehealth appointment. I lean back in my office chair and stretch my arms above me, enjoying the silence for a moment.

In the living room, I find Reid on the couch watching TV, snacks laid out on the coffee table: a mix of healthy things like veggie sticks and a few choice pieces of junk food like chocolate and chips. I snatch a bite-size Snickers and lie down on the couch, my head in his lap, and he runs his hand through my hair with an absentminded air that I know is totally for my benefit. I can see the struggle to ask how it went play beneath his features as he keeps his eyes on the TV, but the tight lines of his body give him away. All of it—the snacks, his waiting for me— is his way of supporting me while I do the heavy work of tackling the trauma each week in therapy.

"Today was a good session," I say. His eyes dart down to examine my face before giving me a soft smile, his body relaxing a little beneath me as he takes stock of my relaxed form. I take a bite of the chocolate and turn to see what he is watching. "Oh, I like this episode!" The chef attempting to cook in the kiddie kitchen looks moments away from losing his mind.

This is Reid's form of therapy aftercare. After every session, he has snacks ready, a TV show that doesn't require a lot of energy to follow, even a blanket close by in case it is a difficult session and I need cuddles and a nap instead.

With Jordan out of my life, so much has changed, and yet so much is still the same. I still work for Heartwood security doing data entry. I never did get my own apartment. The one time I seriously looked into it, Juniper swooped in and demanded I lay out all the pros and cons of living in an apartment vs. staying with Reid. I stopped looking for apartments after that. The shiny engagement ring on my finger doesn't hurt either.

One year to the day we met on the side of the road, he proposed. He took me on a hike where he tried to recreate the day we had our first kiss. It was a disaster, and at the same time, absolutely perfect. It always surprises me just how sentimental Reid is at times.

Jordan being gone doesn't erase the effects he had on my life, nor does it erase the criminal ties he had, but I am dealing with it all the best that I can. Working for Heartwood means that I get to see that his ties go far further than I ever could have imagined, and that in the grand scheme of things, his death left a vacuum that others still fight over. While some of the men at Heartwood, including Reid, have made it their mission to investigate things further, I have chosen to focus on healing. It isn't to say that I'm burying my head in the sand, I am acutely aware of how dangerous the world can be but I'm not letting that stop me from creating the life I deserve.

I snuggle deeper into Reid's lap, turning my gaze from the TV to him. "Want to play tonight?"

About the Author:

Mira Foxx is a neurodivergent, socially awkward introvert who likes books, coffee, and computer games.

She writes emotionally intense and sometimes dark romantic suspense—and the occasional romantasy—delving into the complexities of survival, healing, and the power of trust. Her stories often feature resilient heroines battling the shadows of trauma, fiercely protective heroes dedicated to the heroines, and villains who engage in chilling psychological warfare. If you're drawn to narratives that balance intense darkness with hard-won hope and steamy, explicit romance with complex power dynamics, you'll love her work.

Mira lives in California with her two kids. When she isn't reading, writing, or gaming with her kids, she can be found outside in her garden.

* * *

Sage asked to play. You know Reid didn't say no!

Get the EXCLUSIVE, ultra-steamy bonus epilogue scene detailing their intense BDSM encounter, told entirely from Reid's perspective! This scene is ONLY available to Mira Foxx's newsletter subscribers.

This special content is a thank you for joining the community. You'll also be the first to hear about new books and other exclusives!

Sign up for Mira Foxx's newsletter and claim your scene: https://BookHip.com/XPAAWLA *(This bonus scene contains explicit content for mature audiences 18+).*